DEPRECATED

MICHAEL KARR

Keep up with Michael Karr by visiting

michaelkarrbooks.com

ONE

WITH PRACTICE, EVEN killing gets easier. Especially when killing an Elect.

Rylee peered into the thermal scope of her rifle. A scene of purples and blues filled her vision, exposing shapes in the night she could not see without her thermal scope. She scanned up the deserted street but saw none of the warm tones of orange and yellow she sought. Just cold blue brick walls, set with light blue windows, and a black street below.

She held her right hand up to her earpiece.

"Serg," she said, her voice just above a whisper. "Are you sure you caught them on the cameras?"

Her earpiece hissed for a second, then filled with Serghei's voice. "What, you think I made it up? Three Elects cruising around the slums in the middle of the night. You're right, I made it up. Go back to bed."

Rylee rolled her eyes. "Maybe you dreamt it. You do have a wild imagination sometimes."

"I don't dream about Elects. Unless that Elect happens to be female and—"

"Enough chatter, you two." Preston's voice broke into the line. "Serghei's caught something on his cameras. We're going to find out who or what it is. Rylee, I want you to keep moving south. Scan any of the side streets that Serghei's cameras might miss. And stay off your Harley."

"Moving out," Rylee said.

"Feng, you keep scouting the west sector. Serg, keep watching those camera feeds."

"Aye, aye, Captain," Serghei replied.

"And don't call me that."

Rylee stood, slinging her rifle over her shoulder so that the strap ran across her chest. She was on the roof of one of the housing unit buildings in the slums. She sprinted toward the opposite side. Without the aid of her thermal scope, her vision was impaired. There was no moonlight or starlight to speak of. These were shrouded by the perpetual cloud cover that loomed over the city. There were no street lamps or glowing windows, either. Not in the slums at this hour. Only two hours of electricity a day.

Despite the darkness, Rylee ran confidently toward the edge of the building. She'd spent the last two years training her night vision. Even now, she ran with head sweeping back and forth, utilizing her more sensitive peripheral vision to see what lay ahead of her.

As she reached the roof's parapet wall, she sprang onto it, then immediately leaped across to the next building. She landed on one outstretched foot, and kept running, dashing from one building to the next. It was fortunate the buildings were erected so close together. At least, when one needed to jump from one building to the next. In the case of a building fire, it was not so fortunate. Flames could leap just as nimbly.

After the sixth building, Rylee skidded to a stop, tore off her rifle, and scanned the east-west bound street below her with her scope. Her pulse spiked. A small orange glow flashed inside the scope as she swept it over the scene below. With a jerk she focused on the spot. The orange figure scurried out from between two buildings, a greenish object dangling from its snout.

She exhaled, her heart rate slowing.

A rat.

Not what she was looking for. She watched the rodent as it skulked away. Some who lived in the slums would see that rat as a chance to eat that day. An involuntary shudder ran through her, as she began scratching the tattoo on the back of her right hand. She had never known *that* kind of hunger. She hadn't been Deprecated.

Quickly, she finished her scan of the street.

We're taking too long.

Rylee and the others didn't know why the Elects had come into the slums. But at that hour of the night, it couldn't be for anything

2

good. And depending on what it was, these three Elects could be done and gone in a matter of minutes. Time pressed.

Removing the coil of rope and grappling hook from her shoulder, she secured the hook to the wall's parapet. Then let the rope drop down the side of the build. Slinging her rifle across her back again, she took hold of the rope and rappelled down. The five-story drop flew by as though she were falling. She only stopped abruptly just before she reached the street, her gloved hands burning from the friction in the rope. From the street, she whipped the rope so that a wave flowed through it, and a moment later the hook clattered to the ground. She re-coiled it, then dashed down the street toward her next cluster of buildings.

Suddenly, her earpiece hissed. "Bingo!" Serghei's voice came into her ear. "Camera seven. One of the recordings. Not live. They were headed east. None of the other nearby cameras have anything."

"Give us a perimeter to work," Preston said.

A few moment's silence.

"Housing units 43-D, 48-D, 48-M, and 43-M."

"Tripe! Can't you narrow it down?" Feng's voice came over for the first time.

"Sorry, boss. Not enough cameras. We're underfunded, remember?"

"We're not funded," Preston said. "That's close enough. Feng, you take 48-M, moving south. Ry, you take 43-D, moving east. I'll take 48-D and move to intersect Feng. As soon as you have a visual, radio in. Nobody engages until Ry's got them under scope."

"Copy," Rylee replied, tearing down a side street at a full sprint toward the location.

"Can't I rest for a minute?" Feng said, "I've been running in the opposite direction forever."

"Move it, Feng. There's no time for slacking," Preston said.

"You're worse than my boss at the docks. Can I switch jobs? I want Serg's position. He just sits in the hideout and watches movies."

Rylee smiled to herself. She could imagine the exasperated

expression on Preston's face, his head shaking.

"They're camera recordings," Serghei said. "There's a difference."

"Serg doesn't get to shoot Elects," Preston replied.

"Good point. On my way."

"Me too," huffed Rylee. "I'll be there in five minutes."

The line went quiet.

Rylee reached her assigned corner of the new search area and began ascending the nearest building. Halfway up, a sound made her pause. It came from down the street to her left. Dropping back to the street, she unslung her rifle and brought the scope to her eyes. Again, the familiar purple and blue hues of the thermal scope filled her vision. This time, there was something more. Shades of bright orange and vibrant red. The forms were not organic, but angular, manmade. Electrocycles—three of them. Vehicles of the Elect. Perfect for someone not wanting to be heard in the dead of night.

Rylee dropped to her knees, unfolded the bipod attached to the muzzle of her rifle, then flattened herself on the street. Despite the heat her body had generated from her run, she shivered as the cold asphalt leached through her clothes to her belly and thighs.

Jamming the stock of her rifle into her shoulder, she peered back into her scope.

"Targets possibly located," she said into her earpiece. "There are three cycles outside one of the housing units—43-H, I think."

"Good work," Preston's voice came over her earpiece. "Do you have a sighting on the Elects?"

"Negative."

"I'll be there in three minutes. Do *not* engage until I get there. Feng?"

"I'm moving, I'm moving," Feng said over the line, sounding exhausted.

Rylee placed her finger near the trigger of her rifle, but not on it.

Only an idiot goes around with his finger on the trigger all the time. A lesson her grandfather had drilled into her since she was old enough to hold a gun. *Only when you have your target in sight.*

Otherwise, you'll end up shooting something or someone *you don't intend to.*

And where were those targets? She scanned the nearest building. Had they gone inside? The outer door of the building was closed. But that didn't mean they hadn't gone in another way, or were careful enough to close the door behind them. A desire to move in closer surged within her. They could be doing *anything* inside. *Vermin.* She knew it would be futile, though. Three Elects against a single Norm…

She shook her head. A wisp of white moisture condensed in front of her like smoke as she exhaled in frustration. *Where are you, Preston?*

Suddenly, she noticed something she hadn't before. One of the windows. Was it open, or entirely missing its glass? Of the hundreds of housing unit buildings, none of them didn't have at least a few broken or boarded windows. But this one, why would the occupants leave it uncovered? Perhaps if it were in the sweltering heat of summer. Not with the season so deep into autumn.

A mass of yellow and red appeared in the windows. The form moved quickly, climbing out of the window back onto the street. The precise, fluid motion gave the figure away. It always did. Only an Elect moved like that. Another figure appeared in the window and climbed out in the same precise manner. Elect number two. As soon as the second was on the street, both Elects reached back into the window.

After a moment, they started to back away. They were holding onto…*something*. Something warm, judging from the thermal color. Legs?

"Where are you guys?" she said into her earpiece. "I have positive sighting of two Elects. And I have a feeling they're not going to hang around much longer."

Her earpiece cracked and hissed. "Almost there," Preston said. "Another minute."

We may not have another minute. She adjusted her grip on the rifle.

The object the Elects were holding was not fully visible. Another person. A Norm, no doubt. Gagged and bound around the ankles and wrists. She couldn't tell the gender for certain from her current angle. Like Rylee herself, the figure's hair was cropped short. But any girl in the slums would be a fool not to keep it short. The captured figure's body was thin—typical for a Norm. Rylee inspected the upper torso. Still hard to say. At this distance, the thermal image was not well defined. There did seem to be the correct curvature in that area.

A third figure appeared just within the window, holding the captured girl under the armpits. The poor girl was not moving. Practically as rigid as a corpse. Was she unconscious, or under some spell of the Elects? Then she noticed the girl's head move. Not unconscious. Probably too terrified to fight back.

Shoot now, she told herself. She could kill one of them, at least. The others may scurry away like the rat she saw earlier. At least the girl would be safe.

She fixed the scope's reticle over the head of the first Elect and brought her finger to the trigger. She hesitated.

Always be mindful of what's behind your target. Another of her grandfather's unbidden lessons came into her thoughts.

By the time she verified the shot was clear, the Elects had moved. A curse escaped under her breath. Her clear shot was gone. The three Elects huddled around one of the cycles, working stealthily.

They're going to get away.

She moved the reticle to the Elect holding the girl's arms. But the girl's head was too close. If the girl moved suddenly...No, the shot was too risky.

Where was Preston?

They had the girl on the back of the cycle now, the lead Elect already mounted. *He* was the one to shoot. But the girl's back was facing her now. Rylee would only get one shot. The back tire, or one of the other Elects? Airless tires were far too common. Not waiting for anything else, she moved her reticle to the nearest Elect, exhaled, and pulled the trigger.

TWO

THE GUN'S REPORT shattered the silent night like the earth splitting in two. It momentarily deafened Rylee and echoed forcefully off the huddled buildings surrounding her.

"What the blazes was that!" Preston's voice sounded a mile away, even though it came from her earpiece.

Rylee ignored him. Not waiting to see the Elect fall, she jumped to her feet, slung her rifle over her shoulder and sprinted down the street toward the other Elect. The one with the girl was already speeding away. Though its electric motor was nearly silent, the hum of its wheels on the asphalt was distinct.

"Ry, report!" Preston's voice came again. "Are you there?"

"I'm not dead," she replied curtly, not breaking stride.

She needed to focus. Running in the middle of the street like that left her exposed. Not terribly. The Elects weren't carrying rifles. She knew they'd likely have handguns, though. But even an Elect would have trouble hitting a moving target at that distance and in such darkness. The real question was would the other Elect stand and make a fight, try to escape on his cycle, or run away through an alley?

If she were an Elect, she would fight. With their capabilities, she wouldn't be afraid of *any* Norm. Perhaps the PNUs did not eradicate one's sense of self-preservation. Cowards were still cowards.

This particular Elect seemed to be the cowardly sort. As she drew closer to the spot where the two cycles stood and where the dead Elect's body lay in the street, the dark gloom cleared a little. There was no sign of the other Elect. Still, she removed her pistol, a Glock 17, from the shoulder harness she wore beneath her jacket. The worm might be hiding around the corner of the alleyway, waiting for her to get closer.

Two quick bursts of gunshot erupted nearby. Immediately, she dropped to her stomach, pistol aimed at the mouth of the alleyway.

Nothing was there. The shots hadn't come from the alley. She knew that. The sound was too distant. And she had seen no muzzle flash.

"What is going on!" Preston demanded in her earpiece.

"That was me," gasped Feng on the line. "Ran into one of the Elects on his cycle. Why don't those idiots drive with their lights on?"

"Is he dead?"

"No way, man. You know I can't hit nothing moving like that. Scared him off down 21st, though."

"I'm going after him," Rylee said.

Convinced the other Elect had run away on foot, Rylee went straight for one of the two abandoned cycles.

"Rylee, no. It's too dangerous," Preston said, voice urgent.

"Sorry, Preston. I'm not going to let them take that girl."

Rylee straddled the cycle and turned it on.

"Rylee!" Preston's voice was a near growl.

"There's another cycle here. The third Elect ran off on foot heading north." With that, she gunned the cycle's throttle and rocketed down the street.

For a few seconds, she fumbled with the controls before she got the headlights turned on. It was too late to worry about who might see her. Already she saw windows faintly illuminated with a sallow glow. Hand-cranked lanterns. Just like the ones she and her grandfather used at night when their power was shut off. The windows flew by in a blur.

She smiled. The cycle was fast. It was different than riding her Harley, but fast.

On her left, she passed Feng trying to wave her down. She didn't stop. There wasn't time. Having Feng along might help, but she likely couldn't afford the added weight. If she detected correctly, these cycles lacked the torque to carry heavy loads. She hoped that would slow down her prey enough to give her an edge.

"Sorry, Feng," she said over her radio. "No time to stop."

"That's right," he said over the line. "Go have all the fun without me. Make me run all over the blasted slums."

An intersection approached. Rylee cut the throttle, leaned so her left knee almost skidded on the asphalt, then accelerated out of the turn.

"Serg?" she said into her earpiece.

"Right here," he replied.

"I need a route."

"What's the magic word?"

"Or I'll shoot you in the crotch when I get back to the hideout."

"That's more of a phrase, but it will work. One second. Let me see...no...not there...Ah! Your best bet is to cut him off at Holgate or Plum street."

"Got it."

Rylee gunned the throttle.

"I'm on the other cycle," came Preston's voice suddenly. "I'm coming to help."

Good. Because she had no plan for what to do once she caught up to the Elect. All she knew was that she couldn't let him take that girl. Whoever she was, she didn't deserve the fate that undoubtedly awaited her if the Elect got away. No one did.

Rylee's jaw muscles tensed as she leaned deeper into the cycle and torqued the throttle even more.

Cold, moist air tore at her hair and the back of her jacket. But she scarcely noticed either the wind or the chill.

She reached Holgate and turned onto it, barely letting off the throttle.

"I'm on Holgate," she reported. "Now what?"

"He should be—"

"There!" she shouted as the Elect, girl, and cycle raced across one street over. "Never mind, I found them. Heading north on...er...something. Heading north."

Too addled to think about street names, she leaned her cycle into another turn, following the wake of the Elect. Her headlights shown on him as she pulled up from the turn. He was already a few hundred yards away. The girl was clinging to the back of the

Elect, her thin white shirt and pants flapping madly in the wind.

Rylee gunned the engine. As she had hoped, she made steady gains on them. Not quick enough to evade notice. Evading an Elect's notice in a high-stress situation was harder than trying to dupe her grandfather. Within a few moments, she was trailing them closely.

"Okay Serg, any ideas what to do now? I'm right behind them."

She couldn't shoot him from the back. The girl was still in the way. Almost anything else she could think to do would likely make the pair crash. A crash that would surely kill the girl. The Elect might walk away from it.

"You could try flashing him," Serghei said. "That might make him slow down."

"Oh, you're so helpful."

"Hey, it would make me slow down."

"Rylee." Preston's voice. "Do see if you can slow him down. I'm going to try cutting him off. Maybe take a few shots at the street ahead of him. Just to spook him."

"I'll see what I can do."

Great. Wasting bullets. If she had to shoot, she'd prefer to aim directly at the Elect.

Drawing out her pistol, she took aim just to the right of the cycle. The kickback from the shot threw her hand back more than she expected. Why would anyone try to shoot one of these things with one hand? It was hard enough aiming a pistol with two hands when stationary, not to mention traveling at eighty miles-per-hour.

She didn't see the bullet strike, but the Elect's cycle swerved to the right. Again, she took aim, this time on the left side, and fired. Ready for the flail of the gun in her hand, she controlled it better and saw a spark ignite off the street. The Elect swerved right. What if one of the bullets ricocheted off the street into a window? At least she was shooting down-street.

Her shots had done their job. The Elect's speed decreased some. She lifted her pistol to fire again. Without warning, the Elect reached back his arm. It fell over the shoulder of the girl, pointing directly at Rylee. The slight shimmer of a gun's barrel reflected the light of her headlights.

"Desolation!" she shouted.

With a jerk, she leaned hard to the right, just as the Elect fired the shot. What kind of pistol was it? It was hard to tell in the low light and from her angle. But the grip…

Stop it! An Elect is shooting at you and you're trying to figure out what kind of pistol he has?

The Elect hadn't even turned to look at her as he shot, yet he had aimed straight at her.

How are they so precise?

"Did you just say *dislocation*?" Serghei asked.

"Yes! I'm going to dislocate your nose if you don't leave me alone. I'm being shot at." He knew that's not what she said.

"You know, the nose doesn't have a socket. So, you can't technically—"

"Hold on, Ry," Preston's voice broke in. "I'm almost there."

Right. No problem.

The Elect fired another shot. Again she dodged…barely. But he predicted her maneuver, immediately following up with a second shot. Something struck the top of her shoulder. It didn't knock her back though. She tested her arm. Did the bullet just graze? How did he shoot so well like that, and one-handed?

This was insane. She was going to get herself killed if she didn't do something. Time to waste more bullets. Swerving hard to the left, she fired off two rounds. Then swerved to the other side, and fired off three more.

How many rounds was that? Six? Seven? She fired again. It was working. The shots were keeping him busy enough to prevent retaliation. This wouldn't last, though. He'd figure out she wasn't trying to hit him.

Where was Preston? They were running out of time. Soon they would be out of the slums. And the closer they got to the boundary the more likely they'd run into Regulators. That would only bring them trouble. Already a full squadron could be heading their way.

The Elect got off a shot at her. It whizzed past her head, a sharp whistle sounding in her ear. She couldn't keep this up. What if…

Without stopping to talk herself out of it, she gunned the engine. More rapidly than she expected, her cycle brought her alongside the Elect. Not bothering to aim properly, she fired a single round at the Elect, then squeezed the left brake handle as tightly as she could. With a lurch, she fell behind him. Despite the Elects enhanced reflexes, she had apparently caught him off guard.

The bullet struck the Elect somewhere on his side. He nearly fell off his cycle from the impact. Yet he managed to stay on.

How did he—

She ducked as he swung his arm around and unleashed a torrent of bullets at her. One struck the front-right fender, almost hitting her knee. She slammed on her brakes even harder. Another bullet struck the windshield, passing through, barely missing her face. The shot made her jerk hard left. Her front tire struck a pothole. In vain she tried to compensate. But the bike was already tilting, her rear tire starting to slide. She felt the loss of control, and panic gripped her.

There wasn't enough time to power out of it. She was too close to the buildings. If her back wheel struck the wall, she would be smashed against the bricks. Only one way out. Pulling hard to the right, she laid the bike down. With a force that whipped her neck like a flimsy cord, her back slammed against the pavement.

I don't even have on a helmet, she thought as sparks from the side of the cycle's aluminum body sprayed like fireworks across the asphalt. Luckily, she managed to not get her leg pinned under the cycle. Her body slid free of it. Still, she fought to keep her legs from being mangled by the street's coarse surface. Beneath her back, pinned between flesh and asphalt, she could feel her rifle being ground to powder. The sound made her wish she were sliding on her face instead.

After what felt like minutes, she stopped sliding.

Body trembling, she lay on the icy street, unmoving. With a frazzled brain, she attempted a mental triage of her wounds. At first she felt nothing but shock and cold. Then the pain ruptured through the barrier formed by her adrenaline. Her thigh and left forearm felt like they'd been fried by a thousand volts of electricity. Her spine felt like someone had rammed railroad spikes into it. But she was alive.

The Elect was alive, too. And getting away with his prize.

From up the street, a screech of wheels made her jerk her head in that direction. Through the gloom she couldn't make out anything.

Gunfire erupted suddenly.

"Rylee, where are you?" It was Preston's voice in her earpiece. "I need backup."

Had he managed to barricade the road?

There was no time to ask questions. Or to worry about her injuries. A shootout—a duel—with an Elect was an extremely dangerous thing. Even if most Elects were idiots and held their guns with just one hand, they could still be surprisingly accurate.

Forcing herself to move, Rylee rolled onto her front and pushed herself up onto all fours. Her back screamed in pain. Then she unslung her rifle. She forced herself to put off inspecting its damage. It was still in one piece. It would fire—maybe.

Placing the bipod legs on the street, she painfully leaned over her rifle. Within the thermal scope, she found the Elect crouched behind his cycle, exchanging gunfire with someone she couldn't see. The girl was behind him, lying on the ground, her hands trying to shield her face and head. Screams split the air between the sharp bursts of gunfire. Where was Preston? And why wasn't that Elect incapacitated, or dead? She'd clearly struck him in the side with a bullet.

Could the PNU suppress pain to such a degree? Maybe. The PNU only controlled the brain. The Elect's blood loss should still slow him down. Unless he wasn't bleeding, because he wore a tactical vest. Bulletproof. Only Regulators wore those.

Taking aim at his head, and hoping her rifle still worked, she pulled the trigger.

The Elect's head rocked forward, and his body slumped to the street.

Rylee exhaled in relief, resting her forehead on her rifle's stock.

"Rylee? Was that your shot?" Preston's voice came into her

earpiece.

"You owe me one," she muttered.

"No kidding. Good job."

"Not to spoil this beautiful moment," Serghei's voice crackled over the line, "but Houston, we have a problem."

"What now?"

"Regulators."

THREE

"HOW MANY?" PRESTON asked over the line.

"Oh, one or two squadrons," Serghei said calmly over the line.

Rylee groaned. "You've got to be joking. One or two *squadrons?*"

"Would I joke about something like this?"

Rylee rolled her eyes.

"How close?" Preston asked.

"Eh, two minutes. If you're lucky."

"Ry," Preston said, "my cycle's Swiss cheese. Is yours operative?"

Rylee let out a deranged laugh, casting a glance over at the gray mass smashed against a wall. Its front wheel was obviously bent beyond repair. "You might be able to salvage a few bolts from it."

She could almost hear Preston shaking his head as he evaluated their plight.

"The dead Elect's cycle might work," he said after a moment. "You could use it to return the girl, then lead off some of the Regulators."

"No, you take her," Rylee said. "You're...," she grimaced as pain jolted through her back, "closer."

Preston noted the brief pause in her reply as she tried to talk through the pain. "Ry, what's wrong? Are you hurt?"

"Just go. I'll be fine. Nothing's broken." *I hope.*

"Stay put. I'm coming for you."

Her earpiece went silent. She decided not to argue. If she and Preston got into a stubbornness fight, the Regulators would have them detained long before either budged on the matter. And with the Regulators, there would be no question as to their conviction and summary execution. No evidence required.

Taking a deep breath, Rylee slowly lifted herself from the street and stood on shaky legs. After all she'd done tonight, standing felt like the greatest accomplishment. Her left forearm and hip still burned. Was there any skin left? She didn't dare to inspect the spots now. And she suddenly felt glad for the darkness. With one hand, she slung her battered rifle back over her shoulder.

Down the street she saw a headlight come to life. A bright bluish light. Within a few moments, the headlight started to grow larger, until the cycle was stopped on the street beside her.

Preston motioned with his head to the back of the cycle. "Get on."

Rylee looked at him incredulously. "There's no way we're all going to fit."

"We'll squeeze. It will work."

"Am I supposed to sit on your shoulders?"

"Fine," he said, setting the cycle's kickstand and climbing off. "You drive. I'll go on foot. Get yourself back to the hideout. I can keep the Regulators busy."

Rylee's eyes drifted from Preston's determined face to the frightened, shivering girl on the cycle. Now that the girl was closer, she could see her face more clearly. Lexi Bransen. The Elects always managed to find the pretty ones. Lexi was sixteen, if Rylee remembered correctly. Only two years younger than herself. Yet Lexi still seemed like just a young girl to Rylee. Young and innocent. A slender beam of pure light in a dark world. And a beautiful one. She thought about the girl, arms wrapped tightly around Preston as he drove her home.

Not going to happen.

"Okay," she said, straddling the cycle and fighting back the pain that seared up her side as she did so. "See you back at home." It wasn't really home. But she didn't want to give Lexi any clues about their hideout.

Then she flipped up the cycle's kickstand, and raced off down the street. Lexi instantly wrapped her arms around Rylee and pressed into her back. Pain surged through Rylee's body, momentarily making her vision go fuzzy.

"Not so tight," she gasped as loudly as she could.

Lexi's hold lessened slightly, but there was still a constant throbbing in her back.

Rylee didn't speed like a maniac with a death wish this time. She took care to avoid most of the cracks and ridges in the streets that still remained from the earthquakes of Desolation. As it was, running over a bit of gravel made her clench her teeth in pain.

"Feng?" Preston's voice came unexpectedly into her earpiece. "Where are you?"

"Oh, so did you decide that I'm still part of this team?" Feng still sounded out of breath. "Never mind me, I've just been chasing down an Elect alone and *on foot*."

"Very noble," Preston said. "Now get you and that wisecracking Chinese tongue of yours back to the hideout. And watch out for the Regulators."

"Don't worry about me. The Regulators won't come near me. I smell too much like fish."

The line went dead.

Within a few minutes, they reached Lexi's street. As they drew nearer to the girl's own building, more and more windows glowed with weak, sallow lights.

Great! The whole neighborhood was awake. Now she really wished for a helmet.

She stopped in front of Lexi's building and the girl climbed off. A light shone from Lexi's open window. Shadows traced along the walls of the room within.

Lexi cast a longing glance at it, then turned back to Rylee.

"Thank you," she said, almost too sweetly. "I don't know —"

"If you wish to thank me, you'll keep your mouth shut. You never saw me."

Movement caught Rylee's eye. A head poked out of Lexi's window. A man, his mouth gaped open.

More witnesses. Not good.

"Lexi?" the man said. "What in the world is going on?"

Time to leave.

Without saying another word, Rylee twisted the throttle and sped off into the night.

Now came the gamble. Preston offering the cycle was both a

blessing and a curse. A blessing because she didn't think she could have made it back to the hideout on her own. Scaling buildings was out of the question in her current condition. Even if her rope hadn't been shredded. A fact she would have to try and hide from her grandfather. The cycle was a curse, though, because now she had to do something with it.

If she left the cycle lying outside their hideout, it would be as good as suicide. The Regulators would find it, and then find their hideout. And then…the Elect Hunters themselves. That was what they called their little gang. The Elect Hunters. A morbid name. Serghei had unofficially given the moniker to the group two years ago when they decided to try and do something to fight back against the Elects. To fight against the growing tide of atrocities done to the Norms. It was as important to protect their gang as it was the people of the slums—more so.

The best course of action was to take the cycle far away and destroy it. Sink it to the bottom of Lake Washington or the Sound. Both were out of the question. Unless she was willing to sacrifice herself to do it. Her wounds needed medical attention. She could feel warm blood oozing down her leg . Perhaps she could hide it in an alleyway and dispose of it later. In her exhausted state, brain muddled by pain, she reasoned this to be her best option. Maybe Preston could do a better job of disposing of it when he returned to the hideout.

She drove within two blocks of the Elect Hunter's hideout, just along the border of the industrial district, where row after row of dilapidated warehouses provided refuge for illegal activities, Deprecates, and rats. Rylee deposited the cycle in a narrow alleyway, behind an old garbage dumpster, long since looted of its trash. Then she dragged herself the rest of the way to the hideout, each step adding to her pain.

Slumping against the door frame, she banged on the rusted metal that served as door to the warehouse. She tapped her earpiece. "Serg, it's me. Let me in."

"Password?" He said a moment later.

"I hate you and your passwords."

"Let her in, Serg," Preston said over the line. "She's injured."

Almost immediately, she heard the clanks and screeches of rusty steel, as Serghei unbolted and opened the door. Weak light spilled out into the alleyway. A lanky figure appeared in the doorway and hurried her inside.

"Gunshot wound?" Serghei asked, as he took hold of her shoulder to give her support. "Broken femur? Cracked skull?" He asked it not out of concern or worry. No, he sounded eager. Too eager.

"Just some scrapes and bruises," Rylee said through clenched teeth. Now that the adrenaline from the night's activities was wearing off, she felt the pain more acutely. "I laid down the Elect's cycle. Slid a good way."

"Wicked!" he said.

Wicked? Where did Serghei come up with these expressions? Of course, she knew exactly where they came from. Serghei's movie collection. The boy was a living catalog of old movies, which he'd collected over the years during his scavenging runs.

The word sounded especially odd spoken with his accent. A Romanian accent, Serghei claimed. But they all had their doubts about that. Both Serghei's parents were Romanian. But Serghei had been orphaned at age two, and raised here—far away from whatever was left of Romania—in the nursery with hundreds of other non-Romanians.

They walked down a short corridor, through another door, before coming into a large room. Rylee winced as the lights assaulted her eyes. Despite its size, the room was stuffed with things. Serghei's things. His treasures. Old electronics equipment that hadn't worked in twenty years, stacks of old hard drives pilfered from abandoned computers, cases of *very* flat Mountain Dew, piles of something called DVDs, and on and on.

Feng was already in the room, resting in one of the hole-ridden love seats and drinking a can of the flat Mountain Dew.

Rylee's throat constricted at the mere thought of drinking it. Preston drank the stuff too. She didn't know how they managed it.

Feng raised the can to her as she walked in. His usually pale face was red, and his jet-black hair lay matted against his forehead, wet with perspiration.

"Welcome back," he said without energy. "Thanks for saving some fun for the rest of us."

"You think nearly getting shot by an Elect multiple times, then crashing a cycle is fun?"

She unslung her rifle and eased into one of the chairs. Beneath her weight, the ancient springs in the cushions threatened to puncture the worn upholstery and prick her backside. That would feel like a massage compared to the pain she felt now.

Feng crushed the now-empty Mountain Dew can in his fist. "If it means massacring a few tripe-face Elects…"

Feng, whose parents had immigrated from China before he was born, actually did speak his parent's native tongue. But unlike Serghei, he did not speak with a foreign accent.

"Well, next time," she said, grimacing as she adjusted her left leg, "I'll let you have all the fun. Besides, we're trying to protect our people, not just kill Elects."

Feng tossed the can onto a pile of other crushed cans along the back wall. "Speak for yourself. I just want 'em dead—all of them. Every…last…one." He spoke this last bit through gritted teeth.

Rylee decided to drop the subject. They'd had this argument before. Feng had his reasons for despising the Elects. His own sister, a few years older than he was, had been taken on a night like tonight by a few sex-crazed Elect adolescents. Feng had tried to fend them off, but was too young and weak to do anything to save her.

"Any word from Preston?" she asked, knowing there hadn't been.

"Probably out being a hero, like always," Feng said.

Serghei came over to her then with a metal box in his hands—his first-aid kit, as he called it. Whatever that meant. Setting the kit down on the concrete floor beside her, he began inspecting her leg.

Rylee did the same. It was the first time she'd really gotten a look at it since her crash. Though she was not surprised, she still moaned within when she saw the gash in her pants. Not because of the torn and bloodied skin it exposed. No, that would heal—she hoped. The pants wouldn't. She only owned two pairs of pants. These were her nicest. Tough and warm. It was difficult to come by new clothes in the Post Desolation Reconstruction Alliance. Well, nothing was truly *new* anymore. Not like her grandfather remembered.

Maybe they could be mended.

"Did you leave any asphalt on the road?" Serghei said. "I can't tell if I'm looking at your leg or a chunk of the street."

Rylee didn't respond. She was in too much pain to feel like dealing with Serghei's humor. Not with Preston still out there and that cycle nagging at her thoughts.

"I'll need to clean this," Serghei added.

"Can't you just wrap a bandage around it?" she said, feeling a surge of pain just thinking about scrubbing the wound clean.

"Oh, sure. Not a problem. Dirt and asphalt, they accelerate the healing process. How could I have forgotten that?"

Rylee sighed. "Fine, do what you have to do."

"I'm going to have to cut away this pant leg. Unless…you'd prefer to take them—"

"Just cut them," she snapped, knowing exactly the alternative Serghei was about to suggest.

Serghei opened his first-aid kit and began riffling through it. He produced a pair of blunted scissors and began snipping away at the leg of her pants.

Rylee sucked in through clenched teeth as he pulled the fabric away from the wound bit by bit. For all his joking, Serghei really was a decent medic—considering his lack of training. And she trusted him. That was something hard to come by. Trust.

"Tripes, Ry!" Feng said suddenly. "What happened to your rifle?"

Rylee grabbed the weapon leaning against her right leg. With her own injuries, and everything else on her mind, she'd forgotten about her rifle. Feeling more afraid to look at its damage than her own, she slowly lifted it. She turned it over in her hands, letting the light shine fully on its side. Deep grooves marred the chassis, stock, and barrel. Much of the black anodized finished had been scraped away, leaving behind raw steel. The synthetic stock showed the most damage. By some miracle, the scope had not broken free. Later, she would have to realign it.

Rylee groaned. "How am I going to hide this from my grandfather?"

The old Winchester bolt-action rifle had belonged to her grandfather before he gave it to her. Part of his extensive gun collection that he managed to save from before Desolation came. In fact, all of their guns, including her own Glock had come from her grandfather's collection. Most people had lost everything but the clothes on their bodies. But her grandfather had been more prepared than most.

"Just tell him the truth," Feng said. "Most of it, anyway. You crashed your Harley. Got hurt, and damaged your rifle."

"And when he sees that my Harley is undamaged?"

"Please!" Feng said, leaning back and placing his hands on the back of his head. "That old bike of yours doesn't even look like it should still run."

Rylee shot him a cold glare but didn't respond.

Static filled her earpiece suddenly, then Preston's voice broke in. "Ry, what did you do with that other cycle?"

Both Serghei and Feng looked at Rylee. Rylee put her hand to her earpiece. "I stashed it behind a dumpster, near the hideout. Why?"

"Tell me you're joking," Preston said, frustration edging his tone.

"No. Why? What's going on?"

Rylee started to feel panicked. What had she done?

When Preston's voice returned, he sounded calmer. But there was a definite gravity there. "The Regulators. They've found it. And…they've made an arrest."

FOUR

"Look, everyone just go home for the night," Preston said, now sitting on the faded green vinyl couch in the Elect Hunter's hideout. "There's just a few more hours until daylight. We all need rest. We have a full day of work ahead of us." He took a long gulp of Mountain Dew.

"Sleep?" Serghei said, looking up from feeding his pet rat. "Who needs sleep? Work will always be there. Movie, anyone?"

"Speak for yourself," Feng said. "Some of us have real jobs. I'm out of here."

"Lathering yourself with halibut doesn't count as a job," Serghei retorted.

Feng only muttered something about hating fish, as he continued to walk away. It was true that Feng always smelt of fish. Some kind of fish. Salmon, lingcod, halibut. He worked on a fishing boat.

Rylee didn't move from her place in the old love seat. Her leg and arm were now dressed and bandaged. Serghei had even stitched the leg of her pants back on. Though, even to her untrained eye, the stitching looked questionable. She doubted the repair would survive the next time she sat down. But neither her pain nor her pants kept her anchored where she was.

She just sat there, scratching at the tattoo on the back of her hand. The tattoo didn't itch. Not anymore. When she first got it, back when she was seven, it had itched for weeks. Some kind of allergic reaction to the tattoo ink.

She never liked having the tattoo on the back of her hand. Without it though, the Alliance would refuse to recognize her as a legal member. No barcode, no rations.

Serghei loved to talk about the barcoded tattoos. A science-fiction cliché, according to him, right out of one of his old movies.

Whatever that meant.

"We can't do anything about it now," Preston said, reading the miserable look in her eyes. "It wasn't your fault. The blame is mine. I knew you were injured. I shouldn't have left you like that."

Rylee shook her head. "There wasn't room on that cycle. You know there wasn't."

"I could have sent Feng to intercept you. He could have disposed of the cycle properly."

She felt a modicum of consolation at Preston's attempt to place the blame on himself. It didn't surprise her that he would try to. He always took responsibility for the group's failures. This time, though, she wouldn't allow him to take the blame away from her. Nothing he said changed the fact that her actions had led to the arrest of one of their own people. She didn't argue further, though. What good would it do?

"You're sure you didn't see who it was?" she asked him for the second time that night.

Preston hesitated for only a fraction of a second. Someone who hadn't know him his whole life probably wouldn't have noticed it.

"It was too dark, Ry," he said, his voice heavy with weariness from the long night. "We can't know anything for certain right now."

His green and hazel-twined eyes met hers. He offered her a smile that didn't quite brighten those eyes. Not one of his smiles that drew people in, that made you forget that this was Preston Hyde. The boy—man really—who had plenty of reasons to never smile.

She sighed. What were they doing? They were just kids. She, just turned eighteen. Preston a year older. Feng, seventeen, and Serghei, sixteen. Maybe they were stupid to think they could fight back against the Elects.

"My offer still stands," Serghei said, beaming sincerely at both of them. "Stay and watch a movie. I think something light is in order. Perhaps, Citizen Kane?"

Rylee wrinkled her nose at the idea. "You call Citizen Kane light?" She had only seen the black-and-white film once. And that was enough for her. Nothing particular from the movie stood out to her. Only how depressing it was. She preferred the movies Serghei found with happy endings. Not that such things existed anymore.

"Come on, it's a classic."

"Serg," said Preston, sounding lighthearted for the first time all night, "that movie was made over a hundred years ago. It's a fossil."

"Fossil! No, no, my friend. One day you and I will have a serious talk about this matter."

"Right," replied Preston, downing the rest of his Mountain Dew in one gulp, then rising from the couch. He stretched, letting out an exaggerated yawn. "Well, I can't stick around either. Come on, Ry. I'll help you get home."

Rylee laughed. "Are you going to carry me over the puddles too? My *hero*." She pretended to swoon, like the women often did in Serghei's ridiculous movies.

Preston laughed—a real laugh. "No. But if you keep acting like that, I might shove you into one."

"Just because I'm injured, doesn't mean I can't break your nose...again."

Unconsciously, Preston grabbed his nose. It was still slightly crooked. She hadn't actually meant to break it the first time. A sparring accident. At least, that's what she had told herself—after she had calmed down. At any rate, a crooked nose complemented his rugged appearance. His tangled russet hair, his square jawline, his stubbled chin and calloused hands. His eyes were the only physical part of him that wasn't rough. No, his eyes were soft. Warm. Familiar.

Preston and Rylee left Serghei at the hideout. Whether he actually intended to spend the rest of the night watching one of his movies, they didn't know. The hideout doubled as Serghei's home, after all. He had no family. No parental unit. Nothing.

Despite their relative confidence that the Regulators had withdrawn from the area, they moved cautiously through the streets, silent. And Rylee's leg forced them to go at a snail's pace. It pained her to walk far more she would admit to Preston. Several times, she felt tempted to drop to the street and sleep there for the night.

If she didn't fear what would happen to her, she might have done it.

When they finally reached Rylee's housing unit, Preston ventured to speak, though softly. "You sure you'll be alright to work tomorrow?"

"What choice do I have?" she said. "I'll be fine."

"Besides," she added, her voice growing serious, "I'm more worried about what Regulation will do tomorrow with...whoever it was."

"Forget about that. There's nothing you can do. Besides, it'll probably all blow over. They don't have any evidence against anyone."

"You and I both know Regulation doesn't *need* evidence."

"I know. I know," he said, nodding his head. "But listen. You saved that girl tonight. Think about that. Now, try to get some rest. I'll see you in the morning."

He reached out and took her hand in his. It engulfed her own, warming it like an oven. A different sensation, making her whole body come alive, accompanied that touch. If she weren't marked with bruises all over her body, he probably would have hugged her.

"Everything will be fine," he whispered.

Then he turned and slipped away into the waning night.

Rylee snuck back into her apartment through the door. Though riskier, she didn't know if she could have managed climbing back in through her bedroom window. She had plenty of practice sneaking in and out. And even with an injured leg, she moved as quietly as a cat stalking a mouse. Her grandfather's bedroom door was closed, as always when he slept. She crept passed it and carefully opened her own bedroom door. Once inside, she stowed her things, making sure to hide her scarred rifled. Then she laid onto her cot and attempted to sleep, knowing full well nothing good would come in the morning.

FIVE

W<small>ILLIAM</small> G<small>RAYSON</small> S<small>TEELE</small> rubbed his eyes, yawning. He swiveled in his chair, turning to face the floor-to-ceiling windows that covered most of the southern wall of his office. Standing and stretching his lower back, he walked up to it and looked out. The windows commanded a respectable view of the city, perched on the fifteenth floor of his father's building. Not as high as his father's office on the eighty-ninth floor, which was almost as high as the clouds that perpetually plagued the region.

William didn't mind the clouds. Not usually. Often, they reflected his own mood. Gray. Brooding. Shrouding something from the rest of the world.

Those clouds seldom released the rain they obviously carried. An odd phenomenon that even his father's climate experts couldn't explain. Once one of the rainiest places on the planet, in the days before Desolation, the Alliance now thirsted for moisture of any sort. Ironically, he could look out the west-facing windows of his father's building and see no end of water. The Puget Sound. A vast inlet of saltwater, fed by the Pacific Ocean. If only that water would deign to evaporate, form clouds, and dump its payload over the entire region…

But Will had other matters to occupy his thoughts. The weather he could not control.

Turning his back to the city, he yawned again. A sure signal of an overheated brain. He knew he should take more frequent breaks. That was one thing he'd never been good at. Especially when he was so close to a breakthrough like this. There was just one more hurdle standing in his way.

He connected wirelessly to the neuro-synaptic simulator—the NSS—through his PNU-enhanced brain and halted the simulation of his most recent code changes. The NSS was a physical piece of hardware—one of the few in the building. It was slower than a real brain. But it was much safer than testing prototype code on a live subject. Not that such hadn't been done before. Rookie programmers always believe their code to be bug-free. Such a thing didn't exist. Not from rookies *or* from seasoned veterans. Not even from prodigies, like himself, who had been coding before they could read. Even with the massive simulators, static code analyzers, and automated threat modelers, bugs—vulnerabilities—always lurked somewhere in the code, waiting to be exploited. He excelled at that—exploiting vulnerabilities. And of all William's skills and virtues, it was the one his father valued most.

PNU. Programmable Neurotronic Unit. The name never failed to grate his sense of linguistic aesthetics.

He took off his white lab coat. A pointless article. No one in the labs needed physical symbols to identify scientists or engineers or security personnel. Everyone's profile was embedded into their assigned security certificate. The Central Molecular Nanotechnology Engineering Laboratories issued the certificates to everyone authorized to access any part of the building. Without it, doors wouldn't open. Walking into one of the clean rooms, William could instantly scan the workers' certificates using the microscopic transmitter/receivers embedded within his skin. The data from the certificates would then be routed via his nervous system to his brain, and picked up by his PNU. The names, job titles, security access level, etc. would all be presented to him.

He tossed the lab coat onto his chair. No one needed a lab coat here. His father liked order, though. If you asked William, the man was obsessed with it. But then, one had to be a little obsessive to do what his father did.

William walked over to the door, turned the metal handle, and stepped out into the hall. The thought of the archaic door handle often made him smile in amusement. His father loved to philosophize about trivial objects like doors and door knobs.

People used to believe the future meant doors that slid open automatically, computers and touchscreens on every accursed gadget, and flying cars. At this point, his father would shake his head. *Those people lacked vision. They didn't understand that the future was right here.* Then he'd tap on his right temple. *You put technology in the right place. Where it can change the world. There's nothing futuristic about doors that slide open. Any idiot can build that. But who really wants it? Imagine if every door in this building were an automatic sliding door. That's nearly a thousand doors. A maintenance nightmare. Mechanical things break. Increase the complexity of that mechanism, and you increase the risk of it breaking.*

Put your technology where it matters.

Of course, his father wouldn't stop there. He'd go one for another twenty minutes about the future. About how *everyone* got it wrong but him.

Despite the fact that William had heard his father's speech so many times he could quote it verbatim—hand gestures and facial expressions included—he happened to believe his father was correct. For all he didn't agree with his father, this was one of the few he did agree with him.

William stepped into the elevator and pressed the button for the sixty-fifth floor. A moment later, the doors—sliding, automatic doors—opened to his studio apartment. He stepped inside onto the polished walnut floors, a full wall of windows greeting him with the same somber gray light from outside.

Lander was there, reposed on the sofa mounded with enough feather pillows to soften a jump off the top of the building. Though his eyes were open, he didn't respond to William's presence as he walked into the room. For several moments, William just stood there, looking at his friend. At nineteen, Lander was two years William's minor. But sometimes that age gap felt like two decades. Especially at moments like these, when Lander's mouth hung open slightly, his eyes focused on objects only he could see, occasionally muttering something William tried not to hear. At least, Lander had his clothes on.

William said Lander's name. No response. He shook his head and sent an interrupt message directly to Lander's PNU. William knew how to send messages that would bypass any blocks Lander might have enabled while he was *busy*. Of course, Lander could beef-up his message blockers with his own code, if he wasn't so lazy.

The message wouldn't be presented within Lander's vision as text for him to read. That was a primitive notion of technology. Another one his father liked to discuss at length. Reading was slow. Cumbersome. The PNU allowed William's message to flow directly into Lander's own thoughts. No visual clutter. No reading.

"I hope you have something important to say," said Lander, his voice flat.

"I just thought you might like to know that there's a *real* person in the apartment with you."

"So considerate of you."

"Hey," William said, holding out his hands, "I'm just trying to prevent an embarrassing situation…for both of us."

"You can join if you want. You know I'm always willing to share."

William raised an eyebrow. "So there's more than one, is there?"

"No," Lander said, shrugging his shoulders. "But you should see her. The most gorgeous woman on the planet."

"That's not saying much. Now that the earth's population is one-hundred-thousandth of what it was before Desolation."

"She's more beautiful than any woman who ever lived."

"You do realize that she is not even a real woman?"

Lander grinned stupidly. "I know. She's better. She never nags me, she's only there when I want her, plus she looks, smells, and *feels* just like the real thing."

William didn't respond. They'd had this conversation before. Lander was addicted to the simulated companions—the SimComps—that his PNU enabled. The PNU applications could augment any of the user's senses. If the user wanted to see a field of flowers growing on his floor, the PNU could do it. Trick the brain into believing it saw flowers. The user could smell the flowers and feel them brushing at his ankles. Lots of people, like Lander, used this capability to make their fantasies become as close to reality as possible.

And it was all possible thanks to the PNU.

William sat down in one of the wingback armchairs across

from the sofa. He didn't have the energy to get into a debate about the virtues—or lack thereof—of the SimComps. He didn't even have the energy to get up and get an energy drink. Truth be told, there were worse preoccupations involving the PNUs. He was all too familiar with those as well.

"How are things going with your current project?" William asked, his tone casual.

Lander leaned back on the sofa, clasping his hands behind his head. "That's classified information. But I will say that your father is pleased. Yours?"

"Same."

Like William, Lander was another one of his father's tools. Neither of them had any dissolutions about that. Of course, that wasn't their official job title. Each had a cover project that the rest of the engineers and scientists believed they worked on. And, as a strict rule, neither was allowed to discuss their work with the other.

So long as they did what William's father asked of them, they basically got to do whatever they wanted. If ever they wanted to break off their arrangement...well, William didn't like to consider that.

That didn't change the fact that William almost always discovered what Lander was working on. And Lander discovered what William was working on. This time, though, things were a little...different. William couldn't quite put his finger on what that difference was.

"By the way," Lander said, "Adrianna stopped by."

William groaned. "Fabulous."

"What? I don't know what your problem is, mate. As far as the real deal goes, they don't get any better than Adrianna."

William shook his head. "Have you ever considered that there's more to the opposite sex than..." He hesitated.

"Sex?" Lander offered.

"Never mind. I forgot who I was talking to." He stretched, yawning again. Then he stood. "I'm going to go eat something. I can't remember when I ate last."

"Eat later. You need to relax. Come on, I have just the thing."

Ignoring his friend's invitation, William walked wearily over to the kitchen. He had no interest in Lander's form of relaxation. Besides, he couldn't relax, even if he wanted to. He wished he understood why. Maybe once he completed this latest assignment, he'd be able to relax and feel like everything was normal again. Deep down, though, he knew that wasn't the answer.

SIX

DESPITE HER FATIGUE, Rylee found only a few fitful minutes of rest before her grandfather was rapping on her bedroom door, calling her to breakfast. Rylee beat her head against her home-made pillow—a few bits of rags sewn together, then stuffed with discarded lint from the wash house.

So that her grandfather didn't come barging in to check on her, she muttered a semi-intelligible "I'm awake." Then forced herself to sit up, biting back a scream of pain that burned in her throat. Once upright, she exhaled and just sat for a moment, breathing in and out, eyes closed.

You can do this, Ry. Ignore the pain. Ignore the pain.

Making as few movements as possible, and gritting her teeth the whole time, she undressed. The cold air groped at her bare skin, and she started to shiver. No electricity at nights meant no heating. She stuffed her torn jacket and her pants into the box that served as her dresser, and started the slow process of pulling on her spare clothes.

A second knock rattled her door. "You awake in there?" her grandfather called from the other side.

"Just a minute."

Trying to ignore the pain in her arm, she pulled on her faded green sweatshirt. A Seahawks sweatshirt. The one she refused to wear except on wash days. Maybe the sweater would distract her grandfather from asking about her jacket.

The oversized sweater tended to put her grandfather into nos-talgia mode. Taking him back to the days before Desolation had destroyed everything he'd known. Back when the Post Desolation Reconstruction Alliance was a city called Seattle. Some people still called it by its pre-Desolation name. Others called it the Puget Sound, referring to the ocean inlet whose waters formed the western border of the city. Most simply called it the Alliance. Her grandfather remembered the days before the Alliance better than most. He could talk about Seattle Seahawks football games for hours, once he got going.

Rylee knew practically nothing about either the Seahawks or football. Or even the way things had been before Desolation. She had only been two years old when most of Seattle had been destroyed by a massive earthquake. As far as the rest of the world was concerned, Seattle was lucky. It had been one of the last areas to fall—to truly experience the wrath of Desolation.

Rylee finished lacing up her black leather boots, then walked out of her room, making sure to close the door behind her. Her grandfather was seated at their small kitchen table, hunched over a chipped plate, dolloped with a clump of cold refried beans. She knew they were cold because they had no means to cook anything.

Her grandfather looked up at her and frowned. His grizzled hair was disheveled as usual, and a tuft of it stood up on the side of his head, trained by his pillow during the night. Except for being a bit shorter in length, his beard matched his hair, both in sloppiness and color. Rylee imagined her own dark hair didn't look much better.

Forget showering in the morning. Her grandfather often spoke of doing so before Desolation. Those were in times when the water came from the pipes steaming hot. In the slums, if the water came out at all, it was as frigid as jumping in an ice-covered lake this time of year. She only forced herself to shower once a week—or two—because she eventually grew tired of her own stench. She called it her *two minutes of torture*. Like rubbing fistfuls of snow all over her bare body. She shivered at the thought.

Her grandfather showered more often than she. But then, her grandfather was probably the toughest sixty-year-old she knew. A Norm his age had to be. Or he would have been Deprecated years ago.

Those hard, chiseled lines of her grandfather's face frowned as he took in the sight of her. "What did you do?" he said, digging his spoon into the beans and taking another bite. He hadn't asked as though he were concerned or even that interested. But there was definitely a subtle edge of accusation in his voice.

"What do you mean?" she asked, taking her seat at the table and biting back the jolt of pain that shot through her leg as she did so.

"You never wear that sweater, you knucklehead," he said gruffly. "Not unless you're trying to butter me up, or distract me from something."

Rylee felt her insides burn a little. She took a bite of the cold beans and immediately swallowed. It was amazing what you could eat when you didn't give your taste buds time to process the food. "I ripped my jacket," she said, making her voice sound casual. "It was a stupid accident. I'm going to see if Serghei can patch it." At least, that last part was the truth.

Her grandfather grunted, then took a swig of water from his cup. "What kind of accident?"

Rylee shrugged. "Caught it on something, wire or something at work."

He grunted again.

Rylee's stomach knotted up inside. And her breakfast wasn't the cause. This was her grandfather, her only family in the whole world. And she sat there, lying to him.

"When I was a boy," he said, "parents often chided their children for carelessness with their things. 'Clothes don't grow on trees' they'd tell them. Now they don't even come out of factories."

"I'm sorry, grandpa," she said, her voice showing the sincerity that she felt. "I'll try to be more careful."

Taking two more spoonfuls of beans, Rylee stuffed the remainder of her breakfast into her mouth, drank some water, then rose to leave.

"I've got to get to work," she said. She was more than anxious to get to the Workers Square to hear if there was any news about last night's events, and to avoid further interrogation about her jacket.

"Aren't you forgetting something?"

Midstride to deposit her dirty dishes in the sink she stopped, and let her shoulders droop.

Why does he insist on doing this?

She turned back around and seated herself again. "Right," she said. "I forgot." Couldn't he let her go just *one* morning without this ritual?

Clearing his throat, her grandfather reached into his pocket and drew out a palm-sized book. Its brown leather binding was as worn and creased with age as her grandfather's skin. He riffled through the delicate pages until he came to the spot that he'd been looking for. It was a book he called the Bible. Actually, as he liked to explain, it was just part of the Bible. The New Testament. And he insisted on reading a verse of it to her every day.

Rylee tapped her foot on the floor as he began to read. But before he could get a word out, the sirens started blaring.

* * *

Norms flooded Workers Square, their necks craned toward the platform at the north end. The air still pulsed with the sirens, demanding the attention of all denizens of the slums. Above, the gray clouds hung low, like a blanket of smoke threatening to smother them all.

Rylee scratched the back of her hand as she and Preston took in the scene from a rooftop. Other Norms lined the rooftops of the other buildings surrounding the square. Otherwise, she and Preston wouldn't have risked standing out so much.

Not every Norm in the slums could fit into Workers Square, no matter how tightly the people crammed together. Even though the sirens meant everyone *must* come to the square. But enough would be there to be effective. Effective at conveying whatever message the CA desired for them. That message would reach the ears of the others, like her own grandfather, who ignored the sirens, from the mouths of the many who were present.

Inside, Rylee secretly wished she possessed the strength to stay away. More often than not, a call to Workers Square meant some alteration in rationing, an extension of work hours, or some method of further burdening the Norms. Other times, it was merely for the CA's propaganda machines to bolster the CA, to celebrate the gains he had made in rebuilding all they had lost.

Order will save us.

That was the mantra that had been pounded into her skull since she was old enough to go to work in the fields. It accompanied all messages like the one she feared was coming.

Order will save us.

She repeated the words in her mind, and scratched at the back of her hand. Just being near Workers Square brought them unbidden. Sometimes the acrid words almost reached her own lips.

Workers Square. As a child she had come to the square every morning. She was only six when she first went to work—weeding, pollinating, planting—until her fingers and knuckles bled. That was the rule, though. The order of things. In her mind, she pictured her first day waiting nervously in the square, before piling into the back of a large truck crammed with mud-sodden children. That was the day she met Preston. He was a seven-year-old, with a year's more experience. Even at that young age, he had shown confidence and leadership. He had helped her more than she could say in those first few weeks.

She and Preston were no longer field workers. Like many children, they had moved on to apprenticeships once they turned ten. Preston worked as a mechanic, repairing the decrepit fleet of trucks, construction vehicles, and farming equipment that the Post Desolation Reconstruction Alliance operated. Rylee worked as a journeyman electrician. Rarely did she have reason to come to Workers Square these days, where the trucks picked up field workers, scavengers, loggers, and other laborers in the mornings.

"That green looks…impressive on you," Preston said.

Rylee looked down at her sweatshirt and frowned. She had almost forgotten she was wearing the hideous thing. "Impressive?" she said, raising an eyebrow at him.

"Sure," he said, grinning. "It makes you…stand out."

She jabbed him with her elbow. "Stand out? Wow, thanks. You sure know how to make me feel better."

Preston was laughing too hard to say anything back. Despite herself, and the pent-up anxiety she felt, Rylee let herself smile a little. Preston was so...serious most of the time, stolid. At times like these, you would think he didn't have a care in the world. He did it for her. He always knew what she needed. How could she help but love him for it?

The drone of the crowd below suddenly changed pitch. Rylee turned her gaze toward the square's platform. A line of men garbed all in black, with tactical vests and assault rifles, marched across the platform. Regulators. They halted so that they formed a protective barrier between the crowd and the platform. A moment later, a figure stepped out.

Garrison Pike, Chief Regulator of the Post Desolation Reconstruction Alliance. He walked with his head held high, his movements fluid and precise. If his walk and his slicked hair didn't give him away as an Elect, his clothes did. A long forest-green coat, fastened to the top of his throat with silver buttons—not a single patch, stain, or tear to be seen.

A hush fell over the packed crowd.

The knot in Rylee's stomach doubled. Presence from the Chief of Regulation could only mean one thing.

"Fellow members of the Alliance," he said, his hand clasped behind his back. Though he spoke without a magnification device, his words amplified and echoed through the square and adjoining streets with unnatural force. Serghei had commented on this apparent phenomenon more than once. The Elects, he had explained, could wirelessly interface with amplifiers mounted around the square. That was the gist of what she understood, or cared to understand. Serghei, of course, could talk about the Elects' abilities for hours.

"Members," Garrison Pike repeated, not an ounce of warmth in his words. "You have been summoned here this morning so that you might witness justice being served."

A murmur rose and fell from the crowd below.

"Last night," he went on, "two of our members were murdered in cold blood on these very streets."

More murmurs.

Rylee's heart began to race.

"Two members who have served the Alliance with much vigor,

and who might have gone on to do great things..."

Why was he going on about this? In the last two years, Regulation had never responded like this to the killing of an Elect. Sure, they had performed investigations and issued warnings to the people of the slums. Nothing ever became of it, though. The Regulators knew precisely for what purpose Elects came to the slums. Any who came deserved what they got. If not worse. Why this, though? First, an arrest. And now a public denouncement by the Chief Regulator.

"The Alliance will not tolerate such heinous crimes. This was not simply an attack on two individuals, but an attack on all of us. An attack on all we are trying to rebuild. An attack on the order. And thus we charge Vincent Bowen for the murders of Private Ian Gyles and Commander Michael Pike."

The pronouncement hit Rylee like a bullet in the chest. She rocked back, nearly tripping over her own feet. Eyes wide, she turned to Preston. Had she heard correctly? His eyes, too, gaped wide.

It was true, then.

I killed the Chief Regulator's son.

SEVEN

NOW SHE UNDERSTOOD the prompt backlash from Regulation. The Chief Regulator's son, a Regulation squadron commander. She'd killed the Chief Regulator's own son.

Rylee closed her eyes and squeezed them tightly together.

What did I do?

She should have let him get away with Lexi. That was him she had pursued on the cycle and then killed after Preston had barricaded him. She felt very little doubt of that. A squadron commander. It explained the tactical vest that she suspected he had worn. And why, even for an Elect, he handled his pistol so deftly.

"Order will save us," Garrison Pike declared, voice booming through the square. *Order will save us.* Few good things bore the CA's seal of *order.* "Those who commit such crimes rebel against that order. They threaten our very survival."

Pike made a curt gesture, and two Regulators moved in response. A few seconds later, they hauled a gangly figure onto the platform and forced him to his knees in front of the crowd. The figure looked out at the crowd, hands bound behind his back, mouth gaping.

"Boney?" Rylee said, unintentionally speaking aloud. Preston nudged her to keep quiet. She couldn't risk saying anything incriminating. Even if they were relatively far away from any Regulators.

Boney? She repeated in her mind, completely shocked. She knew Boney. Everyone knew Boney. Everybody liked Boney. *She* liked Boney.

When Rylee was younger, for several years, she had seen him as a lunatic. Always smiling and being friendly to people in the streets. She had seen him as someone to avoid. No one acted like that in the slums. Then one day she had seen him give a can of food to a hungry-looking child. Over the years, she had witnessed him performing similar acts of kindness on numerous occasions. And her fear of him soon transformed to admiration.

Now the poor man knelt on a concrete platform, frightened, accused of killing two Elects. Behind him stood a merciless judge. A judge who apparently didn't care if no evidence was found against Boney.

"Commander Michael Pike's cycle was found stashed in an alleyway behind this man's housing unit," went on Garrison Pike. "We also found a shotgun in this man's possession. We believe he perpetrated the murders in order to steal the eloctrocyle."

A shotgun? Any idiot could tell you that Michael Pike's wound was not from a shotgun.

Boney shook his head violently. Eyes wide.

"For his crimes, the penalty is death."

Cries of dissent rose from a few in the crowd. But they were weak and quickly died down. All knew the law. There were no prisons in the Alliance. There was no food to waste on criminals while they sat in a prison cell. Execution or Deprecation. Those were the only sentences leveled. At least, for the Norms—the Normals, the expendables.

Rylee gripped the lip of the roof's parapet. Her legs had turned to mush. Had Regulation even bothered to investigate why those Elects were in the slums in the first place? Of course, they hadn't. Order? Let the Elects do whatever they pleased. *That* was the order of things.

She couldn't let this happen. An innocent man—a good man—was about to be executed for her crimes. How could she just stand there and watch? She should cry out, admit her guilt. No, not guilt. She was guilty of no crime, no more than Boney was. She had *stopped* a crime.

Say something! Denounce them. Let the people hear the truth.

But she only stood there, watching. Inside, her indignation fought to overcome her fear, fought to quell the sickness in her stomach that the very thought of doing anything produced.

Do something!

In the end, her fear won out.

And she watched. Watched as Garrison Pike withdrew a pistol from within his coat. Watched as Boney's lips sputtered and trembled, as if attempting to form a few last words of defense. Watched as Pike pointed the gun directly at the back of Boney's head.

No!

A piercing *crack* split the air like a thunder strike. It echoed over and over and over, cutting deep into Rylee's heart.

Boney's body fell forward onto the platform. Dead.

She had killed him. As surely as if she had held that gun to his head and pulled the trigger.

From below, a cacophony of sound rose from the crowd. Cries of dismay, gasps of horror, and shouts of rage.

Rylee turned away, her eyes burning. Rage and despair roiled inside her. She set off across the rooftop, not knowing where she was going. A firm hand gripped her upper arm, holding her back.

"This is not your fault," Preston whispered forcefully into her ear.

Rylee tore her arm away. "The devil it's not!" She kept on walking. Why hadn't she stayed away from the square? Perhaps if she hadn't heeded the sirens, she would have never known. Never seen the damage she had caused. Behind her, she heard Preston calling after her. Words she refused to hear.

* * *

That night after work, Rylee went home and holed herself up in her room, refusing to come out. Ordinarily, she would have spent some of the evening with her friends in the crew. Just thinking about them made Boney's terrified face fill her mind. Her grandfather attempted to get her to come out numerous times. If nothing else to eat her supper.

How could she eat? She'd seen much of death in her life. Even public executions. None of those had ever affected her as Boney's did. It wasn't simply because it was Boney, though. She had been the reason he'd been killed. If she'd never pulled that trigger. If she hadn't chased after the Chief Regulator's son. If she'd come forward and taken the blame…

For so long, she'd always thought herself brave. Chasing after Elects, fearlessly protecting her people. Now she saw her true nature. She was a coward. A coward not just with blood on her hands. Innocent blood. And there was nothing she could ever do to wash it away.

Sometime during the night, Rylee fell asleep. She left her earpiece turned off, sitting on her shelf.

Sleep brought her no rest. Her dreams were nothing more than an extension of her waking thoughts. Boney's face flashed within her mind relentlessly.

In the morning, she left for work, refusing to either eat breakfast or listen to her grandfather's Bible verse.

Outside, she shivered as the morning air penetrated her thin sweatshirt. She paused a moment and looked around. The street, the buildings, the ever-brooding sky all looked the same as the day before. Yet everything felt different.

She walked around to the side of her building, back behind an older metal dumpster. A tattered and faded blue tarp draped haphazardly over a pile of boxes, cans, and other unseen objects. With a yank, she pulled away the tarp, revealing her bike. A '32 Harley Davidson Sportster. The sight of it made her momentarily forget her troubles. Not that the bike was much to look at, with its rusty frame, chipped paint, dented and scratched gas tank, and bald tires. But it was all hers. And it could drive like the Devil's chariot.

Few people in the slums owned any kind of vehicle. If they did, most wouldn't be able to supply it with the gasoline needed to run it. Yet her grandfather managed to keep well enough stocked to drive her Harley to work almost every day of the year.

Unchaining the wheels and handlebars from the dumpster, she straddled the bike. Then she went to work reconnecting the bike's ignition wires. The bike's original keys were long lost. So, her grandfather had rigged the ignition to not need a key.

Wires properly connected, she turned the modified switch. Her Harley came to life with a roar that rattled her bones. Here was power those electrocylces would never know. Electrocyles. Another stab into her fresh wound.

She gunned the throttle and tore out of the alleyway.

Rylee had lived nearly her entire life in the slums. Her grandfather had brought her here a year after Desolation first struck Seattle and the outlying areas. By then, much of the population had already been wiped out. And these buildings—pre-Desolation government housing—had mostly survived the earthquakes and floods. Survivors filled them up, seeking shelter and food. Of late, though, this place felt more like a prison than a home to her.

Her current jobsite was in the Elect sector of the city. They were rewiring a building that the CA wanted to restore. An old skyscraper, relatively undamaged by Desolation's earthquakes and storms. The building stood thirty stories tall. Its glassy exterior, pockmarked though it was, reflected the black clouds which loomed low enough to swallow it whole. A fire had destroyed five stories of the building. According to the engineers, though, the building's steel structure was still sound.

Not that she cared if it collapsed. The CA wasn't restoring it for Norms to live in. Let the building topple and kill the whole Elect population.

Hal met her as she drove into the construction zone at the north end of the building. He towered over her, smiling through his ginger beard.

"Morning," he said roughly, as she dismounted from her bike. "A little early today."

Most days she would be glad to see Hal. As far as bosses went, she definitely couldn't complain. Today she cringed inside at the thought of human interaction. She nodded, and hoped he didn't try any small talk. Not that he tended to say much more than necessary to get a job done.

"I'll need you to work with Sophie today," he said. "Once she gets in, grab a coil of THHN wire and go to work on section fifty-eight, on the ninth floor. Drew's got the diagram. And be careful. We've got some live wires running through that section."

Rylee's heart sank. Sophie was fine enough to work with, though she did tend to gossip the entire time she worked. Usually,

Rylee didn't mind hearing the gossip. Today, the thought of hearing Sophie's prattle all day *and* keep her own winces of pain hidden was enough to make her contemplate driving her Harley off the closest pier.

Within a few minutes, a truck full of other workers rumbled into the construction yard. Sophie, along with several other of the electricians, climbed out. Hal barked out instructions and assignments to everyone, and workers started preparing to enter the building.

Rylee didn't go find Sophie, but stood in the yard and waited until the girl sought her out. At about sixteen, Sophie was two years Rylee's junior. Sophie's appearance always amused Rylee somewhat. Sophie wasn't bald. But she kept her blonde hair trimmed so short, she looked it.

"Are you awake in there?" Sophie said, handing Rylee a hardhat.

Rylee shook her head, as though just startled from sleep. "No," she said. "I'm fine." She grabbed the hardhat from Sophie and pulled it onto her head. "Let's go."

They began their ascent up the service stairs to the ninth floor. Almost as soon as they entered the stairwell, Sophie started to run her mouth. Her words echoed off the narrow walls, pressing against Rylee's overloaded brain. Plus, walking up the stairs was killing her leg. She didn't even know what the girl was talking about.

When they were about to the seventh floor, Sophie said something that snapped Rylee's brain to attention.

"What was that?" she said, stopping and turning to look at Sophie.

Sophie wrinkled her brow. "Didn't you hear about Garrison Pike, the Chief Regulator?"

Rylee frowned. "I saw the execution yesterday, Sophie," she muttered in reply. Then turned and started climbing the stairs again.

"No," Sophie said. "Not that. Garrison Pike is dead."

"What!" Rylee whipped back around to face the girl.

Sophie smiled. It was the smile that always accompanied her

best pieces of gossip, when she knew she had her audience's rapped attention and would give anything to hear more. But Sophie didn't toy with her this time, making her squeeze everything out of her drop by drop.

"Garrison Pike is dead," she repeated. "Last night, someone murdered him."

EIGHT

"I HEARD THE same thing," Serghei said, his Romanian accent sounding stronger than usual. "I say, good riddance to him. He was so concerned about justice being served. A twisted irony, do you not think?"

Though Rylee didn't care a bit about Pike, the news troubled her. Their whole crew was together at their hideout—Serghei's place. That morning, she had had no intention of seeing any of them today. Yet, after what Sophie had told her, she wanted to confirm the news with another source.

"Any word as to who did it?" Preston asked, sitting in his customary spot on Serghei's couch.

"Supposedly, it happened in his sleep," Serghei said, feeding a potato skin to his pet rat.

"Man, I can't believe you waste food on that rodent," Feng said, shaking his head in disgust.

In reply, Grant hissed at Feng, baring a pair of yellow teeth, dripping with rat drool.

"His name is Grant," Serghei said, stroking the rat's patchy fur. Serghei had named the rat after an old actor—Larry Grant, or something like that. It also had one black, skeletonized robotic leg. Serghei's own handiwork.

"Just keep that mangy disease ball away from me," said Feng, recoiling.

Serghei held out the bit of potato skin to Feng. "You would rather eat it, would you? I acquired it from a garbage scavenger. Undoubtedly remnants of an Elect's three-course meal. Maybe even from the CA's own kitchen. As it's likely mingled with raw meat and produce, it likely carries but two or three harmful bacterium."

Serghei smiled broadly, that goofy smile that only belonged to

47

him. Feng shook his head as he settled back into his seat. "Dude's got problems." Rylee heard him mutter under his breath.

Serghei went back to feeding his rat. Feng went back to sipping his Mountain Dew. And Preston just sat there.

"Aren't any of you the least bit concerned about the ramifications of this?" Rylee blurted out, her voice edging with a hint of hysteria. "I killed Michael Pike. A squadron commander. And look what happened. They didn't have any evidence against Boney. Yet they killed him just to make a point. What do you think they'll do when the Head of Regulation is killed?"

Rylee felt her face burning with the heat of her anger. And she found herself fighting back tears.

Preston reached over and placed a hand on her shoulder. She pulled away from his touch.

"Serg," Preston said, ignoring her coldness. "You've mentioned before about hacking into Regulation's systems to steal reports. Is that actually possible? Could we look up what they know about the murder?"

Serghei bobbed his head a little. "Anything's possible, is it not?"

"How feasible, then?"

"We have no network in the slums, as you know," Serghei said, his voice rising a few notches like it always did when he talked about his nerdy stuff. "Regulation headquarters has a private network. It does link to the external network used by the rest of the Elect populous. Two issues there though. Both networks are heavily monitored. Elects can connect to their network wirelessly through their PNU-enhanced brains. I don't happen to have any PNUs lying around. I'm not sure of what sort of handshake protocol is involved when they connect to the network, but I assume an issued certificate is required. Spoofing that...forget it. Unless, of course, we could find someone to issue us a certificate. But we're more likely to get promoted to Elects than for that to happen.

"Now, there are, I believe physical servers which make up that network. Unless the CA's brain is it. And I wouldn't put it past him. What better way to monitor *everything* in your city? Assuming that is not the case, locating the servers and gaining access to them would likely take considerable time. And then after that, there is still the problem of breaking through Regulation's fire-walls. However—"

"Forget I asked," Preston said, cutting him off. "I think we get the point." He shook his head and sighed. "I'm sorry, Ry. I don't think there's anything we can do here. Even if we could learn something, I doubt it would make much difference. I don't think you need to worry about this, though. Regulation would have a blasted hard time linking anyone in the slums to the murder."

That was true. Garrison Pike had been killed in his apartment. Not even the Elect Hunters had ever attempted to infiltrate one of the Elect buildings. Unlike the slum's housing units, the Elects' buildings boasted security systems to prevent unauthorized access.

Preston leaned forward and ran a hand through his russet hair. "Well, the good news is that there's one less Elect in the world."

"You said it, brother," Feng said, raising his can of Mountain Dew. "One less we have to kill ourselves."

Rylee's stomach twisted inside. Could she kill another Elect? Did she have the will to continue as an Elect Hunter? All that they were doing—all that they stood for—came into question now. She understood the others and their motivation.

Feng's hatred of the Elects was justified. One of them had taken his sister when he was younger. They found her body a few weeks later in a back alley of the slums, her flesh mangled and torn in ways Feng refused to talk about.

Preston's older brother had been killed by a group of Elects who just wanted to try out a new PNU-enhancement that gave them Kung Fu abilities. The Elects had tied up Preston and forced him to watch as they punched, kicked, and elbowed his brother again and again. Even after Preston's brother collapsed and his chested stopped moving, the Elects continued to batter his bloodied face.

Serghei? Well, Serghei just loved using his *toys*. It seemed to her that this was all a game to him. Strategy, tactics, outwitting the enemy—these were all things that excited Serghei. He never shot anyone. Never went out on the streets to hunt.

What about herself? What drove her to hunt the Elects? Certainly she'd witnessed enough of their atrocities. Senseless killings like the one that took the life of Preston's brother. That was not the first time such a thing had happened. When the Elects stole young girls or women, it always made her sick. They didn't always know what became of those abducted. Sometimes they were merely raped and cast back onto the streets. Most of the time, they didn't come back. Theories abounded on that topic. One rumor—the one which she most believed—is that the Elects used a modified PNU to take control of their minds. To turn these girls into their slaves. The thought made Rylee sick inside. She knew exactly what kind of slave these teenage Elects would make of a girl like Lexi.

It boiled her blood. Why did the Elects feel the need to do such things? According to Serghei, their PNU-enhanced brains allowed them to see, hear, and feel whatever they wanted without having anything physically there. That was the point of the Elects. Their PNU gave them whatever they wanted. The perfect human—more than human. Then why did they insist on taking from the Norms? That is what drove Rylee, what fueled her passion to fight against them. At least, that's what *had* driven her. Was it still enough?

"You did the right thing killing those Elects," Feng said. "So, they killed one of us in retaliation. So what? They're killing us anyway. How much longer would Boney have lasted? No one in the slums is safe. We're all just an injury, an illness, a twisted Elect's whims away from death or Deprecation. But you got two of them. And one of them was a Squadron leader. You should be proud."

Proud? Proud that she'd been the direct cause of an innocent man's humiliating public execution? Pride was the last thing Rylee felt. Disgust, grief, fury…confusion.

"That was the worst motivational speech I've ever heard," Serghei said.

"Whatever man," Feng scoffed. "Not everything's like those stupid movies you watch."

Serghei's eyes grew wide. "Stupid, are they? In the future, you do not wish to watch them, is that it?"

Feng shrugged and pulled out his pistol. "I didn't say I didn't like them. They're just stupid." He released the magazine, then locked back the slide. The chambered round ejected, and he commenced inspecting the firearm. A Berretta M92 nine-millimeter. Nice gun. "The good guys always win. Which is a load of tripe."

Serghei shrugged. "If movies were all strongly anchored in reality, they wouldn't be so entertaining. Speaking of movies, anyone up for one? Edward Scissor Hands, perhaps?"

"I think we could all use a little distraction," Preston said, tossing his empty can of Mountain Dew onto the pile in the corner.

Rylee didn't object. In truth, she didn't think a movie could distract her from her thought. But it was better than sitting in her room, trying to hold back her tears.

Serghei set his rat back into its cage, then walked over to the wall opposite from where the couch sat, and started thumbing through one of the numerous boxes filled with the shiny disks he called DVDs. She knew he had the boxes organized by decade. After a moment, he pulled out a case and removed the circular disc inside. This he inserted into a small black box. Then he unlocked a cabinet and swung open its doors to reveal a black monitor. With the press of the button, the monitor's black screen came to life. According to Serghei, all of it, was *ancient* technology.

"By the way," Serghei said, turning back to look at Rylee. "I came across a few servers today." He pointed to a stack of thin metallic boxes on his desk. "I plan on extracting their data this week. We might find something on one of them."

She gave him a weak smile. Her thoughts were already back to Garrison Pike's murder. More repercussions were coming, she knew it. What she didn't know is what those repercussions would be.

NINE

CARMINE O'CONNER STOOD inside the stainless-steel elevator car as it ascended to the eightieth floor. Subconsciously, she adjusted her scarlet waistcoat, tugging gently at the front hemline. She also checked the collar of her white blouse, which she wore beneath the waistcoat, fingering the neckline. Should she do up another button?

Chiding herself, she forced herself to clasp her hands behind her back.

This was just another meeting. What did it matter if it was with the CA himself? She would not let that affect her composure. What did it matter that she'd never had a private meeting with the venerable Nathaniel Steele before? As a member of the Advisory Board, she'd been in his presence plenty of times. Still, she couldn't help but wonder at the nature of this meeting. Being called to his office was a distinction reserved for his Chief Advisor, or one of the Lieutenant Advisors. Not a Sub Advisor, like herself. Was there a promotion on the horizon?

The elevator chimed, and the doors to the car parted. She lifted her chin and stepped into a small lobby. The heels of her boots clomped loudly on the polished marble floor. Except for a few paintings on the walls, with abstract colors and shapes, the room was bare. No desk, manned by a dutiful secretary. No chairs or bench for sitting. Just the paintings and a pair of double doors, made of a rich mahogany.

One seldom saw such finery these days. Many buildings had been destroyed by the earthquakes of Desolation. Miraculously, Steele's own building survived with only nominal damage. Had it not survived, things would be very different today. Carmine wasn't entirely convinced that wouldn't be a bad thing.

All PNUs were manufactured in this building. More than once

she'd had explained to her that this building contained the only known cleanroom still in operation on the planet. Without the cleanroom, the PNUs could not be produced. Without the PNUs, their chances of rebuilding — of survival, even — reduced to shreds. Or so she'd been told.

From her point of view, their chances were shrinking smaller and smaller every day. Foul weather threatened the few crops the field workers were able to plant and harvest. Every day, the scavenging crews went out further and further, and came back with less and less. And now, they were killing off each other. In the past few weeks, there had been too many murders.

"Ms. O'Connor, Mr. Steele will be with you momentarily." The message came directly into her PNU-enhanced brain, interrupting her stream of thought. The deep, monotone voice was not one she recognized. Nor did the sender of the message transmit a profile by which she might identify him. Not that it would have mattered much. She didn't know the man. The voice was sufficient to tell her that. Among the benefits of her PNU was the complete and total recall of everything that happened to her. Every conversation, face, voice, action — all stored *safely* within the PNU.

Carmine stiffened her back and straightened her shoulders. Steele evidently intended to make her wait. Likely she was being watched at that moment. Very well. She would wait.

Ten minutes later, the double doors opened swiftly, and two men dressed in gray suits and wearing identical striped ties stepped out. Bodyguards. Mechanically, they moved to either side of the threshold, forming a gauntlet for her to pass through. The right-most bodyguard curtly motioned for her to enter.

Keeping her eyes fixed forward, refusing to allow the bodyguard's gaze to intimidate her, she strode forward. The doors opened into a sweeping room with floor-to-ceiling windows stretching the full length of the back wall. Four more gray-suited bodyguards stood stiffly along the windowless walls.

Carmine fought back the urge to smirk. *A little paranoid, Mr. Steele?*

A man in a double-breasted, royal blue suit with faint pinstripes stood behind a broad mahogany desk in front of the windows. Nathaniel Steele. Chief Administrator of the Post Desolation Reconstruction Alliance. And, as far as anyone knew, the most powerful man in the world. Carmine paused just inside the room, waiting.

"Please, come in, Miss O'Connor," Mr. Steele said in an even tone. Neither warm and inviting, nor cold and hostile. Direct. Businesslike.

Carmine stepped down onto the lower platform that covered most of the room and approached the desk. As she walked, she fought against her natural propensity to divert her gaze downward or to the side. Instead, she kept her eyes leveled on Steele. Confidence was ninety percent posture. Of course, she could have tapped her PNU to calm her nerves and eliminate any outward display of weakness. As a rule, she preferred to rely on her PNU enhancements as little as possible.

Steele watched her like a hawk tracking its prey. Could he sense her own insecurity? Having any Enhanced male look at her always made her uncomfortable. Who knew what they were actually seeing. What false reality their PNUs were creating. She'd heard the stories. Teenage males—newly Enhanced—using their PNUs to visualize the women around them without clothing. And similar such atrocities. It revolted her.

A Persian rug hushed the clomp of her heels as she drew closer to the desk. Just behind a pair of studded leather armchairs, which sat in front of the desk, Carmine paused. Steele nodded, and held out his hand toward one of the chairs. "Have a seat, Miss O'Connor." He did not come around the desk to shake her hand.

"Thank you," she said, following the invitation. Though, it had sounded more like a command.

She crossed her legs and discreetly pulled the hem of her black pencil skirt further down. It didn't quite reach the knees. Careful not to appear sloppy, she perched on the edge of the seat, her back as straight as the CA's blue tie.

She expected him to sit in his own chair behind the desk. He did not. Instead, he came around the front of the desk, and sat on the front of it, his left leg hooked, his other keeping contact with the floor. The pose was semi-casual. But he pulled it off without losing any of his poise. In fact, she found the position sub-tly...commanding. Now, he towered over her. It was a position that said, *I have the upper hand and I always will.*

"You'll forgive me, Miss O'Connor," he said, his voice still even and professional, "if I forgo any pleasantries. I've never been one to comply with social protocols."

He paused, and she nodded in assent.

"I assume you've heard the report," he went on. "Needless to say, I am deeply troubled by this apparent trend, Miss O'Connor."

Mr. Steele stood and walked to the windows behind the desk. For several moments, he stood there, his back to her, the low gray clouds outlining the perfect lines of his suit and slicked hair. She wouldn't be surprised if he commanded those clouds to disperse and they obeyed.

"With Chief Pike's loss," he said, turning abruptly around, "Regulation is in need of a new head. That is why I have called you in today, Miss O'Connor. I want you to fill his vacancy."

Carmine sat up straighter. Not out of pride, but surprise. "But sir..." she said tentatively, "I don't have the background to run Regulation. My duties on the Advisor Board deal primarily with logistics for construction and scavenging. I've never even held a gun before. Perhaps, Straufmann? He has some military back-ground, I believe."

Richard Straufmann, Lieutenant Advisor to the CA. Also, the most outspoken member of the board. He and Steele often clashed on affairs of the Alliance. Surely Steele wouldn't mind moving Straufmann off of the board. For the good of the Alliance, of course.

Steele walked back over, this time coming and standing quite close. Making her wish she had opted to stand.

"I need Mr. Straufmann to stay where he's at. Besides, I'm not asking you to patrol the streets of the slums yourself, Miss O'Connor. I need someone to lead the investigation into these homicides. And you are the person I want to do it. I've been watching you long enough to know I'll see results." He stepped closer, and Carmine found herself looking up uncomfortably into his dark eyes. And when he spoke, he spoke slowly. "I want the culprits found. We can't afford for this to continue. It destabilizes our fragile existence."

He returned to his original spot at the edge of his desk.

"I understand, sir," she said, forcing confidence into her words.

"Damon Gyles will be your aide. He's well acquainted with Regulation operations and procedures. As well as holding guns. Let him take care of the mundane affairs of your job. I want you focused on this investigation one hundred and eighteen percent. Any question?"

"Yes. As far as access to sensitive data and —"

"You have access to whatever you need that is pertinent to the investigation, Miss O'Connor. And if anyone gets in your way, I will personally deal with them."

"Does that include your own labs?"

He leaned forward and his face grew even more serious. "I said *whatever* you need access to. I won't hinder you. But take heed that you don't go on any witch hunts, Miss O'Connor."

"Understood, sir." She stood, and stepped aside of the chair. "I will begin immediately."

"Good. Now, there's one more unpleasant matter we need to discuss before you depart."

Again, he held out his hand toward the chair.

"Have a seat, Miss O'Connor."

TEN

SINCE GARRISON PIKE'S death, two more prominent Elects—and a third no one from the slums seemed to know—had been killed. And not a single arrest made for any of them. With each case, the details from the various rumor mills were sparse. Not even Sophie could provide much more than names of the victims.

Who was behind the murders? Surely, it had to be someone outside the slums. Rylee doubted she and the rest of the crew could pull off a single killing in the Elect sector, much less four. Even with their resources and expertise. If a Norm was involved, he would have to be as resourceful as he was brash.

Regulation never made a fuss about the death or murder of a Norm. But these were important members of the Alliance. They could not be overlooked.

And so Rylee was not surprised to find herself on the same rooftop overlooking Workers Square, awaiting another message to the people. Beside her stood Preston, just as before. This time Feng was there. She didn't know what compelled her to come again, to heed the call of the sirens. Her memories of watching Boney's execution were still fresh and raw. The news couldn't be as bad as last time, could it?

So, she stood there, scratching the tattooed barcode on the back of her hand, and waiting.

"Don't you wish you could gun down all those Regulators?" Feng asked. "From up here, if we had more than handguns, we might be able to."

He spat on the ground, as if he were imagining one of the Regulators at his feet. Rylee shifted a little. Feng's intensity startled her sometimes. Of all the members of their crew, she'd known Feng the least amount of time. Both she and Preston had met him through Serghei. How it was that those two were friends, still baffled her.

"Careful what you say out here, Feng," Preston said. "You never know what they could be using to spy on us."

"Let 'em listen. I ain't afraid of Regulation."

"You don't have to be afraid. But that doesn't mean you have to be stupid."

"You call it stupid. I call it backbone. Anyway, what do you think these tripe faces are going to announce?"

Preston shrugged. "Maybe we're all getting upgraded to Elect status."

Feng snorted. "Serg's dream-come-true. No way I'm taking some PNU pill."

Rylee shook her head. There was no way she would ever become an Elect either. That was the CA's perpetual promise, though. One day, everyone would become an Elect—receive the PNU-enhancements, which—more than wealth, food, and status—separated the Elects from the Norms. Not everyone could receive the PNU-enhancements at once, was the excuse. The Alliance's resources were too scarce. Both to produce PNUs and sustain a large population of PNU-enhanced people required more resources than the Alliance could supply.

Back before Rylee was old enough to remember, the Alliance would elect one or two Norms each year to be *enhanced*. That was how their name came about. *Elects*. But that had not happened in years.

All the better.

A movement near the platform caught her attention, and Rylee's heart quickened. This was too much like the week before. Mental images of that fateful morning immediately flickered through her mind. A contingent of Regulators filed in a defensive line across the platform. An uneasy crowd watched on in silence. A proud figure strode across the platform.

This time, however, the figure was not Garrison Pike, the murdered Chief of Regulation. It wasn't even a man. Part of her expected the CA himself to appear on that platform. Such an appearance by the Chief Administrator of the Alliance would surely portend something terrible. She knew it wouldn't be him, though. The CA didn't make public appearances anymore.

Especially to the Norms.

Rylee didn't recognize the woman. She wore a midnight-blue double-breasted frock coat. The skirt of her coat flared out slightly from her trim waist, its hem reaching the top of her knee-high black boots. Her lips were fastened together as tightly as each of the gold buttons running all the way up to the top of the collar brushing her sharp chin. She looked to be in her thirties.

How could one wear such a coat? Rylee much preferred her own simple jacket. She wore it now. Serghei had managed to mend the torn sleeve and shoulder well enough that the jacket was useable again. And though its smooth, impervious outer shell was now slightly permeable, it still did the job better than wool.

Beside her, Preston leaned in close to her. "That's a member of the CA's Advisory Board—one of the Sub Advisors," he said quietly. "O'Conner, I think her name is."

Well, that was somewhat of a good sign. At least, the CA hadn't sent one of his Lieutenant Advisors. Still, she would have been happier to see a mere messenger, or propaganda functionary.

The sour expression on the woman's face showed she didn't think highly of her task. Like the master's mistress sent to feed the dogs the table scraps. A job better suited for a servant—or a slave.

Just as before, when Garrison Pike had addressed the crowd of Norms in the square, Sub Advisor O'Conner's voice amplified through the square's speakers without the aid of a microphone.

"Members of the Alliance," she said, her words as cold as the morning air. "I come to you this morning on direct assignment from our Chief Administrator, Nathaniel Steele."

She paused. An unenthusiastic cheer sputtered through the crowd, mottled here and there with hisses and boos. O'Conner smiled thinly.

"He wishes to advise all members of the Post Desolation Reconstruction Alliance of the deaths of two important leaders of our Alliance. Prasad Balay, Chief Scientist for the Division of Ecological Development. And Jonathan Breznen, Vice-president for the Bureau of Trade and Commerce."

O'Connor paused.

Is that it? Did they simply call them there to tell them that some more Elects had been killed? News everyone already knew?

It was too much to hope for.

"The contributions," O'Conner went on, "of these upstanding men were invaluable. We publicly recognize them for their loyalty and commitment to the Alliance. Their murders represent a serious crime. One which hinders the work of restoring prosperity to our city and people."

She paused again, looking over the murmuring crowd before continuing.

Rylee's heart sank. This was it. More executions of innocent lives.

"Regulation has assured the Advisory Board that we are conducting a full and thorough investigation of the murders. The perpetrators shall be found and dealt with appropriately. These crimes cannot continue. They threaten our very existence.

"As such, the CA, in conjunction with the Advisory Board, has deemed it necessary to impose new sanctions until the culprits either come forward of their own will, are handed over by the people, or are apprehended by Regulation.

"The sanctions comprehend two parts. One, food rations will be decreased by fifty percent."

Angry shouts erupted from the crowd. Not a few mothers in the crowd held trembling hands to their mouths, likely wondering how they would keep their families from starving on such meager rations. Around the platform, the Regulators tightened their ranks and pointed their assault rifles at the unruly crowd. Gunfire pierced through the noise, as several Regulators fired warning shots into the air.

Rylee shook her head, recalling another of her grandfather's lessons. *A bullet shot into the sky will eventually come down. And it can kill a person just as surely as if you had pointed the gun directly at them.*

Idiots.

The shots had their effect. The people knew the drill. Next time, the warning shots would be fired into the crowd at random.

O'Conner continued, ignoring the crowd teetering on the brink of rioting. "Food rations shall remain fixed at fifty percent until this matter has been satisfactorily resolved. The second part of the sanctions involves Deprecation."

A collective shudder at the mention of that word ran through the crowd.

"In two week's time," continued O'Conner, "if the culprits have not been found, the Deprecation age shall be lowered five years. All sixty or older shall be Deprecated."

Cries of dismay.

Not waiting for the crowd's fury to unleash like a pack of rabid mutts, Chief O'Connor turned on her heel, marched off the back of the platform, and disappeared into a large black vehicle. As soon as she was inside, the vehicle sped off, Regulators trailing in its wake on their electrocycles.

Rylee watched it all in shock, repeating the news to herself as though in a trance. The Deprecation age, unless someone found who was murdering these high-ranking Elects, would be reduced to sixty.

Precisely her grandfather's age.

ELEVEN

WILLIAM SIGHED AND leaned back in his chair, ignoring another of Adrianna's messages. Sometimes he wished he could shut his PNU off...permanently. If nothing else, it would end the constant intrusions into his thoughts. He couldn't though. Of that he felt certain. He relied on its abilities far too much. And, for as much as he complained sometimes, deep down he knew he liked the telepathic abilities his PNU afforded.

He was tired and stressed. That was all. And the thought of dealing with Adrianna didn't help.

The fact that he felt stressed, added to his stress. He shouldn't feel stressed. He'd finished the latest assignment from his father several days ago. After coding for months on end, often working through the night, scarcely sleeping, subsisting off nothing but energy drinks, he ought to be sleeping or relaxing. Anything that didn't involve code or work in any form. But his mind refused to allow either.

Sure, he could utilize his PNU to suppress his anxiety. The PNUs could synthesize any emotion. But doing so for too long could be damaging. As addictive as Lander's own obsession with SimComps. Besides, PNU emotion-synthesis wouldn't solve the underlying problem. That was one thing that could drive him to work all night—unsolved problems. The more challenging and perplexing the problem, the more likely he was to relentlessly pursue its solution.

This wasn't a coding problem. The problem was...well, that's what troubled him. He didn't *know* what the problem was. Only that he felt something amiss. It was the same feeling he'd been having for several days. Of course, he could blame the feeling on the death—murder—of Garrison Pike. There was more to it than that, though.

Swirling around in his chair, he stopped so that he faced the windows of his office. The same gray clouds hung in the sky. No sign of storms, or anything brewing outside. He yawned—his overloaded brain trying to cool down. Perhaps he should respond to Adrianna. She could help distract him.

No. He refused to succumb to that temptation.

He should find Lander. The two of them could do…something. Preferably an activity that didn't involve Sims. In the last few months, the two of them had spent little time together. He didn't know what they'd do. Work consumed so much of his life these days that he struggled to remember what life was like before, when he had more discretionary time.

When they were younger, they enjoyed pranking unsuspecting victims. Regulators were a particularly fun target. They liked hacking into Regulation's *secure* communication channels and sending messages to lower ranking Regulators which looked like they came from a senior officer. Message spoofing. Always good for endless entertainment. One time he and Lander tricked a Regulator into trying to arrest the Chief of Regulation's daughter.

William smiled at the memory. Of course, they'd been caught for that one. A verbal reprimand had been their only punishment, though.

Sending spoof messages between a girlfriend and boyfriend was fun too.

But William was twenty-one, now. And an Engineer Lead at his father's laboratories. The days of programming mice to scare girls in the shower, imitating Regulation officers, and causing breakups between love-struck teens were over. Well, maybe mostly over.

Standing up, he raised his arms, stretching out his whole body. Where was Lander, anyway?

He sent a direct message to Lander using a private protocol they'd created years ago. It permitted them to communicate without anyone snooping. *I need a break*, he messaged. *Where are you?*

He waited for Lander's sarcastic reply, mocking William's full sentences and proper grammar. It was a running joke between them. William refused to compose his messages as though he were some kind of alien toddler who didn't know a single complete English word. To William, there was no excuse for the lazy—often cryptic—lingo that suffused most PNU messages amongst the adolescent population. Maybe forty years ago, when you had to physically type each letter of the word. These days, all you had to do was think it. To William, it was more work to try and think in the bizarre messaging jargon.

A full minute passed. No response from Lander.

Likely too busy with his latest SimComp.

Deciding to go find his friend, William left the office and took the elevator to the studio apartment he and Lander shared. He found it empty, no sign of Lander. And still no response to his PNU message. Where was that idiot?

William went over to the kitchen and opened the refrigerator. A single unopened energy drink sat on the top shelf. The shelf had been practically full a few days ago. Had Lander drunken that many since then? At least, one was left. He reached in and grabbed it.

Unscrewing the plastic cap, he moved to bring the bottle to his lips. But paused. What was that? He turned the bottle around and inspected its side. Affixed to it, edges curling up slightly, was a piece of...*paper*. Paper? Scrawled on the paper in a messy hand were the letters 7-5-M-Y-Z-1. *75MYZ1.*

Had Lander put that there? A *written* note on *paper*? William was so busy puzzling over why Lander would do such a thing that it took him a minute to recognize what was written. When he finally stopped to look at it, he immediately identified it.

Back when he and Lander were learning about data encryption, they'd devised their own custom cipher algorithm. A variant of the old Caesar Shift, but with their own twist. At the time, they thought they were quite clever. Of course, they were only eleven at the time. Their cipher used the standard English alphabet, offsetting it by some integer. The offset-value changed with each cipher, the creator writing it at the beginning of the message. Naïve. The offset-value wasn't completely obvious, though. The person deciphering the message had to divide the value by seventeen to attain the actual offset. Lander had chosen the multiple. Entirely random.

The only part of the algorithm which showed any promise was that vowels could be dropped at the creator's discretion. The only indication of the missing letters would be a string of indices at the end of the message. It mitigated the chance of a quick decipher by unwanted eyes. Though, in reality, any brute-force algorithm could crack the code in a matter of minutes—or less—given a long enough sample of the encrypted message.

Most people, however, wouldn't give this seemingly random scribble of numbers and letters a second thought.

Utilizing his PNU, he deciphered the message. Dividing the prefixed seventy-five by seventeen produced five. That was the offset for the cipher. The trailing single digit *one*, using zero-based indexing, meant that the second letter in the word—a vowel—was omitted. The ciphered text *HDE* flashed within his PNU-augmented vision.

The only logical missing vowel, was an *I*.

HIDE.

TWELVE

DUNCAN'S WAREHOUSE STOOD on the south western-most tip of the old industrial district, far out of the way of Regulation's notice. At least, far enough out of the way that it passed the notice of Regulators making their usual rounds. Or maybe Regulation knew of it but decided to turn a blind eye to it. Of course, if Regulation ever did raid the place, they'd find plenty of Deps—those with Deprecated status, but hadn't been caught and officially Deprecated. Deps usually didn't last long. But Duncan's warehouse attracted them like sewer rats to rotting food.

From the outside, the warehouse looked no different than all the other decaying warehouses. On the inside the building was alive. Alive with propane lanterns hung from the ceiling, which struggled to keep the night's darkness at bay with their sallow glow. Alive with a raucous crowd, faces begrimed and clothes soiled from a long day's work in the fields or the sewers. Alive with smells, sweat and grease and cheap alcohol and bodies that hadn't bathed in weeks. Alive with the motives that drove the people of the slums to Duncan's Warehouse every Wednesday night.

Most people came to Duncan's warehouse to bet on the races or to waste a few rations on a dram of whiskey to chase away the burdens of a hard life. Some came to escape the monotony of slum life. Rylee came for a different reason.

Rylee, Preston, and Feng pushed their way through the crowd waiting for the races to begin. A girl, whose arm was held in a sling, passed them on the right, eyes sunken and dark rimmed. A Dep. Injured and unable to work, the girl had been Deprecated. Rylee didn't need to ask the girl her story to know it. She'd seen it hundreds of times before. Unlike many before her, this girl stood a chance at survival. A pretty face could do that. Deps like her could usually find someone willing to exchange rations for....Rylee didn't like to think about it. If she had rations to spare, she might have shared them with the girl. Given what she was about to do, she definitely did not have any to spare.

In the center of the warehouse, a tall chain-link fence cordoned off the racing rink. At the far end of the rink, was another cordoned off area called the pit. Both fenced areas were topped with razor-wire to prevent tampering and interference. Not that any sane person would tamper with a race. The penalty for such an infraction was a severed hand—which for any Norm was as good a Deprecation sentence as any.

Though Rylee couldn't see him, she suspected Serghei was in the pit at that moment, preparing Grant for one of the races.

"I'll go place our bets," said Preston, shouting to be heard over the din of the crowd.

Rylee nodded her head. With Preston gone, she and Feng continued to push their way through the crowd, in search of a place to watch the race from. They passed a group of Norms seated about a makeshift table—an old wooden cable spool, turned on its end—drinking, and listening to a sailor spew out a tale from his travels. Anytime a ship came into port, you could find sailors at Duncan's warehouse, exchanging stories of the outside world for shots of whiskey.

On more than one occasion, Rylee had listened to those stories. Sea storms with waves that could swallow an entire ship whole. Great cities once home to millions of people, now deserted, but for the bones of the people who died. She never listened for long. It was all death and destruction. And if she listened too long, the sailors started to slur their words and make ridiculous claims that were obviously false.

The sailors were the only ones Rylee knew brave enough to venture out into the outside world. Though, at their core, sailors were just glorified scavengers. Going from deserted city to deserted city, pilfering whatever supplies they could find to trade with the Alliance. From the sailor's stories, very few people lived outside the Alliance. Most sailors had only come across a handful of settlements—twenty to thirty poor souls, fighting to stay alive—

among all their travels. Of course, few sailors lived more than one or two years before drowning, disease, or a pack of feral dogs ended their life.

There was one sailor who'd managed to live nine years out on the seas. People called him Moby Dick. When he came to Duncan's warehouse, people fought to get within spitting distance of the man. *His* glass never went dry.

But Rylee wasn't here to hear a sailor's drunken tale, either. Pushing their way deeper into the warehouse, she and Feng came to a set of metal stairs which took them to a loft. This too was packed with people. Still, they managed to squeeze into a space along the railing.

From this higher vantage point, they had a clear view of the rink. Most of the lanterns in the warehouse hung above the oval shaped race track.

The races were simple. The first animal to cross the finish line after completing the requisite number of laps around the rink won. The number of laps depended on the category. Serghei's rat would race in the rodent division. As such it would only have to complete three laps. In the larger size and weight divisions which included dogs and cats, and the occasional wolf or coyote, the animals had to complete fifteen laps.

The fact that rats, and sometimes wolves and coyotes, were involved didn't make the races particularly unique. It was their common robotic body parts. Like Serghei's rat, all of the animals were in some way modified by cybernetics. Rodent cyborgs. Freaks of nature. The animals were only rivaled in abnormality by their masters. Norms like Serghei—smart enough, resourceful enough, and yet twisted enough to spend their time turning an injured animal into a racing machine.

With a crowd like tonight's, though, she could hardly blame anyone for creating a racer. A hefty winner's cup awaited the victor. A month's worth of food rations, maybe two. And a handful of other valuables—gasoline, ammunition, blankets, cigarettes.

No paper and coin currency existed in the Alliance. She didn't know what Elects used for their currency, but in the slums food controlled everything. And why not? It was blasted hard to get enough of it. And now, with the announced decreases in rations? The worth of food just skyrocketed. Which also meant what she was about to do was insane.

Rylee watched the crowd below press against the fence surrounding the rink, desperate for their chosen animal to win. Was she any less desperate? A heightened tension electrified the air. Much was at stake tonight.

She breathed in deeply and forced herself to stay calm. The pungent odor of the warehouse assaulted her nose. The smell of a hundred different kinds of filth. The warehouse odor only partially overwhelmed the smell of fish coming from Feng, who stood just inches from her.

"Do you really think Serghei's lousy rat can win this thing?" Feng shouted over the crowd. Rylee didn't respond. "If it were my rations at stake, I'd bet on the squirrel—Mr. Rabies, or whatever its name is. Have you seen that thing? All foaming at the mouth. All it has to do is bite all the other racers, and it's game over."

Serghei has to win.

Preston returned from placing their bet a few minutes later, and *made* a spot for himself next to her. Though they were packed so tightly Rylee struggled to breathe, she felt better to have Preston's warm body next to her. She always felt better when he was around. Since that first day when she was seven, alone and afraid, he'd been there for her when she needed him.

Soon the wail of a steel alarm bell signaled the last call for bets to be placed and for trainers to move their animals into position. Rylee watched, scratching at the back of her hand as the trainers entered. The pale, lanky form of Serghei, gingerly holding Grant in his hands, stood out from the other trainers. He looked to be stroking the rat's head and talking to it. Probably giving it a pep talk or some other crazy idea that only Serghei would think of.

Let him talk to it, massage it—whatever it takes. Just so long as that rat wins. Please win.

If she were her grandfather, she'd probably be praying right now. If he were there, she'd probably encourage him to. Not that she believed it would help. Then again, if her grandfather were there and knew she had just bet a weeks' worth of rations on a race, she would be in major trouble. But if Grant didn't win this race and she lost those rations, he would find out eventually. That worry, however, was least on her mind.

With the extra rations they would win, she'd have enough to pay an informant. Only a handful of informants lived in the slums. Among them, there was only one worth his salt. That is, if his reputation was to be believed. Uriah Mounts was his name. Sources claimed he always made an appearance at the races, and that he had connections inside Regulation. If anyone from the slums knew anything about the recent murders, Uriah Mounts was the one. And Rylee intended to suck all the information she could out of him.

There was no way she was going to leave it to Regulation to find the perpetrator of the murders. Not when her grandfather's life depended on it. *Deprecation.* Just another name for death. Any Norm who reached the age of sixty-five was automatically Deprecated. Disenfranchised from the Alliance. Serial number erased from the system. No barcode meant no food rations. By law, Deprecated members were not permitted within the city. Every week, truckloads of fugitives were found and carted off to either be executed or dumped outside the city's border, where armed border guards would ensure they did not return.

No one survived long outside the city. When she was younger, she often saw corpses along the roadside, as the trucks carried her and the other children to the fields each day to work. In the summer, fresh bodies would be engulfed in black plumage, as ravens and vultures picked away the flesh, leaving only skeletons and mangled bits of cloth that had been clothes. Once, she'd witnessed a man trying to get one of the trucks to stop. He ended up crushed behind the truck's wheels. Rylee still could recall the sickening crunch, and the bump of the truck as it went over the man's body.

An involuntary shudder coursed down her back. She couldn't let that happen to her grandfather. She *wouldn't* let it happen.

The next bell rang, signaling the close of the betting office. Below, Serghei and the other trainers placed their animals in their assigned starting gates. A metal grate in the front and back of the gate, kept the animals from escaping or jumping the gun on the race. Once their animals were secured, the group of trainers exited the rink, returning to the pit.

, Rylee gripped the railing in front of her and scratched at the tattoo on the back of her hand. The bell rang a third and final time. Two men lifted open the metal grates, releasing the animals. And the races began.

A deafening cheer shook the whole warehouse as the crowd rooted for their chosen animals. The animals ignored the mayhem, speeding down the track as if chased by a hellcat. Most were deaf already. Either from previous injury or intentional marring.

After the first bend, Grant, Mr. Rabies, and a different rat with gray fur had taken the lead.

Mr. Rabies was a wiry creature with more bald patches than actual hair, and a tail like a rat's. Two robotic hindquarters powered its rears as it raced along, foam seething from the mouth. The mangy squirrel, as Feng said, had a reputation for biting other animals who got in his way. And biting was not illegal. Or clawing and scratching. She'd even seen a mouse nearly win by climbing onto the back of a larger, faster animal. The rules were loose, if not nonexistent.

The animals completed the first lap. Still holding a strong third, Grant kept a steady pace behind the leaders.

"Should have bet on that squirrel," Feng shouted at her side.

Come on! If Serghei's rat lost this race, she swore to herself she'd drown it in gasoline, then set it on fire. That is if her grandfather didn't kill her first.

An urge to shout out loud filled her, to cheer Grant on. She looked around at the maddened, screaming crowd. What good did yelling like a maniac at the animals do? Instead, she stood there, tense as a cord ready to snap.

Maintaining his third-place position, Grant passed the halfway mark of the second lap. One and a half laps to go. Still in the lead, Mr. Rabies scurried frantically, showing no sign of slowing down.

If she had her rifle, she would have been tempted to shoot the squirrel before it reached the finish line. Of course, *that* was illegal.

And she doubted she would make it out of Duncan's warehouse alive. Either the crowd would tear her apart, or Duncan's lackeys would do it.

The rodents completed the second lap. Grant continued to lag behind Mr. Rabies. Rylee scratched her tattoo more vigorously.

Come on, Grant!

The animals rounded the first bend of the third and final lap. Grant was still behind. Too far behind. She'd seen enough of these races to know that the race was over. Her rations were as good as lost. She closed her eyes and tried to pretend she was somewhere else, not watching Serghei's rat lose this life-or-death race.

This couldn't be happening.

She heard the crowd's cheers suddenly turned gleeful.

"Look!" Preston shouted in her ear.

Her eyes shot open, fixing on the rink. Behind the leaders, a chipmunk and a pink rat rolled across the rink, teeth and claws locked into each other.

Great, a fight. Ordinarily, the fights were the only part of a race worth watching. Who cared tonight? Let all the other animals tear themselves to shreds for all she cared. Why should she care? Grant was going to lose. She would lose her rations that they had gambled away. Why had she thought this was a good idea?

Against her will, her gaze drifted back to Grant. Part of her couldn't bear the thought of seeing him actually lose. When she saw him, though, he was no longer in third. No, now he was in second. A *close* second. That's what Preston had been pointing to. Was Grant moving faster than before? A sleeper? Serghei had promised her that Grant was faster than the last time he'd raced. Something about modifications to his prosthesis as well as new sensory input training. Would it be enough?

Daring to hope, Rylee shouted Grant's name. She couldn't bottle it in any longer. She felt she might explode. Her fingernails scratched the back of her hand at a hundred miles per hour.

Grant continued to make gains. The two lead animals reached the midway point. Inch by inch, Grant chiseled away at Mr. Rabies' lead. By the time the pair reached the final bend, they were snout to snout. A large chunk of the crowd began to boo and slap at the fence in frustration.

Rylee gripped the railing.

Out of the final bend, Grant inched ahead of Mr. Rabies.

"Go Grant, Go!" she hollered. He was going to win.

The finish line was just ahead. Less than a quarter of a lap remained.

Then Mr. Rabies jerked to the side and sunk his teeth into Grant's right forequarter. Grant's head twisted violently in pain, and he stopped running. Mr. Rabies let go of the leg and scurried ahead. For a moment, Grant writhed in pain.

As soon as Mr. Rabies tail was even with Grant, however, he paused his writhing and chomped down on the squirrel's tail and held for all he was worth. Mr. Rabies jerked his head back, baring his teeth, but kept moving, pulling Grant with him. But the added weight slowed him down too much. Within a few moments, the gray rat which had been in second place caught up to the pair. The rat scurried around both of them. Just as the rat got around Mr. Rabies, he lashed out his head and grabbed the rat's leg.

The crowd howled with delight and anguish. Rylee felt as if her chest would burst. She hated not being able to do something to help. Action, that was what she excelled at. Not sitting and watching helplessly, as a pair of rats and a squirrel determined her fate.

Suddenly, Grant released Mr. Rabies' tail and shot forward. Before Mr. Rabies could get loose of the other rat to snatch at him, Grant was out of reach. He crossed the finish line, into the protective arms of Serghei.

It took Rylee a second to process what she'd seen. Grant had…*won!* Joy and relief filled her.

All around, torturous cries rose from the crowd. People started climbing the fence. Some started to shake it violently. Others joined in. Rylee's surge of elation died away, quelled by the crowd's response to Mr. Rabies loss. The people. They were too volatile. With the imminent ration reduction, the people couldn't afford to lose.

There was one word to describe the crowd's response. Panic. And a panicked, embroiled crowd unless quickly quelled almost certainly would turn to rioting. But there was nothing to snuff out the people's panic—nothing to hold them back. No squadron of Regulators. Duncan's own lackeys would be insufficient to deal with such a crowd—a tempestuous sea of people.

From behind, Rylee felt people pressing against her, pinning her against the railing. She looked over a Preston, who was likewise trapped. With his elbow, he was attempting to push back. It was futile. There were too many pressing against them. Shouting, yelling, stomping, pressing. Rylee felt the cold steel lip of the railing digging deeper and deeper into her stomach, cutting into her ribs. Each breath was a struggle.

"They're going to crush us like a can of tuna," Feng cried.

She tried to slide her body beneath the rail. It was no use. The rail dug in too deep. Even if she could scrape it over each of her ribs, it would rip her chest off, or catch her under the chin and strangle her.

What to do? *This* was helplessness. What in the name of Desolation were the people on the loft doing behind her?

There was a sudden release of pressure from her abdomen. The feeling of relief was immediately replaced by the sensation of falling. The railing had broken free beneath the force of the crowd. And now Rylee was falling straight down.

THIRTEEN

R YLEE CRASHED INTO a huddle of people below the loft. Beside her, Preston likewise landed onto a few unfortunate individuals. Both struggled to their feet, so as not to be trampled. She tried to reach down to help those she'd crashed into, but was immediately pushed to the side, caught in the current of the crowd.

Preston was forced in a different direction.

She looked for sign of Feng, but didn't see anything. Could he still be on the warehouse floor? He'd be trampled if he didn't get up. Struggling against the current that dragged her against her will, Rylee gradually made her way back toward the spot where she'd fallen.

For each inch she gained, however, the crowd dragged her back another foot. She cursed, but couldn't even hear her own voice above the deafening noise of the mob. If only she could get to Preston. Maybe he could do something. Now she couldn't even see him.

Turning her gaze around, she looked toward the rink. The protective fence was flattened, lying ominously across the rink. Rylee's stomach twisted into a knot. Serghei. She tried to catch a glimpse of the pit. Were Serghei and the other trainers still holed up inside? Or had the crowd taken them in retribution? Through the tall heads around her, she couldn't tell. It was one of the few times she wished she were taller. Tall like Preston.

If it would have done any good, she would have yelled at everyone to stop. If a mob had a brain, it would be the size of a rat's. A rat's brain, with only haphazard sense, and zero reasoning power. The mob was a seething mass of emotions, capable of any violence or crime.

The mob would turn to looting. Those who'd lost their winnings would claw and bite and bash their heads to get it back.

Those who'd won would do the same to get their due.

Rylee only wanted out of that building with all her friends. She was helpless to do either.

Something harder than the side of a leg or a boot struck her thigh. She looked down. One of the makeshift tables was parting the current of people like a stone in a river. On an impulse, she mounted the table, and stood.

The wooden cable spool rocked and shifted more like a storm-tossed fishing vessel than an immovable rock. She assumed a wide stance to keep from getting knocked back into the throng.

From this new vantage point, she could clearly see the pit. Around it, the perimeter fence and barbed wire still stood. The trainers were inside. And one particularly lanky figure. Serghei.

Good. Serghei hadn't been gutted by the mob...*yet.*

She continued to scan, searching for Preston or Feng. For the first time that night, she wished she'd thought to bring her earpiece.

A moment later, she heard screams that pierced through the din. Rylee whipped her gaze in the direction of the sound. A flurry of movement deeper into the warehouse caught her eye. Then she saw orange and red flames dancing among the crowd, black smoke collecting like storm clouds on the high ceiling. One of the warehouse's partition walls was on fire.

Great! Now those who weren't trampled to death, shot down, or killed in one of the hundreds of scuffles, would get roasted alive. Perhaps the fire itself wasn't a huge threat in a metal warehouse with a concrete floor. But the foam insulation lining the walls would burn, and all of Duncan's storage with it. If nothing else, they would all die of asphyxiation from the smoke.

She had to get out of there.

For the first time, she noticed that the current of people rushing around her seemed to be thinning out. Turning back toward where she had last seen Feng, she felt a jolt of relief to see Preston leaning near one of the toppled cable spools.

Leaping down, she descended back into the crowd. This time, she wasn't rammed backward with every step she took. A moment later she reached Preston's side. He was leaning over Feng, who was curled on the floor, partially covered by the large wooden spool. The crude table had likely saved his life.

"We've got to get out of here now!" she shouted, as if they weren't keenly aware of that fact already. Then she caught Feng's expression. It was one of intense pain. "What's wrong?"

Feng just grimaced.

"I think he broke his leg," Preston shouted, his face grim. There wasn't time to think about the ramifications if that were true, though. If they hung around much longer, they'd all be dead. "Let's get him on his feet. He can use us for crutches."

She nodded, and they both placed hands under Feng's armpits and lifted. A few curses flew out of Feng's mouth. Against the pain, Feng squeezed his eyes tightly shut and bared his teeth.

They propped Feng up onto one leg, as he draped his arms over their shoulders. Beads of sweat ran down Rylee's forehead. Already the heat inside the warehouse had grown intense. And the crackling flames were starting to roar like one of Desolation's earthquakes. Rylee coughed. They didn't have much time before the smoke would engulf them. This type of smoke—the type that burned down buildings—wasn't the friendly grayish cloud that gently billows and disperses into the sky. No, this was the black, consuming smoke. Smoke that choked and blinded. Thick as tar.

With Feng resting nearly his entire weight on Rylee and Preston, they started moving toward the exit. Ahead of them, she could see people converging near the exit of the warehouse. Good, at least most of the people weren't idiotic enough to continue looting while the building burned down around them. No doubt there were still some trying to grab what they could. She briefly wondered if everyone would make it out. If *they* would make it out.

Then she remembered Serghei.

"What about Serghei?" she hollered to Preston.

"We can't do anything for him now," he shouted back. "He's smart. He'll get out."

It was a complete lie. She could recognize it in the look on Preston's face. He was trying to protect her.

"I've got to go back for him," she shouted, removing Feng's

arm from around her shoulder.

"It's too dangerous!"

"When did that ever stop me?" she hollered back to him as she turned and raced back toward the rink.

Preston called again, but his voice was carried away in the cross-current of sounds blasting within the steel shell of the warehouse.

The rink was still empty, lantern lights shining down on it, competing with the orange blaze of the fire. Just beyond it, through the chain link fencing, she could see the pit. Figures were inside. Some halfway up the fencing, stymied by the razor wire. Some beating their fists against the links and shouting words she couldn't hear. Others trying to pry up the fence and climb out underneath it.

Racing around to the pit, she found Serghei at the gate, trying to pick the lock.

"Every good heist movie has a lock-picking scene, you know?" Serghei said, sounding far too casual. "They never tell you how difficult it is. Especially, if you have to do it locked *inside* the fence. When I make my movies—"

"Stand clear!" Rylee Shiites, drawing out her pistol from her shoulder holster and taking aim at the lock. She stepped to the side of the lock slightly. This would be by far the stupidest shot she'd ever made.

Bullets bounce. Another of her grandfather's lessons.

Well, she hoped *this* bullet wouldn't bounce at her or anyone else. Not letting herself think about it too long, she steadied her hands and slowly pulled the trigger. New or inexperienced shooters—and even many with lots of experience with hand-guns—overlooked this phase of the process. It did little good to aim and then jerk the gun off target by pulling the trigger reckless-ly. Careful, controlled trigger pulls were the secret to good marksmanship.

The pistol kicked back in her hands and the bullet fired. She immediately leveled the gun again and sighted, just as she had been trained. She felt no pain. The bullet hadn't ricocheted and struck her. Even with her heightened adrenaline, she was sure she'd feel a bullet wound. Hopefully, no other innocent bystander had been struck.

She adjusted her focus from the front sight of her pistol to the lock. Still in one piece. She'd struck it. The lock still swayed on its hasp.

Again she took aim and fired. The lock jumped to life but remained intact. She fired a third time. Still no change.

Desolation! This is supposed to work.

She wished for her rifle. Surely the lock couldn't withstand a direct shot from *it*. A bout of coughs seized her for a few moments. The smoke was growing thicker. There wasn't time for this.

Curse it!

Casting her eyes about, she searched for some other means of breaking Serghei and the others free. Did Duncan really need to lock the trainers in the pit? Maybe it saved them from a hoard of angry gamblers, but it was definitely not going to save them from the fire. She needed a blow torch, or some way of ramming the fence. A forklift. A truck. An Indiana Jones-style boulder.

Great! Now I'm starting to think like Serghei.

Then she spotted something on the floor of the warehouse that gave her an idea. A terrible idea. But it was something.

She sprinted toward it. The heat from the fire was drawing sweat from her body like a water pump. Reaching the nearest makeshift table — the wooden cable spool — she tipped it onto its side and rolled it into the fence. Then she went after four more tables, doing the same thing with each one. Once she had a collection of tables, she went to work on her half-baked idea.

Taking the first spool, she set it up on its side so that it sat like a table.

"Are you planning to have a tea party?" Serghei hollered at her through the fence. "What is it you are trying to do?"

She ignored him and kept working. Next, she grabbed another spool to stack on top of the first one. It was heavier than she counted on. It was just made of wood, wasn't it? Old, dried out wood. Still, she managed to stack it, so that now the tower of spools stood a good six feet tall. Moving quickly, trying to breathe in as little of the smoke-ridden air as possible, she positioned another two spools on the floor around the base of her tower. With the fifth spool, she stacked it on top of one of the single spools.

Smoke continued to choke her lungs. It was bad enough that Serghei had stopped making comments.

Using the spool that was not part of a stack as a stepping stool, she clambered up to the top of one of the double stacks. Then she leaned over, grabbed the top spool from the other tall stack, and lifted.

Her stomach muscles tightened until she felt they would rip apart. But finally managed to lift it. Then she hefted it up into her arms. The motion pushed her off balance. She teetered, fighting to regain her balance. If she fell this time, only an unforgiving cement floor would break her fall. And likely break her skull in the process. Straining all her muscles, and with a cry of force, she righted herself. Then, she heaved the spool over the barbed wire of the fence, into the pit. It landed onto the concrete floor with a loud thud, but miraculously did not split into pieces.

That's one. Oh, blast! The thought of doing that again made her want to collapse and give up. Already her muscles trembled.

She couldn't stop. She had to keep moving. Had to save Serghei. She reached for another spool, just as a fit of coughs seized her body. Still coughing, she tried to pull up. It scarcely budged.

Come on!

She pulled and yanked and cried out in pain. Then she collapsed. It was no use. Her energy was spent. The smoke…it was too thick.

Something grabbed her arm and shook her. "Ry, can you hear me?" a voice shouted in her ear.

She lifted her head to find Preston looking into her eyes.

"We've got to get you out of here," he shouted. He helped her down from the spool. "Can you walk?" She coughed and nodded. "Stay low, and make for the exit. I'll help the others."

Rylee didn't argue. Didn't have the energy for it. Coughing like her body was trying to eject her stomach up through her mouth and bending low, she staggered through the smoke toward the exit, relying on her internal sense of direction to guide her. She only hoped that sense of direction was sure.

After what felt like an eternity, Rylee finally felt a cool air touch her overheated skin. Greedily, she tried to suck in the fresh night air. But her lungs were still working to discharge the smoke clogged inside her.

A scene of commotion dominated the narrow street outside the burning warehouse. Around them, flames cast their orange hue on terrified, angry, or awestruck faces. The flames would continue to blaze, so long as it could find fuel to feed its insatiable appetite. No firemen, or bucket lines, or even rain would come to quench the flames. The first two didn't exist anymore. And the last *virtually* didn't exist.

Somehow, she found Feng amid the crowd, propped up against a building, evidently still in a lot of pain. She dropped to the street next to him and coughed violently.

"Tripe!" Feng said through clenched teeth. "What happened to you? Where's the others?"

Rylee coughed again. "Coming." *Cough*. That was all she managed to get out. She hoped it was true.

For several minutes, the pair of them sat there, silent but for Rylee's coughs. In the background, Duncan's warehouse continued to burn.

Come on, Preston. He had to make it out. If he didn't soon, there would be no getting out for anyone. She chided herself for leaving him. Abandoning him like a coward.

A tall figure moving through the crowd caught her attention. Her heart stuttered in her heaving chest. Could it be? As the figure moved closer, another appeared next to it. Shorter, lanky. Serghei? A second later, she knew. It was them. All alive, including Grant.

Sweat poured down Preston's bright red face as he collapsed to the street next to Rylee. Serghei crouched in front of her, beaming, Grant darting back and forth across his shoulders.

"I was beginning to think you wouldn't make it," Rylee said.

Preston coughed. "Me, too," he wheezed.

"I hate to interrupt this beautiful reunion," Feng said in a strained voice. "But there's an Elect right over there."

Despite her weakness, Rylee shot her head up and drew out her gun. Preston did the same.

FOURTEEN

Rylee didn't know what to expect. A gang of Elects, astride electrocycles? A squadron of Regulators, assault rifles in hand? What she saw were clumps of huddled Norms transfixed by the burning warehouse. A few people nearby who saw Rylee and Preston's handguns cried in protest and fled deeper into the crowd.

"Where?" Rylee said, continuing to scan the crowd for anyone who looked suspicious.

"In the black coat," Feng's strained voice came in reply from beside her.

"There!" Preston said, motioning toward the edge of the crowd.

Narrowing her eyes, Rylee saw him—or her. A black figure, highlighted with vermillion streaks from the dancing flames. He moved with an Elect's signature litheness. How had she not noticed before? The long coat, too. Even in the flickering light, she could tell that it was a finer garment than any Norm would own.

"He's moving," Preston said through a cough, "toward that alleyway," He coughed again. "Come on, Ry. Serg, you stay with Feng."

"Aye, aye, Captain," Serghei said, saluting.

Not wanting to draw more unwanted attention to themselves, Preston and Rylee holstered their guns as they weaved through the crowd toward the alleyway. Several times, the Elect disappeared amongst the crowd, only to reappear a moment later.

They broke free of the crowd, just in time to see the dark figure slip into the shadows of an alleyway.

"You follow him," Preston said. "I'll try to cut him off."

With that, Preston took off running toward the nearest alleyway that the Elect hadn't gone down. Rylee unholstered her pistol and dashed into the alley, pursuing the Elect.

She wasn't entirely prepared for the darkness that engulfed her as she entered the narrow alley between two abandoned warehouses. The lights from within the warehouse and from the fire had spoiled her night eyes. Not for the first time that night, she wished for her rifle topped with the thermal scope.

For a few moments she paused, letting her eyes adjust to the shadows, tuning her ears to any sounds coming from ahead of her. It wouldn't do her any good to charge right into an ambush. For all she knew, the Elect could be pointing a weapon directly at her at that moment. The thought made her skin crawl.

There was a pile of rubble beside her along the wall of the alley. She crouched down behind it and aimed her pistol down the alley. There. Now she had some cover. Though, she'd much prefer it if she could just see the Elect.

A cough escaped her mouth. *Great.* If the Elect didn't know she was there before, he did now.

Her eyes adjusted steadily to the darkness. Forms in the alleyway began to take shape. Ahead, she saw a shadow moving. She trained her gun on it. What if it was Preston? Suddenly, she didn't like this plan of splitting up. Not without their earpieces.

The figure kept moving down the alley. If she stayed put until the Elect reached the end of the alley, Preston would be alone to deal with him. She would have to try and trail him, without any more coughs.

Keeping her gun trained on the shadow, Rylee slipped out from her crude shelter and stalked forward.

She crept as quickly as she dared, needing to move more rapidly than the Elect so that she could be close when he reached the end. Several times she was forced to pause while she stifled a cough.

About halfway down the alley, Rylee's foot struck something. The clatter of the empty aluminum can that followed would have been sufficient to rouse a whole army of Elects. She cursed under her breath, as she dropped to one knee, prepared to return any fire that came her way.

Nothing. All she heard was the pounding of footfall on the asphalt.

Springing to her feet, she raced after the Elect.

Where was Preston? The Elect was getting closer to the exit to the alleyway.

What did Preston intend to do once they caught this Elect? Kill him on the spot? An unsummoned image of a terrified Boney flashed in her mind. Would another innocent Norm die as a result of them killing this Elect?

Suddenly, a blinding light burst to life ahead of her. Preston's commanding voice filled the narrow space. "Don't move! Hands in the air!"

The Elect's figure, now outlined in intense light, halted and slowly raised his arms. There was no weapon in either hand. Instinctively, Rylee moved to the side, out of direct line of fire behind the Elect. On the other side of the Elect, now that the light wasn't shining directly on her, she could see Preston's strong jaw and brow faintly illuminated by the indirect beams of his tactical light.

A tactical light? She'd entirely forgotten that Preston usually carried one in his pocket, even though he seldom attached it to his pistol. Why didn't she have one of those?

"Who are you?" the figure said, still not moving, hands up.

"I'll be asking the questions," Preston replied, sternly.

Seriously? Did he just say that? Evidently they'd all seen too many of Serghei's movies.

"I want you to slowly drop to your knees," Preston continued. "And place your hands on the top of your head. Also, beware that the sharpest shooter in the entire Alliance has a gun trained on your head. Neither of us will hesitate to put a bullet through your skull."

The Elect turned his head to the side, as if to look at her. And Rylee caught a glimpse of his profile. She didn't know any other way to describe it, aside from arrogant, with dark hair and stubbled chin. A face she instantly hated.

Despite the loathing she felt, though, Preston was wrong about one thing. She would hesitate to shoot. Even though it might cost them their lives.

* * *

William reluctantly did as the man ordered. The cold asphalt bit into his knees, the thin material of his trousers doing little to protect his skin. Why hadn't he worn better garments for running away? Next time, he would have to be better prepared for running for his life. And, apparently, for dealing with a gun-wielding Unenhanced. He heard the Unenhanced could be hostile. This was absurd, though. What did they want? It wasn't like he carried cans of food in his pockets.

"I have very little of value," William said, fighting to keep his tone subservient. If it came to it, he would try the authoritative voice he'd learned from watching his father. People responded to that voice. But sometimes that response was the opposite of what you wanted. Safer to appear weak at first. Make them let down their guard.

One Unenhanced with a gun he could have handily dealt with. Two, though? With one standing behind him? The odds were not in his favor. Even with his PNU-enhanced reflexes, his situation was tenuous. He couldn't move faster than bullets. Likely, he could dodge the first shot. But the subsequent ones? That miniature sun burning his retinas didn't help him any either. If he couldn't see the person—watch the movement of his eyes, the subtle twitch of his muscles—it made it blasted difficult to accurately calculate a man's actions.

This situation called for diplomacy.

"We have lots of experience dealing with Elects, like you," the man with the light said. "So, don't try anything."

Elects? Is that their name for the Enhanced? Now that he thought about it, the name did sound familiar. Despite his current dilemma, he found it fascinating that they could tell. He wondered how. This was not the time to ask though. Better to play dumb.

"No, no," he said, making his voice sound pleading. It pained his ego to do it. "I'm no Elect. Honestly. I—I swear." He added a little stutter to his words, for good measure.

"Malarkey!" Light-man retorted. "We could tell just by the way you walked."

85

Could they really? This was something he would definitely have to investigate. That is, if he made it out of this alive. He could write a modification for his PNU that helped him blend in. All he would have to do...*Brilliant, Will! Two hostile Unenhanced creeps have their guns pointed at your head, and you're thinking about a coding challenge.*

His ignorance act was not working.

Time for a different tactic. Make a threat.

Sharpening the tone of his voice slightly, he spoke again, "If I am an Elect, as you call me, then you should know that I can contact the Regulators anytime I want. They'll have my exact coordinates, as well as a live capture of everything I can see and hear. Which would include you."

It was a bluff, of course. There was no way he was going to contact Regulation. He'd be worse off with them than with these two.

"The Regulators are probably already on their way," Light-man scoffed. "To investigate the fire. And little good your recording will do. All they'll see is a bright light."

Alright. So the Unenhanced are not so easily hoodwinked. At least, not this one.

"What are you doing in the slums?" Light-man said.

"Is it against some ordinance of the Alliance for me to be here?"

"We don't care about Alliance ordinances! Now, answer the question."

How to answer that one...

"I came to Duncan's Warehouse hoping to ascertain information," he replied. Which was not entirely a lie. He needed to find somewhere where he could stay—somewhere safe...*ish*. And possibly information on how to get smuggled out of the city.

"Right," Light-man said. "Like where to find a nice young girl to abduct. We kill Elects like you. You think you can come around and do whatever you want with us just because you can get away with it. Some of us are sick of it and are more than ready to fight back."

It was an admirable speech, all things considered. But nothing that would work in William's favor. He had to think of something fast, for he was quickly losing this battle. Would outright pleading forgiveness for all the wrongs committed by his fellow Enhanced do any good? No, that was too expected. And pleading innocence certainly wouldn't help.

If only these two were Enhanced, it would make dealing with them so much easier. He found that surprisingly ironic.

"Look," he finally said, "I've got my own problems to deal with. Shoot me if that will make you feel better. I promise, no one is going to miss me. And I'm really tired of being on my knees."

It was a risky approach. He doubted it would work. Using his PNU to suppress any fear, he stared—well, squinted—calmly back into the blinding light. If they fired, he would try to dodge. Turn and go for the legs of the one behind him. He tuned his ears. Every sound would be vital to his survival.

"Believe me, I'll be very happy to rid the world of another Elect."

"Preston, wait!" came a voice from behind. A *female's* voice. Will hadn't realized a female—a girl—was behind him. Did it matter her gender, though? She had a gun. Yet maybe there was less of an eagerness to kill him, if he read her voice correctly.

"What is it?" Light-man said.

"I think we should let him go."

I like her already.

"What? Why?"

"We haven't actually caught him doing anything. We can't know for sure he'll do anything."

"He doesn't *need* to have done anything. You know that. The fact that he's here means he's up to no good. If we let him go, someone else will pay the price."

"I know, but…" her voice faltered slightly. She sounded like she could be his own age, maybe younger. "Remember Boney?"

"Fine, you don't have to shoot. I will."

"Preston!"

Light-man sighed audibly. "What do you suggest we do with him, then? Just let him go?"

There was a moment's pause. Will hoped the girl would just

say 'let him go.' But that was probably too much to hope for from these two. Should he make his own suggestion?

"We'll escort him out of the slums," she finally said.

"And if he comes back?"

"I'll shoot him myself."

Despite the relative calmness he felt, William winced at her words. Nothing in her tone betrayed a hint of deceit. The girl meant what she said. Perhaps he didn't like her so much, after all.

"Fine," Light-man replied. Preston, she had called him. "Feng ought to love this plan. Go back and bring the others here. We'll wait out in one of these warehouses until the crowd has cleared out, just in case the Regulators show up. I'll stay with *friend* here."

Friend? A sarcastic remark came to him in response. But he restrained himself. Somehow he didn't think Light-man— Preston—would appreciate his humor.

"Are you sure you'll be alright by yourself?" the girl asked.

"I'll be fine. Hurry back, though."

The girl didn't reply, and a moment later he heard soft footfall as she dashed away. *So quiet.* If he hadn't used his PNU to help him filter out other sounds, he doubted he would have heard anything. As he listened, he activated his Accelerated Visual and Sensory Processor—AVSP. He could only run in this mode for so long before his brain overloaded or his PNU ran out of power. The AVSP allowed him to react three times faster than the average human brain, the main component being its accelerated visual processing. The same sort of visual processing that flies innately possessed, and makes most humans look like they are moving through molasses.

This fellow with the gun pointed at him likely possessed above-average reflexes. Even so, William would still have a significant advantage.

Taking a deep breath, he forced his face, his eyes, his posture to look relaxed. He wanted to appear bored, belying the adrenaline that was surging through his body. Once confident the girl was a safe distance away, he lunged forward with a superhuman burst of speed, ramming directly into Preston's legs.

FIFTEEN

WILLIAM HEARD PRESTON'S cry of shock for what seemed like minutes after he had already struck. Then a gunshot, fired much too late. Preston was falling forward, his feet swept from under him by William's blow. Reacting before Preston's body even hit the ground, William turned, and kicked the gun from his hand.

The firearm clattered and clanked as it bounced against the pavement, its mounted tactical light flashing like a strobe as it flipped end-over-end.

Then he kicked Preston in the face. A crack sounded as his boot met Preston's nose. Preston let out a cry of pain. Stepping to his side, William laid a few swift kicks into Preston's ribs. He heard none of them crack. He contemplated kicking harder, but stopped. Someone undoubtedly had heard the gunshot. It was time to leave.

Turning, he made to run. Just as he did, Preston's leg shot up and tripped him. William tumbled forward, but rolled out of the fall and was instantly back on his feet. He turned back to find Preston picking himself off the street, apparently intent on fighting back.

Impressive.

"You devils think you can get away with whatever you want!" he growled, staggering forward. "You killed my brother."

Blood poured down Preston's face. But he kept coming toward William.

Should have kicked harder.

Preston looked in no condition to run. So, William turned and sprinted away.

"Come back!" came Preston's cries from behind him. "Come and fight me!"

William could hear him try and pursue, but in his current state he likely couldn't muster more than a pathetic jog. Rounding a bend, William disappeared down an alleyway. He ran as fast and as hard as his legs would go. One downside to the PNUs is that they couldn't boost his muscle power. They could, however, force the muscles to work at their maximum ability for a long time—essentially until his body collapsed, or his PNU drained of power.

And so he ran.

* * *

Rylee dabbed Preston's bloodied and bruised face with a damp rag. The skin around his right eye wrinkled up in pain. The other was too swollen to show any expression. Blood had finally stopped streaming out of his nostrils. Serghei had set the broken nose a half-hour before.

It pained her to watch. Still, as painful as it was to see Preston like this, it wasn't anything compared to what she had felt when she had heard him screaming at that Elect. The one who got away. The one who would have been dead if it weren't for her own weakness. Never had she witnessed Preston lose control of his emotions like that. Not even the night they had killed his brother. There was such a raw anger. It frightened her.

The crew was back in Serghei's hideout. On the couch sat Feng, his leg propped up on one of the worn armrests. A broken tibia. Not a compound fracture. But broken nonetheless. Serghei had set that bone, as well.

"This is all my fault," she said softly to Preston as she tried to clean his face. He looked terrible. His strong, confident face. Broken. Broken by an Elect she should have shot.

"I'm the leader of this crew," Preston said. "The decision to let him go was mine. There is none to blame but me."

Rylee shook her head. "And if I hadn't said anything…you'd have shot him. And if I hadn't talked us in to go looking for information at Duncan's Warehouse—"

"Oh, I'm totally blaming this on you, Ry," Feng groaned from the couch.

"Are you forgetting about me?" Serghei said from across the

room. He was tending to Grant, who was still on edge after the night's events. "I'd be dead right now if Ry hadn't come to my aide. Grant too."

"Small loss," Feng muttered.

"Small loss, is it?" Serghei cried. "That's gratitude for you. Next time, you can set your own broken bones."

Feng grimaced as he shifted his position on the couch. "Like it matters. It won't heal fast enough. They'll Deprecate me long before I can walk again."

The group fell silent. They all knew it was true. With a broken leg, Feng couldn't do his job. If his supervisor was particularly lenient, Feng might get away with one week of Infirmary leave. But that would require him to report his injuries to the Infirmary. Only the extremely desperate did that. Checking yourself into the Infirmary was the surest way to get yourself Deprecated.

"We won't let that happen to you," Preston said, after a moment. "We'll figure something out." It was just the sort of thing Preston would say. His words, though, lacked any of their usual conviction.

"Like what?" Feng said, his voice bitter.

"We could amputate your leg," Serghei offered, his voice excited. "I have always wanted to try cybernetics on a human subject."

"Just shut up!" Feng cried. "All of you...just shut up! You're not helping one bit."

Rylee looked away from him. It was easier to look at Preston's battered and bloodied face, than to see the anger and bitterness in Feng's. What would happen to his mother if he were Deprecated? Feng was all his mother had left.

It was true that Rylee didn't feel the same bond with Feng as she did with Preston or even Serghei. He was not the sort of person that made it easy to feel close to. His caustic, flippant attitude was deceptive, though. He cared about people. And he was tenacious when they were hunting Elects, even though he would pretend to complain.

Though she felt tears fighting to fill her eyes, she staved them off. Tears wouldn't help Feng. They wouldn't help her own grandfather. They wouldn't bring back Boney. They wouldn't heal

Preston's face. She didn't deserve to cry. All she could do was try to fix what she had broken.

Oh, Desolation! Can things possibly get worse?

That night, Feng slept on Serghei's couch. Preston offered to go speak with his mother so that she knew where he was. But Feng adamantly opposed that idea.

"If I don't show up myself, she'll be all kinds of suspicious," Feng had said. "This won't be the first time I haven't come home at night."

Not knowing what else to do, Rylee went home and attempted to sleep, but found that she couldn't. Every time she closed her eyes, she saw that Elect. And every time, the same desire surged inside her: to shoot him in the head.

Finally, she threw off her patchwork blanket and rose from her cot. She quietly slipped on her boots and stood. Her muscles protested—still sore from her crash on the electrocycle. Ignoring the pain, she took her pistol out from under her pillow and holstered it. Then she grabbed her rifle, shouldered it, and climbed out of her bedroom window.

* * *

Rylee stalked the streets of the slums all night without a trace of that Elect. Many times she wished to use her earpiece to call Serghei. Maybe he'd caught something on his cameras. She resisted, refusing to involve the crew. This was her mess. No one else was going to tidy it up for her.

Deep down, she knew killing this Elect wouldn't fix anything. At that moment, she wasn't listening to that part of her brain—the rational part. She needed vengeance. For Preston's sake. For Feng's. For her grandfather and Boney.

As she walked, she constantly blew air into her cupped hands to keep them from freezing off. Lingering bouts of coughs still afflicted her. Why hadn't she remembered to grab her gloves? Not only did it expose her fingers to the elements, but made it easier for her to scratch the tattoo on the back of her hand. The skin had become red and raw.

Abandoned building after abandoned building, alleyway after alleyway, street after street, she hunted. Her fingers frozen stiff, her throat raw and sore from coughing, her thoughts muddled with drowsiness. Not a trace of the Elect.

Eventually, she became aware of the waning darkness. Morning approached, and she had failed. Almost too exhausted to care, she turned her numb feet toward home. Keeping to the alleyways, with her head bent low, and her hood pulled forward, she trudged back to her housing unit. Except for a cat with a mangled tail that hadn't been caught and eaten yet, and a few mice, she met with no signs of life.

After what felt like hours, she reached her building. Fingers numb with cold, she gripped the icy handrails of the fire escape, and climbed two stories up to her room. Pulling up the window sash, she climbed inside and collapsed onto her cot, her eyes snapping shut like steel traps.

Almost as quickly as they closed, her eyes snapped back open. *Voices?* Someone was talking. Muffled though they were, she could distinguish her grandfather's voice, and one which was undoubtedly not. She slipped out of bed, unholstered her pistol, and crept to the door. Gently, she turned the doorknob and pushed the door ajar.

Through the crack in the door she saw a man sitting at the table in the kitchen. About her own age. With stubbled chin and...*arrogant face.* The Elect!

Bursting through the door, Rylee aimed her pistol directly at the Elect's head and fired.

SIXTEEN

THE ELECT'S HEAD jerked forward. But there was no spray of blood. Rylee moved to take aim again, but the Elect had already slipped under the table.

Desolation! How do they move so fast?

She'd missed the easy shot. Perhaps she shouldn't have made such a hasty entrance. The Elect had plenty of time to react.

Moving into the kitchen, she prepared to take another shot at the cowering Elect.

"Rylee!" her grandfather shouted. "What in the blazes are you trying to do!"

"Kill vermin!"

The Elect toppled the table onto its side, creating a barrier between himself and Rylee. Plates and forks and cups crashed onto the floor, spilling their breakfast with it.

That pathetic particleboard tabletop wouldn't stop her bullets.

"Rylee, stop it!" Her grandfather seized her arm and forced the muzzle of her gun down. "Have you gone mad? Tell me what is going on."

Despite his age. Despite that he was soon to be Deprecated by the Alliance because he was no longer any value to them, her grandfather easily overpowered her. Still, she struggled against him.

"Rylee!" her grandfather said firmly. "This is not what I taught you. I armed you with a gun so you could defend yourself, not kill innocent people."

"He's not innocent." Rylee's chest heaved forcibly as she pressed her lips together.

"You know this fellow? Has he done something to you?"

"I've never seen either of you before in my life," came the voice of the Elect, still cowering behind the table.

"He's an Elect," Rylee said, her eyes fixed with anger at the table, as if she could burn a hole through it with her gaze. "What else do I need to know?"

Her grandfather shook his head. "I know you're upset about the new mandate from the Alliance. But this isn't going to fix anything. You'll have the Regulators crashing down our door any minute."

Then he slowly moved in front of her, until he stood between her and the Elect. His gray eyes, lined with thick veins, bored into her own. Though she tried to look away, she found his gaze held her own, gripping her eyes like he now gripped her arm.

"I want you to hand me your gun," he said.

Like ice melting under the sun's heat, Rylee felt her anger melt away under his gaze. Slowly, she moved her finger away from the trigger, then placed her pistol into the firm grip of her grandfather's hand.

He patted her on the shoulder.

"Good," he said softly. Then he removed her pistol's magazine, and locked back the slide. A single brass cartridge glinted in the dim kitchen light as it ejected from the chamber. Plinking to the floor, it rolled until it bumped against the wall. He walked over and picked it up.

"Now," he said, inspecting the cartridge before loading it into Rylee's magazine, "I believe it's safe for you to come out, Grayson."

Grayson? So, now her grandfather and this Elect—who she should have just killed—knew each other? What in Desolation's Thunder was going on? Had this Elect done something to take control of her grandfather?

"Safety is a relative term," the Elect—Grayson—said from behind the table. "You have a lovely floor. I'm quite content here."

Her grandfather chuckled. "Smart man. Knows better than to show his face to an angry woman. Come on out. We've got to get this mess cleaned up."

Cautiously, Grayson lifted his head over the top of his barricade. Rylee glared at him, and instantly felt her anger surge again. His eyes looked her up and down. His gaze hovered lower mostly, apparently checking to ensure she was indeed disarmed. Once satisfied, he rose gracefully to his feet. To see him move sickened her. Everything about him—his appearance, his movements, his way of speaking—reeked of an Elect.

"I found Grayson, here," her grandfather said, clapping him on the back as though they were old friends, "huddled in an alleyway just next to us when I went for a walk this morning. Said he'd nowhere to stay."

Her grandfather bent over to pick up the scattered dishes on the floor, and scooping up lumps of the spilled pinto beans. Grayson stood the table up, and walked around to help. Rylee watched him.

Seeing the spilled food reminded her of the rations she had lost. How long before her grandfather noticed?

"I invited Grayson to stay with us," her grandfather said. "Just until he can find something more permanent."

"Something more permanent?" Rylee said, staring at her grandfather is disbelief. "He's an *Elect*. He probably has his own building. Why does he need to stay with us?"

"I do have a place," Grayson said, setting a plate back on the table. "I just can't go there right now. It's…complicated."

He looked at her with a face that asked for sympathy. Instead of feeling sorry for him, she just felt like punching him.

"Don't you have other lowlife Elect friends? Why don't you burden *them* instead of *us*? Or do the other Elects not like you either?"

"That's quite enough, Rylee," her grandfather scolded. "I've offered to let Grayson stay with us until he figures things out. He's our guest. I expect you to treat him with some amount of civility. Or, at least, without hostility. Understood?"

He looked at her sternly. Ordinarily, she would have cowed beneath that gaze. Not this time.

"We don't have enough food to feed another mouth," she said between clenched teeth.

Especially, now that I've gambled away a whole week's worth of rations. She wasn't about to point out that fact now, though.

"We'll get by." The fallback response for everything her grandfather didn't know how to deal with.

"Right," she said, pursing her lips and glaring at the Elect. "I need to get to work. Can I have my gun back now?"

"You can have it back once you've proven I can trust you not to harm Grayson."

Little chance of that happening.

Giving Grayson one last glare—which he actually met with an arrogant smile—she turned and stormed out of the apartment, making sure to slam the door as hard as she could.

* * *

William felt glad to see the girl leave. She was psychotic. He looked over at the cabinets along the wall. A ragged hole gaped in the bottom corner of one of the cabinet faces. He was lucky he'd been able to react so quickly. As depleted as his power reserve was, he felt surprised his PNU's AVSP system had kicked in so rapidly. He didn't want to contemplate what would have happened if it hadn't.

Within a few minutes, the girl's grandfather—Kenny, he'd called himself—reemerged from a side room. "Well, Grayson," he said, rubbing his gray beard. "I'm off to work. The pot's in there, when you got to do your business. Don't help yourself to any food. We'll eat supper after sundown. If I were you, I'd stay off the streets and out of sight." Then he turned and walked out the door, leaving William alone.

Grayson. Why had he used that name? Couldn't he have come up with a better alias than his actual middle name? He shook his head at his own stupidity. Even the name Bill was less identifying than Grayson. No one ever called him Bill. Physical exhaustion. PNU-overworked brain. Starvation. They were to blame for his lack of coherent thought.

It was that same lack of coherence that made him think staying *here* was a smart idea. Now he wondered if he shouldn't find a safer place to stay. But where? He'd wandered around the slums the whole night without finding anything better than a bunch of derelict warehouses. Here, at least, there was food—of a sort.

But that girl—Rylee—she had attacked him so readily. It was

like deja vu from last night. Could she be the same girl? He wasn't about to waste precious power reserves to perform a voice match.

The real question for him was, what to do next. If he stayed here, he might avoid starvation. But at the risk of dealing with psycho-girl. Perhaps he should beg asylum from Adrianna. He sighed. As tempting as that sounded at the moment, he knew he couldn't do it. Not until he figured out what was going on, and understood what kind of danger he was in. Besides, going to Adrianna's was a predictable move.

William...no, Grayson. He needed to think of himself as Grayson. Grayson. He was amazed at the cramped confines of the apartment. The rooms felt more like closets than places to live in. As he browsed around the apartment, he contemplated his conundrum. Since receiving Lander's cryptic message on the energy drink, Grayson had heard nothing more from his friend. He considered sending Lander another secure message with his PNU, but dismissed the idea. A waste of power, and likely a waste of time. He'd just have to wait for...something.

Where was Lander? *This had better not be some twisted game he's concocted.* He only wished that were true. Deep down, he knew it wasn't. But what should he do about it?

His bodily and mental faculties were too far depleted for him to assess the problem logically. Noticing a cot on the floor of one of the rooms, he laid down and immediately fell asleep.

* * *

Rylee raced her Harley through the narrow streets as though she were in hot pursuit of an Elect. Weaving sharply in and out of downtrodden clumps of Norms trudging home from work and transport trucks, she earned the angry shouts of many calling for her to slow down.

Not today, she thought, as the chilly November air streamed in through the cuffs of her jacket and up her back. She needed to get home. The thought of that Elect home alone with her grandfather sickened her. For the entire day, she'd been able to think of nothing but that Elect...in her apartment. What was he doing in the slums? He didn't belong. And if she got home before her grandfather, she planned to make sure he understood that. If only her grandfather hadn't confiscated her Glock…

She arrived at her housing unit earlier than usual. It was already dark as night outside, even though it was early in the evening.

Stowing her Harley in the alleyway, she entered the housing unit through the front door, and ascended the two flights of stairs to her floor, then paused at the door. What would she find? The Elect sitting at the table, eagerly awaiting her arrival? Perhaps she should enter through her bedroom window.

Chiding herself for feeling nervous over an Elect, she unlocked the door and shoved it open. She stood on the threshold, taking in the empty kitchen. The apartment was silent. For a brief moment, she harbored the hope that he'd left, for good.

She knocked on the bathroom door. No answer. Then she checked her grandfather's room. Still no sign of the Elect. Her hopes began to swell. Perhaps she truly had managed to frighten him off. Breathing easier, she opened the door to her room so that she could retrieve her earpiece. She stopped just inside the threshold. On her bed lay the Elect, his mouth hanging wide open, his breath even and rhythmic. Asleep.

Her primary instinct was to yell at him to get out of bed. Then she noticed something leaning against her makeshift desk that made her smile. Her rifle.

SEVENTEEN

CREEPING AS QUIETLY as the wooden floorboards would allow, she made her way across her room. How had she forgotten about her rifle? She didn't need a handgun to kill the Elect. Though a few of the floorboards betrayed her presence, the Elect didn't stir. With her eyes fixed on his face, she slowly passed the cot, *her* cot. It disgusted her to see him sleep there. Even sleeping, he looked arrogant.

The familiar cold metal of her rifle's barrel felt good in her hands. Just to be armed again felt good. All day at work she'd furtively felt at the spot under her left arm where her pistol always hung. But it wasn't there. Well, what she was about to do wasn't going to help earn back her pistol. At that moment, she didn't care.

Turning around, she brought the stock of her rifle to her shoulder and aimed the barrel at the slumbering Elect. She didn't peer through the scope. At this range, there was no point. Placing her finger on the trigger, she breathed out slowly. Her heart pounded in her chest.

Unintentionally, she found herself studying the Elect's features. His dark hair looked nearly black, and was cut short—an Elect's haircut. His pale skin was slightly darker around his mouth and chin, as a new beard started to grow. His jawline lacked the strong, stone-carved lines that Preston's face bore. Instead of a pronounced square jawline, the Elect's narrowed gradually into a rounded chin. Soft. A face designed to lure in innocent girls. Just as his closed eyelids and drooping mouth were supposed to make her hesitate at shooting him.

She gripped the rifle tighter with her left hand and began to squeeze the trigger.

"You wouldn't really shoot a man in his sleep, would you?" The voice made Rylee jump. It had come from the Elect. Though, his eyes were still shut. "Because, that would be just a tad on the rude side. Inhospitable, some might say."

"It's also rude to sleep in someone else's bed without asking first," Rylee snorted.

"I knew you wouldn't mind. So, I didn't bother."

He smiled, his eyes still closed. An urge to punch him squarely in the mouth surged inside her. How could he be so arrogant at a time like this?

"Your grandfather's going to be disappointed when he comes home and finds a bullet in my head."

"He'll get over it."

"Let me just say, there's no one I'd rather shoot me in my sleep than you. By the way, I unloaded your rifle while you were gone."

"What!"

Rylee turned her rifle over and released the magazine. Empty. To be sure, she pulled back the rifle's bolt. No round ejected. She cursed.

For the first time, the Elect opened his eyes and sat up, still smiling. "I took the liberty of unloading it about an hour ago, when I got up to go to the loo. You know, it's dangerous to leave a loaded firearm lying around like that."

Ignoring him, Rylee went to her desk and opened the rusted metal toolbox where she kept her extra munition. It was empty. Whirling around, she pointed the rifle at the Elect.

"What did you do with it?" she demanded.

"You do realize that rifle is still not loaded, right?" he said, raising his eyebrows. "I just point it out because you seem to think I should be afraid of it." He smirked, drawing in his lips.

"Just tell me what you did with my ammo."

"You know, I think you should work on your negotiation skills. Because, you see, I feel like—as foolish as this may sound—that it wouldn't be in my best interest to comply with that demand."

He smirked again.

"And *you're* not making me want to shoot you any less."

That wasn't the only ammo in the apartment. Her grandfather had his own cache of them, hidden. There were some .308 rounds in there, she knew. If she could find them. She stomped toward the door. Before she reached it, she heard a sound that made her halt midstep. A second later, she heard the door to the apartment squeak open, followed by the heavy footfall of boots. Her grandfather.

She frowned and spun back around. "Today, you got lucky."

"As fun as this little game of yours is for me," he said, "I'd be happy to tell your grandfather about it." He smiled broadly. "I'm sure he'd love to hear about it, too."

Too annoyed to respond, Rylee deposited her rifle back in its place, then walked out to greet her grandfather.

Rylee ate her dinner that evening mostly in silence. She didn't feel like talking, especially with that Elect around. Grayson. Her grandfather called him Grayson. That bothered her. The way the two sat there chatting and laughing like friends...He was the enemy. Why couldn't her grandfather see that? Not only was Grayson sitting at their table, talking, but he was eating their food. Food which they were in short supply of. Food of which there was not enough to spare.

Besides the fact that he was an Elect, what aggravated her the most about having him there is she felt like a babysitter. She couldn't go anywhere, because she didn't trust him alone with her grandfather. She needed to go to Serghei's to check on Feng. And the crew needed to plan their next move to find out who was behind the recent murders. Because if they didn't, her grandfather would be Deprecated in a matter of weeks.

Just after dinner, as it always did, the electricity shut off.

"I'll go get the lantern," her grandfather said. His chair squeaked against the floor in the darkness.

"Is this a normal occurrence for you?" Grayson asked. He sounded surprised.

Rylee rolled her eyes, even though no one could see her do it. Of course, Grayson was oblivious to this fact. He probably had electricity flowing every minute of the day, pipes bursting with heated waters, a bed piled with soft blankets, and an endless supply of food—fresh food, not expired cans of beans and corn.

"Electricity's regulated here," her grandfather said. "This time of year, we get about two hours a day." A thump sounded on the table, followed by a whirring and a bluish glow from their hand-cranked lantern.

"How are these buildings heated at night, then?" Grayson asked.

"They're not," her grandfather replied.

Grayson didn't respond. He looked shocked. That gave Rylee some satisfaction to see. As a Norm, she might have little in the way of possessions and comforts. But compared to Grayson, who apparently couldn't fathom surviving without indoor heating, she was tough.

Rylee's grandfather stopped turning the lantern's crank and sat back in his chair. Rylee had hoped that with the shutoff of the electricity her grandfather would call it an early night. Instead, her grandfather started asking Grayson questions about his childhood and other things that Rylee couldn't care less about. Rylee sighed, and sunk down into her chair.

The evening passed like mold growing on the bathroom ceiling. Rylee felt like impaling herself with a fork, just to get Grayson and her grandfather to quit jabbering. Her grandfather was a quiet man, by nature. He did have his moments, though. Why did *now* have to be one of them…with this Elect? What would the others think if they knew she and her grandfather were entertaining an Elect at that moment? What if Preston discovered it was the same Elect who gave him a broken nose? Rylee's heart stuttered at the thought. He couldn't find out. No one could.

Somehow the subject of religion came up while her grandfather and Grayson were talking.

"I don't know that I've ever met a true believer in God, or in *a* god before," Grayson said, acting annoyingly interested. "I personally know little about pre-Desolation theology. Just heard a few rumors here and there. Tell me, how does your belief in a supreme, omnipotent being reconcile what Desolation has done to mankind? I believe Christians called their god merciful."

That did it. With that one innocent question, a lengthy theological debate ensued.

Rylee wanted to shove electrical wires into her ears.

Finally, finally, finally, the discussion died down. Her grandfather yawned, wished them both good night and left the table.

"Wait a minute," Rylee said, speaking for what seemed like the first time that night. "Where's *he* going to sleep?"

She pointed disdainfully at Grayson as though he were a rancid hunk of meat. Grayson merely raised his brows and looked quizzically back at her.

"I'll let you two figure that out," her grandfather said, leaving them alone as he went into the bathroom.

Great! Leave me to deal the nuisance.

"I guess that means you're sleeping out here tonight," she said. "I'm sure you'll find the floor as comfortable as your own bed."

Grayson feigned a smile. "You're too kind."

"You could sleep in a tub of acid for all I care." Rylee stood up from the table. "And if you try to come into my room tonight—"

"You'll shoot me with your...empty rifle?"

Rylee pursed her lips and felt her nostrils flare as she exhaled forcefully. "Just stay out. And stay away from my grandfather."

With that, she marched into her room and slammed the door shut.

Rylee sat on her bed staring up at the ceiling, waiting, listening. A solid hour later, she decided their *guest* must be asleep. She reached over and grabbed her earpiece from her desk. Next she grabbed her grappling hook and rifle. Even if it wasn't loaded, she didn't want Grayson getting a hold of it. Then she quietly pulled up her window sash and climbed out into the night.

A frigid gush of air chilled her ears and nose as she stepped onto the fire escape. Closing her window again, she turned and began ascending the metal stairs. At the top, she unslung the grappling hook and cord from her shoulder. The fire escape ladders only reached to the topmost windows of each building. She could have jumped from the top of the railing to the building's parapet, but she preferred using her grappling hook and rope.

Swinging the grappling hook around a few times, she lofted it into the air. With a light clank, it struck the top of the roof. She pulled the cord tight to secure the hook onto the lip of the parapet, then climbed up the rest of the way to the top. Once on top of the building, she touched her earpiece and spoke softly. "Preston?

Serghei? Is anyone on the line?"

Several seconds passed. She began to fear they were all asleep. If she spoke loudly, she could probably wake Serghei. Of all the crew members, she most expected him to still be awake. She wasn't sure if he ever slept.

The earpiece hissed in her ear, then Preston's groggy voice came over the line. "I'm here. What is it, Ry?"

An immediate rush of warmth filled her just at the sound of Preston's voice. Her earpiece hissed again. This time Serghei's voice came over the line. "Present." Serghei's voice sounded faint, as if he were whispering. "The little grumpling is asleep on my couch. What news?"

"Um...Serg," she said tentatively. "I was hoping just to talk with Preston."

"Right," he replied over the line. "I understand. Fully. I'll just go back to painstakingly hunting through petabytes of old data searching for your parents."

Rylee rolled her eyes and smiled to herself.

"And just for your knowledge," he said, coming back on the line. "I absolutely will not be eavesdropping on your conversation. Feel free, then, to share your most intimate feelings."

The line went quiet.

"Are you on top of your roof, Ry?" Preston asked.

"Yes."

"Be there in five minutes."

Five minutes later, Preston pulled himself up onto the roof and sat down next to her on the parapet.

"I brought popcorn," he said, pulling out a small plastic bag from his jacket pocket.

Rylee let out a tiny squeal, as she snatched the bag from his hands and started devouring its contents. "Where'd you get it?" she mumbled, her mouth full of the delicate white puffs.

Popcorn was one of the few treats she'd ever known. Her grandfather sometimes told her stories about eating candy bars, chewing gum, and other sugary items she'd never tasted. Before Desolation, people had an abundant supply of any kind of food they wanted. There were even places called restaurants, where you could go any time of day and buy whatever food you wanted. There was also something called ice cream that was often in Serghei's movies, that Rylee had always wanted to try.

For her, popcorn was as good a treat as anything she knew.

Preston shrugged. "I have my sources." That probably meant Serghei had procured it during a scavenging run. "Sorry it's not warm. I popped it a while ago." He paused for a moment. "I expected to see you tonight at Serg's. Is everything alright?"

Rylee froze. She realized she hadn't come up with a story for where she'd been all night. Why hadn't she? She had all the time in the world while Grayson and her grandfather talked it up. There was no way in Desolation she was telling Preston the truth, though. Preston's cries of anger from last night still haunted her thoughts. Even in the darkness, she could see Preston's bruised and swollen face.

"I just…couldn't get away from my grandfather tonight," she said. Well, it wasn't a complete lie. It still jabbed her in the stomach. For as long as she and Preston had known each other, she could never remember lying to him before. Not about anything important. "How's Feng doing?" she asked, wanting to change the subject.

"I stopped by his mother's place today. I told her Feng's been injured, and that we're taking care of him. I also told her he would be okay. Which, I don't know is true." His voice faded off a little as he said these last words. "She told me that one of Feng's supervisors stopped by and issued Feng a formal citation for missing work. He has four days to get back to work or report to the Infirmary."

"I felt so bad," he went on. "You should have seen the look in her eyes. I could barely take it."

For a long moment, neither of them spoke. Rylee had stopped eating the popcorn. Her stomach didn't feel like it could handle food at that moment. She looked out over the tops of the buildings, towards the Elect sector of the city. Standing tall, mottled with numerous illuminated windows stood Steele Tower, the CA's own building. While the heat and electricity was shut off for all but a few hours during the day in the slums, his building never went without.

"What are we going to do for him?" Rylee asked, speaking at last.

"Serg's working on some kind of splint that will allow Feng to walk without putting pressure on the broken bone. He's not sure if it will be ready soon enough, though."

"And if it's not?"

"We'll hide him. The Regulators will never look for him at Serg's. I've already decided that I'll split my rations with him. And do what I can for his mother."

Of course, Preston would volunteer to share his rations with Feng. Share his already limited rations. Rations he needed to give him energy for his job. A job that left him drenched in sweat, even with winter fast approaching, and had transformed his arms muscles into chiseled hunks of stone.

"He'll be a fugitive...for the rest of his life," she said, stating what they both already knew. "That will be tough on his mother."

"It's better than the alternative."

It was an alternative she wished her grandfather would entertain. Her attempts to bring up the topic after the new mandate was made had been fruitless. He was far too proud for such a *cowardly* act.

"What do you hope for?" she said.

"What do you mean? For Feng?"

"No, I mean..." She hesitated, feeling her cheeks flush. "Forget it," she finally said. "It's stupid."

"Nothing you could say would be stupid," Preston replied, nudging her with his shoulder. "What is it?"

"I don't know," she said. "Sometimes I feel like I'm living in a dream—a nightmare. And one day, I'll wake up, and things will different. Serg...he always talks about how he wants to make movies. Bring back Hollywood. Just like things were before Desolation. Do you have hopes?"

Now that she had asked it, she definitely felt foolish. Preston didn't mock the question, though. He seemed to be considering his response.

"That's a tough one," he said, after a few moments. "I guess, I hope that one day my dad will forgive me, and treat me like a son again."

He wrapped a strong arm around her, and Rylee felt her pulse flutter, the way it always did when she had physical contact with Preston. Of late, that contact had been more and more common. A few weeks back, Preston had actually kissed her on the lips. She could still feel that kiss. It thrilled her and worried her all at once.

Physical affection was a dangerous toy for them to play with. The Alliance regulated all births, and had zero tolerance for unauthorized pregnancies. Rylee had known plenty of women and girls forced to abort the babies they were carrying. In some cases, the Alliance simply Deprecated the pregnant mother.

"What about you?" he asked.

Rylee shook her head. "Right now, I have a hard time looking past all my problems. I don't feel like there's room for hope."

"What about that picture of your parents?"

"That seems really unimportant right now."

It should be unimportant. What difference did it make whether she ever saw a photograph of her parents? It wouldn't change anything. Wouldn't bring them back. Wouldn't help her come to know them any better than the stories her grandfather told her did. And yet, it was important to her. She couldn't really explain why. Perhaps it would prove that they had been real. That once, life really hadn't been the way it was now. People used to smile, and have families, and play at parks.

That's what Serghei was doing for her. Often during his salvaging run, he'd come across old computers that had not been destroyed in the floods, earthquakes, and wildfires of Desolation. When he does, he removes their hard drives and brings them back. Some of the disks have restorable data. He takes those and runs some sort of algorithm on them to find any information on Hannah Lynn Day or Asher Kyle Day—her parents. In particular, a photo.

Serghei believed strongly that on some hard disk in the area a photo must exist. People used to store their entire lives on computers. The best hard disks to search were those from old datacenters. But such hard disks had become harder to come by, as the

Alliance tended to requisition them.

Still, she hoped.

Her parents had both been killed in an earthquake. She was just a toddler. They had been on their way to a place called Leavenworth for a romantic weekend getaway. Their first since Rylee had been born. It was just a short drive through the mountains, from Seattle where they lived to Leavenworth. But the earthquake struck just as they were traveling through Stevens Pass. Their car was crushed by a boulder.

Rylee was too young to remember their deaths or the earthquake, whose scars could still be seen wherever you looked. In the cracked and splintered streets, the collapsed buildings and bridges. She could only remember the storms that came later. The wildfires. The food shortages. The loss of her home, and her toys.

They called it Desolation. Though, it wasn't a thing—or even a single event. Five years of relentless earthquakes that yielded mile-wide chasms in the earth, floods that engulfed entire cities and states, storms that sent down bolts of lightning like the heavens were at war with the earth and whose winds could level entire forests. Mother Nature gone mad.

Natural disasters, as they were called before Desolation, had been common enough. But never had they struck with such fierceness and frequency. For years, the planet was thrashed. At first, cities and countries managed to curtail the effects of the destruction. People were rescued, electrical grids restored, bridges rebuilt, roads repaired, supply chains reestablished. Eventually, though, there were too many people to save. Too many roads to repair. Too many shelves to restock with food.

Gradually, a century-old infrastructure broke down. Commodities stopped flowing. World economies collapsed. Governments disbanded—what good were laws when there was no way to enforce them. Wildfires burned. Floods rose. The earth fractured. Disease swelled. Hunger spread. And people died in droves.

By the time Desolation's fury subsided, earth's population of twelve billion people had been almost entirely annihilated.

Nathaniel Steele, CA of the Alliance, is credited with saving the lives of most of the people who make up the Alliance today. His company, Steele Corp., was developing a new nanomolecular vaccine to combat the spread of various diseases during the early years of Desolation. The vaccines were effective, but by the time Steele Corp. received approval from the FDA, the global distribution and mass production of the vaccine was all but impossible. So, Steele ordered the vaccines be distributed to local hospitals in Seattle and surrounding areas. Later, Steele distributed food from his own personal stockpile of food stores. Rumors claim he'd stockpiled five warehouses full after the first few storms of Desolation hit—before anyone knew just how bad things would become. He also took charge of the city of Seattle, organizing relief efforts, and bringing order to a city in chaos.

To many, Steele was a hero. To her, he was the one threatening to take away her only surviving family member. At that moment, she'd give up ever seeing a photo of her parents if it would just save her grandfather. Wishful thinking. That sort of thinking wouldn't save her grandfather. Only action would. If she only knew *how* to act...

"I know this is going to sound selfish of me to bring up," she said hesitantly. "But how are we going to save my grandfather from Deprecation?" She couldn't keep her voice sounding a tad hysterical. "If we don't figure out who's behind these murders soon, they're going to take him. I can't talk him into running away. And I'm all out of ideas."

"It's okay," Preston said, his voice confident. "Serghei has a plan to help with that. We'll discuss it tomorrow night. Can you make it?"

She nodded. "I'll be there." *One way or another.*

EIGHTEEN

GETTING HER GRANDFATHER out of the apartment proved easier than Rylee anticipated. Several weeks had passed since her grandfather had gone over to Lloyd's for a game of Dominoes. Lloyd was an old friend of her grandfather. They enjoyed getting together and reminiscing about the days before Desolation.

Her grandfather had said he wasn't really in the mood for it. Too tired. But after she pestered him sufficiently, and laid on a guilt trip about how she wanted to go out but didn't want to leave him alone, he'd finally relented.

"Fine, I'll go, if it makes you happy," he had said. "If I didn't know any better, I would have said your grandmother taught you how to nag me like that."

That comment saddened Rylee. She'd never known her grandmother either. At least, she didn't remember her. She was too young. Like her parents, her grandmother was dashed out of her life by Desolation.

With her grandfather out of the apartment, she made preparations to leave.

"And where are you off to?" Grayson asked, as she slung her unloaded rifle over her shoulder. Even though she still didn't have her ammunition back, she hoped the appearance of the rifle would dissuade any creeps from trying anything with her.

"That's none of your business," she said, not bothering to look at him.

"I need sugar," he said.

She paused, looked up at him, and blinked. "*What?*"

"Sugar. I need it. Can you get me some?"

"Look, I don't give a rat's tail what you need. I'd really love it if you went away, and left me and my grandfather alone."

She grabbed her earpiece, and put it in place. Then, she made for the door. With a side step, Grayson barred her way.

"Get out of my way," she growled.

He held up his hands. "How about a trade. You get me some sugar, and I'll give you back your bullets. I'll even put in a good word with your grandfather. Maybe he'll give you back your little pistol."

For a moment, she considered him. His dark brown eyes looked pleadingly into hers. Eyes the color of dog feces. Eyes she would never trust. She shoved past him.

* * *

"The brace is fairly simple in concept," Serghei explained, holding up a piece of paper with some hand-drawn diagrams done in pencil. "Two exoskeleton supports run along the inside and outside of the leg, and are secured at five points with straps. A hinge at the knee permits the leg to bend. Now, here's where the magic happens. The lower portion of the supports connects to a small platform, with approximately the surface area of the bottom of the foot. However, this platform extends a few millimeters beyond the natural length of his leg, you see? When he steps, the platform will hit the ground, and not his foot. Any pressure will run the length of the supports, and be taken up by his upper leg. This should facilitate walking without stressing the fractured bone. Though, the rigidness of the foot platform will mean he will walk with a noticeable limp."

Serghei beamed at them proudly. Rylee looked back at him dubiously. The idea seemed good, but all she saw on Serghei's cluttered workbench was a scatter of random pieces of metal, screws, and some tools she couldn't identify.

"So, how's it going?" she asked.

"Terribly," Feng said from across the room, on the couch.

Serghei shrugged. "Well, the straps that hold the supports onto the upper leg are proving difficult. I don't have all the tools and materials I'd like to have."

"Can we get them?" Preston asked.

"Not a problem. We just need to break into one of the Alliance's machining shops and steal a two thousand pound CNC machine."

"You can borrow my backpack," Feng said.

Rylee didn't laugh, but she was glad to see Feng was somewhat back to his old self. At least, he wasn't yelling at everyone to leave him alone.

"If anyone can make it work, you can," Preston said, picking up a long metal piece and inspecting.

"I still think it would be easier if we amputated his leg at the knee," Serghei said. "Then we could just carve him a prosthesis out of wood. He'd be a real pirate. We could even give him an eye patch. He does work on a boat, does he not?"

"Just keep working on your plans here," Preston said, setting down the piece of metal. "Now, I think Rylee's anxious to hear your plans to help her grandfather."

Swiveling around in his chair, Serghei stretched his long arms above his head, then stood up. A yawn escaped his mouth.

"Wouldn't you guys rather watch a movie?" he said. "I discovered a few new ones on our scavenging run today."

"Serghei, this is really important," Rylee said. "There's only a few days left." She hadn't meant to sound so petulant. Like a whiny child. But she did feel desperate, and in little mood to put up with Serghei's humor.

"Fine, fine. All work and no play makes Jack a dull boy. First, I require a little hydration."

Serghei stood and walked over to his stack of Mountain Dew. Grabbing a can from one of the open cases, he cracked it open and took a long swig. The brightly colored can caught Rylee's attention as if she'd never seen one before. Those drinks were loaded with high-fructose corn syrup. Serghei had talked about it before. It was essentially like guzzling sugar. She thought of Grayson's plea for sugar. His bargain. All she would have to do is take him one of the cans and she could get back her ammunition.

Unlike the other members of the crew, she never drank the stuff. Once had been enough for her. If she asked for one, would the others be suspicious? And if she asked for it, but didn't drink it? Maybe she could sneak one while they weren't watching.

Great! Now, I'm plotting how I can steal from my friends to feed an Elect. She could tell them her grandfather wanted it. He would drink it...if she gave it to him. Which was worse, lying or stealing? Or she could just come clean and tell them about Grayson. Sure, that would go over like Desolation's storms. Especially with Preston. No, they didn't need that distraction right now.

"Throw me one of those too, Serg," she said, trying to sound nonchalant.

Serghei paused with the can still pressed to his lips, and raised an eyebrow.

From her side, she could feel Preston staring at her, too.

"It's for my grandfather," she said. "I thought it might help if I need to butter him up."

Her heart beat against her rib cage, protesting against her decision to lie. What else was she to do?

Serghei shrugged and tossed her two cans. Hastily, she stowed them in the pockets of her jacket, hoping everyone would quickly forget about them.

Following Preston's lead, they congregated around Serghei's couch. Serghei brought over the stool he used at his workbench, since Feng took up all the space on the couch.

"I have a plan," Serghei said, his Romanian accent flowing thicker as he tried to sound dramatic. "It's very simple, actually."

"Just like your plans for my leg brace?" Feng asked.

"Any idea is more than we have right now, Serg," Preston said. "Let's hear it."

Serghei took a gulp of the Mountain Dew, and let out a loud belch. "I realized last night that we have been looking at this problem from the wrong angle. Hitherto, we have been thinking about how to find the culprits behind the murders so that the CA will halt the Deprecations. A fine goal. But if we get to the root of the problem, we see that it is nothing more than an accounting issue."

An accounting issue? Rylee looked across to see Preston's face reflecting the confusion she felt.

"Uh...what does that mean exactly, Serg?" Preston said.

"It means that if the Alliance doesn't know Ry's grandfather is sixty, then he won't be Deprecated next week, you see?"

"Tripe!" Feng cried. "Why didn't we think of that? All we have to do is tell the Regulator's he's younger, and they'll leave him alone. Maybe you can talk to my supervisor, while you're at it. Tell him I've actually been working." Feng shook his head in disgust.

"We don't tell anyone anything," Serghei went on, unperturbed. He held up his fist, the tattooed barcode on the back of his hands facing them. "This barcode matches an ID in a database held by the Alliance. That ID maps to data about the individual. Birthdate, for example. We alter the data, we save Ry's grandfather."

"That sounds promising," Preston said, but Rylee could tell he was fighting to hold his skepticism at bay.

Rylee didn't speak, thinking it best if she just kept her mouth shut. Otherwise, she feared her feeling of hopelessness would catch, like a bad cold. But, Desolation! Did Serghei honestly believe they could gain access to the Alliance's databases and modify her grandfather's personal records?

"So, how do we do it?" Preston said.

Serghei smiled. "We break into Regulation headquarters."

"But you said yourself before that it would be too hard, and take too long."

"Well, I've changed my mind. As I said, it's all how you look at a problem. Furthermore, the playing field has changed slightly in our favor."

"How's that?"

"Now we can walk in the front door, uncontested. You heard the announcement. Regulation is asking for tips from anyone regarding the homicides. Just like us, they're desperate for information. They'll take anything. And you, Preston Hyde, are going to go there and give them one."

NINETEEN

CARMINE O'CONNOR SAT at her desk inside Regulation head-quarters rubbing her temples. A bad habit of hers she employed when she felt overstressed. One in a leadership position, such as hers, should avoid such idiosyncrasies. Those under her might interpret them as weakness or uncertainty.

Of course, her PNU could keep her from falling back to such habits when her natural inclinations tried to kick in. But there it was again. She didn't want to rely so heavily on her PNU. To her it felt superficial. It wasn't her willpower changing herself. It was her PNU changing her. A subtle distinction when the PNU was bound to the neurons in her brain. But it was there.

Over a week had passed since Steele had appointed her the new Chief of Regulation. A job she felt unqualified for. Still, she committed to the job. If she must track down the killer by patrolling the streets every night herself, she would do it.

Not that it would do her any good. As yet they had no viable lead on who the murderer was. No plausible link between the victims. No common theme in the killings themselves. Except for maybe bafflement.

The perpetrator had hitherto left no shred of tangible evidence. No fingerprints. No footprints. No camera footage. No witnesses. Nothing but corpses.

Garrison Pike: dead of apparent strangulation. Prasad Balay: dead from suffocation by a pillow. Jonathan Breznen: dead from possible poisoning. The autopsy reports were still underway to confirm the poisoning.

Thanks to the victim's PNUs, Forensics had been able to salvage most of the victim's recent memories and replay them. Until being appointed as Chief of Regulation, she'd never truly valued the memory extraction capability the PNUs enabled. Despite that capability, however, she felt they were no closer to cracking the case.

In the strangulation case, Pike saw a masked figure attack. Then the attacker's bulging outstretched arms—supposedly with his hands wrapped around Pike's neck, while Pike clawed at the arms, trying to get free. Then the scene went black. Garrison Pike dead.

In the pillow case, there was...wait, did she just refer to it as the *pillow case? Desolation!* She'd actually been calling it that to her officers. The Balay case. There. *That* would help her not sound like a complete moron.

In the Balay case, Prasad Balay saw nothing. The pillow apparently covering his eyes. Only muffled screaming could be heard.

The poisoning case was trickier. The effectiveness of memory extraction decreased after death. Or, at least, that's how she had understood it from the forensic technicians. The number of recoverable memories decreased as a function of time since the victim's death. They'd presented her with formulae, and other technical nonsense. Bottom line, they couldn't replay far enough back to know when the victim—Jonathan Breznen—might have ingested the poison.

At that moment, Carmine was going through the mind-numbing task of hunting through the victims' medical histories, personal effects, interrogation reports from friends, colleagues, neighbors, and bosses. All in hopes of uncovering a solid link between the victims, or a potential suspect. Whoever was committing these murders was excessively thorough.

But Carmine would catch him—or her. Failure was not an option.

There was the rumored disappearance of William Steele, the CA's son. Could he be behind the murders? Thus far, her investigation had not led her in that direction. Perhaps it was time to visit Steele's laboratories.

She stood up from her desk. She wasn't sure why she even had a desk. All the information she needed for the case were stowed away in her PNU. There were no physical documents to read or handle. It did give her somewhere to rest her arms, and something to sit behind to assert her authority.

Placing her hands on the small of her back, she stretched, yawning. She glanced around her office. The show of authority would have been more effective with a larger office. This one felt more like a prison cell. In truth, it was only slightly smaller than her previous office. This new one had as much light as an underground tunnel. It smelled only nominally better. When she first moved in, the place smelled as if a two-week-old fish were tucked away in one of the desk drawers. Pike must have enjoyed eating codfish in the office. A few *hours* of scrubbing had helped lessen the odor's potency.

Speaking of fish, she couldn't remember when she last ate. Perhaps she should...

A knock sounded at her door.

With her PNU, she scanned who it was before the door opened. The profile image of a red-haired officer flashed before her. Complete with name, rank, and other pertinent data. Karl Meister, Sub Agent Second Class. Age nineteen. He looked more like fifteen.

Why was a Sub Agent knocking on her door? Gyles must be on his break. Her *aide* did his best to shield her from...well, everything that happened at Regulation. It wasn't hard to understand why. Damon Gyles thought the job of Chief of Regulation should have gone to him. Not an outsider like herself, with no experience running such an operation. Aside from doing the actual investigation work, Carmine found herself spending considerable effort asserting her leadership.

Gyles needed the most reminders. More than once, she'd threatened to report him to the CA. An empty promise. And he likely knew it. If she took her grievances to Mr. Steele it would only give credence to Gyle's unspoken claim: that she couldn't handle this job. Once she had thoroughly proven him wrong, *then* she'd have him demoted. She smiled at the thought.

At least one message—that she preferred face to face contact, rather than PNU communication—was getting across to some people. To this Karl Meister, anyway. It wasn't that she didn't value the convenience of PNU communication. She used it frequently. But if a thirty-second walk could put the real, tangible person in front of her, to her it was worth the minuscule effort.

She straightened her jacket and called for Meister to come in.

Meister's profile picture failed to do justice to the quantity of freckles on his face. Nor did it quite capture the shocking brightness of his hair. Nor the way he fought against his natural inclination to avert his eyes from her as he entered her office.

"What is it Meister?" she asked, keeping her tone authoritative, but not so harsh that the boy wet his pants. All her actions needed to tell those beneath her that her time mattered.

Meister's gaze momentarily dropped to the floor. But when he spoke, his voice was relatively solid.

"A tip's just come in, Chief," he said. "I thought you'd want to hear it yourself."

Chief. The title still sounded odd to her. Despite that, she took pride in it. Some of her annoyance at Meister softened.

"We've received countless tips," she replied. "What makes this one special?"

It was true. Since soliciting the general public for information on any of the recent homicides they'd received a deluge of tips. Thus far, all of them worthless. Every Unenhanced in the city wanted to help. It was easy to understand the reason. Put a gun to a man's head and ask him for information, and he'll give it to you. Even if he doesn't have it, just to save his skin. Well, the reduced rations and accelerated Deprecation timetable had put a gun to the head of everyone in the slums.

"There's a girl here, from the slums," Meister said.

What else?

"She claims she saw who shot Commander Pike, Chief."

"Agent Meister," Carmine said, fighting to keep her tone from betraying the full extent of her annoyance. "This would not be the first time we've had eye-witness claims. We've had people claim their own neighbors were the culprits. What's so convincing about this girl's story?"

Meister shifted uncomfortably. "Two reasons, Chief. First, I can tell she doesn't want to be here."

A questionably sound reason.

"Second, she knows that Pike was shot in the head."

Carmine studied the junior officer for a moment, thinking. That last reason might hold its own weight. The general public did not have access to autopsy records. From the reports of that night, Regulation arrived on the scene within minutes of the killing. Before that time, a citizen of the slums could have inspected the body, then disappeared. She thought it unlikely. From what she understood of the Unenhanced, they locked their doors, closed their windows, and pretended nothing amiss was going on outside.

Should she personally interrogate the girl? Undoubtedly, it would prove an utter waste of precious time. Unfortunately, her curiosity was now piqued. *Curse this junior officer.* Later. She'd find a way to reprimand him later.

"Very well," she said. "Send the girl in."

A moment later a waifish figure with blonde hair as short as a young boy's stepped into her office. The girl bowed her head. One look at the girl and Carmine knew she'd made the wrong choice. Had Meister actually gotten this little doll to talk? Perhaps Meister had imagined it while admiring her pretty face.

"Have a seat," she said, pouring some warmth into her tone. One harsh word and the girl might crumble to bits. The girl's red eyes told her she'd been crying already. *What have I gotten myself into?*

The girl took a seat in the chair opposite from Carmine's desk. The metal springs in it squeaked in protest. Carmine made a note with her PNU to have the chair oiled. Taking her own seat behind the desk, Carmine cracked a smiled at the girl.

"My name is Carmine O'Connor, Chief of Regulation," she said. "I realize this must be difficult for you. Understand though that the Alliance highly values your help. Any legitimate information you can provide us will benefit all members of the Alliance. Including yourself."

A sniffle escaped the girl's nose, which she wiped with the back of her hand.

"I'm Lexi. Lexi Bransen," she said. This information Carmine already knew from the report Meister had transmitted a moment before.

"Can you tell me why you came to us, Lexi?"

"My dad," she said, voice quivering like Desolation's tremors. "He made me come."

Please, do not start bawling like a newborn in my office.

"My agent tells me you saw who shot and killed Commander Michael Pike," Carmine said. "Tell me where you were."

Again, the girl sniffed. "I was on the back of his cycle."

"What!" Carmine couldn't help but gape at the girl. Realizing how unseemly that was, she closed her mouth and rocked back in her chair. Reactions like that would only encourage the girl if she were lying. "I'm sorry. You say you were on the back of Pike's cycle? How did that come about?"

"He kidnapped me…from my room."

Carmine compressed her lips. Yes, a believable story. The atrocities of the Enhanced males—mostly adolescents—were well known to her. And often such crimes went unpunished. If this were true, then Carmine genuinely felt sorry for the girl. Michael Pike, though? A Regulation Squadron Commander?

"There were two others with him," Lexi went on.

Two others? Now *that* was news. The Regulators had found two Enhanced males, both shot in the head. This was the first she'd heard of a third. Unfortunately, those bullet holes in their brains had damaged their PNUs sufficiently as to make the memory extraction impossible. Otherwise, they would have already known about Lexi, and been able to corroborate her story.

A third kidnapper? If there had been another there who'd escaped, it would make sense that he wouldn't come forward with information. Given the nature of their little escapade into the slums…well, best just to keep quiet.

"What happened then?" Carmine asked, now honestly wanting to hear the rest. "I know this is hard. You're doing very well."

Though still visibly upset, Lexi continued with her account. "The three of them came into my bedroom while I was asleep. I woke up with a gag around my mouth, and hands grabbing me, pulling me. I tried to break free, but they were too strong. One of them whispered in my ear to stop squirming or they'd kill my parents.

"They carried me through the window and put me on the back of a cycle. A gun fired next. I didn't see who fired or who got hit. The cycle I was on zoomed us down the street. Then I think someone was chasing us. The one driving the cycle, he started pointing his gun and shooting at whoever it was.

"What happened next is all a little blurred. I was just so scared."

Carmine leaned forward, and placed her clasped hands on her desk. "Just do the best you can."

The girl nodded. "Next thing I remember, we were stopping abruptly. Something blocked the road."

Yes, that piece of the story checked out, too.

"Then, there was a lot of gunfire. I felt like it was coming from everywhere. I didn't see who was shooting. Suddenly, it stopped, and someone—a boy I knew—was helping me up from the street telling me I was safe now."

A few tears streamed down the girl's cheek. "They were just trying to help me," she sobbed. "Please, you can't do anything to them. They saved me."

"They?"

Lexi nodded. "There was a girl, too. She took me back to my apartment."

"Lexi, listen to me," Carmine said, her voice edged with urgency. "All I need from you are their names—this boy and girl who saved you. We just want to ask them a few questions."

"Please! You can't get them in trouble. I saw what happened to Boney."

Well done Chief Pike. Pinning the murder of his son on some random, innocent man wasn't such a brilliant tactic after all. Now she would have to use more persuasive methods to get this girl to divulge any names.

"Listen, Lexi," Carmine said. "I know times must be tough for you and your family right now." She leaned in closer. "If you help us, I'll see that your family's rations are…supplemented. You won't go hungry. I can promise you that."

It was a generous offer. There wasn't exactly food to spare. Hopefully, it would pay off.

From the expression on the girl's face, Carmine could tell she was waging an internal battle with herself. She felt confident the girl would give in. The fact that she was at Regulation headquarters providing a major tip against her will was a testament to her father's control over the girl.

"I don't know the girl's name," she said, at last. "I've seen her before, though. The boy...his name is Preston. Hyde is his last name, I think."

In shame, the girl bowed her head. Carmine couldn't help but feel pity for the girl. Michael Pike and his accomplices deserved to die, if Lexi's story was true. And this Preston Hyde might be a hero. On the other hand, he might also be a murderous criminal. The Alliance would view him as nothing less than a dangerous vigilante. Either way, she would find out.

Using her PNU, she composed a quick message and sent it to one of the squadron commanders. "Report to me immediately. I have someone I want you to bring in."

TWENTY

SERGHEI HAD BEEN droning on for a good half-hour, throwing out technical terms and acronyms which sounded like gibberish to Rylee. He was attempting to explain his plan for infiltrating Regulation Headquarters. Rylee still had no idea what the plan actually was. Finally, Preston cut him off.

"So, what does all this have to do with me going to Regulation headquarters?" he asked.

"Patience, Iago," Serghei said, almost certainly referencing another film. "I was just getting to that. Ry," he added, turning to her. "On a scale of one to ten, how confident are you that you could temporarily shut off the main power to Regulation head-quarters?"

"Uh, if I knew where the building's electrical closet was and could get to it, then a ten. No doubts."

"Good," Serghei replied. "Then all we have to do is research where the electrical closet should be, and we're all set."

Preston furrowed his brows, sucking on his lip. "I'm not quite following you, Serg. I'm afraid you're going to have to spell the whole thing out for us, minus the first bit about servers and certificates."

"There are still a few details we must iron out," Serghei said. "But the basic idea is this: You and Ry go to Regulation headquar-ters on Saturday under the pretense that you have a tip for them. Ry will claim to be there as a tagalong. While Preston's interrogat-ed, Ry will ask to use the restroom. From the restroom, she'll climb up into the ceiling through a vent shaft. It's a classic method from the all the action films. From the ventilation system, she'll navigate to the electrical closet, cut off the power, then activate this little guy."

Walking over to his bench, Serghei retrieved a small metal box. Returning, he held it out for them to see. Rylee didn't know what she was looking at, other than a metallic device that fit in Serghei's palm. His expression, though, indicated that they should be impressed.

"Looks nice, Serg," Preston said. "What is it?"

Serghei raised his eyebrow. "Our very own rogue server. It's something I've been fiddling with for a while. Putting together spare parts from the salvage runs."

"Aside from the fact that I have no idea what that is, when do you have time to do all of this stuff? Don't you ever sleep?"

"Two hours a day, sometimes three," Serghei replied proudly. "It all depends on where the salvage run takes us."

"So, you only sleep in the back of the truck, with the rest of the salvagers?"

"It's a little bumpy, but it gets the job done. All the others know that Grant stays in my coat. So, none of them try to steal my contraband. Otherwise, Grant will gnaw off their fingers."

"Can we get back to the plan?" Rylee said, really not wanting to hear more about Serghei's sleeping habits. Or any of his habits, for that matter. "So, it's a rogue server. What do we do with it?"

Brightening at the mention of the device in his hand, Serghei started back in enthusiastically. "You," he said, pointing to her, "just turn it on. Here." He pointed to a small switch on the side of the device. "Once turned on, you must restore power to the building. That is all."

Serghei stopped and looked at them expectantly, as if that were the end of his plan.

"What do we do after that?" Preston asked.

"You get out of the building," Serghei shrugged. "However you can."

"And the...rogue server?"

"Right. Ry will leave it there—hidden somewhere inconspicuous. If I'm not mistaken, once the power is shut off to the building, Regulation's local servers will also go down. I'd be highly surprised if they had backup generators just to keep their servers running. The main Alliance servers are in the basement of Steele

Tower. *Those* likely have backup power. But this is beside the point. Once the power comes back on, the Regulator's PNUs will seek to re-establish the lost connection to those servers. If we're lucky, a few of them will attempt to connect to our rogue server, thinking it a legitimate one. When that happens, it will attempt to exploit the vulnerabilities I mentioned earlier."

"If we're lucky?" Rylee said. "You mean you're not sure that thing will work?"

"Not at all. Without reliable data about their system, it's impossible for us to know how best to hack into it. I know I love my films, but those old movies showing hackers breaking into some top-secret server...they make it look like all the hacker has to do is type fast and they'll get in. Like they had magic keyboards or something. It's not like that. It's far, far more complicated. First you must discover a vulnerability in the system — however small. Non-trivial. Then you must figure out a way to exploit that vulnerability. Also, non-trivial."

"Sounds like a really solid plan," Feng said. "We're all as good as Deprecated."

"What's the harm if it doesn't work?" Serghei asked. "We're no worse off than we are today. And all that you two have to do is get this little guy into Regulation headquarters."

Preston's eyes met Rylee's. He wanted her confirmation before agreeing to the plan. There was a fair amount of risk involved. Could she infiltrate Regulation headquarters, find the electrical closet, and shut off the power? All without getting caught? That she didn't know. But if it meant saving her grandfather, she would try it. She only wished Serghei's part of the plan were more certain.

"I want to try," she said softly. "I've got to try something. I'll go in alone if I have to."

Rubbing his stubbled chin, Preston studied the contraption in Serghei's hand. "What about that thing?" he said. "We don't have to get it out? It wouldn't be traceable back to us?"

"Regretfully," Serghei replied, frowning, "the server stays. Should it be found, I've taken precautions to ensure it won't lead anyone back to us."

"Okay," Preston said. "Let's move forward with this plan. There's still some details we'll need to work out. But we have a few days to do it. We can do this."

Conviction filled his voice when he said those words. *We can do this.* Whether real or forced, Rylee didn't care. Just having a plan, having her amazing friends made her believe it was true. For the first time since she heard the new mandate to cut rations and increase Deprecation, she felt hope. A faint glimmer of hope. That was enough for her.

Wanting to be home when her grandfather returned, Rylee decided to leave. "I've got to go," she said. Preston looked at her. It was evident in his expression that he wanted her to stay. "My grandfather…" she said, hoping everyone would fill-in an excuse in their own minds. But Serghei was already talking about watching a movie. And Feng, she was sure, didn't care. Preston reached out and grabbed her hand. "I'll see you tomorrow," she said. "Promise." Preston frowned slightly, but didn't protest.

With a twinge of guilt, she stood, shouldering her empty rifle, then exited Serghei's room. Out in the hallway that connected the inner warehouse room to the outer door, she patted her jacket pockets, confirming she still had the cans of Mountain Dew. Now she could get her ammunition back.

Now with the prospect of having the means to kill Grayson, the thought of actually doing it made her uneasy. She'd seen him eat. Seen him sleep. Seen him laugh. If she hadn't known he was an Elect, he would have been just another person to her. But he wasn't. Of that she knew without the slightest doubt. Still, the thought of killing him…killing *this* Elect…

Desolation! If only Grayson acted differently. No, he had to treat her grandfather with respect. Talk to him like a friend. The snake. He was probably doing it just to lure them into disillusionment of safety.

Midway to the door, Rylee froze. Had something just moved in the shadows ahead? To keep snoopers away, Serghei hadn't wired any lights outside his room. Now she wished there was at least one. Gradually, her eyes adjusted to the darkness. Yet she saw nothing more.

Serghei's cameras would have picked up an intruder. And he always kept the outside door bolted shut.

Steeling herself, Rylee walked forward. There was nothing there. Reaching the door, she grabbed its handle. Something pressed against her from behind, as a cold hand clapped over her mouth.

TWENTY-ONE

RYLEE'S IMMEDIATE REACTION was to scream and bite down on her assailant's hand. Instead, she relaxed her body, even as a hand grasped her left arm and hot breath slithered across her neck. A surprise attacker almost always had the advantage. The best way to turn the table on such an attacker was to surprise them back—by not fighting back.

It worked. Within a moment, the grip on her mouth and arm both slackened. Now it was time to strike. Before she made her move, a voice in her ear stopped her. "It's me, Grayson. I'm not going to hurt you."

Grayson? What was *he* doing here? Well, it didn't matter why. This was a perfect opportunity to rid herself of him.

"I'm going to let go of your mouth," Grayson whispered in her ear.

Go right ahead. Then she could call for Preston.

She felt Grayson's hand tentatively slip away from her mouth. Then he released her arm.

Whirling around, she faced him. In the darkness, she could just make out his features. His expression was calm. Trusting. Why did he think he could trust her?

Now! Call out. It could all be over then and there. All she had to do was call for Preston. His gun hadn't been confiscated or its rounds unloaded. *Just call out.*

"What are you doing here?" she found herself asking. "How did you get in here?"

With his hand, he motioned for her to go outside to talk. The last thing she wanted was to have a secret conversation with an Elect. Why couldn't she summon the courage to call for Preston? Was it because she needed to keep Grayson hidden from Preston and the others? What if they somehow discovered that Grayson had been staying with her for days? Or was there something else? No, of course there wasn't.

With a sudden urge to slam the stock of her rifle into Grayson's nose, she pushed open the door and strode outside. The frozen night air didn't dampen her rising anger as she walked through the back alley. White plumes of chilled breath rose above her as she huffed forward. Behind her she could hear Grayson following. Good.

She intended to give Grayson an earful, if not a broken nose. Not here, though. If Serghei reviewed his camera footage from tonight, he would see a figure following her. She didn't want to be caught talking to that figure. Consorting with the enemy.

Not until she had stepped around a corner which she knew wasn't monitored by Serghei's cameras did Rylee stop and face Grayson.

"What do you think you're doing!" she demanded.

"What do you think *you're* doing?" he replied. "You're not actually going to go through with that insane plan? Break into Regulation headquarters?"

"What! You were spying on us?"

"Like any lousy—what do you call me—Elect would do."

"Just leave me alone." Shoving him hard in the chest, she turned and continued down the benighted street.

"I can help you, Rylee," he called from behind.

"I don't want your help," she muttered to herself, lengthening her stride.

From behind, she heard Grayson following her. *So persistently annoying.* Why was he doing this? And how had he followed her without her noticing? The thought of him stalking her stoked her anger.

She contemplated taking her rifle and swinging it at Grayson's head. If she swung hard enough maybe...no. His reflexes were much too fast for that. *Curse it!* She started to run, just to put distance between her and that creep behind her. Not until she reached her housing unit did she stop. She entered through the front door, and found it empty. *Great.* More time alone with her new stalker. For a moment, she considered locking the apartment door behind her. That idea made her smile.

She thought of her grandfather's reaction. Maybe she could claim Grayson tried to hurt her, or touch her. More lies. Of course, it was doubtful that her grandfather would believe such as story when he saw that Grayson's arms were still intact. Grayson *had* stalked her. That was something.

With a shrill groan, she turned on her heel, strode into her room, and slammed the door shut. She wanted to scream. She wanted to shoot Grayson.

Unslinging her rifle, she leaned it in its usual place by her desk, then collapsed onto her cot. A hard object jabbed her in the side as she did. Reaching for the spot, she felt a cylindrical object through the fabric of her jacket. The Mountain Dew. In the heat of her frustration, she'd forgotten about the drinks in her pockets.

Now she only wanted to pour the cans' contents onto the floor in front of Grayson and watch him try to lick it up like a starving mutt. Or peg him squarely on the forehead with one of the cans.

From the other room, she heard the sound of the apartment door open and close, then footsteps sounded on the floor. Was it too much to hope that the footsteps belonged to her grandfather? That Grayson had managed to get himself lost on the way back? Or that he tripped over his own arrogance and bashed his brains against the asphalt?

Apparently, it was. Those footsteps didn't belong to her grandfather. No, those footsteps belonged to a pesky Elect.

An Elect who had her ammo.

She sighed. She'd gone through the trouble of lying to her friends to get the stupid Mountain Dews. Might as well go through with her plans.

Exiting the room, she found him standing in the kitchen. He didn't greet her with his typical smug smile. Instead, it looked almost…lost?

"Here," she said, tossing the can at him. "That's the best I could do. Now where's my ammo?"

She'd hold onto the other can for now, in case she needed to bargain again.

Studying the bright green can, Grayson turned it around in his hands. His face brightened with sickening satisfaction as he read the back label. Then he cracked it open and took a long swig. Almost immediately, he began coughing uncontrollably. When he finally stopped, he shook his head and screwed up his face.

Despite herself, Rylee smiled. At least someone else shared her dislike for the drink.

"Wow," he said, smacking his lips, "that's really something. It's perfect, though."

Then he took another long gulp, which threw him into another fit of coughs.

Rylee waited impatiently for him to finish the entire contents of the can. When he was done, he looked at her and smiled. "I needed that. Thank you."

Part of her was curious why he needed sugar so badly. Was this a quirk of Elects Serghei had failed to mention? She refused to gratify her curiosity. Instead, she folded her arms and raised her eyebrows expectantly.

"Ah, right," he said, clearly reading her body language. He turned, opened the cabinets above the kitchen sink, and pulled out two boxes of ammunition.

"What!" Rylee exclaimed. "They've been in there the whole time?"

"The whole time." He smiled and held out the boxes to her.

Snatching them from his thieving fingers, Rylee turned to go back to her room.

"I meant what I said earlier," he said from behind, his tone serious again. She paused but didn't face him. "I can help you."

"I do not want—nor will I ever want—your help." She walked into her room, closed the door, and attempted to go to sleep.

She awoke with a start the next morning. For a moment, the grogginess kept her from registering the buzzing noise coming from somewhere within her room. It took her only a few seconds to realize it was her earpiece.

Scrambling out of her bed, she jammed it into her ear and tapped it. "Serg?" she said, her voice gravelly.

"Good morning Vietnam," Serghei's voice hissed in her ear. "We've got a problem."

"A problem?" Rylee rubbed her eyes and yawned. If there were Elects to deal with, that was a problem she would welcome.

"It's the Regulators," he said. "They've apparently decided to do the Deprecations ahead of schedule."

"What? How much ahead?" Rylee felt her heart burst into a rapid pounding in her chest.

"Today—now. They're already in the streets."

TWENTY-TWO

RYLEE DIDN'T HEAR anything that Serghei said after that. The Deprecation…today? That couldn't be. It was four days early. And her grandfather…

Hands shaking, she grabbed a box of ammunition and began loading rounds into her rifle's magazine. Five rounds. She needed a high capacity magazine. Or her Glock. That would give her another sixteen rounds. Slamming the magazine into the receiver, she charged out of her room, rifle gripped in both hands.

The lights in the kitchen were off. In the shadows, a startled Grayson bolted up from his bed on the cold linoleum floor. "Seriously?" he said, when he saw her. "We're going to play *that* game again?"

Rylee ignored him.

In her ear, Serghei was trying to tell her something. Yanking the earpiece from her ear, she tossed it across the floor. Then she pounded on her grandfather's door.

"Grandpa!" she shouted. "You've got to get up."

Before she could pound on the hollow door again, it opened with a jerk. Her grandfather stood just on the other side of the threshold, his gray hair disheveled and his Bible in one hand. Sallow lantern light spilled out from behind him, casting his concerned face in shadows.

"I am up—" he said, cutting his words short as his eyes fixed on the rifle in her hands. "What in the devil are you doing, Rylee?" His voice was commanding, distrustful. Just as it had been the morning she tried to put a bullet through Grayson's skull.

"The Regulators," she huffed, as though she'd been sprinting for the last hour. "They're in the streets."

Her grandfather shook his head. "What are you babbling about? The Regulators are always in the streets."

"No," she said, her voice edged with pleading. "They're making the next Deprecation run. Don't you understand? They're coming for you."

He lifted his lower lip in response, but otherwise looked completely unfazed. Didn't he understand? They were coming *now*.

"We have to do something," she pleaded. "You have to hide. I'll fend off a full squadron of Regulators if I have to."

The kitchen light came on. Power restored to the slums. It illuminated her grandfather's face. That hard, stern face. The face of the man who had taken care of her since she was a baby. The man who had taught her how to survive in this harsh world. Her only living family. Her only link to her dead parents. To a world she couldn't remember, but longed for every day. She couldn't lose him.

"It's alright, Rylee," he said, softly. "We knew this was going to happen one day. You'll get along fine without me."

"No," she said, her voice trembling. "I need you."

He placed a firm hand on her shoulder. A hand she knew to be strong and unwavering. Just like the man to whom it belonged.

"I won't let them take you without a fight," Rylee said.

"You have to."

"Why? You've always taught me to fight. Why not now?"

"Because it won't do any good, Rylee. We may kill a few Regulators, but more will come. Then we'll both end up dead. I'm not about to let you throw away your life just to save me."

"What life?" Rylee said, extending her arm toward the door. "One where I have to live in fear of being Deprecated just for getting sick or injured, or just being too old? One where Elects prowl the streets at night like wolves, preying on innocent girls? Where I may never be able to have kids? Where I have to wonder if I'll have enough food to eat each day? What kind of life is that?"

"You, Rylee Loraine Day, make of your life what you will. Your circumstances don't define who you are or who you'll become. Unless you let them. Which you won't. You're stronger than that."

For several moments, neither spoke. Her grandfather's eyes gazed into her. There was a firmness in them, of course. Behind that, though, she saw sadness. This wasn't easy for him. Why should it be?

"Loraine," he said at last. "That was your grandmother's name."

"It was?" Rylee genuinely didn't know. Her grandfather never spoke much about her.

"I should have told you a long time ago. A prouder grandmother there never was. Many times after her death, I've thought how unfair it was that she died and not me. She missed watching you grow up. It was hard for me too, Rylee. I didn't know if I could get by without her. But I did."

Not knowing how, Rylee found herself in her grandfather's embrace, and she was hugging him back fiercely. She didn't remember the last time her grandfather had given her a hug. That just wasn't his way. It just made this one all the more meaningful.

The stomp of heavy boots came from the stairwell. Gently, her grandfather forced her to let go of him. With an incline of his head, he motioned to her room. "Go put it away," he said. Reluctantly, she obeyed, returning her rifle to her room. When she returned, she just stood there, waiting, scratching the back of her hand. Her eyes momentarily flicked up, catching Grayson staring at her. He looked uncomfortable. Why did *he* have to be there? Of all people to share her final moments with her grandfather, did he have to be an Elect?

Outside, the boots grew louder. Then the door shook as someone pounded on it. Rylee turned to her grandfather, her heart racing. He nodded to her, then went to answer it.

How could this be happening? Every part of her longed to fight—needed to fight. To do something to save her grandfather. Was she truly going to stand there watching while they took him away?

Calmly, her grandfather unbolted the door and opened it. Two armed Regulators pushed their way inside, the muzzles of their assault rifles pointed threateningly. They would use force, if necessary, to perform their duty.

"It's okay, boys," her grandfather said. "No one here's going to fight you."

He cast Rylee a stern glance.

Convinced the place was secure, one of the Regulators pointed the muzzle of his rifle at her grandfather. "Check his code," he said.

The other Regulator let his rifle hang by its shoulder strap as he grabbed her grandfather's arm and pulled back the sleeve of his sweater, exposing the tattoo of black lines, underscored by a thirteen-digit number. Silently, the Regulator stared at the tattoo, as if studying it. Rylee knew the man was scanning it with his PNU-enhanced brain. The data retrieved from the barcode would reveal who her grandfather was, and that he was scheduled for Deprecation. Rylee bit her upper lip. This was what Serghei's plan was going to fix. So that when they scanned his code, it would come up negative. Why did they have to do the Deprecation early?

After what seemed like much too long, the Regulator let go of her grandfather's forearm. "He's clean."

"What do you mean?" The first Regulator demanded.

The other shrugged. "I scanned him. He's not up for Deprecation."

Despite her utter shock, Rylee managed not to gape in disbelief. Had Serghei managed to do something after all? Is that what he had tried to tell her? No, Serghei had acted just as surprised as she was.

The Regulator, who appeared in charge, shoved his comrade aside and took hold of her grandfather's arm, and inspected the tattoo. Not once did her grandfather show surprise or anger. He remained stoic, letting the Regulators do as they wanted, never speaking. After several moments, the Regulator cast her grandfather's arm away, a disgusted look distorting his face.

Then he looked slowly from Rylee to her grandfather. He grunted. "Anyone else here?"

"No," her grandfather replied.

Looking displeased, the Regulator made a curt gesture to the other and the two filed out. In the wake of the Regulator's retreat, her grandfather slowly closed and bolted the door. Then he turned, and his eyes narrowed. "What in the blazes just happened there?"

Rylee gasped for air, as though her head had been under water the entire time the Regulators were there.

"Perhaps a system malfunction," Grayson said. "They happen on occasion."

Rubbing his gray beard, her grandfather seemed to be considering that possibility, before finally shaking his head. "Well, I'm not about to go argue with them. Let's eat breakfast. We're going to be late for work."

And that was it. He accepted whatever happened and didn't appear to question it further. Rylee wasn't satisfied. What happened just now was no glitch in the Alliance's system. As little as she knew about PNUs or computers or any technology, she knew enough to know that scanning a person's barcode and retrieving their personal data was the simplest of tasks. It wouldn't have failed...twice. No, unless someone had deliberately or accidentally modified her grandfather's data, something else had happened. Those Regulators came directly to their apartment for a reason. From the sound of their boots leaving the building, theirs had been the only apartment to check.

Something fishy was going on. And she had a pretty good idea who was to blame.

She turned and looked at the reason, sitting there at her kitchen table, arms folded, yawning like he hadn't slept all night.

TWENTY-THREE

"SO THIS IS what peanut butter tastes like," Grayson said, licking another spoonful. "I had no idea."

"Wait a minute," Rylee said, unable to keep from acting interested, "you've never had peanut butter before?"

"My father's allergic to peanuts," Grayson explained. "To my knowledge, I've never eaten a peanut in my life."

"That wasn't uncommon," her grandfather said. "Before Desolation, seemed like half the population was allergic to peanuts. Couldn't send kids to school with peanut butter sandwiches. Or take peanuts on planes. Or have peanut breath in a hospital. Ridiculous. Everyone was afraid someone would go into anaphylactic shock, die, then sue them."

Grayson nodded his head knowingly. "It's pretty serious for some people. My father always carries around an epinephrine injector, just in case. When I was about twelve, he made me super angry. So, I snuck into his bedroom, took all his injectors, and replaced the medicine inside them with water. I secretly hoped he would accidentally be exposed to peanuts, go into shock, then try to use one of the useless injectors." Grayson shook his head, smiling. "I was *that* mad at him. He'd probably have died if that happened. I was scared stupid after that. So scared I never told him what I did. For all I know, he's still walking around with those same useless injectors."

"Wow, that's really awful," Rylee said. "Even for an Elect."

Grayson's dark eyes flashed on her. "Well, you already know we Elects are scum."

Rylee didn't respond. The hint of irony in his voice wasn't lost on her. What had he done? More importantly, why had he done it? She'd wait until her grandfather was gone to confront him.

Clapping Grayson on the shoulder, her grandfather said,

"None of us is perfect. Neither are we defined by being an Elect or a Norm." He gave Rylee a stern look of disapproval. "Now, it's time to get moving."

Retrieving his Bible from his bedroom, her grandfather read a verse of scripture, offered a prayer—offering gratitude to God for being spared another day—then left for work. Rylee promised that she was leaving just as soon as she put on her boots.

And after I make Grayson talk.

As soon as the door banged shut, Rylee pounced. "What did you do with those Regulators?"

"Whoa, whoa," Grayson said. "We need to work on your people skills."

"I don't have people skills. Now, tell me what you did."

"Or you'll...shoot me? Because that's how you thank people here."

Rylee let out a sigh. Must she truly act nice to him?

"Fine. I'm sorry. I just have to know what happened."

Grayson raised his eyebrows, nodding appreciatively. "That's better. See, it's not so hard."

"It would be a whole lot easier if you weren't such a jerk."

"Oh, now we're regressing a little."

"Stop it! Are you going to tell me or not?" Had she actually just stomped her foot like a spoiled child? *Desolation*, how he could infuriate her!

The grin on Grayson's face vanished. "I'm sorry," he said, actually sounding sincere. "I have a bad habit of being a jerk. I often take jokes too far."

Rylee didn't respond. What could she say? *I still think you're a jerk?*

"What I did with those Regulators," he went on, "was stall them. They'll be back again once they figure out your grandfather was not brought in. That's why we need to work together."

"I don't understand. How did you stall them? You didn't even talk to them. Did you hack into the system?"

He shook his head. "No, I didn't hack into the system. Doing so without leaving a trace is...complicated. And especially risky for me. What I did, I call a Real-time Altered Reality Attack. R-A-R-A."

"Catchy name," Rylee replied dryly.

"Give me a break. I write code, not marketing copy. Anyway, it was something I was developing before I...left. As far as I know, no one but my father knows about it. It's essentially a PNU virus. I'll spare you the technical details. Essentially, any user who's attacked by it, will have his PNU controlled by the attacker."

Rylee wrinkled her brow. "You mean, you took control of those two Regulators?"

Grayson weaved his head. "Not exactly. I couldn't control their bodies. Not directly. However, I could override the visual system of their PNUs, for example. When they looked in this room, they didn't see me. I used my PNU to send them an altered version of the room, which excluded me. Likewise, when they scanned your grandfather's barcode, the data returned was the correct data. However, I modified it in real-time to show him being five years younger than he is."

He paused. Rylee just looked at him. Stunned. The idea sounded too farfetched to be real. Then again, Rylee didn't understand how the PNUs worked in the first place.

"Are you still controlling those Regulators?"

"No, I severed the link as soon as they walked out the door. The virus isn't perfect. It puts tremendous strain on the attacker's PNU, especially with more than one person being attacked. My PNU had to process nearly three-times the amount of data." He yawned again. "And the longer I keep it up, the more difficult it becomes to ensure there're no discrepancies in their reality once I sever the link."

"Why did you do it?" she said.

His dark eyes looked back at her, and for the first time she didn't feel any repulsion to look back. When he spoke, his voice was soft. "Because your grandfather didn't deserve Deprecation. And I hoped, in some way, it might atone for my own mistakes."

"Thank you," she said, surprised to hear those words coming out of her mouth.

"You owe me no thanks. I'm glad that I could be here to help. But, you're welcome, all the same."

An awkward silence fell between them after that. Rylee didn't know what to say. It was easier to treat him like a rat, than to be civil. Now she felt like she had on her first day as a field worker when she was just a little girl; small and insecure.

"I'd better get to work," she finally said, moving to grab her boots from her bedroom.

"Can we talk later?" he asked. "About what to do next, that is."

"We'll see," she said, hurriedly pulling the boots onto her feet. She needed time to think about…everything.

"Sure," he said, appearing in her doorway. "And one other thing: would it be possible for me to shower or something? I haven't bathed in days, and I stink so badly, I can scarcely bear to breathe."

Finishing lacing up her boots, Rylee stood and walked out of her bedroom. He moved to the side to let her pass, and she pretended to take a whiff of him.

"I've smelled worse," she said. "But be my guest. There's a basin and a hand wand in the bathroom. The water should be just above freezing. Knock yourself out."

"Yes, I remember seeing that in the bathroom," he replied. "I guess I was hoping there was something…ah…different."

"Sorry, the Slum spas are closed weekdays." Then she left the apartment, and closed the door behind her. To her surprise, she found that a smile was tugging at her lips.

* * *

Grayson stared at the closed door until his eyes grew blurry. "That is one odd girl," he muttered to himself. He shook his head violently, trying to wake himself up. That little foray with the Regulators had sapped all his energy. He needed sleep and, regretfully, more sugar. Could psycho-girl get her more of those drinks? The peanut butter did contain sugar. That helped. Still, he would need more. Especially, now that he'd spent most of his reserves on that little stunt he just pulled.

It was a risky thing to do. In all of his testing, he'd intentionally ignored any scenario involving multiple simultaneous victims. It was not among his father's specifications, and Grayson frankly didn't think it could work. Too much of a resource drain. It had worked, though. Barely. He only hoped that those Regulators wouldn't suspect any PNU manipulation. That would certainly compromise his current location.

Too late to stress over that now.

He needed to figure out what was going on. After his PNU had recharged last night, by extracting electrons from his body's blood glucose, he'd attempted to contact Lander again. Still nothing. With every day that passed, Grayson grew exponentially alarmed.

Had Lander been caught snooping? Could knowledge of Grayson's RARA virus be so important that his father would feel threatened by it? The RARA virus wasn't *that* dangerous. He'd already contemplated potential exploits. Nothing stood out to him as particularly egregious. Sure, the virus had the potential to cause someone to have an accident—an even fatal one. But any investigation into a death caused by it would certainly yield a discrepancy between reality and the actual cause of death. His father was too smart to do something so reckless.

No, Grayson's RARA virus wasn't behind the murders. Was it?

What if there was another part to the virus? A part that Lander had been working on? It would be smart of his father to divide up a potentially lethal virus into two apparently innocuous ones. If Lander and Grayson were ignorant of each other's work, it would eliminate suspicion. If only he knew what Lander had been working on...

There were two ways to find out: squeeze it out of Lander or hack into Lander's secure server. As much as it concerned him, option one was out. That only left hacking into Lander's server, which required directly connecting to his father's network. That was something he couldn't do, even if he was willing to risk detection. He'd need to get into his father's building for that. First, though, he needed closure on Lander. And he intended to use Rylee to do it. He knew she was going to hate it.

* * *

Rylee shook her head violently. *Focus, Rylee! Or you'll get yourself electrocuted.*

She'd seen it happen once before. A careless journeyman who thought the wires he was handling weren't hot. He didn't bother to test them with his multimeter—the simplest of tasks. One that would have saved his life. That would have saved Rylee from having to watch helplessly as his body convulsed violently on the floor.

That image helped to refocus her mind on the task at hand. Still, when she wasn't actively handling wires, her mind drifted back to the events of that morning. What was she going to tell the others? Serghei knew that her grandfather was supposed to be Deprecated. Now, she wished she hadn't thrown her earpiece across the room. She hoped it still functioned. And Preston? If Serghei told him, he would be sick with worry over her.

Her stomach twisted. More lies.

On their break, Sophie prattled on about the usual gossip. Rylee only half heard anything. The sorts of topics Sophie usually went on about didn't interest Rylee. Then Sophie said something that caught her attention.

"From what I heard, no one has seen him for over several days," Sophie was saying.

A group of four other workers was huddled around Sophie, rapped by this new piece of gossip. Rylee sat alone, on the perimeter.

"Where do you think he is?" a girl named Veronica said.

"Maybe he's dead," Sophie said with a wicked smile. "It's too bad, I've heard he's kind of cute."

"Please!" an older worker named Jay exclaimed. "He's an *Elect*. A pampered prince. Not a bit of man in 'em."

"Says the twenty-five-year-old who still can't grow a decent beard," Sophie said.

The others laughed, while Jay rubbed his patchy stubbled chin, pretending to not be embarrassed.

"Who are you talking about?" Rylee said, once the laughter died down. "The one who's missing."

"Didn't you hear me?" Sophie replied. "The CA's son, that's

who."

The CA's son? "What's his name?"

"William, I think."

"See?" Jay replied. "That's a wussy name right there."

The group continued to joke, but Rylee zoned out again. *William.* Well, at least the names were different. But...could Grayson have lied about his name? Was he the CA's son? The idea seemed ludicrous. Of all the people in the city, surely the CA's own son wouldn't need a place to stay, need to hide from...whatever Grayson was hiding from.

That evening, she rode home on her Harley with her brain saturated with questions. Questions only Grayson could answer.

Outside, it was as dark as night, the sun having retreated below the horizon before she got out of work. Perhaps more than anything else about this time of year, she hated that the most. Between the perpetual gray clouds and shortened daylight hours, it felt like the night never ended. Just like her own life; she wondered if she would ever see the sunrise again.

At her housing unit, she found the door unlocked. Alarmed, she reached for her pistol. *Curse it!* Still confiscated. Loud voices sounded from the other side of the door.

Throwing the door open, Rylee found Grayson standing in the kitchen, hands raised defensively as Preston leveled a pistol to his head.

TWENTY-FOUR

"STOP, PRESTON!" RYLEE'S shout filled the small kitchen.

Grayson turned to her. "Hey," he said. "I thought you two might be friends. You share the same meeting ritual."

"Shut up!" Preston demanded.

Keeping his pistol trained on Grayson, Preston jerked his head in her direction. In his eyes, she saw that same hatred she heard in his voice the night Grayson escaped from them. Preston's face still bore the bruises from that night. A jolt of fear momentarily paralyzed her.

"Do you know who this is?" he growled. "He's the Elect who broke my nose. The one who should be dead right now."

He returned his gaze to Grayson. Rylee could see the veins in Preston's hands bulge as he tightened his grip on the gun. This was not the calm and collected Preston she knew so well. This was the Preston who had given way to pure anger. Anger over a ruthlessly murdered brother. Over a father who had beat him again and again because of it. The one Preston had suppressed for years.

"I know," Rylee said, as steadily as she could manage, as she took a few cautious steps forward.

"You *know?*" Preston snapped, adjusting his grip on the pistol. The muscles in his jaw hardened. "Then what is he doing here?"

"Please, put the gun down, Preston. I can explain."

"Explain what? That you have an *Elect* in your house? And you knew about it!"

"He helped us."

"Helped you? *Him?*"

Rylee moved in closer. She was halfway across the room to where Preston stood. If she could just get there before he did anything rash...

"He kept my grandfather from getting taken by the Regulators this morning. You can't hurt him. He's not like the other Elects. He's…good." Even as the word fell from her lips, she couldn't believe she was the one who said it.

She moved closer. Almost there.

"*Good*." Preston spat the word. "He's an Elect, Ry. They're all bad. His kind killed my brother, just because they could—just for fun. And you're trying to tell me this one's your friend now? I found him sleeping in your bed. Is he your lover, too?"

"No, Preston, he's not." A few more steps. Gently, she touched his back. "He's just…it's complicated. *Please*, just leave him alone."

Preston dropped the gun and turned to her. His eyes looked into hers. In them she no longer saw anger. No, the anger had been replaced by something much worse. Pain.

"Fine," he said, pulling away from her. "Keep your Elect boy-friend."

Shoving his pistol back into its holster at his waist, Preston pushed passed her toward the door. Rylee grabbed his arm to stop him, but he yanked it away.

"He's not my boyfriend," she said. Preston didn't stop. "Don't leave."

Just before he reached the door, Preston paused and spoke over his shoulder. "I thought you trusted me, Ry. We could tell each other anything." He reached for the door handle and turned it. "I guess I was wrong."

"Preston, don't…"

But it was no use. He was gone.

Her stomach felt sick. How had she let this happen? Had Preston discovered Grayson yesterday, she would have gladly watched him pull the trigger. Now…everything was blasted complicated.

Rubbing her eyes, Rylee sank into one of the kitchen chairs.

"It might help if you told him you tried to shoot me in the head the first time you found me here," Grayson said.

"Just be quiet," she muttered. "You can't understand what Preston's suffered because of your kind."

"How can you say that? How can you hate someone just be-cause they're an Elect?"

147

"You don't get it, do you? When Preston was twelve, a group of Elects—teenage boys—broke into Preston's bedroom, bound and gagged him and his older brother, then kidnapped them. The Elects took Preston and his brother to the top of one of the housing units. There, they untied Preston's brother and took turns fighting him. Apparently, they had some new martial arts enhancement for their PNU they wanted to try out. Preston, still tied up, was forced to watch.

"His older brother was strong. He fought back. But he was no match for five Elects, all with new fighting enhancements. They beat him again and again and again. Preston cried for them to stop. But they didn't stop until his brother was dead.

"After that, Preston's father blamed him for not doing something to help his brother. He went a bit mad. Started spending their food rations on cheap liquor. He often gets drunk at night, and then he'll beat Preston and tell him it's his fault his brother's dead."

Rylee sniffed, and her lips started to tremble.

"And after all that," she went on, "Preston is still the best person I have ever met. He is kind and considerate and—of all things he shouldn't be—relentlessly positive."

"I'm sorry," Grayson said quietly. "I don't know what else to say."

"There's nothing you can say, or do," she replied, shaking her head. "There are hundreds of other lives that have been destroyed by Elects."

Standing, Rylee exhaled sharply. "I've got to go talk to him."

"Okay," Grayson replied. "I'll just stay here, then. If you don't—"

A buzzing sound made him stop.

It took Rylee a moment before she realized it was coming from her earpiece. Rylee scanned the floor and spotted the thumb-size device sitting in the corner. Hurriedly, she picked it up and positioned it inside her ear. With a tap, she activated it.

"Ry here," she said.

Over the line Serghei's voice crackled to life. "Uh...I know you had a tough morning with your grandfather, and all. So, you probably don't want to talk, but…"

"Spit it out, Serg."

"Well…have you seen Preston? He's not answering his ear-piece."

"He was here. He's gone now."

"Ah, that could be a problem."

"Problem? Why, what's going on!"

"Regulators. They're stopped outside Preston's housing unit. I saw them on my way home."

Rylee cursed as she went to grab her rifle before making for the door. "Keep trying him, Serg," she said. "I'm going after him."

"Right," Serghei replied, then the line went dead.

Bursting out into the dark street, Rylee made for her Harley. Then she thought better of it. Preston's housing unit was only a few blocks away. She could run there almost as swiftly, by taking back alleyways. Plus, the roar of her bike could attract unwanted attention from the Regulators.

Veering left, she bolted down an alleyway, startling a stray cat.

Oh, Preston! Don't go home yet. She didn't know why the Regu-lators were outside Preston's housing unit. As likely as anything, they were there to bring in someone else in for Deprecation. But what if they weren't?

Rounding another corner, she slipped on some loose gravel, bashing her knee onto the asphalt. Instantly, she was back on her feet, sprinting. Ignoring the pain.

The closer she drew to Preston's housing unit, the more her hope faded and her dread grew. Where *was* he? Already back in his apartment, safe from any molestation by the Regulators? Still on his way, about to enter his home and be trapped? Wandering the streets in a deep pocket of the slums?

Surely Preston wouldn't tramp boldly into a housing unit sur-rounded by Regulators, too disillusioned to notice them, or care. Would he?

One more turn.

And then she was on his street, a few hundred yards from Preston's housing unit. Still no sign of Preston. Pale lights from windows shown down, feebly holding back some of the darkness.

It was not yet the hour for the electricity to be shut off. Slowing her pace, Rylee moved closer to the walls of the buildings, where the shadows were deepest.

As she drew closer, she saw the silhouette of vehicles in the gloomy street outside Preston's housing unit. A van without back windows, and a group of electrocycles. No sign of any Regulators.

Where are they?

The front door of the housing unit burst open. Several dark shapes emerged. Their dark uniforms melded with the night. She could still make out the precision in their movements, as well as the familiar shape of their assault rifles. One day, she would have to get herself one of those rifles.

Two more Regulators, followed the first two. There was a figure between them. Rylee caught her breath and forced herself to stifle a cry.

Preston.

His head was bowed. But she knew that hair. That strong chin. Those weight-bearing shoulders. They were escorting him out of the building. But why? What had he done?

Then she realized. Preston had done plenty. And so had she. Had someone ratted them out? Who?

There wasn't time to try and figure that out. Preston needed her. There wasn't anyone else in the Alliance who could save him right now.

Removing her rifle from her shoulder, she brought the trusted weapon up to her cheek, her finger along the trigger, her right eye to the scope. Murky blues and purples framed the orange and yellow outlines of the Regulators and Preston. She fixed her reticle on the right-most Regulator holding Preston and moved her finger to the trigger. She wouldn't be able to eliminate all of them before they returned fire. Perhaps it would be enough, though, to allow Preston to escape.

Slowly, she squeezed the trigger. Before she could fully engage the trigger, a force rammed into her on her left, knocking her deeper into the mouth of an alleyway. Only stunned for a breath of a moment, she turned and struggled against her assailant. Thrusting her elbow out, she struck something solid. Probably ribs. Her attacker let out a sharp grunt of pain. Not waiting for whoever it was to recover, she swung the butt of her rifle around to strike his head.

Her attacker ducked, grabbing her rifle and yanking it free of her grasp.

Blast! Now running wasn't an option. She really needed her pistol back. If she got out of this, she would have to work on that.

She moved to try and take out one of her attacker's knees.

"Rylee," her attacker hissed. "It's me."

Rylee paused. "Grayson?"

"Yes. Now stop fighting. You've already given me a nasty bruise on my side."

"Give me back my rifle," she said, lunging for it. "I need to help Preston."

Grayson jerked it away. "You'll get both of you killed."

"Not before I kill a few of them." Again, she tried to grab her rifle free from Grayson's grip. He dodged and put out a blocking hand. Knocked off balance by the blow, Rylee fell to the ground.

"There's a better way to help him," he said.

"What is it? Stand here and watch like cowards as they take him away?" Picking herself up, she moved closer to him, but didn't attack. "You may deal with your problems by running away and hiding, but I fight back. Now, give me my rifle."

The heat of her anger singed her words. Every second she spent fighting with Grayson, meant another second lost to save Preston. Already, it might be too late. She threw a punch at his face, but he easily dodged it. *Blasted Elect.*

"Listen," Grayson replied, his voice frustratingly unperturbed. "You've got to trust me. I can help. Just like I helped your grandfather. I promise you, I'll help you get Preston back. But if you go gunning down Regulators, more will come. They'll find you. They'll find him. If they cared enough to track him down now, they will do it again. Trust me."

The sound of a car door slamming shut stopped Rylee's heart. She pushed her way passed Grayson and peered out from around the mouth of the alleyway, just in time to see the van and its escort of Regulators drive away.

For several moments, Rylee stood there, her breath coming out in short bursts of white clouds. Gone. Preston was...gone.

She whirled around to face Grayson, chest heaving. "If anything happens to him, I swear...I'll make you pay dearly for it." She would also never forgive herself.

"Look," he said, "they're probably bringing him in to investigate his connection to the murder of Michael Pike." He held up his hands to stop her from saying anything. "I don't know if he is—nor do I care. However, if I'm right—and he is—then they'll want to link him to the other murders. Which they won't be able to do without some heavily-fabricated evidence. It won't work."

"What are you trying to say?"

"Only that we have a few days. They won't publicly execute him, because it would be an embarrassment to the Alliance when the murders continue—which they likely will. Also, most of the Elects will no doubt reject the ruse. More likely, they'll deal with him quietly in the next Deprecation run. We have some time—that's my point."

Rylee crossed her arms and glowered at him. "You said you could save him. What's your plan? Don't tell me you *don't have a plan.*"

"I have a plan...partially."

"Partially!" she shouted. "We just let them take Preston away because you partially have a plan!"

"Unless you want the Regulators to take us too," he growled, "I suggest you keep your voice down. Look, unlike you, I don't go making snap decisions without all the data. I have a plan for *our* next course of action. And it involves you taking this."

In the darkness, she saw him reach into the breast pocket of his coat and remove something. It was too dark for her to tell what it was.

"And what is *that*?" she said.

"This..." He stepped in closer, until his face was just inches from hers. "This is what turns people into Elects."

TWENTY-FIVE

"ARE YOU DEMENTED? There's no way in Desolation you're turning me into an Elect." Rylee stepped away in disgust, as if the very scent of the object Grayson held in his hand wreaked of decaying flesh.

"I thought you wanted to help Preston. To help your grandfather," Grayson said.

"Don't try to manipulate me. I'm not going to become one of *you*."

Turning around, she started marching down the alleyway. She would go to Serghei's place. Together, they'd come up with a real plan. Abruptly, she halted and turned back around.

"I'll have my rifle back, now," she said, her tone as icy as frozen steel.

Wordlessly, he held it out to her. She snatched it away, then turned and started walking again.

"I need your help, Rylee," he said from behind her.

"Don't care," she called back.

"You can't do this without me. You don't know what you're up against. You can't just shoot away all your problems."

Rylee kept walking. She didn't shoot her rifle at all her problems. She used her pistol, too. When her grandfather didn't confiscate it, that is. But how *would* she solve this problem now? If only Grayson hadn't interfered, Preston might be free.

Become an Elect? Of all the loathsome, half-baked, arrogant ideas…

Did Grayson think he could get her to magically trust him enough to let him desecrate her brain, then use his Real-time Creep Virus to control her? *Not going to happen.*

Behind her, the sound of footfall told her that Grayson was following close behind. For a person who'd managed to sneak up

153

on her twice, he sure did walk like a full squadron of Regulators. Was he *trying* to make his presence known? A fleeting thought came into her mind to give a quick kick behind her. She didn't bother. He would dodge it.

What would it be like to react so quickly, with such precision? A tantalizing thought.

No! I won't become a monster just to have amazing reflexes.

It would be so much easier to kill Elects. *Other* Elects.

No. She wouldn't even consider it. The idea was too repulsive.

"Are you willing to let your grandfather and Preston die simply because you're afraid of the very thing they need?"

She stopped midstride and whipped around. "I am not afraid of you or your PNU or any blasted Elect. But I am not going to become the one thing that I hate the most. I'll find another way to save Preston and my grandfather."

"Rylee, the PNU wouldn't change you unless you allowed it to. Honestly, most men can't handle the kind of power the PNUs give. That's the problem. It's not the PNU changing them. It just makes it easier to see who they really are. I don't think the PNU will turn you into what you fear. You'll still be you. You'll still hate the sight of me. And you'll still have no sense of humor."

Almost against her will, she smiled. And she wanted to punch him for it. She shouldn't be smiling just after Preston had been taken by the Regulators. Preston. Her Preston. Who had always, always, always been there for her. And now that he needed her…she didn't even begin to know what to do.

"At least give me a chance to explain my idea. You owe it to your grandfather and Preston to understand all the options."

"I'll give you a chance to run, before I rid the world of one more Elect," she said, lifting the muzzle of her rifle to Grayson's chest. "This time, I know it's loaded."

"He'll be Deprecated before the end of the week, unless you listen to me," Grayson said, unfazed by the rifle pointed at his heart.

"I will find another way," she growled. "Serg and I…we'll come up with something." She said it more to convince herself. They could save him, couldn't they?

"And what will that plan be?" Grayson scoffed. "Shoot people? Not every problem can be solved with a gun, Rylee."

"Go choke yourself," she hissed, then turned and stormed away.

He followed her. Not closely, but he followed her all the way to Serghei's place. *Fine. He can see how much Feng likes Elects.*

She tapped her earpiece. "Serg, let me in?"

A moment later, her earpiece hissed. "You do realize," Serghei said, "that you have a stalker following you?"

"I know. Now, open the door." She was beyond caring if anyone else knew about Grayson. What did it matter now that the Alliance held Preston in custody?

A few clinks and rattles sounded behind the outer door to the warehouse, then it squeaked open. Serghei pointed his nose out into the dark alley. "Welcome," he said. Then he looked past her to where Grayson stood behind her. "Is your stalker coming in, then?"

Rylee pushed past Serghei. "Honestly, I don't care. He's just a parasite. An Elect. Let him in. Maybe Grant will chew off his face."

"I'm here to help your friend," Grayson said. "My name's Grayson."

Rylee turned to see Grayson hold out a hand for Serghei to shake. Serghei just looked back at her, his brows knit together in confusion. Rylee let out an angry groan, then turned and proceeded to Serghei's room.

"I sense a really fascinating story here," Serghei said from behind. "This could be better than an Alfred Hitchcock film."

Leave it to Serghei to think that having an Elect follow her home was fascinating. She charged into Serghei's lantern-lit room, and immediately began pacing the floor.

"I guess you saw that they got Preston?" Feng was sitting on the couch, leg propped up, Mountain Dew in one hand.

"Yes, I saw," she said. "And it was all *his* fault." She shot a stiff finger at Grayson as he and Serghei entered the room.

Grayson held up his hands defensively, smiling. "What'd I do?"

"Who's this tripe face?" Feng said.

"He's the Elect who broke Preston's nose," she said. "And now he's trying to ruin my life."

"What!" Despite his broken leg, Feng was up from the couch in an instant, his Berretta pointed directly at Grayson. "Why the blazes is he here?"

Grayson took a step back. "Man, Rylee," he said. "You and your friends, and your little get-to-know-you game...Look, I'm here to help Preston. You need my help. If you shoot, Preston's as good as dead."

Feng looked at Rylee, keeping his gun trained on Grayson.

"I helped save Rylee's grandfather," Grayson added.

"What's this tripe face talking about?" Feng's face was flushed with anger, and the muscles in his arms were so tense his veins looked like they would burst from his skin. Despite her frustration with Grayson, she couldn't suppress the surge of fear that Feng would actually harm him.

"Leave him alone," she said, careful not to let her voice betray her concern. It wasn't hard. She was genuinely annoyed with herself for being so weak. "He's telling the truth. He did stop the Regulators from taking my grandfather this morning."

Feng looked at her as though she'd just confessed that she secretly loved Serghei. "Are you trying to tell me that he's your boyfriend, or something?"

"No!" Rylee cried. "He's just a...I don't know...friend."

"So, you're friends with Elects now?"

"No...no..." Did she really have to have this discussion twice in one day? How did she explain what Grayson was? She didn't even understand it herself. "Look, just put down the gun, Feng, and I'll explain everything."

Feng looked at her skeptically. Finally, he let down his Berretta and carefully lowered himself back onto the couch. "This is messed up, you know that right? We're supposed to kill punks like this."

"Yes, but is it not much more interesting this way?" Serghei said. It was apparent from his tone that he was enjoying this twisted turn of events a little too much. "Drink, anyone?"

Seeing that Serghei was going for his stash of Mountain Dews,

Grayson lifted a hand. "I'm parched."

Great. Give him more fuel for his stupid PNU.

"What's wrong with you?" Feng said. "Treating him like a guest, or something...*Idiot*"

Since Feng had stopped pointing his gun at Grayson, Rylee had relaxed somewhat.

"We're waiting on this story, Ry," Feng added.

Right. Just what she wanted to do: confess to Feng and Serghei how her life had become entangled with an Elect. The kind of people they'd hunted down and killed. She needed their help, though. She'd need to convince them that she was still one of them...*without* getting Grayson killed in the process.

She started her story with everything that happened after she'd left the hideout following their very first encounter with Grayson. She told them how she'd prowled the streets until the early morning hours, looking for him, wanting to avenge Preston. She told how she'd come home to find Grayson sitting at her table with her grandfather, and how she'd tried to shoot him, but her grandfather stopped her. She told them how Grayson had — somehow — stopped the Regulators from taking her grandfather for Deprecation. She skipped over her deceits about the Mountain Dews, and how Grayson stopped her from shooting at the Regulators sent to collect Preston. Her intention was to make Feng less hostile, not more.

"Of all the people in this gang," Feng said when she'd finished, "you're the last one I'd expect to do us all like you've done. It's harsh, Ry."

"I'm sorry," Rylee said. And she did feel sorry. She'd never wanted to deceive any of them. Especially not Preston.

"How exactly did you dupe those Regulators?" Serghei asked, apparently unbothered by her deceptions. "Did you hack into Regulation's systems?"

"No, that would have been traceable," Grayson said. "I—"

"Can you two be nerdy later?" Rylee interrupted. "We need to focus on Preston. Serghei do you have any ideas?"

"Doesn't your friend—er—acquaintance here have connections in the Elect world?"

"I'm not exactly free to move about, at the moment. That's why I'm in hiding. However, I do have an idea."

"Which we have no interest whatsoever in hearing," Rylee put in before Grayson could go on. She didn't even want to hear him mention her becoming an elect again. "There's got to be a way that we intercept the Deprecation trucks, or something."

Grayson walked over and sat in Preston's usual spot, exchanging a distrustful glance with Feng as he did so. "You could try that," he said.

"But?" she replied, reading in his tone that he knew something she wasn't accounting for.

"First of all, you won't know for sure when they'll take care of the next round of Deprecations. Could be the end of the week. Could be in two weeks."

"We could rig a camera to monitor Regulation headquarters," Serghei suggested.

"Fine," Grayson said. "You'll have to be ready at a moment's notice. The real problem is that those trucks are well-guarded. Two Regulators up front, in the cab. And two or three in the back. This wouldn't be the first time someone has tried to save a loved one from Deprecation. And don't be surprised if the Regulators use Preston or the others as human shields."

Rylee didn't reply. The idea of someone using Preston as a human shield paralyzed her. No, she couldn't go through with a plan that put Preston in so much danger. She was a skilled marksman, but under that kind of stress...even the best could make mistakes.

"Well," she said, unconsciously scratching at the back of her hand, "can't we break into Regulation headquarters and bust him out?"

"Ah, a jail heist," Serghei said, excitedly. "Classic!"

"You want to break into a building full of Regulators?" Grayson said, his voice dripping with cynicism. He took a casual swig of his Mountain Dew.

"Why not?" Feng said. "We go in, guns blazing. Shoot up some Regs. And we can use *this* tripe face as our own human shield." He jabbed his thumb in the direction of Grayson.

"You keep calling me that name. Does that even mean any-thing?"

"Shut it, tripe face!"

Grayson just shook his head.

"Not to be a doubting Thomas," Serghei said, tentatively, "but Feng's not in any condition to engage in a gunfight. Even with the brace I made, he struggles to walk."

"Whatever. I can fight."

Serghei didn't say it, but they all knew that he was useless with a firearm. And despite Feng's bravado, she knew that it would be suicide to bring him on such a mission. It would be suicide even if Feng weren't injured. She scratched at her tattoo. This was pure torture. A nightmare. Preston was in the custody of Regulation, and she had no way to save him. Why had she let him go? Why hadn't she stopped him?

"If I had a few weeks," Serghei said, "I might be able to devise a plan which doesn't involve extermination of all the Regulators, but it would be too late by then."

"What about your original plan?" Rylee asked. "The one to hack into Regulation's systems."

Serghei shook his head ruefully. "Insufficient, I'm afraid. For one, the word is that Regulation has stopped taking tips. Too many bogus leads. Secondly, we don't know how to access the holding cells in the basement of Regulation headquarters. I suspect the locks for those will not be tied to the building's main power."

Was there nothing they could do then? No, she refused to ac-cept that. There had to be a way.

As if in answer to her thoughts, Grayson spoke. "I respect your ingenuity. Unfortunately, even if you manage — by some miracle — to rescue Preston, that won't be the end of it. They'll eventually tie him to one of you. To Rylee, or her grandfather. Then they'll come after you. You may be able to hide for a while, but sooner or later, they'll get you. Then it will be over for all of you."

"That's a risk we're willing to take," Rylee said. "We're not going to abandon him just because it's dangerous."

Grayson waved his hands. "I'm not suggesting you give up. Not at all. But, if you want to help him, you need to do it the right way. And for that, you need my help. You need this."

From the breast pocket of his coat, he drew out a thin glass vial, and held it up between his thumb and forefinger.

"I'm not letting you turn me into an Elect." Rylee nearly shouted as she said it.

"Wait, wait, wait a moment," Serghei stuttered. "*That's* a PNU? That's all that's needed to make someone an Elect?"

"That's all," Grayson said. "With this you'll have access to information and locations not possible otherwise. With it, I'm confident you and I can find out who's behind the murders. If we do that, it will be easy to get Preston exonerated."

"Why don't you turn Serg into the Elect," Rylee said. "He's the one who loves Elects."

"Yes," Serghei replied eagerly. "Imagine the things I could do with a PNU-enhanced brain…"

Grayson shook his head. "Unfortunately, in my haste to get away, I didn't pay attention to the PNU I was stealing from the labs. It was made for a female."

"I see," Serghei said, dejected.

"What does it matter who it was for?" Rylee said. "The PNU will still work, right?" She couldn't believe she was even talking about this. Even if it was Serghei who would take it, she didn't really want him turning into an Elect either.

"Actually, the PNUs are tuned differently for the male and female brain. Generally, male and female brains are *wired* differently in some areas. The PNUs account for that difference in wiring. It might work okay in a male brain, but it could have some unintended consequences."

"Man, if Serghei starts liking boys," Feng said, "then I'm gone."

Grayson shook his head. "That wouldn't happen. However, there's another issue. This PNU has a specific certificate and profile that's directly linked to one Leah Morrison. Any network access done with the PNU will log her name as the accessor. Likewise, if we have to infiltrate Regulation, any of the Regulators will be able to access your PNU's profile and see your name, age, gender, etc. You need to use it, Ry."

He held out the tiny vial to her. "It's the only way to save Preston."

She stared at it, the sullen lantern light glinting off the glass like a yellow jewel. It was so small—innocuous. How could something so small cause so much grief and pain?

"Don't do it, Ry," Feng said. "Don't become one of them."

"Just because you have a PNU-enhanced brain," Serghei said, "doesn't mean you'll become *like* them. You'll still be Rylee. Still be one of the good guys. But with awesome abilities. You'll be able to shoot a fly off Preston's shoulder from five hundred yards away. You'll be unstoppable."

"Stop it, you two," she said, holding up her hands. "Please, I just...need to think."

She ran out of the room, out of the warehouse, bursting out into the night. The rush of cold air soothed her burning cheeks. Rylee looked up into the night sky covered with murky gray clouds. Neither the moon nor the stars were visible. Just like always. She felt a surge of hot tears forming in her eyes. But she fought them back.

She would not permit herself to cry. Tears could not save Preston. No, Preston needed action. He needed her to forget about herself and do what it takes to save him. That's what he needs. What he deserves. If there was any other way...

Clinching her fist, she turned and strode back into the warehouse.

"I have one more question," she said, as she entered back into Serghei's room. Grayson looked up at her in surprise, as if he didn't expect to ever see her again. "Once this is all over, can the PNU be...removed?"

Grayson nodded his head slowly. "It can be disabled, such that it's virtually removed, yes."

Rylee swallowed. "Okay. I'll take it."

TWENTY-SIX

"Do you see any other Elects nearby?" Grayson whispered from her side.

Rylee went to peer around the corner of the wall against their back.

"No!" Grayson said, pulling her back into the shadows by her shoulder. "Not like that. Remember what I taught you?"

Sighing so that he could hear her annoyance, she tried the technique—or whatever you called it—to inspect her surrounding for other Elects.

"We're particularly interested in Regulators."

"Great. My favorite people," she muttered.

Rylee had practiced this. Even become fairly good at it. Using her new PNU. She hated it. Every time she utilized its capabilities, she felt appalled. Appalled to be her. Appalled to be one of *them*. Appalled at herself for not being able to come up with a way to save Preston without Grayson's plan. She still didn't know if she was making the right choice. Or even if she trusted Grayson.

The PNU commands—as Grayson called them—were supposed to be like extensions of her own thoughts. Like telling your hand to form a fist or your toes to curl. Only there weren't any muscles involved. And the PNU automatically compensated—somehow—for her brain's lack of *muscle memory* using the commands. The PNU had a multiplicity of autonomous operations which didn't require her direct control. These she was learning about.

Now she needed to instruct her PNU to tell her about any nearby Elects. Her natural inclination was to speak aloud. That wasn't necessary.

I hate *this.*

If only Grayson didn't have to go around the Elect sector of the city with his PNU deactivated. It wasn't safe for him to have his PNU active. Someone might detect him. As yet, he'd failed to fully explain why that was a problem. He was hiding something from her.

Issuing the command, Rylee didn't have to wait but a fraction of a second. Her vision filled with faint lines and shapes—pale blues, outlining the walls of the buildings around her. The augmented vision momentarily gave her vertigo. How could she ever get used to this? She was being shown the buildings beyond the wall, which currently obstructed her *actual* vision. Literally, she could scan the street around the corner without actually seeing it.

Only lines of inanimate objects—that's all she saw along the street. All clear there. She turned her attention to the building. Lots more lines, punctuated here and there by bright green figures—outlines of people. Other Elects. Great. A building full of Elects. Just where she wanted to go.

Reds. She was looking for the color red— an indication of Regulators. *Probing*, Grayson called it. The method that allowed her to detect the nearby presence of other Elects. What Serghei wouldn't give to have that technology.

"It looks clear," she said, speaking over her shoulder.

"Good," he replied. "Follow me. Keep probing for Regulators."

Grayson skirted around her, and dashed across the street. Despite her augmented vision—or whatever Grayson called it—she still turned her head to look down the street before following. She followed Grayson to the right of the building, down an alleyway. He stopped midway down it. A door stood in front of them. *Morgue*. Her PNU forced the word into her thoughts.

A chill ran through her at the thought of going inside. A room specifically for dead bodies. Even though they were all likely the bodies of Elects, it still creeped her out.

"Open it," Grayson instructed.

"I hate you, by the way," Rylee said in response.

"It would be awkward otherwise. Now, open it. *Please*."

This was one of the reasons Grayson needed her help. To open doors for him. Like some sort of servant. There was more to it than that. Or, at least, that's what he had explained to her. Her PNU would unlock doors. Grayson had described to her the full technical details. Sufficient to make her want to beat her head against a wall, and to make Serghei drool.

All she really remembered is that her PNU was meant for someone else. As soon as she opened that door, it would log her entry. That's why Grayson needed her. If he used his PNU to open the door, the elusive *someone* would know he'd been there tonight.

Grabbing the metal door latch with her gloved hand, Rylee paused. As soon as she touched it, something happened in her mind. A tugging, almost. She didn't quite know how to describe the sensation. Only she knew instinctively that it came from her PNU. The door wanted information—credentials—from her. Credentials she had to relinquish. Not understanding quite how she did it, she let go of the requested data. Instantly, the door clicked. She turned to the door latch and pushed the door ajar. Magic.

Despite hatred toward the Elects and the PNUs, she couldn't help feeling a sense of awe at what she could now do.

Rylee felt for the pistol beneath her jacket as she pushed further inside. Three days had passed since Preston had been captured and she'd agreed to Grayson's plan to make her into an Elect. In that time, Grayson had taught her how to use her PNU. And she'd done little else but practice using the accursed thing. The only bright spot in that whole time was that she'd managed to convince her grandfather to return her Glock.

Those three days had felt like an eternity. Her mind refused to rest. Refused to stop worrying that they would be too late to save Preston. That any minute, the Regulators would come back for her grandfather. Supposedly, what they were doing now would help both her grandfather and Preston.

The door led them into a dark room. Much to Rylee's surprise, the air within was only slightly warmer than the frozen air outside. She shivered, not from the cold though.

Behind her, the door clicked and thudded as it closed them inside, making the darkness complete.

"Help me look for a light switch," Grayson whispered from behind.

"What? You mean your precious PNU can't turn on the lights, too?"

"Actually it's *your* precious PNU. And that's a very good question. If you ever get a chance, ask my dad about it some time."

"Found it." Grayson's proclamation was followed by a faint snap and a flood of blinding white light.

Shielding her eyes, Rylee let out a cry of shock. "Ah, that's bright!" She'd never seen lights so bright before. Not artificial lights, anyway. Occasionally, the sun made such appearances outside. It would probably take her night vision a full week of pitch blackness to recover from this exposure.

Once her eyes acclimated sufficiently to the lights, Rylee looked around. There wasn't much to see. A wall lined from top to bottom with large steel locker doors. A few steel tables. On one of the tables, there was a green sheet of fabric, laden with a neat row of shiny implements. Scalpels and other tools that made Rylee's skin crawl to think of their use.

"You should stop probing, by the way," Grayson said, moving over to one of the lockers. "It's generally considered rude or suspicious behavior."

"And breaking into a morgue is not?" she quipped.

"No argument there. I'm only suggesting that it might draw unwanted attention."

Though she liked the idea of being alerted early of someone's unexpected intrusion on them, she agreed that it would be foolish to advertise their own presence. Focusing her thoughts, she instructed her PNU to stop probing. The blue lines of her augmented vision faded away, leaving her feeling relieved and a bit lethargic.

"Done," she said.

"Good. Now, can you see about accessing the morgue's internal records? There ought to be an inventory of recent admissions and where they are stowed."

Rylee furrowed her brow at him. "An inventory? As in an inventory of dead people?"

"What do you want to call it, a guest list?"

An unbidden smile cracked Rylee's lips. "Fine, you win. We'll call it an inventory. Not that it really matters. I have no clue how to access it."

"Just try a few commands. The PNU is designed to work intuitively. Think about what you want, and there's a good chance the PNU will figure it out."

Right. Super intuitive. Maybe for someone who was used to having their brain possessed by another lifeform.

Again, Rylee focused on her thoughts. *Show morgue inventory,* she thought. Though, it was a little different than merely thinking. The best way she could describe it was pushing the thought out, as if to do something outside of her body. Of course, that didn't make any sense at all. Since everything was happening within her brain.

Whatever she did, it worked. In her vision, overlaid on the world around her, six of the lockers illuminated with a hint of yellow. Her eyes instinctively fixed on one of the lockers. As she did so a name instantly formed in her mind. Garrison Pike. The name induced a flood of toxic emotions, which she fought to contain.

There was other information there too. She could *sense* it there. Like an unfocused object in her peripheral vision. Only, it was an unfocused thought.

"Okay," she said slowly, "I think I have it."

"What did I tell you?" Grayson said. "You're a natural Elect."

She shot him a withering glare, but didn't reply.

"Can you find the most recent…uh…guest that checked in?" he asked.

"There." She pointed to one of the lockers on the middle row, close to where Grayson stood. "Two lockers to your left."

She took a step backward as Grayson walked over to the locker and pulled it open. Though Rylee had killed her share of Elects, she preferred the idea of kissing Serghei's rat over looking at bodies that had lain dead for several days or weeks. Steeling herself, Rylee walked over and stood next to Grayson.

From within the open locker, Grayson slid out a long steel table. On it lay an equally long white bag. Any fool would know what the bag contained. Apparently unaffected by such thoughts, Grayson located the zipper's tab, unzipped it part way, and peered inside. A white face, swollen and rigid peered back. The sight made Rylee jump back in horror.

She looked at Grayson. He seemed to be paralyzed by what he saw. For a long time he stood there dumbly, unmoving.

"It can't be," he muttered after some time.

"Who is it?" she said, her voice coming out in a whisper.

"You tell me. What does the inventory say?"

Having forgotten about her abilities, Rylee quickly recalled the list. The augmented vision returned and she read the name aloud. "Lander Vance Wilson."

In reply, Grayson's head dropped to his chest. "How could this have happened?" he muttered.

"You knew him, then?" Rylee said, immediately regretting it. A stupid question. Of course he knew him. Why else would he look so wretched?

"I've known him since we were just children. No closer friend do—did—I have in the world."

Rylee didn't want to feel sorry for Grayson. That would show she cared, however minutely, about what happened to him. Yet she couldn't help feeling a pang of sadness for him now. Grayson didn't deserve this.

"I'm sorry," she said.

Grayson shook his head and laughed. Not a laugh of joy, but a deranged sort of laugh. "He always was a bit reckless, but I never thought—"

He broke off and they both turned toward the door. Someone was outside.

TWENTY-SEVEN

CARMINE BRISTLED INSIDE, but held her tongue.

"I put you on this case because I knew I would get results, Miss O'Connor," Mr. Steele said, his tone reflecting the hardness in his eyes. "Did I err when I promoted you?"

Inside, Carmine flinched at the edge in his voice. She didn't gratify him by letting any of that show on the outside. She would stay calm, confident.

The CA had called her into his office to receive a personal report on the progress of the case.

"No, sir, you did not," she said, voice even. "I *will* discover who's behind the homicides. You have my word on that."

"I'm glad you're so confident, Miss O'Connor. But I don't care one bit about your word. I want results. So far, all I have is important members of our Alliance getting killed right from under our noses. One of my own engineers among them. And now my son has gone missing. What the devil are you doing?"

Steele slammed the palm of his hand onto his desk.

Carmine narrowed her eyes and gave him a cold smile. She wouldn't be cowed this time. She only wished that she was standing, so that Steele couldn't tower over her like a thundercloud. She filed a reminder away in her PNU to ensure she remembered next time she met with Mr. Steele.

"We are investigating every possible lead," she said.

"Not good enough."

"We have a few suspects with probable cause," she went on unperturbed, "but no evidence yet to make an arrest."

"Still, not good enough."

"Our forensics team is painstakingly attempting to extract the PNUs in the victims, in case there is a new kind of PNU virus we're dealing with."

"That could yield results. But it will take too long."

"We've also brought in a young man, an Unenhanced," she said. Steele raised one eyebrow expectantly. She hadn't planned to bring up Preston Hyde. Frankly, she wanted to release him. "We received a tip from a member. The young man's linked to the murder of Commander Michael Pike and Ian Gyles. He may be linked to the other homicides. Possibly a crime ring. From our interrogations, we've learned that he didn't work alone. Though…" she hesitated. *How to phrase this without sounding weak?*

"Though, what?" Steele demanded.

"He's proved impressively resilient to our interrogation techniques. Thus far, he's managed to hold out any names from us. We will get them, though."

Yes. Now she would ensure she squeezed the names out of him. She'd not yet permitted her officers to use their full arsenal of tactics. Steele didn't need to know that.

For a few wordless moments, Steele considered her. She met his gaze. Finally, Steele move from his position in front of his desk to his windows.

"What's his name?" he said, still facing the windows.

"Preston Hyde."

Another moment's silence. Carmine knew that Steele was accessing the young man's records. A scant record. Most records for the Unenhanced were.

A minute later, Steele turned away from the window. "Bring him to me," he said.

"Sir?"

"Bring Preston Hyde to me."

* * *

Rylee drew out her pistol and pointed it directly at the door. The door swung open as if in slow motion. In fact, everything around her seemed like it was moving slower than it should. Not herself, though. She moved like a burst of electricity. This wasn't just adrenaline. The PNU. How did it…

The form of a person, a lanky boy with bushy brown eyebrows

filled the doorway. He wore a white lab coat.

Her finger moved to the trigger. She hesitated.

As if from far away, she heard a long drawn out, "stoooooop!"

The bushy-eyebrowed boy raised both arms.

"Don't shoot!" came Grayson's voice again, this time not quite so far away.

The boy in the doorway didn't appear threatening. Rylee relaxed her grip on her pistol and moved her finger away from the trigger. Instantly, time sped back up. The world around her returned to moving at a normal rate.

"Sorry about that, Ron," Grayson said. "She has this thing about pointing guns at people."

The boy—Ron—looked from Rylee to Grayson, arms still raised, face ashen. His spectacled eyes, which were already opened wide, grew even wider when he fixed on Grayson.

"Wil—"

"It's me," Grayson said, cutting off Ron. "Grayson. Don't tell me you don't remember my name."

Ron just looked at him with a puzzled expression on his face.

"Don't worry," coaxed Grayson. "No one's going to hurt you." He shot Rylee a disapproving glance. "Come on in."

Grudgingly, Rylee lowered her pistol, but didn't holster it. Grayson may think this scrawny boy with the bushy eyebrows wasn't a threat, but he was still an Elect. And now that she understood firsthand some of the capabilities of the PNU, she definitely wasn't about to let down her guard. For all they knew, Ron had already notified the Regulators of their presence. Hopefully, she had frightened him sufficiently, that the thought hadn't entered his brain.

Warily, Ron stepped inside and closed the door behind him. For the first time, Rylee noticed that he gripped something in his right hand. Something edible. Bar-shaped, and wrapped in a dark brown wrapper, that was pulled back part way. The letters were obscured. A hunk of the brown stuff was missing. No doubt the missing chunk was being digested by Ron's stomach at that moment.

Rylee's own stomach growled. Ever since Grayson turned her into an Elect, she'd always been hungry. Of course, it didn't help that rations for the Norms were down to almost nothing. Grayson had explained to her that the PNU required electricity to operate. Using some sort of magical process, it converted glucose into electricity. A fascinating bedtime story for Serghei. All she understood is that she needed more food. Which was just about the worst punishment you could inflict on a Norm.

"Ron and I went to school together when we were younger," Grayson explained, as if she cared. "We're old friends."

Taking a bite of the bar in his hand, Ron sputtered out a few intelligible words. "What are you doing here?"

"I need you to tell me everything you know about the recent deaths...the murders," Grayson said, his tone serious.

Ron walked over to the open locker, where Lander's body lay on the metal table. As he passed, he watched Rylee out of the corner of his eye. "I'm not really allowed to disclose that information."

"I know, Ron," Grayson said. "I respect that. We don't want to get you into trouble. I'm asking as a personal favor. We're trying to figure out who's behind the killings. There can't be anything wrong with that, can there?"

Ron looked back and forth rapidly between Rylee and Grayson, like an animal that can't decide which of its predators is most dangerous. Rylee felt sorely tempted to use her pistol as a motivator. Although, maybe with someone like Ron, he would just end up passing out.

Finally, he fixed on Grayson, taking another large bite of his bar. "I'll tell you what I know," he smacked nervously. "Just...you can't tell anyone you were here or what I told you."

Grayson held up his hands. "Listen, I don't want anyone to know I was here either. Or even that you saw me. Do we have a deal?"

"Deal," Ron said with a bob of his head and a nervous glance at Rylee. Then he turned back to the body on the table. "This one," he went on, his tone suddenly becoming more academic, "died of apparent drowning. His body was found floating beneath one of the piers at the docks. Based on the temperature of the water, its concentration of salt and other chemicals, and the amount of flesh decay, I estimate he's been dead about seven days. No signs of physical injuries which might indicate foul play. Although, if he didn't know how to swim, someone could have easily pushed him into the water. Unlikely, though."

"Do you know if they were able to extract any of his PNU memory?" Grayson asked, moving closer to Lander's body.

Ron shook his head. "Dead too long."

Rylee noticed that Grayson's face looked pale. This was still hard news for him to accept. And yet he went on, trying to learn what he could from Ron. "Any evidence of a new PNU virus causing this?"

"That depends on what kind of evidence you want. No incontrovertible proof. No empirical evidence, anyway. I'm no forensics expert. Nevertheless, to me, all these killings are a little too clean."

"How's that?"

Ron adjusted his spectacles. "Take Garrison Pike's death, for example. I have a buddy who works for Regulation. He did the memory extraction and analyzed it. The victim was strangled to death. My autopsy confirmed it. The memory playback confirmed it. A dark figure, face covered, approaches on the street and starts strangling. Two things don't add up though.

"First, not a speck of evidence was ever found confirming there was another person on that street with the victim. No footprints, no DNA, no hair follicles—nothing. Fine. Maybe the attacker was super thorough."

"Or the Regulators were sloppy with their investigation," Grayson added.

Ron chuckled. "I'll give you that one. How about this, the marks on Pike's neck...they matched the victim's own hands."

"You think he strangled himself? That's not possible. He would have passed out before he could finish the job."

"Exactly. All of this, to me, suggests evidence of a new virus. Though how it actually works is something I haven't figured out. Surely, the PNU couldn't control the victim's body after he lost consciousness."

Rylee shifted anxiously. This conversation was taking too long. What if someone else showed up unexpectedly? Plus, she didn't believe any of this was going to help Preston. Every moment they spent theorizing about someone's cause of death, the less time they had to save Preston.

Still, she held her tongue. She had promised Grayson they'd do this his way — for now.

"What about the other deaths?" Grayson asked.

"In my opinion," Ron said, "Pike's was the most interesting. Prasad Balay was apparently smothered by a pillow in his own bed, yet no evidence of anyone breaking into his studio was ever found. The memory extraction from that victim was basically worthless. The pillow blocked the victim's vision."

"So, you think the victim smothered himself with his own pillow?"

"You're the PNU engineer, not me. Could someone build such a virus?"

Grayson looked down at the body of his friend, apparently considering the question. "It's nothing like what I've ever heard of," he said at last. He looked as though he might say more, but he held back.

"There was a poisoning, too," Ron continued. "Dr. Mei Lin, entomologist. Died of ingesting chlorpyrifos, a common pesticide."

"Couldn't she have ingested it by accident? I assume she worked with lots of pesticides."

"You *could* argue that it was an accident. Until you look at the amount of the chemical she consumed. Five hundred milliliters. Did she think she was consuming an energy drink? Unlikely. Her colleagues claim Dr. Lin was always extremely careful when dealing with hazardous chemicals. She didn't even allow workers to drink water in the labs. And yet the poison was found in her coffee mug. Furthermore, unless she guzzled her coffee in one breathless gulp, there's no way she could have drunk so much chlorpyrifos without noticing."

"Unless a PNU virus caused her to ignore the taste," Grayson said softly, as if talking to himself. "Was suicide ruled out?"

"No previous signs of depression. Also, from her memory extraction, forensics detected high levels of confusion from the victim just prior to death. And it was a painful one. Lots of vomiting. Had she poisoned herself intentionally, she wouldn't have been wondering what was happening to her. Additionally, she sent for help."

Grayson's jawline tightened and he shook his head bitterly before speaking again. "Thank you, Ron. You've been more than helpful." Then he turned away from Lander's body and moved toward the door.

Rylee followed, watching Ron as she moved toward the door.

"Ah...one more thing," Ron said, the timidity in his voice returning. Grayson halted, cocking his head to show he was listening. "If someone should check the access logs for the door..."

"They'll show an individual you never saw in here."

A frantic laugh—or maybe it was a cough—escaped Ron's mouth. "Very good. Just checking."

Out in the street, Grayson marched forward, steps careless of any possible danger lurking in the shadows or around corners. Rylee hurried to keep up with his long purposeful strides. The bright lights of the morgue having destroyed her night vision, she felt blind in the dark alley.

"Well, what next?" she said.

Not stopping or turning to look at her, he simply said, "We go to a party."

TWENTY-EIGHT

"ADRIANNA SAYS SHE'LL be there in ten minutes," Rylee announced as she and Grayson strode through the Slum streets toward Serghei's place.

"I'd give her an even twenty," Grayson said. "Always fashionably late. Everything is fashionable, with Adrianna. Utter nonsense if you ask me."

"Does that mean she always wears fancy clothes?" Rylee had caught glimpses of Elect women before. That O'Connor lady, for example. They always looked…different. Like they *wanted* the men around to notice they were female.

But the idea of being fashionable was not something Rylee understood. Was it like some of the women she saw in Serghei's movies? Dressed so that it would be impossible to conceal a gun, ride a motorcycle, or even chase after an Elect?

"It means," Grayson replied, "that she dresses in a manner that's…distracting. Especially at parties like the one we're going to. You'll see for yourself soon enough."

A thought that gave Rylee that pit in her stomach again. Were they truly going through with this plan? How did she keep letting Grayson talk her into these things? She was supposed to hate him. First the PNU. Now this? Scratching the back of her hand, she increased the pace of her stride.

"Your friends…" Grayson began tentatively. "Do you think they'll be a little less…hostile, this time?"

Rylee shrugged. "Feng will probably still want to shoot your brains out."

"Oh, good," he replied feigning joviality in his voice. "I was beginning to miss having a gun pointed at me every few hours."

"Hey!" she exclaimed, shooting him a glare. "Keep that up, and I might not stop Feng this time."

"I'm in earnest. There's no other person on this planet I'd rather have point a gun at me than you."

"Shut up," she said, sending him tumbling to the pavement with a shove.

"See," he called back to her as she kept walking. "Always charming."

And Rylee found a smile creeping onto her lips again.

They found Serghei and Feng both in the hideout, just as Rylee expected. Feng was testing out the latest version of the brace Serghei was constructing for him. Despite a look of disgust directed at Grayson, Feng remained calm.

"You mean a girl is coming here?" Serghei said when she told them about their plans. "A *female*...Elect?" The way he said it, you'd have thought she'd told him the girl was going to be *his* date for the night.

"Arriving any minute," Grayson said. "We need your place to get ready for tonight."

"An Elect girl...coming here?" Serghei didn't register anything else they said. Instead, he went to work tidying up his room. Which didn't make a bit of difference. Piles of junk still looked like junk, however you stacked it. Of course, to Serghei they were piles of precious junk.

"Who cares if she's a girl?" Feng said, plopping on to the couch and working at the straps of his brace. "She's still one of them."

Rylee flinched inside at the comment. Now she was one of *them*. An Elect. A traitor.

Five minutes later, Adrianna arrived. A black SUV pulled up to the warehouse. The rear door popped open and a long slender leg, armed with a deadly looking stiletto heal shot out. Grayson dodged to keep from getting skewered. Then a figure shroud in a dark hooded coat stepped out, and shoved a loose bundle into Grayson's arms. Fumbling with the bundle, Grayson got the car door closed, and the SUV drove off, as silently as an autumn breeze. An electric-powered vehicle. The darkness rendered it impossible to tell for sure, but Rylee didn't see a driver. She'd heard of the autonomous cars— self-driving—in the Alliance. A few had survived Desolation and were still operable.

"After you've avoided me like you have," Adrianna said, her voice smooth as peanut butter, "I shouldn't even be talking to you. And then you have the nerve to ask me to come to…" She looked around her as if she were standing in a sea of human waste. "*Here.*"

"And I'll repay you adequately," Grayson said, laying a hand on her shoulder and moving her toward the alleyway. "That is, if I live through all this."

"Where are you taking me?" She sounded as if she thought she was about to be murdered.

"Relax, Adrianna. Rylee, here, carries a gun. If you're nice to her she might not shoot you."

Rylee smiled, but didn't say anything. In truth, she felt sorely tempted to pull out her pistol just to frighten the girl even more.

"I see your little sojourn into the slums hasn't cured you of your sarcasm," Adrianna snapped.

The trio entered the warehouse, Grayson muttering assurances to Adrianna the whole way.

Serghei's eyes nearly leaped from their sockets when they walked inside, and his mouth drooped open. His eyes were transfixed on Adrianna, who strode into the room, swinging her hips as if she were trying to knock over the furniture with the shockwave from their wake. Turning up her sharp bejeweled nose, she looked the room over, before firing an angry glare at Grayson.

Grayson gave her a half-hearted grin and cleared his throat. "Adrianna," he said, "I'd like you to meat Serghei, Feng, and Rylee." He held out his hand to each one of the companions in turn.

"Fang?" Adrianna said with a scowl. "Like a wolf? What kind of name is that?"

Uh, oh! Wrong thing to say.

"It's not Fang!" Feng shouted, springing to life from the couch. "It's *Feng.* I'm not no animal, man. Tripe! I thought Elects were supposed to be smart. Feeeeng. With an 'e'."

Placing her hands on her cocked hips, Adrianna snorted. "Right." She turned back to Grayson. "So, where's this girl that I'm supposed to dress up for the party?"

"Right here," Grayson replied. "It's Rylee."

Adrianna studied Rylee with a look of pure bewilderment. Rylee could feel her cheeks start burning.

Yes, I'm a girl, Rylee wanted to say. Sure, she intentionally tried to hide her gender. But having this...woman, who oozed femininity from every square centimeter of her sparkly body, fail to recognize Rylee as a fellow female irked her in the extreme.

"This will be loads of fun," Adrianna said dryly, as she slipped off her coat and deliberated on which surface was the least filthy to set it on.

Off to the side, Serghei wobbled like he might melt, as he took in this new sight of Adrianna. With the coat removed, Adrianna's dress—or lack of it—was fully exposed. The tight, shimmering fabric, wrapped around her curvy body, exposing more skin than it covered. The green hue of the dress matched the streaks of green lacing through her blonde hair, which cascaded in a torrent of curves over her bare shoulders and back.

"Is there even a bathroom in this hole?" Adrianna asked.

"Down the h-h-hall," Serghei stammered out, his mouth still gaping.

"Fabulous," Adrianna said, smiling venomously at Rylee. "Shall we? Will, bring my things, darling. I'm glad I didn't come unprepared."

Will. She called him Will. William. That was the name Sophie had mentioned, wasn't it? She didn't have time to deliberate the matter further, for Adrianna was leading her by the hand out of Serghei's room.

As soon as Rylee registered Adrianna's hand, she snatched hers away and stormed ahead to Serghei's bathroom. The only physical contact she wanted with Adrianna involved disfiguring the girl's perfect nose with her fist.

If possible, Adrianna looked even more disgusted by Serghei's bathroom than anything she'd seen thus far. "Oh, that is vile!" The girl plugged her nose and began rummaging through one of her bags with her free hand. A moment later, she pulled out a clear bottom of liquid, angular in shape, and started spritzing its contents into the air. After dousing the air to her satisfaction,

Adrianna declared, "I suppose that will have to do."

Rylee took a whiff of the treated air. The scent of it was…sweet. More than that she couldn't say. It didn't remind her of anything she'd smelled before. Certainly nothing from the slums ever smelled like that. Rylee felt like gagging.

Having tainted the air with her spray, Adrianna looked around her, a look of disgust still plastering her face. The look suited her.

"Please tell me *that* is not the bath," she said, pointing to a small tub in the corner.

"It is," Rylee replied. "Why don't you try it out? Maybe the cold water can wash some of that sparkly stuff off your skin."

"I am not touching anything. And just so you know, that *sparkly* stuff is called body spray." She cocked her hips, as she ran the back of her hand delicately down the length of her forearm. "All the men love it. Including my Will." She lifted her gaze to meet Rylee's eyes, and gave her a smug smile.

At her side, Rylee's hands clenched into fists. Had Adrianna just claimed Grayson as hers? So what? What did it matter if Grayson had a girlfriend? Let him have fifty girlfriends for all she cared. Grayson meant nothing to her. Nothing more than a tool to help her get back Preston. Because Preston was worth saving. *She* had Preston. A better man than Grayson could ever hope to be.

"The bath is for you," Adrianna said, pulling out an armful of various colorful bottles. "You *cannot* go to the CA's birthday party smelling like a Slum dweller."

Slum dweller? Digging her fingernails into her palms, Rylee contemplated drilling her fist into Adrianna's face. Had she actually promised Grayson she wouldn't hurt this…this skin exposing, hip swinging, sparkly tramp?

Taking a deep breath, she forced herself to stay calm. If she broke Adrianna's nose, she wouldn't have the help she needed to get ready for the party. Then she couldn't help Preston and her grandfather. She was doing this for them. She could do it. Afterward, she could break Adrianna's nose. Something to look forward to.

"These are for your hair," Adrianna said, handing Rylee two bottles. "Use this one first." Then three more bottles. "This one's for your body. And this one's for your face. After you're done, you can put on this." She pulled out a fluffy pink…something, and handed it to her. "Don't take all night." Then she exited the bathroom and closed the door.

Great. A bath. The last thing she wanted to do was bathe. What did it matter if she didn't smell like someone had dropped a nuclear perfume bomb on top of her? She wasn't going to try and attract anyone. Especially if that someone was an Elect. And there would be hordes of them, from what Grayson had described of the party. But she did need to blend in, not draw attention by smelling like she never bathed. For Preston. She was doing this for Preston.

Placing her pistol and holster on a shelf above the tub, she stripped off her clothes, stepped into the tub, and turned the knob for the faucet. A black tube connected the faucet to a hand-held wand. A few echoed gurgles from the pipes and a stuttering stream of water poured out. Squatting in the narrow tub, she began to rinse her skin. She drew in a sharp breath as the near-freezing water bit at her skin. Instantly, her teeth began to chatter and her shaking hand struggled to keep hold of the wand.

With the dirt and grime more or less rinsed from her body, she started on her hair. Every time she washed it, she felt grateful it was short. Less to wash. She applied the goopy contents of the various bottles to her hair, hoping she was doing it in the right order. Each bottle contained a different, overwhelming scent. How could so much sweet-smelling stuff even exist?

Hair done, she washed the rest of herself with whatever strange soap came from the bottles, shut off the water and reached for the fluffy pink thing.

It turned out to be a robe. Shaking uncontrollably, she managed to wrap it around her body and tie it up at her waist. The pink fabric felt warm and comfortable, in a bizarre sort of way. Though, strictly speaking, she was dressed, she didn't feel like she was wearing anything. Clothes were not meant to feel like this.

"Done," Rylee growled, once her teeth stop chattering.

"That was…fast," Adrianna said, as she opened the door and stepped back inside. She looked Rylee up and down with a critical eye.

"The liquid ice from the faucet tends to speed things up," Rylee said.

"Well, you smell better, anyway." Adrianna fumbled through her bags again before producing a small silver box. "Now, it's time for the fun part."

Where I punch you in the nose? "Which is?"

"Makeup, of course. Sit."

She pointed to the toilet. Serghei's toilet. Lovely. At least there was a seat lid. Slamming the lid down, Rylee sat. As she did, the robe slipped open at her knees, revealing her legs. Adrianna gaped at them as though she'd just witnessed a murder.

"What are you staring at?" Rylee said, quickly covering her legs again. What was her problem? Adrianna had enough of her legs on display to make you wonder if she'd forgotten the lower half of her dress.

"Your legs," Adrianna said, as if that what explanation enough. Rylee just raised her eyebrows. "Don't you ever shave or wax them?"

"Do what to them?"

Adrianna let out a moan that sounded like a cat dying. A sound Rylee had heard many times before. Then she huffed, and returned to her bag. "I was wrong," she said, pulling a yellow cylindrical container from her back. "This will be the fun part…for me."

TWENTY-NINE

WHAT IN THE NAME of Desolation were those two doing in there? Grayson tapped his foot impatiently. Were those screams he heard? And were they Rylee's or Adrianna's? Perhaps it was a mistake to let Rylee be alone with Adrianna after all.

More screams. Should he check on them? His PNU enabled him to communicate with either one of them without words. Rylee was still getting used to this new form of communication. She could use the practice.

Another scream. Then again, maybe he didn't want to know what was going on. Plenty of time remained for them to make an appearance at his father's birthday party. The thought made him anxious. Going tonight was a huge gamble. Practically, anyone of importance—and a fair number of unimportance—from the Alliance would be in attendance. More than likely, the murderer included. Lander's murderer. Grayson himself might very well be targeted.

A risk he must make. A risk he hoped would yield results. Most of his plan relied on Rylee for it to succeed. Was she ready? Admittedly, she could use more training with her PNU. Time they didn't have. Another opportunity like this would not present itself anytime soon. By then, he would likely be dead.

He turned his attention away from these uncomfortable thoughts, and to the other occupants in the room. Feng still sat on the hideous couch, his foot propped up, and an angry expression pointed at him. Serghei—the amiable one—was feeding a rodent of some sort.

"Is that a rat?" Grayson asked. He moved in for a closer look. He hadn't noticed it the last time he'd been there, when Rylee decided to go along with this crazy plan.

"This is Grant," Serghei replied brightly.

"But his leg…a prosthesis?"

"I prefer the term cybernetic."

Grayson examined the artificial leg with admiration. The mechanical work was impressive. Intricate. With tiny actuators and motors all working in efficient harmony as the rat scurried back and forth across Serghei's shoulders.

"You built that?" Grayson asked.

"Every last joint and gear. It took months."

"Impressive."

"Listen," Grayson continued, "I was wondering, if you could spare any more of those drinks of yours. Rylee and I are sure to need the energy for our PNUs tonight."

"Be my guest, mon ami. What's mine is yours."

"Thanks," Grayson said, walking over to the bright yellow boxes and grabbing two of the cans. He downed the contents of one—as quickly as he could manage—then pocketed the other.

The clomp of high heels on the concrete floor made him turn around. Adrianna strode into the room, the sequins of her turquoise dress catching the dim light like a galaxy of tiny stars. Her gait was calculated—just like her tiny dress, hair, makeup, and perfume—to entice him. That was Adrianna's way. That was what she did. Entice. Yet his eyes were drawn to a different figure entering the room. A figure with dark chocolate hair and swathed in a sleeveless dress, with gold sequined top and frilly white lace skirt.

He raised an eyebrow. Rylee? Not possible. He'd expected a change, of course. But this…this was nothing short of a complete transformation.

"Put those tongues back in your mouths, boys," Adrianna said, as she stepped to the side and held out her arms, showing off her handiwork. "I hope you gave this girl a decent security update, Will. Because every guy at that party is going to try to infect her with a date-rape virus."

It didn't happen often, but Grayson didn't know what to say. He noticed, too, that both Feng and Serghei were staring, and not at Adrianna. Not that she rivaled Adrianna. Not when it came to raw enticement. Rylee possessed a simpler beauty. An honest beauty. Wholesome.

"She's had a mani, a pedi, a waxing, a facial. Plus a coiffure. Makeup. And a dazzling a-line gold dress, with belted waist. Which shows off her adorable waistline perfectly."

"What the blazes did you do with Ry?" Feng said.

"It's me, you idiot," Rylee snapped. She shifted a bit uncomfortably, obviously unused to this kind of attention. "Stop staring, or I'll give you another—permanent—injury."

Yes, it was definitely Rylee.

"Beauty that bites," Adrianna said, folding her arms with satisfaction and giving Grayson a cocky smile. "Not too bad, don't you think?"

Grayson moved closer, wanting to get a better look. Feeling like he wanted to be closer. To wrap his arms around that waist and...*Stop it!* What was he thinking? This was psycho girl. The same one who'd tried to shoot him—twice. Besides, women always complicated things. They were a distraction. He couldn't afford distractions right now.

"I was hoping you'd help her fit in, Adrianna," he said. "Not catch everyone's attention."

With amber eyes, outlined in dark makeup, Rylee caught his gaze. "I look ridiculous," she said, trying to tame her skirt.

"You look anything but ridiculous," he said. "Distracting is the word I was thinking."

From behind him, Adrianna let out an exaggerated *humph.* "Here, take this," she said. "You'll probably need it more than me." With that, Adrianna slipped down a garter holster from her upper thigh that was somehow hidden beneath her dangerously short skirt and handed it to Rylee.

Rylee took the holster, and drew out a palm-sized silver pistol. She gave Adrianna a questioning glance.

"Hey," Adrianna replied, "I'm not quite as helpless as I may seem. Don't lose it. I'm rather fond of that little gun."

Rylee didn't respond, as she was already engrossed in examining the weapon. She removed a slim magazine from the gun. "A Kimber," she said. "Nineteen-eleven-style. Single-stack .380 auto.

Six rounds, plus one in the chamber. Aluminum frame. Rosewood handle. Integrated laser sight. I prefer a little higher caliber bullet. I'm also not used to an external safety."

"Well, if you don't want it—"

"No, no, I'll take it," Rylee said hurriedly.

Turning away from the peeping eyes of all the males in the room, Rylee strapped the holster onto her leg. When she turned back around, she looked more confident than before. And not a soul could tell that beneath the frilly, delicate fabric of her skirt, a dangerous weapon lay concealed.

"Well, my work here is done," Adrianna said. "I expect you won't let my work go unrewarded, William. You can repay me later." Then she brushed past him, leaving the scent of strawberry sherbet hanging in the air. As she passed Rylee, she whispered in her ear loud enough that Grayson could hear. "Don't let him break your heart, darling. He's good at it."

So saying, Adrianna pulled on her pea coat, and strutted out of the room.

"That girl's crazy," Feng said, when she was fully out of ear-shot.

"I like her," Serghei replied, his tone wistful.

Grayson turned and noticed that Rylee was looking *him* over.

"What?" he asked.

"Are you going looking like that?"

He looked down at himself, felt the overgrown stubble on his face. Even during his usual stints of personal hygiene laziness, he didn't allow his facial hair to get this far out of control. "I see how it is," he replied. "Now, you don't want to be seen with me. All this time, I thought you were above such shallow prejudice."

Grayson bathed, combed his hair, and dressed into the oxblood suit and tie Adriana had brought him. His growing beard stayed. Among all the personal-grooming accouterments that she brought, Adrianna had neglected to bring him a razor. Which might prove a boon, in the end. Perhaps no one would recognize him. Of course, that was wishful thinking. His father, for one, would know the moment he stepped into the building. PNU active or not.

His first brazen signal of his whereabouts Grayson had performed just ten minutes before, when he remotely hailed his car to come to the slums to pick up Rylee and him. No better way than that to say, 'I'm here. Come and get me.' A calculated risk. He hoped it proved worth it.

His black Tesla sat waiting just a few warehouses down from Serghei's place, headlights off. An autonomous vehicle didn't need headlights. And he and Rylee didn't need the attention the lights brought.

The pair climbed into the back of the sedan, and Grayson wordlessly instructed it to take them to his father's building.

Next to him, wrapped in a wool overcoat that left her legs exposed, Rylee sat shivering. Grayson shook his head. Adrianna's fashion always lacked practicality. He instructed the car to turn up the heater.

"Are you clear on the plan?" he said. Of course she was. Her PNU-enhanced memory ensured she wouldn't forget the slightest minutia of the plan. He still liked the verbal confirmation. "Once you're in the labs, I won't be able to contact you without putting both of us in jeopardy."

"I'm clear," she snapped.

Still he persisted in his redundant instruction. If nothing else, it made him feel better. "Remember that the PNUs can only reliably process so much data at once. If you have to fight another Elect, use that knowledge to your advantage. If all his processing power is focused on dodging bullets, for example, he'll be slow to respond to a different kind of attack. Creativity and surprise are your allies. Though, please do use Adrianna's gun as a last resort. I know how you like to—"

"When were you planning on telling me that you were the CA's son?" she blurted out.

The question came out of nowhere. Perfect. Just what he needed right now. He sighed. "What difference does it make who my father is?"

"Well, when he's the most powerful man in the Alliance, and the one responsible for ordering the Deprecations and the ration cuts, it makes a big difference. You've been lying to me this whole time. Your name's not even Grayson."

"Actually, Grayson's my middle name. So, it's not a complete lie. Besides, doesn't this just make it easier for you to hate me more? That's what you want, anyway."

It was not a fair response. She'd acted somewhat civil—for her—the last few days. But he was in no mood to try and seek forgiveness for his deceits.

"If your father's the CA," Rylee went on, apparently not willing to let the argument go, "then couldn't you just get him to release Preston and stop the Deprecations? Or are you too much of a coward?"

Grayson looked away, out the darkened windows of the car. Shame burned within him. *Yes. Yes, I am a coward.* He'd always been one. Not tonight though. He would face his fears. Face his father, or whoever wished him dead.

"I don't always agree with my father," he finally said, softly. "I seldom do, in fact. Coding is the one topic we can share without breaking into a heated debate. The problem is, I suspect my father might be behind the murders. And if that's the case, then he wants me dead, too. So, I guess you have something in common."

"Why would he want you dead?"

Was that concern in her voice? Or just incredulity? He shrugged his shoulders. "That I don't know. I'm still putting all the pieces together. Maybe I'm wrong. Lander's death...there's something screwy going on."

The car pulled to a gentle stop in front of Steele Tower. The lights from the building's lower floors shown out into the night like a beacon. A beacon of death. Grayson shivered.

"Look," he said, "I'm sorry I kept my identity hidden for so long. You haven't exactly made it easy for me to tell you things."

"You do realize, that you just blamed *me* for *your* actions."

"It's a talent I have. Ready to go meet my dad?"

"Only if I get to shoot him in the head."

"Well, before you do," he said, pulling out the can of Mountain Dew, "drink this."

THIRTY

IN ALL HER life, Rylee had never beheld such extravagance. The great room, a hall really, with its sweeping double staircases and marble floors, sparkled with thousands of soft golden lights. From deeper within, music thumped out a mesmerizing beat.

But nothing dazzled as much as the people themselves. Especially the women, whose gowns shimmered and flaunted their figures, just as Adrianna's had. The hairstyles were as varied as the cacophony of colors from the dresses. Wrapped around their heads. Braided in intricate patterns. Piled up, and held together with flowers or feathers. The men too were finely appareled. Though, their appearance was severely muted by the women's.

Rylee felt a surge of insecurity. She did not belong here. This dress she wore did not belong on her body. Even though it covered more than Adrianna's, she still felt naked.

"Stay calm. You look stunning," Grayson whispered in her ear, as he hooked his arm for her to take.

Despite the fact that she was angry at Grayson, his words made her heart momentarily flutter. No, she was just nervous being at the party. She hated Grayson, *so much*. She was doing all of this for Preston and her grandfather.

Taking his arm—only because they needed to look like a couple—she and Grayson weaved their way deeper into the sea of glamorous people.

As they walked, Rylee's feet began to protest. How did women bear to walk in heels? They were torturous. And there was no way she could run in them. What was the point? Despite the pain of them, she managed to walk without making a fool of herself. A trick of the PNU?

Eyes. So many eyes. The eyes followed her and Grayson, turned in their direction, as the couple passed. Several men smiled at her, their eyes furtively taking her in. These smiles weren't friendly smiles. There was something hidden behind the glowing white teeth. Rylee understood well. And coming from Elects, it sickened her. She knew what men like this were capable of—all too well. She'd killed men like this.

Several people called Grayson's name. It wasn't *Grayson*, though. Just as Adrianna, they called him Will. Grayson ignored most of the shouts, and kept moving them deeper in. Rylee felt like she couldn't breathe. So many people. So many smells, lights, and sounds. Notifications bombarded her PNU. Probes of her profile. Images of men she didn't know without their shirts on. And other things she didn't understand. It was maddening.

Don't accept anything. Not even a probe. The words—*thoughts, really*—came into her mind, as though Grayson had spoken to her alone in an empty room. *The last thing we need is for you to be infected with a virus that has you getting friendly with random strangers.*

They walked over to a long wooden table brimming with more food than Rylee had ever seen in her life. The entire slums population could live off of that much food for a month. Most of the food she didn't even have names for. Compared to this, the people in the slums ate like dogs.

One thing was for certain, that table didn't contain anything with peanuts, recalling what Grayson had told her and her grandfather about his own father's peanut allergy. It seemed ironic to her now that the most powerful man in the Alliance was deathly allergic to something so small and innocuous.

Grayson took two fluted glasses filled with a bright blue substance and handed one to her. *Don't drink it*, he spoke into her mind.

If she wasn't supposed to drink it, then why the blazes had he given it to her? She liked to keep her hands free. If she had to draw her pistol quickly, she didn't want a glass of undrinkable blue liquid slowing her down.

She looked at him expectedly, waiting for an explanation about the drink. But he didn't notice. Tension accentuated his jawline, and his eyes were fixed elsewhere. Rylee followed his gaze, but through the crowd she didn't see anything that should merit Grayson's reaction.

"My father doesn't waste time," he muttered aloud. Then he took her hand in his, and communicated through the PNU. *Remember to stick to the plan—whatever happens.*

With a subtle nod, Rylee acknowledged the instruction. She might have said something, but she felt inexplicably frazzled by finding her hand clasped into his. If he had attempted to touch her like that a week ago, she would have kneed him in the groin. Now? His touch felt warm and...*sweaty.* Or maybe that was her hand. Regardless, now her heart was working harder.

Two men in gray suits emerged from the crowd, and planted themselves in front of the pair. They wore impassive expressions, though one of them attempted a smile. These men carried handguns beneath their suit coats. Hip holsters. The minutest bulge of the fabric gave it away. Most people would never give it a passing thought.

"Your father's quite anxious to see you, William," the man with the false smile said. "Allow us to escort you to him."

It was more than evident in the man's tone that this was no request. It was an order. One that these men were prepared to carry out by whatever means they deemed necessary.

"Your friend may come, too," he added, inclining his head toward Rylee.

With a squeeze of her hand, Grayson shouldered his way through the two men, pulling Rylee with him. "No need fellas," he said in a jovial tone that belied the tension streaming from his hand into hers. "We'll find him just fine. You stay here and try some of the punch."

As much as she disliked having her back to the two men, she allowed herself to be led away by Grayson, and managed not to glance back. A man with a gun didn't bother nearly as much as a man at her back with a gun. Within a few feet, however, she and Grayson were engulfed in the sea of revelers, cutting them off from the two men.

Grayson weaved them through the crowd. More shouts and eyes and intrusive PNU notifications assaulted her from everywhere. Rylee's head spun from it all. Soon, they mounted one of the sweeping staircases, which led to the second-floor mezzanine. A furtive glance down into the crowd showed that the two gray-suited men were following. Noting the extra weight and pressure on her upper leg, Rylee again felt relief at having Adrianna's pistol—however small. Maybe she would need fewer rounds now that her brain was PNU-enhanced.

An intimate gathering of partygoers occupied a portion of the mezzanine overlooking the lower floor. Though dressed as finely as anyone at the party, these commanded a more serious air. The women's skirts covered more of their legs. Their necklines left more to the imagination. And overall, between the fabric of their dresses and their comportment, they *sparkled* less. The men, too, bore a certain gravity about them. One, who seemed to grip everyone's attention held up his glass of champagne when he saw Grayson and Rylee approaching.

"There's my son now," the man said. "I told you he wouldn't miss his own father's birthday party."

The CA. Chief Administrator of the Post Desolation Recon-struction Alliance. Despite her loathing for this man, she suddenly found her legs felt like rubber. And it wasn't her shoes. With a quick inhale, she steeled herself and walked forward.

Briefly, she wondered what would happen if she drew out Adrianna's pistol and shot their illustrious leader in the head. She knew precisely what would happen. Those men in the gray suits, they would gun her down before she put her finger on the trigger. Along the periphery of the group, she spotted other men in the gray suits. Bodyguards. No doubt with the most advanced PNU capabilities possible.

The CA broke free from his flock and clapped a hand on Gray-son's shoulder. "I've been waiting for you," he said, smiling. But his words lacked any warmth that one might expect from a father-son reunion. For a moment, he and Grayson had a private conver-sation—or battle—with their eyes. Eventually, the CA's gaze broke off and fell on Rylee. "And who is this beautiful young lady?"

Grayson pulled her closer, wrapping his arm around her waist. "Father, this is Leah."

Rylee forced a smile.

"I don't believe I've had the pleasure of meeting you before," the CA said. "Welcome to my little celebration."

"Thank you," she said, wanting badly to spit in his face.

"Ms. O'Connor was just asking about you, Will," the CA went on more loudly, as he clasped a firm hand on Grayson's shoulder and ushered him closer to the little congregation of followers. "She's been worried that you might have disappeared for good."

Grayson let out a chuckle. "Well, you know me and my work," he said. "Sometimes I get so consumed that I forget to go to the bathroom."

"I can see that you've forgotten to shave, as well," the CA said.

The little group shared a laugh. All but the gray-suited body-guards and that woman...Ms. O'Connor. Her lips were pressed tightly together into a smile that was miles away from reaching her eyes. Rylee recognized that woman. From Workers Square...that day they announced the cut in rations and increase in Deprecation. Oh, if only she could kill the whole lot of them!

An alert within her PNU startled her from her mass murder daydream. Time for her to make her first move. She excused herself from the group, under the pretense of needing to use the lady's room. As she left, Grayson placed a gentle kiss—a believable kiss—on her cheek.

Rylee felt both cheeks burning as she strode away from the group. That kiss had felt so...What did it matter what it felt like? It came from Grayson. It felt like slime on her skin. Slime. Really terrible slime that she wanted to forget immediately.

Focus. She needed to focus.

Her PNU guided her to the women's restroom. It was located down a long carpeted hallway with dark wood paneling and soft lighting. The lavish hallway reminded her of her dress. In both, she felt out of place. Entering the bathroom only served to heighten her sense of not belonging. Never had she been any-where with a *separate* bathroom for both men and women. And as she pushed open the door, heel's clomping loudly on the polished tile floor, she noted that she'd never seen a bathroom like this before. Everything shined, bright and clean. So big, too. Bigger than her entire apartment.

Locking herself into one of the stalls, lest someone come in and wonder what she was doing, she waited. Seven minutes to go.

When those seven minutes expired, she would have precisely sixty seconds—one minute—to exit the bathroom, walk down the hallway, turn down a different hallway, and enter the main doors to the laboratories nestled within the building. In that one-minute window, she would be free from the prying eyes of the CA's security crew. At a specific time, Grayson planned to set off a small device—an EMP bomb. Electromagnetic pulse bomb.

Curse it. Now her PNU was making her remember things she didn't even want to remember. She didn't even know what an electromagnetic pulse was. Only that it messed with electronics and—as it turned out—PNUs.

For one minute, anyone within fifty feet of Grayson would suffer temporary PNU failure. Which meant that the CA's guards, whose augmented vision received live feeds of all the cameras in the building, would not see one of the partygoers in a gold dress stealing into the laboratories.

All Rylee had to do was get through the doors within that minute. After that time, the effects of the EMP would wear off, and the guard's PNUs would resume their normal operation. No problem. She didn't even have to break in. Just like the door to the morgue, the doors to the laboratories would recognize her security certificate and automatically unlock for her.

Two minutes.

Rylee longed to scratch at the back of her hand. Her tattoo lay concealed a layer of Adrianna's makeup, to hide the fact that she was a Norm.

The one part of their plan that they had not fully addressed was what would happen if anyone got suspicious when she didn't return in a reasonable amount of time from the restroom. Grayson suspected—hoped, really—that no one would pay her a second thought. Out of sight, out of mind. Just to be safe, she would need to be quick.

One minute.

Time to move. She flushed the toilet for effect, unlocked the stall door, washed and dried her hands with hand towels that were impossibly soft, then stepped out into the hallway. She stopped in the doorway. Standing on the opposite wall, arms folded, was a man. He wore a shiny gray suit and a leer on his face. Rylee ignored him and turned to stride down the hallway.

"The parties back this way, doll." A rough voice came from behind her. It didn't entirely match the word *slimy* that she'd already associated with him, but it was close enough.

Rylee continued to ignore him, and kept on walking. Time was literally ticking. As much as she would love to introduce this Elect to her new friend hiding under her skirt, she simply didn't have time. Besides, a gunshot would be too loud. Even from a .380.

"I can show you a different party," he said, this time his voice closer. "I promise you'll like it."

Leave me alone! Rylee kept on walking, increasing her stride.

Behind her, she could hear him still pursuing. Suddenly, a hand grabbed her forearm and jerked her backward. She found herself whipping around to face the smiling sleazeball—one of Serghei's words.

"Where are you going?" His breath smelled like one of Adrianna's perfumes. Rylee gagged.

She tried to jerk away, but the man held her with a viselike grip. "Relax. I won't hurt you. Relax."

He reached for her with his other hand. Something pricked her arm. A strange sensation washed over her. Calmness. She relaxed her arm and stopped fighting to free it. Why wasn't she fighting? Why did she feel so calm?

"Good," the man breathed. "See? I am as harmless as a newborn. You can trust me."

He was harmless. Yes, she could see that now. She *could* trust him. Why hadn't she seen that before?

"Come with me," he said gently. "I will take you someplace safe."

He placed one hand on the small of her back, low. She felt herself moving with him, away from where she had been going.

Something was wrong. But everything about how she felt told her everything was right.

No, this couldn't be right. Why was she trusting this man? Yet she couldn't make herself do anything else. So she kept walking, moving farther away from wherever she had been going. And she didn't care.

THIRTY-ONE

"YOU DON'T NEED to worry," the man repeated. Rylee felt herself slipping into deeper relaxation. "Your friends will not be worried about you. No need to tell them where you are."

Friends. *Grayson. The PNU.* Something clicked inside her brain—faint—but she knew what she needed to do.

Focusing all the brainpower she could muster on her current state, she tried to regain control of her PNU. Not complete control. Only enough to shut it off. To deactivate it.

Deactivate. Deactivate. Summoning the thought from deep within the fog of her mind, she struggled to push them to her PNU. *Deactivate.*

Finally, something snapped. A flood of adrenaline consumed her calmness and docility. Not giving the man with his slimy hand on her time to realize what had happened, she lifted her leg and brought it down, stabbing his foot with the heel of her shoe. A trick she'd seen in one of Serghei's movies. He'd be proud.

The man let out an angry cry of pain.

Not allowing him even a second to recover, Rylee followed the heel jab with an elbow to his chin. The contact was solid. A crunch sounded in her ear. A grunt of pain. He staggered backward, and she turned to run. She still had time—though precious little—to make it. She fully remembered her task now.

Strong arms seized her from behind, holding her in a bear hug that forced the air from her lungs.

"I was going to be gentle," the man growled. "But now you force me to be rough."

Rylee threw her head backward, intending to bash his nose or teeth. But her neck only whipped, her head hitting nothing. *Curse these PNUs.* His reflexes were too good. One of his hands moved from her middle to her throat, and started to squeeze. Using her manicured nails as weapons, she clawed at his hands. Still, his grip held firm.

Again, she tried to jab his foot. He easily evaded. It was growing harder for her to breathe. If she didn't do something fast, she would be unconscious, or worse.

Think, Rylee. Think.

The pistol!

If only she could...*there.* She broke her right arm free, and started blindly swiping at his head with it. He dodged without difficulty. But it didn't matter. She merely wanted to distract him. To get him to expend precious PNU processing power on avoiding her harmless blows.

Slowly, carefully, she moved her left hand down, down. For the first time that night, she felt grateful that her skirt was so short. With shaking fingers, she grabbed the pistol from its holster strapped to her thigh and pulled it free. Blackness started to creep into the edges of her vision. She had to do something *now.*

The pistol in her left hand—the wrong hand—she pointed the muzzle at the floor, hoped she didn't hit her own foot, and pulled the trigger. Whether the shot was true or not, she didn't know or care. The earsplitting bang of the gun startled her captor just enough that his grip loosened. Like a feral cat, she ripped herself free of his grasp, whirling around as she moved away. Bringing the gun up as she spun, she fired off two rounds, sweeping from left to right.

The creep managed to dodge the first shots, but the second caught him in the chest. A grunt forced its way from his lips, and he sank to the floor, eyes wide.

Then Rylee turned and ran. Whether the gunshot wound proved fatal, she didn't know. And she wasn't about to waste another bullet. It was enough to stop him. That's all that mattered. Kicking off her accursed shoes, she reactivated her PNU and dashed forward.

Rounding a corner, she entered the hallway that connected to the laboratory. She could only hope that by a profound miracle she still had time, and that no one heard the gunshot. Maybe Grayson's EMP frazzled hearing, as well.

Her PNU vision glowed inside her mind, illuminating the doorway up ahead that she needed to reach. How much time?

Five seconds.

She wasn't going to make it.

Willing her legs to move faster, she ran with every ounce of strength she could summon.

Three seconds.

Come on…

She nearly collided with the door when she finally reached, the door handle jabbing into her side. It didn't matter. Her hand was on the handle. Instantly, the same exchange she experienced at the morgue started. The wordless request for her security certificate. Her relinquish of it. The click of the door as it unlocked.

A push. And she was inside, panting heavily. She checked her time. Three seconds over.

Blast it! Had they seen her through the cameras? That perverted jerk in the hallway…of all the girls to try and ensnare at the party, why did he have to choose her? Now she wished she'd spent another bullet on him. Right where he really deserved it.

She re-holstered Adrianna's pistol. The subcompact semiautomatic had just saved her life. Maybe Adrianna wasn't as bad as she seemed.

Four rounds remained in the gun. Way too few. If the guards had spotted her, and were coming after her, she'd need to make every shot count. What she wouldn't give to have her rifle at that moment. *Curse this dress.* It barely hid her own body. If she could have worn Norm clothing, she would have been better armed. And that creep in the hallway probably wouldn't have tried to…do whatever he was planning.

This was no time for cursing her absurd wardrobe. She needed to act—quickly. She strode deeper into the lab. If the guards came after her, she could claim she panicked, trying to get away from Sleazeball in the hallway. Which was not entirely a lie.

Before her, a white corridor stretched for a good fifty yards. White tile floor. White walls. White ceiling and lights. White. She blinked a few times. Rylee had never seen so much white before. If possible, it was brighter than the bathroom.

Numerous doors lined both walls, at uneven intervals. She stopped at the first on the left, opened it without the need for PNU nonsense, and stepped inside. A large storage closet. She scanned the room quickly, and spotted what she was looking for. A short rack of white lab coats, all neatly hung in a row. Taking one of the coats, she pulled it on over her dress and stepped back into the corridor.

Should she see any other workers in the lab, the white coat was supposed to help her look less conspicuous. Because a girl wearing a lab coat over a party dress, excessive makeup, and no shoes would not look the least out of place. Right. Well, she would just have to hope that everyone else was at the party.

A bank of elevators stood at the end of the corridor. Her destination was on the fifteenth floor. As she made her way toward them, she activated her PNU's probing mechanism. It would alert her of any others around. Grayson had told her this was a normal practice in the labs. Unfortunately, this would also mean anyone else probing the labs would see her. A trade-off. Just like Adrianna's pistol. Sacrifice handling, firepower, and capacity for concealability.

Reaching the elevators, she called it by pressing one of the buttons. Vaguely, she realized this would be her first time riding in an elevator. Probably her last, too.

A ding and a glowing light alerted her that one of the cars had arrived. The left-most elevator doors parted, and she stepped inside and pressed the button for the fifteenth floor. Rylee breathed out, releasing some of the tension in her muscles. Maybe she could do this, after all. Maybe she wouldn't get caught.

As the elevator doors closed, she watched the corridor, eager to see it disappear. Without warning from her PNU, the laboratory doors at the opposite end of the corridor burst open, and several gray-suited bodyguards spilled in.

The elevator doors shut a second later. But not before the gray suits saw her.

Would they know what floor she was going to? They could probe her. That was as good as knowing. Why hadn't the gray suits appear in her probe? Did they have some sort of immunity to it?

Her stomach lurched as the elevator zoomed upwards, and her mind reeled to come up with a plan. How many of the gray suits had she seen? Five. Wow, her memory—even under duress—was amazingly accurate. *Calm. Be Calm.* Immediately, she felt calmer. Maybe too calm. Was her PNU doing this?

A plan. I need a plan.

The elevator stopped moving with a jerk. She looked up. It wasn't on the fifteenth floor. Or any floor, for that matter. She jabbed frantically at the buttons. Nothing worked. Voices reached her from somewhere down below. Muffled men's voices. She couldn't make out what they were saying.

How to get out? If the gray suits had stopped the elevator, could they also recall it? She didn't want to find out.

If there was ever a time for her PNU to come to her rescue, it was now. Nothing came.

She looked up and noticed a recessed square in the ceiling of the elevator car. The escape hatch. Could she escape through that? According to Serghei's movies, it was possible. Of course, according to Serghei's movies people could also fire a .45 pistol with one hand and easily hit someone over forty yards away. Total tripe. Just as shooting that padlock had proven.

Still, she didn't see any other options. The ceiling was just out of reach, if she stretched out her arms and fingertips. Jumping up, she pushed against it with the flats of her hands. The escape hatch jostled slightly, but didn't fly open as she hoped. Was it locked? Again, she tried, this time jumping higher and hitting it harder. Same result. Again. Nothing.

Of course it would be locked. *Curse elevators and the person who invented them.* She should have taken the stairs. Stairs didn't stop letting you go up and down at the whim of gun-toting gray-suited Elects. What next? What good was her blasted PNU if it failed to do anything for her now?

Maybe she could shoot a hole in the ceiling. A stupid idea. Not only did she not have near enough bullets to try it, but she didn't know what the car's exterior was made of. The bullets could ricochet. And bouncing bullets were not cool.

Couldn't *her* PNU control the elevator, too? If she figured out the magic commands, maybe she could override what the gray suits had done.

Focusing her thought on her PNU, she attempted a few commands. *Go up. Up. Tenth floor. Open…*

Abruptly, the elevator dropped downward, sending her stomach colliding with her lungs. She gasped, and held out her hands to steady herself, her reflexes responding with Elect speed. But as quickly as the car dropped, it halted again. Rylee looked around, suspicious. Had she done that?

Then the display over the doors indicated the fifth floor. A ding sounded. Not waiting to see what would happen next, Rylee drew out her pistol, pressed herself into the corner, and aimed at the doors, just as they began to open.

THIRTY-TWO

ONLY FOUR ROUNDS left. Four rounds and at least five grays suits. Perfect. If she managed not to get killed, she planned to let Grayson know how much she hated his plans.

The doors moved like they were being open by slugs. Her PNU-accelerated visual processing, spurred by her surge of adrenaline, made everything appear to move slower than it actually was.

Did a line of gray suits stand waiting for her on the other side of that door? An empty corridor? An unsuspecting lab worker who called the elevator?

Whoever it was, they likely wouldn't expect to find a girl wrapped in a lab coat around a party dress, gun blazing. For that was exactly what she intended. Surprise was her only ally. If it was even possible to surprise an Elect already on alert.

Rylee adjusted her grip on Adrianna's pistol. A smaller gun meant a smaller grip to hold. The doors crept open. A sliver of light divided the reflective steel surface of the doors. Wider. An inch wide.

She still didn't see anything. Nothing that could be a person. Wider.

Still no one.

Wider.

Just open already.

By the time the doors were mostly halfway open, she realized she wasn't going to get an easy shot at anyone. Likely, they waited on the periphery of the doors, out of the line of sight—and gunfire. They would have the advantage of surprise in that case. Unless…

Without giving it a second thought, and as the doors continued to draw apart, she ducked, and charged forward.

Rylee didn't slow down as she crossed the threshold to the

elevator. Or as she turned to the side, pistol raised, and fired. Not pausing to see if the gray suit standing there was hit, she turned a full one hundred and eighty degrees, letting off another round at the gray suit on the other side. That gray suit returned fire almost the same instant, but she dodged—*how* did she dodge? This wasn't possible. What she was doing wasn't possible. How did she move like this?

The other three gray suits...where were they?

Springing toward the gray suit who'd just fired at her, she raised her gun with one hand and fired. But it was only a diversion. At the same instant, she kicked, striking his right knee. With a grunt, the gray suit went down. Then she whipped around and fired off her last round at the other gray suit.

He'd only held off shooting at her for fear of hitting his comrade. More often than not, bullets passed through human bodies without trouble—especially with the wrong kind of ammo.

The gray suit dodged and returned fire. She moved to the right, anticipating the shot, while she kicked at the gun in the fallen gray suit's hand. She needed that gun. Another shot fired at her. Dodged.

She couldn't dodge all day. And the cursed gray suit on the floor wouldn't let go of his blasted gun.

Focused on the gray suit firing at her, she didn't notice the hand until it had already grabbed her ankle. Before she could even attempt to jerk herself free, the gray suit on the floor gave a powerful tug that yanked her legs out from under her. Even as she fell, her PNU took control of her muscles as it calculated her landing. A fall like that ought to have caused her to crash into the polished floor, her shoulder taking the full brunt of the blow. Instead, she rolled out of it, her hand and arm expertly guiding her to a smooth landing, as though it were a maneuver she'd practiced a thousand times before. But the injured gray suit was already prepared for her.

A mace-like fist slammed into her side. Pain rippled through her body. And she doubled over.

No pain. No pain. Ignore it! Desperate, she tried to fight back the pain. She felt like she couldn't breathe. She kicked her leg, hoping to strike the man in the jaw. He caught her foot, and jerked, twisting it into an unnatural angle. Pain exploded from her leg. She cried out, believing her bones would splinter and break at any moment.

Too much! Too much pain. She was useless. She couldn't move. Pain.

From someplace far outside her abyss of agony, she heard voices. Nothing made sense. Then the pain in her leg subsided. Her side still throbbed, but she was free.

Pushing off the floor with a burst of energy, she turned and hunched, ready to fight back. What she saw made her heart freeze.

Preston stood in the middle of the hallway, his eyes wide, a gray suit behind him, the blade of a dagger resting beneath Preston's chin.

"That's enough, Miss Day. I don't want to have to bring harm to your friend."

Rylee shifted her eyes, scanning the scene. The other three gray suits were now present. And Grayson. And the CA. He was the one who'd spoken. He stood, looking at her with a placid expression on his face, his hands clasped behind his back. Despite the CA's imposing posture, and the guns trained on her, her eyes locked back onto Preston.

Still alive. Relief flooded her. But what was he doing here? What was the CA doing with him? And why had the CA called her by her last name, her real last name?

She lowered Adrianna's gun, activated its thumb safety—even though it was empty—and dropped it to the floor. She wouldn't fight anymore, not while they held Preston like that.

"I appreciate your cooperation," the CA said. "Now, you'll come with me up to my office for a little chat. I assure you, Mr. Hyde will be well taken care of."

The gray suits ushered her into an elevator car. Rylee felt a surge of panic at being separated from Preston so soon. She tried to say something, but the grey suits moved her too quickly. In a flash, Preston was gone.

Rylee's mind was so frazzled by the turn of events, that she was only vaguely aware when the elevators stopped, and the gray suits forced her out of the car. And not until they exited did she notice Grayson was also being led. The gray suits took them into a room that seemed as expansive as Duncan's Warehouse.

"Have a seat, please," The CA said, gesturing to some padded chairs in front of a desk. Rylee glanced at the chairs. They were chairs that didn't have holes in their upholstery, or boast hideous, faded colors.

Neither she nor Grayson sat.

"Let Rylee go, father," Grayson demanded. "She hasn't done anything wrong."

"There's a body with a bullet hole in its chest that would indicate otherwise," the CA replied calmly.

"He attacked me," Rylee said, finally breaking out of her stupor.

"I don't doubt it," the CA replied. "William will go and explain your story to Chief O'Connor, who is more than anxious to know your whereabouts right now. He's not needed in our little discussion, anyway."

"What's this all about?" Grayson said.

"I have a few questions for Miss Day," the CA replied. "Nothing you need to concern yourself with."

"Malarkey!" Grayson snorted. "What's really going on?"

"That's my business, son. Now go and tell Chief O'Connor that Miss Day will be down shortly. We need to treat any injuries she suffered during her attack."

"I'm no fool, father. I know you're involved in the murders—somehow."

The CA didn't even flinch at the accusation, but only raised his eyebrows. "That's immensely clever of you," he said, his tone mocking. "But you're powerless to either prove it, or do anything to stop me. Now go."

Grayson's nostrils flared as he silently considered his father. Then he turned, casting Rylee a furtive glance, and walked out.

"Sit," the CA commanded, once Grayson was gone.

Rylee obeyed. She was glad to sit. What had just happened? Grayson outright accused his father of being involved in the murders, and his father didn't deny it?

The CA sat down on the front of his desk, unbuttoning the top two buttons of his suit coat. He neither smiled nor scowled. Yet his look made Rylee shiver inside. "I'm not one for drama, so I won't hold you in suspense," he said. "I have an important job for you."

He paused. So much for nixing the drama.

"I need you," he finally said, "to kill my son, William."

What! Rylee inhaled as though that gray suit had punched her squarely in the gut again. Kill Grayson? His own son?

"Why?" was all she could stammer out.

"That's my own affair. However, as soon as you kill William, I will exonerate Preston Hyde for any involvement in the killing of Michael Pike, and I will ensure your grandfather is removed from the Deprecation list. Permanently."

Permanently remove her grandfather from the Deprecation list? And let Preston go free? How could she hope for anything more. Except...

"How do I know you'll keep your word?" she said.

"You don't," he said, and then leaned in menacingly. "But, if you don't, I can guarantee neither one will make it through the end of the week."

The CA stared at her, and Rylee stared straight back. She knew he spoke the truth. His cold, hard eyes told her that he wouldn't hesitate for a moment. This was a man who was willing to kill his own son. She looked away.

"What will happen to me?" she whispered, not really wanting to know.

"Miss Day, you can't possibly be hoping for salvation now. You're much too deep in."

Involuntarily, Rylee shuddered. It was all too clear to her. The CA planned to frame her for the murders, or at least as an accomplice. A scapegoat. And, unless she was willing to let her grandfather and Preston face Deprecation, there was absolutely nothing she could do to about it.

"I'm giving you forty-eight hours, Miss Day," the CA said, leaving his perch on the front of his desk and strolling around to sit in his own chair. "If it eases your own conscience about killing my son, you should know that he's not without his own level of culpability in the murders. In fact, he played a rather vital role. It's unfortunate that he must die, but it's the way things are. I've finally come to peace with the decision, I'm sure you can too. Now," he added, standing again, "if you don't mind, the Chief of Regulation is downstairs waiting for you." He held out his hand for her to accompany him out of the office.

THIRTY-THREE

GRAYSON NOW KNEW his father was behind the string of murders among the Enhanced. He knew it. Those dead included Grayson's best friend, Lander. The thought made him squeeze his hands into fists. Even though he wasn't a fighter—not like that, anyway. He would fight back, in his own way. Bring down his father.

The fact that he was still alive baffled him. Sure, he'd been hiding until tonight. But his father had just held him in his control and let him go. Well, technically he wasn't free. Not so long as he remained in his father's building. As he considered it, though, he knew his father wouldn't do anything to him now. Nothing that would bring suspicion to the illustrious Chief Administrator's head.

No, his father would devise some other means. If he hoped to stay alive, he'd have to figure out by what means. And soon.

That was something he couldn't worry about right now. He still needed to know how his father was getting away with the murders. Lander's work. If only he could get to Lander's office...

Only one problem with that plan. Miles. One of his father's bodyguards. Of course, his father hadn't trusted Grayson to return to the main floors and talk with Chief O'Connor on his own. That's why he ordered Miles to escort him.

Fighting or outrunning Miles were absurd ideas. How Rylee had fared so well against two of his father's men still amazed him.

"I need to stop by my apartment," Grayson said, intentionally not making it sound as though he were asking for permission. "It will only take a minute."

"That's not what your father instructed," Miles replied.

"Yeah, well, since when have I followed my father's instructions?" They stepped into the elevator and Grayson pressed the button for the sixty-fifth floor. "Don't worry, I won't snitch."

Beside him, Miles frowned and let out a little growl of annoyance. But the man didn't argue further. There were some perks to being the CA's son.

The elevator opened, and they stepped out into Grayson's apartment. A wave of remorse and longing washed over Grayson as he strode in. Though less than two weeks had passed since he'd run away, it felt as if he'd been gone for a year. He ached to go indulge in a long, steamy shower, then collapse onto the sofa and fall asleep. For a few moments, he might have been able to pretend that everything in his life wasn't garbled beyond recognition.

Things wouldn't ever be back to normal. Not now. Not with Lander gone. Never again would he walk into this room and catch Lander lost in his infamous virtual conquests. Never again.

Grayson shook his head, pushing away these thoughts. He wasn't here to reminisce, or even to take a shower.

"I just need to grab a few items," he said, walking over to the kitchen.

"Like another one of your EMPs?" Miles replied, falling in behind him. "I'm not letting you out of my sight, Steele."

"Does that mean you're going to follow me into the bathroom? Is my dad paying you enough for that?"

Miles grunted.

Grayson wasn't entirely sure his father *earned* such loyalty from Miles and the other bodyguards, or if it was the result of PNU preconditioning. Brainwashing.

Walking over to his dresser, he opened up one of the drawers, and started rummaging around. Out the corner of his eyes, he saw Miles tense. "Relax," he said, as he pulled out a few pairs of boxer shorts. "You won't believe how badly I need a fresh pair of underwear." He shook his head as he screwed up his face in disgust. "I'm actually going commando right now. That's how bad it got." Though he did—desperately—need clean undergarments, he mainly hoped this diversion would put Miles off his guard a little.

"I don't want to hear about your hygiene problems," Mile said. "If you're finished, let's go."

"Just need to stop at the throne. Coming?"

"I'll wait outside the door," Miles grumbled.

Grayson tsked. "My father would be so disappointed in your lack of commitment."

Once inside the bathroom, Grayson locked the door and focused his PNU. He'd spent a considerable amount of energy just keeping his nerves under control at the party, and trying to protect Rylee without drawing suspicion. A failed effort. The EMP did its job well, but it instantly put his father's men on alert once the effects wore off.

If only he could have used his RARA virus to ease them out of it...But there was no way he could override that many PNUs simultaneously. His brain would have overheated in a matter of moments. That is, if his PNU didn't run out of power first. No, it was best done targeting one or two others. His PNU could handle the extra load of just one target. One target was simple. A target like Miles.

When Grayson opened the bathroom door and walked out, Miles didn't say anything. Miles didn't follow him. Not even when Grayson pushed the button of the elevator, and stepped inside. And he wasn't going to. Because Miles didn't see Grayson leave. He only saw a closed bathroom door, from which the occasional grunting noise emanated.

* * *

Rylee didn't know what to think, what to feel. Had the CA of the Alliance really just blackmailed her into murdering his own son? Was Grayson truly guilty of involvement in the murders? If so, he deserved to die. They *all* deserved to die. Every last Elect. Just as she'd always believed. Why had she trusted Grayson?

Chief O'Connor pounced as soon as they emerged from the labs. The CA fended her off.

"Let the poor girl be, Miss O'Connor," he said, putting his arm around Rylee's shoulder and moving her through the press of Regulators. "You can interrogate her another time. She's had a very traumatic night. And I take full responsibility. For it was at my own party."

O'Connor did not give up so easily, though. "Need I remind you that there is a dead body in your hallway? This is a homicide. And it is my duty to investigate it."

The CA turned and pointed his finger at O'Connor. "There's nothing here to investigate. A young lady was attacked by some sicko. And she defended herself. We should all be grateful she was prepared for it."

"With all due respect, sir, it is my job to determine whether or not this was a simple matter of self-defense."

"No, Miss O'Connor, your job is to ensure the people are safe. Safe from the individual responsible for murdering my people. And so far you're doing a pathetic job of it. Now, let the girl go. You're just embarrassing yourself."

Chief O'Connor stared back at him, her eyes narrowed disdainfully. But she didn't reply. Lifting her chin sharply, she turned and retreated.

Rylee was relieved to see the woman leave. Though, why that was, she didn't know. The CA was the one to fear. *He* was the monster killing off his own citizens. To O'Connor's face, he'd accused her of failing to find the murderer. If she only knew that he was standing right in front of her...

Grayson was nowhere to be seen. No surprise there. It figured that he'd abandon her now. Truth be told, she didn't want to see him. She still didn't know what she thought about him. Other than the fact that she hated him. Better to not think anything. Not *feel* anything. It would make killing him less painful.

Partygoers gaped at her as she and the CA descended the stairs and retrieved Rylee's coat. For the first time that night, she wondered how she looked. With a discreet glance, she noted that her dress—Adrianna's dress—was torn. The pretty Elect would be upset for certain. Rylee didn't care. Let Adrianna be livid with her. Let the whole world be livid with her. It didn't matter. Nothing could make things worse than they already were. So, let everyone gawk.

The CA helped her into her coat.

She let him. She shouldn't let him. She should break each of the five fingers touching her. She should denounce the CA in front of all these people. She knew it would be useless. Knew that whatever she said, he'd find a way to discredit it. He was the CA. He controlled the Alliance. Just like he controlled O'Connor. Just like he was controlling her now.

A black car pulled up in front of the building and the CA helped her into the back. "See that you get plenty of rest," he said, his voice sounding incredibly sincere. "And please let me know if there's anything further I can do for you. Rest assured, Chief O'Connor shall not molest you further." And with that, he smiled a smile so warm that it gave Rylee the chills. Then he closed the door, and the driverless car drove away.

Rylee sat back in the plush seat. The cool leather felt soothing on her overheated skin. Her mind felt fatigued, overworked from the events of the night. She needed another of Serghei's Mountain Dews.

Through her PNU, the car requested a destination. *Home*. She wanted to go home. She wanted to forget this night had ever happened. She wanted to eat cold beans and listen to her grandfather give meaningless prayers and shiver herself to sleep on her cold cot.

She gave the location of her housing unit to the car. In response, it turned to the right, heading in the direction of the slums.

Closing her eyes, Rylee attempted to shut out the cruel world she saw outside the car's windows. Her PNU did not comply. It allowed her to recall everything with sickening clarity. Did the PNU have the ability to make her forget everything?

Without warning, the car screeched to a stop. Rylee leaned forward sharply, pulled by the force of her momentum. She quickly glanced around for the cause of the sudden stop. Ahead, cast in the white glow of the car's headlights stood Grayson.

THIRTY-FOUR

CARMINE CHAFED WITH each step she took, as if Mr. Steele's words had transformed her satin dress into sandpaper. She'd had enough of his condescending treatment, his outright scorn of her handling of the investigation. She refused to cow to him any longer.

Something about that girl…the circumstances of the attack, and—most of all—Steele's emphatic defense of her was not right. Why hadn't he allowed her to ask a few simple questions? At the very least, she would have liked the girl's PNU profile. As it was, she didn't even know the girl's last name. Leah, was what William Steele had called the girl. The only records returned from her database search of Enhanced citizens with that first name returned a girl a few weeks shy of being Enhanced.

This could not be the same. For the girl tonight—Leah—was clearly Enhanced. Had the name been an alias? A moniker? If so, who was she really? A girl who knew how to use a handgun, that was for certain.

Mr. Steele had told Carmine to leave the girl alone. No, he did more than that. He tried to manipulate her—bully her—into dropping her interest in the girl. Could it be that he was hiding something? Forcing her off the trail of a potentially important lead, by humiliating her in front of her officers? Perhaps. The idea felt too conspiratorial. She saw no clear connection between what had occurred tonight and the murders she was investigating.

It could be an utter waste of time. At this point though, if it defied Steele, she would gladly take that risk.

Below her, the party throbbed like a living creature, mostly oblivious to the drama that had unfolded a short while before. Mounting the stairs that led to the main floor of Steele Tower, she sent a message to one of her commanders. *Follow the girl.*

Rylee wondered if her car would obey her if she ordered it to run over Grayson. She didn't do it. Before she knew it, Grayson was climbing into the back seat of the car. He sat down next to her, and the car rolled onward.

"Well, that didn't go quite as smooth as I planned," Grayson said. He let out a half-hearted chuckle.

Rylee just looked out the windows, feeling her anger rising just to hear his voice. That voice which had lied to her. Were there more lies waiting to spew out of his mouth? Technically, he hadn't *said* any lies. She understood that. They were all unspoken lies.

A sin of omission is no better than a sin of commission. A lesson her grandfather often liked to refresh her on.

"Solely out of curiosity," he said, "what exactly happened with that Elect? You know, the one you shot in the chest? We all heard the gunshots."

"You tell *me* what happened," she bit back. "Some slime-ball pokes my arm with something, and suddenly he's luring me away like I'm his personal slave."

"Ah, I see now. He gave you a nanotronic sedative—of sorts. He couldn't control you, exactly. Just render you more...compliant." He sighed heavily. "I'm really sorry about that. I didn't...I can't tell you how worried I was when I heard that gunshot."

"Thanks so much for your concern. Don't worry, I kept to your stupid plan, despite that creep. Little good that it did."

"I didn't mean..." he trailed off, pausing. When he spoke again, his tone was colder. "So, did my father turn you against me so easily, then? I'm very aware of how persuasive—even manipulative—my father can be. He always sprinkles some truth with his lies. It can be difficult to tease the two apart."

"A trait you seem to have inherited," she snapped, still not looking at him. If only she had a loaded gun right now, she'd be sorely tempted to do exactly what the CA asked of her. Unfortunately, though the gray suits had returned Adrianna's gun to her, she didn't have any more ammunition. Adrianna really needed another thigh holster to carry an extra magazine or two.

"That's a fair accusation," he said. "I deserve that, and worse. At least give me a chance to defend myself. I think I at least deserve that."

"You deserve a bullet to the head. You and every other Elect. Maybe not Adrianna. But only because she gave me her pistol."

"Good," he said. "I'm glad we're back to how things used to be between us. It was starting to get awkward not having you threaten my life all the time."

"Keep being a jerk," she said. "It will make things less complicated for me."

Outside the car, the lights of the Elect sector vanished as the car crossed the threshold into the slums, plunging them into darkness. To keep anyone from seeing the car, she ordered it to turn off its headlights, making the darkness complete.

"Hey," Grayson replied, "I'm just doing what apparently I'm best at. By the way, you did look stunning tonight. I'm trying to make up my mind about whether it will be nicer or worse to die at the hand of a pretty girl. At the moment, I'm leaning toward better. That way, the last thing I see in this life wouldn't be some ugly dude's face."

Rylee's heart stuttered. Did he know what his father wanted her to do? How could he? He wasn't there. Perhaps he'd figured it out on his own. The CA was Grayson's father, after all. Twisted brains thought alike. But if he knew that, why wasn't he running? If he thought that she wouldn't do it…

"Your silence is not very reassuring," Grayson said, after a few moments.

She didn't reply. What should she say? Her thoughts and emotions were in a fierce battle—and she had no idea which side was winning.

"I know I don't deserve it," he went on. "But would you at least tell me what my father said, so that I can have a chance to defend myself? I can probably guess at it, but I'd rather hear his side first."

There was a pause. Rylee deliberated. She knew she shouldn't say anything. If Grayson managed to shatter her current impression of him, it would make it all the more difficult for her to save Preston. Almost against her will, though, she found herself speaking. "He said you developed the virus that's been killing the Elects. Is that true?"

"Unfortunately, I believe it is. In part, anyway. I was a...somewhat innocent player in my father's scheme."

"Somewhat?"

He let out an audible sigh. "For some time, Lander and I have done special coding projects for my father. My father doesn't ever tell us what a particular piece of code is for. But usually, I figure it out. Sometimes, like this time, it's after the fact. However, it's never been anything so serious. I expected it to be the usual fare: blackmailing an Advisory Board member, spying on a potential threat, doing cover-up—nothing I'm proud of. If there's anything I've learned from my father, it's that running the Alliance is a messy business. But I swear, I had no idea my father would use my work the way he did—to murder."

"You created a virus capable of killing other Elects for your father and you didn't think he'd use it to kill?" It was an absurd idea. If Grayson knew his father so well, he'd know what his father was planning.

"That's just it. He couldn't use the virus I created to kill someone. Not without immediately revealing that a virus was used. It would have been too risky for him to try it just using my code."

"So, now you're saying that you didn't write the virus?"

"Confusing, I know. And I was confused until just a few moments ago. I managed to sneak into Lander's lab and access his hidden files. I haven't fully inspected Lander's code, but I think I have enough to know what happened. You see, my father is paranoid. Always has been. If you put all your data in one location, it can all be lost...or found, in this case.

"There are two parts—three really—to the virus that's behind the murders. At any rate, that's my theory. Apart, they are relatively innocuous. But most of all, wouldn't draw suspicion. My part of the virus, you already know about. I've just discovered what Lander's part was. It was actually an extension of work one of the engineering teams has been working on for some time.

They've really been pioneering into a new frontier of PNU engineering.

"I'll spare you the details. Suffice it to say, it deals with controlling the involuntary functions of the body. Heart rate, for example."

"So, the virus can...speed up someone's heart?" Rylee asked, failing to grasp the import of this discovery.

"Or slow it down. Slow it down so much that it stops."

Rylee felt the impact of those words, like they had stopped her own heart. It took her a moment to realize that the car had also stopped. Through the dark tinted windows, she peered out. Faintly, she made out the outlines of familiar buildings. They were in front of her housing unit. Home. She longed for it.

"Why does your father want you dead?" She knew she was better off without an answer to that question, but she wanted to know. What drove a father to want his own son dead?

A bitter-sounding laugh came from Grayson. "What, you find it difficult to believe that someone other than you wants to kill me? I think that's the first compliment I've received from you."

"Can you just be serious, for once?" Rylee said. "I'm in no mood for your humor."

"Right, attempting not to be a jerk. Well, he wants me dead for the same reason he wanted Lander dead. Too much liability. If one of us squealed, that would be very bad for my father. Not to mention, killing me would help alleviate any suspicion that he was the culprit. Because, what kind of father could wantonly kill his own son, right?"

"I don't buy it," she said. "Your father wouldn't kill you just so no one would suspect him of the killings. There's got to be some other reason."

"That, and I'm excessively annoying, as you already—" He paused. "Right," he went on. "I'm being serious." He let out a sigh. "My relationship with my father was never great. I think it has something to do with my mother's death."

"Your mother?"

"Most people have them, you know. Well, mine happened to die giving birth to me. It was before Desolation, when there were good hospitals with advanced medical technology. At a time when, at least here, dying through childbirth was extremely rare. But it happened to my mother. Secretly, I believe my father's always blamed me for her death. If he had had a choice, I know he would have chosen her over me.

"My father's always like being in control of things. In control of his company back before Desolation. In control of the people around him. In control of the Alliance. I broke his control of things."

The story left her a bit unsettled. If all Grayson told her was true, then she actually felt sorry for him.

What if Grayson was lying?

"I have to think about this," she said after several moments of silence. She opened the car door to leave.

"I'm not sleeping on your kitchen floor tonight, then?"

"No," she replied, then shut the door and strode away from the car.

The frosty night air blasted her as she left the car's cozy interior. She still wore Adrianna's dress *and* the accursed shoes. In all the madness, the shoes had been returned to her. She didn't remember when that happened, or who brought them. Awkwardly, she ascended the metal fire escape and climbed in through her window.

Her grandfather was long asleep. Not bothering to remove the frilly dress, she threw herself onto her cot and tried to find sleep. All she found were questions swirling in her brain. Around and around they went until she felt dizzy from it. *Preston or Grayson? Preston or Grayson?*

More than the question themselves, it troubled her that she had to ask the question.

THIRTY-FIVE

RYLEE'S FIRST SURPRISE was that she woke up. That implied she'd actually slept during the night. Though, by how tired she felt, it was likely little more than a few hours—if that. A pounding headache urged her to shut her eyes and go back to sleep. But a pounding at her door refused to let her. Where was that pounding coming from? She wished it would stop. Then there was a voice. She barely registered the words. But the voice…

Her grandfather!

The realization jolted her out of her sleepiness as though she'd been electrocuted with a hundred and twenty volts. He would barge in if she didn't come out soon. Come in and see her still wearing Adrianna's dress. On top of all else, that was the last thing she needed.

Hurriedly, she shimmied out of the sparkly gold and white lace and satin, and pulled on her spare clothing, trying to think of a good reason why she was wearing them—again.

Stashing the dress under her blanket, she opened her bedroom door. Her grandfather's gray eyes met her as she entered the kitchen. They immediately took her in. The subtle furrow of his brow told her he noticed something out of place. Her mind raced. Was it just her clothes? Had she forgotten to take something off? Put something on? She looked down, attempting to appear casual, unconcerned. Relieved, she saw that she had pants on.

And then she remembered. The makeup. She hadn't bothered to wipe away the dark stuff around her eyes, nor the glossy gold on her lips.

"You smell like a bowl of overripe fruit," her grandfather said, turning his attention back to his breakfast.

Argh! She'd forgotten about the perfume, too. What would she have done about it anyway? Jump in one of the dumpster bins outside? Borrow one of Serghei's rat-smelling sweatshirts?

"Um...Serghei gave me some new soap he found during one of his scavenging runs," she said, lying. Her stomach twisted up inside. "I guess it does smell a bit different."

Her grandfather looked up from his breakfast, just long enough to fix her with a scowl. "I'm no fool, Rylee Day. And I don't appreciate you lying to me either. Now, sit and eat your breakfast."

"Just let me run to the bathroom," she said, turning to leave.

"Fine," he replied. "But don't waste time rubbing that mascara from your eyes. I've already seen it. When you're finished, you can come tell me what's going on."

Though she inspected her facial appearance in the cloudy and cracked mirror above the sink in the bathroom, she didn't scrub the makeup from her face. Why bother? Her grandfather had already seen it. And what would be the point of hiding it from anyone in the slums? Sure they would wonder if Rylee was exchanging her body for extra rations. Let them wonder. It was not as if protecting her reputation could save her from the CA.

She was on the brink of tears when she returned to the breakfast table. Her grandfather looked as calm as a windless morning. He continued to eat.

"You're in trouble," he said, between bites. It wasn't a question. Did he suspect the same thing the people of the slums would assume?

She didn't respond. Nothing she said would matter. It couldn't fix her problems. *He* couldn't fix her problems. Not like he'd been able to do when she was just a little girl. He could fix a scraped knee or a blistered hand. Remove splinters. Build furniture out of garbage. Fix her Harley. Repair the safety on her rifle. Even cut hair—sort of. This was a problem, though, he couldn't fix or mend or repair.

"Well, whatever your problem is," her grandfather said when he realized she wasn't going to talk, "starving yourself is not the answer."

Picking up her fork, Rylee poked at the pile of reconstituted potato flakes on her plate. Her brain told her she ought to be hungry. Ravenous. Her stomach disagreed. Still, she took a bite to appease her grandfather.

"You don't have to tell me what's going on," he said after a few moments. "Heaven knows I've never been one to be open with my feelings, either. But I want you to know that if I can help you, I'll do whatever I can."

Despite herself, Rylee let out a bitter laugh. "There's nothing you can do. Nothing anyone can do."

"That may be true. But there is one who can help, who does understand." He slid something across the table, closer to her. She didn't have to look up to know what it was.

A sigh escaped her lips. "Even if there was a God, I think he must have forgotten about us a long time ago." The last thing she wanted to talk about was her grandfather's wacky notions about faith. Nonsense—all of it.

"Maybe it's the other way around."

"You haven't forgotten and he hasn't done any so-called miracles for you. What's the point?" Why was she even arguing about this? The time she had with her grandfather was limited and precious. She didn't want to waste it debating about the existence of God.

"Miracles don't have to be grand or spectacular to be real."

"I'd like the miracle of having the CA choke on his own tie," she muttered.

"And you think that would fix everything?"

She shrugged. "It would be a good start."

"Maybe. But it might not solve as many problems as you think."

"What's that supposed to mean?"

"It means things could be a lot worse. We have food to eat, a place to sleep, and work to keep our minds busy. That's more than anyone can hope for in times like these."

Rylee scooped another bite of the potatoes and shoved them in her mouth, casting her grandfather a dubious look. "Are you kidding me? You think what the CA has done is good? A few days ago, you were inches away from being Deprecated—just because you were *too old*. Not to mention that while *we* live in squalor, the

Elect go to parties, dine on three-course meals, and can literally get away with murder. So, I fail to see how the CA's death could not be the best thing that ever happened."

Her voice had risen to a near shout, so that when she stopped, a heavy silence hung between them. When her grandfather finally replied his voice was calm.

"I'm not saying there's not injustice. There's always been injustice of one form or another. I do miss the old days, when we had more freedom. I miss fly fishing on the Skykomish River for salmon in late summer, and eating barbeque. I actually miss mowing my lawn—though I always complained about it."

He sighed, shaking his head. "Now you've got me all nostalgic. Look, some men, unless compelled, won't lift a finger to work for themselves or their family. There can't be any tolerance for that. Not with how fragile our existence is now. Order. That's one thing I agree with the CA on—"

"What! You *agree* with the CA?"

"Now, calm down. I do think his punishments are far too harsh. There ought to be exceptions made for the aged and infirm. But, look, what if something did happen to the CA, who would take his place? Would the new leader be better? And what if the entire Alliance collapsed because the people rose up and rebelled? Would the scavenging routes keep running? Would the fields continue to get tended? How long before we ran out of food?"

"So, you're saying that what the CA's done is good?" Rylee couldn't believe the words that were coming out of her own grandfather's mouth. How could he say such things about that awful monster?

"I'm saying, we should be grateful for what we have now. I don't like the CA. I'd punch him in the face, if I had the chance. But if something happened to him, I don't know what would come of it—except for chaos." Then he looked at her intensely. "If you're going to fight, though, Rylee Lorraine Day, then you need to know what you're fighting *for* and not just what you're fighting against. And I'm not going to tell you not to fight, because that would be like me telling the wind not to blow."

There was a pause, and Rylee considered her grandfather's

words. She was having trouble making sense of it all. Did he somehow know her plight? Did he want her to fight?

Her grandfather pushed out his chair from the table and stood, taking his empty plate. "It's time for work."

Just like that, their moment was over. It was back to business. Back to life. Back to the mundane. Back to the forced servitude. Work or be Deprecated.

As he always did, her grandfather pulled out his Bible and read a verse, then offered a prayer. Rylee usually ignored the prayers. Today, she listened. Not because she believed, but because she loved her grandfather. And this could be the last time she ever would hear him pray. He prayed for her. He petitioned his god to give her peace and an answer to her problems. By the end, Rylee was fighting back tears.

After he was finished, her grandfather rose from the table, kissed her on the top of her head, and left for work.

A part of her didn't want him to go, wanted to tell him everything. Force him to make the decision for her. To force him to fix this.

She shook her head. No. That would never do.

The message that pushed itself into her thoughts made her jerk her head up. She still wasn't used to communicating via her PNU. Not that she wanted to get used to it. At times it was downright disturbing, like having someone implant thoughts into her brain. She knew who the message was from before she accepted it.

Rylee: Serghei, Feng, and I have a plan. Will you come to Serghei's place?

Grayson. Her heart and her mind were still at war over him. Frankly, she didn't know what to think or believe. Part of her didn't know if she could face him again already. Part of her didn't know if she could stay away. If she stayed away she didn't have to worry about killing him. If there was no opportunity, it wouldn't matter what she decided. Then again, now her curiosity was fully piqued. What kind of plan could Feng possibly have agreed to that involved collaboration with Grayson?

The sound of the apartment door closing as her grandfather departed snapped her attention back to the real world. For a few moments, she stared at the door, contemplating.

Work. Why go to work? It's not like it would keep her from Deprecation. It was time for action—whatever action that was. And she might as well start with hearing Grayson's plan. Before she left, she grabbed her rifle and her Glock.

THIRTY-SIX

CARMINE HAD REQUESTED an hourly report from Commander Harris concerning the activity of Leah—young Steele's date from last night's party. In blatant disobedience to Mr. Steele's request, she ordered Commander Harris to follow the girl as she left the party in one of the CA's own vehicles. That order had already borne fruit. And it gave Carmine intense satisfaction.

According to the report, the vehicle picked up William Steele shortly after leaving Steele Tower, then proceeded on to the Slum district. There, the girl exited the car and entered into one of the housing units through a window. William Steele did not get out of the car, which drove off heading toward a different portion of the slums.

Carmine reproved herself for lacking the foresight to send out two officers originally. Commander Harris could have sent the other officer to follow the car after the girl exited. The commander did call in one of his patrol officers to locate the vehicle. But William Steele had thus far managed to elude them.

A minor setback. They would find him yet. As long as they continued to follow the girl, Steele would eventually pop back up. Carmine didn't have any doubts about that.

Thus far, the girl had not left the housing unit. During the night, three other officers joined Commander Harris. Together, they staked out the girl's housing unit. Unless the building possessed a secret tunnel out of it, the girl was still inside. Which likely could only mean one thing: the girl lived there. But an Enhanced living in the slums? It didn't make any sense. It was possible the girl was merely hiding there. Hiding from what, though?

The housing records indicated that the particular apartment the girl was seen climbing into was assigned to one Kenneth Jones and his granddaughter, Rylee Lorraine Day. Unfortunately, the Alliance didn't keep visual records for the Unenhanced. Carmine wanted a photo of that granddaughter.

Carmine sat up straighter and breathed in deeply, forcing herself to remain calm. Patience would be her ally. But it was difficult to remain patient when a flood of suspicious evidence linked to the CA was flooding in. Evidence she fully intended to use against Nathaniel Steele. Make him pay for his insults.

She took another breath.

Not yet. They had not found anything condemning...yet. It would come, though. She felt it.

Though there was little information about this grandfather and his granddaughter, one of the investigators had noticed that the grandfather should have been Deprecated during the last round of Deprecations. A mere oversight, or something more? Their records indicated that he was indeed on the list.

Something was definitely going on there. And she would get to the bottom of it.

A smile touched her lips. Now, she would prove her worth.

Only one thing troubled her about the girl from the party. The CA went out of his way to keep Carmine from doing her job, demanding she leave the girl alone. It was almost as if he were goading her. Did he actually want her to follow the girl? If so, why?

A PNU notification interrupted her thoughts. It was from Commander Harris. Another report. It came in without her explicit acceptance of the communication, as she'd previously granted his messages priority access.

Commander Harris reporting. The target has been spotted leaving the housing unit. She is dressed...shabbily. Transmitting live visual.

Carmine's vision flashed as she instantly saw what Commander Harris was seeing. One of the nondescript housing unit buildings, with its brick exterior, square shape, and boarded windows. Out of the front door, strode a girl. She wore a faded green sweatshirt that looked a few sizes too big. Carmine couldn't help but gag at the color. The girl's short chocolate brown hair, had obviously not been brushed that morning. But her untidy appearance could not mask the fact that this was William Steele's date from the party.

If only...Carmine's gaze followed the length of the girl's right arm, from her shoulder to her hand. Was it there? The girl's hand was angled just slightly away from Harris's line of sight.

Commander: can you get a clear visual of the back of her right hand? She communicated back to Commander Harris using their PNU link.

I'll try, came his reply.

Carmine's own view of the hand zoomed in suddenly, the vignetted corners of her vision indicating that the commander was now looking through a pair of binoculars. Still, the girl's hand was angled away from the commander's line of sight. It looked like there could be something there. Suddenly, the girl entered an alleyway, turning her back to the commander.

Carmine let out a curse under her breath. Only by exerting a high level of self-control did she restrain herself from ordering Commander Harris from nabbing the girl right then and there. An order which might spoil everything. Patience.

Switching visuals to McCormack, came the commander's message.

Carmine's view of the girl flickered and changed. It took her a second to register what had happened. She was now looking at the girl from the front, walking toward her, deeper into the alley. Again the vignette of her vision indicated the magnified view of binoculars. Carmine didn't know where McCormack was located, but it had to be far enough away not to draw the girl's suspicion.

Wherever it was, the location was perfect. Carmine fixed her attention on the back of the hand. Yes, there was definitely something there. Still, she wanted a clearer view.

As if in answer to the request, the girl reached over her left hand and scratched the back of the right, turning it just enough so that Carmine could clearly see it. There, on the girl's pale skin were the dark lines of a tattooed barcode.

So, William Steele's girlfriend really did live in the slums. Carmine froze the image of the barcode, used her PNU to scan it, and retrieved the associated records. An instant later, the scan and retrieval completed.

Name: Rylee Lorraine Day.

Carmine smiled.

Follow her, she ordered, then severed the communication link.

THIRTY-SEVEN

RYLEE LISTENED THROUGH her earpiece for Serghei's instruction to move in. It felt good to have it in again. Even with the static, she much preferred it to the disturbing thought-intruding communication of her PNU.

Two days had passed since Grayson had contacted her about the plan he and Serghei contrived. The plan that—despite her better judgment—she had agreed to. She knew she should have stayed away from Grayson. *Why* couldn't she? In the last forty-eight hours, she'd had countless opportunities to pull out her pistol and end it all. It would have been so easy. Not like what they were about to do.

This was by far the stupidest thing she'd ever done. Stupid in the way that Russian roulette is stupid. Only what they were about to do could hurt a lot more people. Why in Desolation's Thunder did she let Grayson talk her into it?

She sat astride her Harley, parked inside an abandoned building near the border between the slums and the Elect district. The building used to be some kind of office space. A large open floor, now scattered with a few desks that had been smashed by gangs delighting in destroying things. The rest of the desks had likely been looted over a decade before. Dust, shattered glass, and papers littered the floor.

Through one of the lower windows, its glass broken long before, she peered out into the street. Evidence of the previous night's storm was everywhere. Toppled garbage bins, more busted windows, bits of trash plastered against the sides of buildings. They called such storms Wake Storms, sent to remind the people of the awful destruction Desolation had caused. The gale-force winds had kept her up most of the night. That was the lie she told herself, anyway. Truth be told, she doubted she would have slept at all had the night been quiet as a whisper.

Apparently, the lack of sleep showed in her appearance. Enough so that her grandfather had brought up how tired she looked as they sat and ate their breakfast of peanut butter. He *never* did that. And she'd gone plenty of nights without any sleep before.

A mental image of her grandfather suddenly filled her vision. It was so clear and vivid, she almost thought he was there with her. Yet another PNU trick? Her grandfather had discovered the depleted food rations. The ones she'd lost betting on a rat race when Duncan's Warehouse burned to the ground. Instead of accusing her, or demanding answers, or punishing her, he'd simply gotten out a jar of the peanut butter. "Looks like it's a special day," he'd said.

Even now she could taste the sweet flavor on her tongue. It made her think of that first day she'd met Grayson. If she'd managed to kill him that day, would she be in this mess right now? Probably not. Her grandfather, though…he'd be Deprecated. Grayson saved him. Grayson had also lied to her, and was an Elect, and…She didn't want to think about Grayson. It only made her mad at him for not being there for her to be mad at. Or…something like that.

Argh!

She scratched the back of her hand. The spot was bright red and sore. There wasn't anything else to do. Just wait, and *not* think about Grayson.

Twenty minutes later, her earpiece hissed and came alive with Serghei's voice. "The eagle has left the nest. I repeat, the eagle has left the nest."

"The eagle?" said Rylee. "What are you talking about?"

"The CA," Serghei replied. "He's left the building. Time to move, folks."

"Why do you call him an eagle, man?" Feng's voice broke over the line. "How about Tripe Face?"

"Your suggestion lacks roots in any established colloquialism," Serghei said. "Additionally, that phrase was never once used in any movie."

"Who *cares*? The idiots who made those movies were all tripe faces anyways."

"Guys?" Grayson's voice came over the line. "Can we stay focused here?"

"Aye, aye, captain," Serghei said.

A half-smile formed on Rylee's lips as she rolled her eyes. It almost felt like the days before everything had become so…messed up. Freakishly, Grayson sounded like Preston. At least, with the whole stay-focused bit. This time, though, they weren't just hunting down a few cocky Elect teenage boys. This was serious business. And she didn't even have her rifle to help.

"I'm moving out," Rylee said, starting up her Harley with a roar.

"Good luck, everyone," Grayson added, and the line went silent.

Leaning the bike so it was fully upright, she flipped back the kickstand, then shoved her helmet on. Then she rumbled out of the building, out through a doorless threshold, out into the street, toward the last place she wanted to go.

* * *

Grayson stood on the grass of Mt. Pleasant cemetery, at his feet the granite headstone engraved with his mother's name. Sophie Lynn Steele. Unlike the other headstones in the small cemetery, hers was free of the moss that had overtaken the grass, headstones, and rotting benches.

He had never known his mother. And frankly knew little about her. He knew she had dark hair, the same color as his own. That she was prettier than a man like his father deserved to have. That she attended The University of Washington, and earned a Bachelor's of Science in Biomechanical Engineering, followed by a Master's degree in Synthetic Neural Engineering. After which, she was hired by Steele Corp as a Junior Engineer. Ten years later, she married his father. Five years after that, Grayson was born. The same day she died.

Twenty-one years ago. Grayson's birthday had never been celebrated. It was a death day. November sixth. The day his mother died. The day he planned to kill his father. Of course, if he failed, it would likely become his own death day.

He thought about his mother. He didn't have any personal stories about her. He didn't know what her favorite food was, what her hobbies were, or what she did for fun. His father never spoke to him about such things. Vaguely, he wondered if his mother would forgive him for what he was about to do. Wherever she was. He didn't believe in an afterlife. There was no empirical evidence of one. Still, he found some comfort in imagining his mother—or some form of his mother—still existing in another sphere of existence, however irrational that notion was.

"I wouldn't do this if I knew another way," he whispered, as if she could hear. "He's a broken man. And he's dangerous."

He hugged himself, trying to dispel the sudden chill that came over him. A weak, but biting wind pushed at his back, a reminder of last night's storm. He couldn't help but view the storm as a fitting portent of what this day would bring.

The earpiece crackled and hissed. "Motorcade heading west," Serghei said over the line. "Estimated arrival in four minutes." The earpiece felt so…archaic to him. It was awkward too, like having a giant fly stuck in his ear, buzzing around. But Grayson had been too preoccupied with the problems, to code up an interface between the earpiece radio feed and his PNU. He reached up and adjusted it in his ear, wondering if he should have altered his priorities.

Four minutes. Could he actually go through with this? More importantly, would his plan actually work? There was a high probability it would fail miserably. In his mind, he analyzed all the variables. All the unknowns. There were too many.

He'd spent the last two days and nights coding, with a meager hour or two to sleep each day. Physically, he was exhausted. Mentally, he was drained. The only thing that had kept him fueled and functioning was Serghei's stock of Mountain Dew.

The situation was tenuous, at best. Years of experience told him the worst kind of code was hacked out by young hotshot coders who neglected sleep and personal hygiene.

But he had no other option. If he hoped to stop his father, he needed to employ his RARA virus on more than two targets. More than three. Six, to be precise. His father and his five bodyguards. Until a few short hours ago, that would have never been possible.

Either his PNU would have overloaded and shutdown, or else failed to process fast enough, fracturing any sense of reality.

With his last-minute, untested, semi-coherent modifications, all that had changed. At the heart of it, the concept was so simple he wondered he hadn't considered it originally. The model went back to the early days of computer science. Something called a distributed system.

The idea was that a big computational task could be broken down into lots of smaller tasks and distributed across multiple computers. The individual computers would solve their subtasks in parallel, then combine their results.

Simple, effective, and—he believed—capable of being utilized for his purposes. Only the other *computers* would be PNUs. The PNU of the infected target, in addition to experiencing an altered reality, would also involuntarily lend processing power to infect other targets. Enabling Grayson's PNU to do less processing.

Theoretically, that's how it would work. Theoretically. In about one minute…

The faint hum of approaching vehicles made him turn around. Three black cars drove up the street. His father's motorcade. His father came, just as Grayson knew he would. Just as he came every year on the anniversary of his wife's death.

The motorcade stopped at the border of the cemetery.

Grayson clenched the grip of the pistol concealed in his pocket and pushed down his fear. Time to put his code to the test.

THIRTY-EIGHT

RYLEE PARKED HER Harley on the south side of Steele Tower. She saw no point in trying to stash it someplace inconspicuous. Not when she was planning to waltz into the building in the full light of day. Pulling off her helmet, she jogged around to the front of the building, where she entered through the prominent glass doors of the main entrance.

Her thoughts flashed back to the night of the party. Everything came back. The lights. The music. The leering faces. The man who'd tried to abduct her. The bloody bullet hole in his chest. All of it. Had only two days passed since that night? What little sleep she'd managed to get since then had been riddled with nightmares of this place.

She willed herself to keep breathing, to slow down her careening pulse.

No receptionist greeted her in the main lobby, the way she'd seen it done in many of Serghei's movies. In a world where a person's presence and identity could be known without verbal or visual communication, such jobs were redundant.

Mounting the stairs, she climbed to the second floor. Though the room below and the mezzanine above were not brimming with drunken Elects, she still felt as if she were being watched. Likely, she was. At least, the CA and his gray suits weren't in the building. Still, with a single thought, which was becoming second nature to her, she activated her PNU's probing capability. She recalled Grayson's warning about probing. Politeness and protocol could go to the devil. She didn't want any surprise run-ins with *any* Elect.

The doors to the laboratories accepted her PNU credentials without protest. No alarm. Grayson hadn't been sure if her credentials would still work. The CA could have revoked her access after the incident at the party. Though, the fact that he hadn't made her life easier unsettled her. Could this be a trap?

"I'm in," she whispered as she tapped her earpiece to activate the microphone.

"10-4," Serghei replied in her ear. "I'm monitoring the building's entrance."

"Thanks," she muttered. *Not that it will do much good.* If the CA's bodyguards returned while she was still in the building, she'd be trapped. Just like last time. And that had gone so well.

Inside, she didn't bother donning the white lab coat. Her PNU-augmented vision showed her numerous people working in the lab room off the main hallway. Both the hallway and elevators looked clear. Steeling herself, she walked toward the elevator bank. It was time to find Preston. Again.

* * *

Grayson remained standing by his mother's headstone as his father and his bodyguards approached. The look on his father's face showed that he was not surprised to see him at the cemetery.

Miles, the bodyguard who Grayson had tricked into letting him get away, planted himself in front of Grayson and looked down at him with an angry scowl. "Spread 'em," he said roughly. Grayson was not surprised by the request. Fine. He knew his code still worked on one person.

Grayson lifted his arms and widened his stance, as Miles started patting down his chest. To Grayson, though, it felt more like the man was trying to collapse his rib cage.

"Let him be, Miles," said his father. "Do you really believe my own son would try and harm me? Especially here?"

Miles hesitated before giving Grayson one last *pat* to the sternum then backed away. Grayson gave the bodyguard an obnoxious grin, as the man assumed his usual stance: hands clasped together at his front, feet shoulder-width apart.

His father stepped forward and placed a hand on Grayson's arm. He wore a long charcoal gray coat, buttoned all the way up to his neck. Grayson thought about how odd it was to see his father outside. Rarely did his father leave the polished interior of Steele Tower, out into the harsh world—into reality.

In unison, they turned and faced the headstone. Neither spoke. For a fleeting moment, Grayson felt as if everything was back to normal. That this man who stood next to him—the man who he called father—was not trying to kill him. That they were a father and son, together to honor the memory of a wife and a mother. And then the moment vanished, as Grayson remembered why he was there.

His father rarely spoke when they visited the cemetery. Except to call them to leave. He never shared anything about the woman buried beneath their feet.

Grayson broke the silence. "Do you think she would have wanted you to kill the son she died giving birth to?"

It was a calculated question. A cruel question. A desperate plea for sanity. But it just might—on this day of all days—touch on his father's emotions enough to have the desired impact.

Grayson turned and studied his father's face. His father's eyes remained fixed on the headstone, mouth screwed up, as if he'd just bit into something disagreeable. Grayson knew the face. It meant his father was chewing on his anger, preparing to respond in his customary calm manner. It also meant Grayson's effort to wake up his father to his madness had failed.

"Do not speak as if you could even begin to care for her, William," he responded. And the words shocked Grayson with their coldness. "You have no idea what I suffer at her loss. Nor what I suffer for what I must now do."

"Don't insult me!" replied Grayson. "You'll be happy to be rid of me. Admit it. You've always resented me. As if *I* had killed her."

Wrong thing to say. Grayson knew it. Angering his father even more was not going to solve anything. But he couldn't resist. For so many years he'd longed to say these things. Now, he found he couldn't keep his feelings bottled up any longer. Besides, it wasn't as if he was actually going to succeed in dissuading his father. He knew that even before he tried.

His father turned his gaze on him. In his eyes, Grayson saw

fire. "I could have been rid of you years ago if I had wanted it, son. You can trust that."

"So, all those years of letting me live atone for what you're doing now?" Grayson scoffed. "You're so magnanimous, father."

Well done, William. You're just making it easier for him to go through with his plans. He needed to talk rationally with his father, not goad him on. That was something he had always struggled with. His ability to goad his father just came so naturally.

"You think I find joy in any of this?" his father asked. "That I *wanted* things to be this way? I loved your mother more than you can ever hope to fathom. Scarcely had we been married a few years when she was stolen from me. Just as Desolation stole my dreams for the PNUs to change the world. Everything I worked for all those years—gone. All I have left is an ungrateful people to take care of, and a son who never loved me. A son who ought to bring me joy."

"You never exactly made it easy for me to love you," said Grayson, his tone subdued.

The fire in his father's eyes died away, replaced by…sadness? "I guess that's one of the reasons I loved your mother so much," he said softly. "She loved me, despite the fact that I am not easy to love. But if you think that incessantly pushing you to test the limits of your abilities was for lack of love, then you are unequivocally mistaken."

"Yes, father. I'm afraid I must have mistaken the act of trying to have me killed for something other than love. Thank you for that clarification. I see now how much of an idiot I've been."

His father ignored his sarcasm. "There's an old story that people of faith used to tell. I don't draw the same conclusion as they, but it will illustrate my point just as well."

"A story?" Grayson asked. Was his father actually going to moralize right now? Apparently, he was. For he continued talking without pausing.

"There are various versions of the story. But the basic idea is that there was a drawbridge operator, whose job it was to ensure that at certain times each day, the drawbridge was lowered so that the passenger train could cross the river. One day, the operator took his young son with him to work. At one point during the day, the son was playing under the bridge and managed to get himself trapped in the mechanical gears of the bridge. The father struggled to free his son. Soon he heard the whistle of an approaching train. If he did not lower the bridge, the people aboard would plunge into the river below, and die. Yet, if he lowered the bridge, his son would be crushed to death by the gears." His father paused for a moment, then asked, "If you were the operator—the father—what would you do? Save your only son, or save the lives of hundreds of people who blindly put their trust in you?"

Grayson blinked. So, *this* was what kept his father going? What assuaged his guilty conscience at night? The predicament was disturbing. How could anyone answer that?

"I'll tell you what the man did," his father continued without waiting for Grayson to answer. "He had mercy on the people on the train. The people heading home to all of their loved ones. He sacrificed his own son to save so many others. He exchanged all the potential heartache, tears, and anguish of complete strangers for his own."

"You're not God, father," Grayson said. "It's not your job to save everyone. Plus, in that story, the father didn't have an alternative to killing his son or letting the people die. You do. *You're* choosing to kill me—your son."

"Do I have a choice? If people discover what I've done there will be mutiny. Everything we've built up will crumble and fall. I cannot let that happen, Son. Don't you see?"

A gust of wind struck them from the west. An icy winter wind. Yet it did not chill him half as much as his father's words. His father truly saw himself as some kind of savior for the human race.

"This is better than watching The Godfather," Serghei's voice hissed in his ear. Grayson almost jumped in surprise. "You're dad's Vito Corleone, and you're Michael. Classic. Anyway, I'm deploying Grant."

Perfect timing. Serghei's pet rat would be there in a few minutes. In the meantime, he just needed to keep his father talking. However disturbing that might be.

"No," Grayson replied. "You don't just want to save the people of this city. Not for any altruistic reasons. You just want to restore what you lost. Desolation took from you your dream of a world filled with your PNU, with Enhanced people. A world transformed—and you the creator of it. You would have been famous, wealthy beyond imagination. But that will never happen. Not in our lifetime. Maybe in a century from now."

His father shook his head, and his jaw tightened. Again, his gaze fixed on the headstone.

"It was never about fame or money. You don't know me, if that's what you believe. I wanted to prove to everyone that they were wrong. Since the inception of my research into the PNUs there have been critics, naysayers, even opponents. I fought with the board of directors for years to fund the research at Steele Corp. My own company didn't believe in the PNUs. They wanted to stick to developing new nanomaterials and nanochemicals.

"I was forced to fund the research and development myself. And all the while, the nanoscience community laughed on. Their skepticism, their taunts—they only fueled my desired to prove them all wrong. Even now, some on the Advisory Board think we ought to halt further development. A waste of resources, they claim. But they are wrong. We need the PNUs more than ever before.

"A single PNU-enhanced mechanical engineer can do the work of ten regular engineers, performing calculations, discovering design issues, and building blueprints faster than ever. Doctors can perform operations better than any robot ever could. The examples go on and on."

"And yet it hasn't saved us from all starving to death," Grayson replied. "You know, if all you wanted was to tighten rationing, Deprecate a few of the Unenhanced, and kill me, you could have found an easier way to do it. You didn't have to hatch an elaborate, circuitous plot that involved killing off your own Regulation Chief, and other important members of the Alliance. That's what I still don't fully understand."

"If you poked your head out of your hole once in a while, and looked around at what's going on, you might have figured it out on your own. Most of the Enhanced who met their untimely death, were reporting symptoms that were going to make it difficult for me to continue our PNU research."

"Symptoms?"

"Dementia is the main one. Type-2 diabetes another. We have evidence which suggests—for some users—the PNU can cause the development of these diseases. I have a group working to remedy this issue. Still, it will be several years before we have a cure and can broadly distribute a patch."

"And so you killed off anyone exhibiting these problems so that no one would have evidence to condemn your PNU. How merciful of you to end their lives like that for them."

"Why did you come here?" His father suddenly demanded. "Your remarks are beset with your usual insolence. If you came here in hopes of changing my mind, you're doing a shoddy job of it."

Tell me about it.

"You expect me to come here and kiss up to you? Come now, Father. I'm not that pathetic. I'm here to tell you the truth. What you're doing is wrong. But I can see that you're beyond hope of reason on this matter."

Grayson suppressed the urged to steal a glance over his left shoulder. He knew Serghei's rat would be approaching from that direction, from behind a tree where he'd hid it after Feng dropped him off. Unless, of course, it decided to scurry off in the completely opposite direction. Serghei had spent the last few nights training the rat here at the cemetery. Serghei had assured him *Grant* would do fine. Grayson didn't share Serghei's confidence. If only he'd had had ready access to the labs, he could have programmed the cyborg rodent. Too late now.

"By the way," his father said, his tone conversational, "I know that your little girlfriend is in my labs at this very moment. Did you honestly think I wouldn't be monitoring the security certificate of a stolen PNU? She'll never get her friend out. Our dutiful Regulation Chief has been spying on her, just as I knew she would do. A squadron of Regulators is already on its way to Steele Tower. I also have a little surprise for her. You can't win this one, son. It's over."

Rylee? Blast it! He thought his father wouldn't bother himself with her. Maybe his father was bluffing about the surprise. Trying to fluster him, get him to cooperate. Should he call her off? If she left now, she might get out. She'd hate him because she didn't save Preston, but she'd be safe. Safe. He could live with himself if—in the end—she was safe. Who was he kidding? Unless he succeeded right now in stopping his father, she'd never be safe.

Despite his inner turmoil, Grayson didn't give his father the pleasure of looking shocked or afraid. Fixing his father with a steady gaze, he said, "Unfortunately for you, I inherited your tenacity. I'm far from ready to give up."

At that moment, one of his father's bodyguards let out a shout. "What the…"

Time for the show.

THIRTY-NINE

RYLEE STEPPED INTO one of the elevators and pressed the button for the sixteenth floor. Her heart thundered in her chest with enough force to rival any storm Desolation could dish out. The sixteenth floor. It was Grayson's best guess as to where Preston might be located in the building. Grayson had emphasized *guess*. There were eighty floors in Steele Tower. And Preston could literally be on any of them.

Great plan, Grayson. I hate you so much...

The elevator doors closed, and Rylee's stomach bottomed out as the car lurched upwards. Riding in the elevator made her mind flash back to the CA's party. Instinctively, she placed her hand on the grip of her pistol concealed beneath her jacket. *Her* pistol. Not Adrianna's tiny squirt gun. After she'd come home wearing makeup like a tramp, her Grandfather had given her Glock back. She honestly hoped that she wouldn't need any of those rounds this time. Especially since Preston would be unarmed.

The elevator chimed, snapping Rylee's mind back to the task at hand. The display above the doors indicated she had reached the sixteenth floor. A quick scan showed her that no other Elect was waiting on the other side of the elevator doors. Despite her PNU's reassurance, she kept a firm grip on her pistol.

When the open doors revealed an empty corridor, she let out a gush of bated breath and she loosened her grip on her pistol. Stepping out of the elevator, she headed left, following Grayson's directions.

The sixteenth floor, in addition to numerous offices and simulation labs, contained several testing and observation rooms. That's what Grayson had called them. The *testing* rooms were where they put test subjects when they were trying out some new form of PNU. The rooms were secure—just in case something went wrong.

Right.

According to Grayson, the testing done with new PNUs was highly confidential, and highly unethical, at best.

Each testing room was supposed to be adjoined by an observation room, which permitted the scientists to easily watch the test subject, like Serghei stuffing his pet rat in a cage. According to Grayson, the rooms were rarely used, as new PNUs take months — or years — to develop and manufacture. And he wasn't aware of any scheduled testing anytime soon. So, the rooms should be left alone by any of the normal staff. A perfect place to lock up Preston.

Rylee strode down the clinically white corridor, walking as quickly as she dared to avoid looking any more conspicuous than she already was.

At the end of the corridor, a single door barred her way. She grabbed the handle. Immediately, her PNU received another security challenge. Just as instantaneously, her PNU supplied the requested security certificate, and the door clicked open.

Inside, she was met with a long wall extending in both directions, with gray doors set at even intervals. According to the instructions from Grayson, these were the testing rooms. Even though her PNU granted her access to this part of the building, her PNU's internal schematic of the building did not show the rooms beyond the gray doors. Just a long, empty corridor labeled as a construction area.

Someone really didn't want people snooping around here. Likely, the CA himself knew about everyone who entered here. This thought made the hairs on the nape of her neck stiffen. It also prodded her to move even quicker.

How many doors were there? Ten? Fifteen? Vaguely, Rylee wondered who the tests subjects were. Unsuspecting Norms? The thought made Rylee's anger flare.

Preston. She needed to focus on Preston.

Where would he be? She didn't want to waste time checking every single room. But what alternative did she have? Start shouting his name in hopes that he would hear? That would be a good way to get everyone's attention on the entire floor. The rooms beyond the gray doors could very well be soundproof. But this corridor? Doubtful.

Not wanting to waste time deliberating, she went to the nearest door. Maybe whoever locked up Preston opted for convenience over difficulty of discovery. Opening the door, which again requested her security certificate, she peered inside. The room within was gray. A minor relief to her eyes after the blinding whiteness of the corridors. Furnished with a bed, sofa, table and chairs, the room looked more comfortable than any apartment in the slums.

"Preston," she called out softly, even though the room was obviously empty. No reply. She shut the door and moved to the next door to her right. Empty. And the next…nothing. After five more empty rooms, she moved back to search the other half of the hallway.

With each empty room she found, the franticness of her search increased. What if Preston truly wasn't in this part of the building, or even in the building at all? Grayson hadn't suggested anywhere else to search. She opened another door. Empty.

Three more rooms remained.

By the last room, she felt positively desperate. Like a starving animal hunting for food. With trembling fingers, she snatched at the door handle and yanked it open, practically shouting Preston's name across the threshold. No reply came. Her eyes took in the room. Bed, sofa, table, chairs. Empty. Her heart sank into her stomach.

He wasn't there. He truly wasn't there. She turned back around to the corridor, looking around wildly in case she'd missed another door. Missed a sign…something. But there wasn't any-thing else. This couldn't be happening. She needed to find Preston *now*. There wasn't time to search every blasted room, office, closet and lab in the entire building. Grayson's father and his gray suits would be back soon. And she wouldn't get another chance like this again—ever.

At that moment a familiar hissing filling her ears, then Serghei's voice. "I hate to be the bearer of bad tiding, Ry. But you are about to have unwelcome company. I advise you leave. *Now*."

"The CA can't be back already."

"It's not the CA, sweetheart. Regulators. A whole squadron of them."

Rylee cursed. "I can't leave now. I haven't found Preston." *Did he just call me sweetheart?*

"This is not a good idea. They *know* you are there. Find an emergency exit and get out."

Rylee bolted for the door connected to the main corridor. Not to leave though. The Regulators would still have to find her in the building. She had a few minutes. She would find Preston, somehow. And then...well she would figure that out once she got to that point.

The real question remained: where to find Preston. If she were the CA—if she were a twisted, sadistic leader—and wanted to secretly stow someone away, where would she put them?

Unexpectedly, her PNU informed her of an incoming message. From Grayson? Was he okay? The message, though, didn't just interrupt her thoughts, force itself into her brain, like Grayson's messages always did. This was different. Her PNU informed her that the message originated from an anonymous sender.

Anonymous? What other Elect could possibly be sending her a message? And an anonymous one at that. She recalled Grayson's warning from the night of his father's party. He had given her explicit instruction not to accept any unsolicited communications. Now, however...there was no one around. No one who knew she was in the building. Except for the squadron of Regulators. Or possibly the CA himself.

She continued striding down the hallway, toward the elevators, trying to ignore the message. Willing herself to tell her PNU to reject the message. Every logical part of her told her she should reject it. Grayson's warning told her she should reject it. Yet something else inside her longed to accept it. Precisely the wrong thing to do.

Ignoring logic, caution, and common sense, she accepted the message. Instantly, a single word flashed into her mind.

Eighteen.

That was it. That was all the message said. *Eighteen.* And still no indication as to the sender. What did it mean? Perhaps the message had been sent to her erroneously. If Grayson were around, he could likely bore her to death about how and why that was virtually impossible.

Reaching the elevators, she pressed the button to call one of the cars. A second later, a ding sounded, and the doors to her right opened. She dashed inside and went to the panel of buttons. Her hand hovered over the numbers. Which floor? As if pulled by an invisible force, her finger stopped over *18*. Without thinking, she jammed her finger into it.

Eighteen. Floor eighteen. It all made sense. Now she understood the message. Not only that, but she suspected she knew who sent it. The CA himself. This was a trap. A trap that she voluntarily walked right into.

FORTY

THE ELEVATOR CAR couldn't move fast enough. Had it been attached to a rocket, it still would have been too slow. Never mind the fact that she was almost certainly being played by the CA, and lured into a trap.

Scratching the back of her hand furiously, she watched the display above the doors lazily tick off the floors. Had the elevator gotten slower?

Regulators were already in the building. Her probe was specifically configured to warn her of their presence. Currently, they were still on the main floor of the building. Within minutes, they would have the entire building locked down. All main exits and emergency outlets blocked off. Other Regulators would track her down. She couldn't hide her presence. Even the elevators checked her security certificate before allowing her to access a floor. They would know precisely where she was going.

Again, her hand gravitated toward her handgun. This time she unholstered it. She wasn't going down without a fight.

Eighteen.

The elevator chimed, and the doors began to slide open. Even though her probe indicated no one was on the other side of the doors, she couldn't risk being ambushed. And with Regulation already hunting her in the building, she couldn't care less if she spooked an unsuspecting lab worker.

Her gun held up, finger on the trigger, she waited for the elevator doors to open. She couldn't help but note that she was violating at least two of her grandfather's rules for gun safety. Never point your gun at an unknown target. Finger off the trigger until ready to shoot. In general, good rules to follow. In this situation, she'd rather not worry about shooting an innocent Elect. They all deserved a bullet to the chest, anyway.

Nobody greeted her on the other side of the elevator doors. Still, she remained alert, cautiously moving along a side wall of the elevator toward the opening. The elevator had opened directly to an open room, as big as the CA's. Floor-to-ceiling windows made up the far wall, peering out into gray clouds. No sign of anyone.

The elevator doors began to close. She cursed and darted through them, sweeping her muzzle to her right as she exited. Her world slowed as her PNU detected her burst of adrenaline and kicked in slow-motion mode, as she called it. Her muzzle followed her gaze as she scanned the room, taking in details that should have been impossible for her to process so quickly. A sofa and coffee table. A large oriental rug. A few crumbs on the polished hardwood floor. A lacquered table laid with a recently eaten meal. A bar and stools. A figure sitting on one of the stools.

Immediately, her three-dot sights locked onto the figure. But her finger paused on the trigger. Startled green eyes stared back at her. Eyes she knew better than any others.

It was Preston.

He looked at her, mouth hung open as though he were seeing a ghost.

"Ry?" he said, his voice echoing the shock on his face. "What are you...how did you get in here?"

"Let's talk about that another time," she said. Preston still didn't know about her new abilities. And this was certainly not the best moment to bring it up. "Isn't there someone guarding you?"

He jumped off the stool he'd been seated on, hurrying over to her. "No. There's no point. The only way out is through that elevator." He held his arm out to the elevator she'd just exited. "And it won't let me call a car."

Rylee spun around to face the closed metallic doors.

"Which means now we're both trapped in here," Preston said. His voice betrayed an emotion Rylee seldom witnessed from Preston. Defeat. Her own heart sank. Was that the trap all along? Lead her into a room she could never get out of. Why hadn't she thought of blocking the doors from closing?

"You're certain there's no other way in or out?" she said, knowing what the answer would be.

"Not unless you brought a two-hundred foot rope."

In pure desperation, she strode over and rapidly punched at the buttons to call the elevator.

"It's useless," Preston said. "I've tried them a hundred times, at least."

But then her PNU received a certificate request, just as always. A moment later, the elevator dinged, and the doors slid open.

"How in the…" Preston began.

"Come on," Rylee said, grabbing him by the arm and pulling him into the elevator. Inside, she punched the button for the first floor, then the button to close the doors. As they slowly closed, her mind raced. Was there no trap, then? Did the CA want her to rescue Preston and not get caught?

Get caught. Idiot! The Regulators. For a minute, she'd actually forgotten about them. The CA likely knew the Regulators would come. Maybe even sent them himself. They had to get off this elevator now. Seventeen. She punched the button for it. It was their best option.

"What are you doing?" Preston cried.

"The only place this elevator will take us is a Deprecation truck. We'll have to find another way."

Ten seconds later, the doors opened again and the pair spilled out. Then Rylee had another idea. "Hold on." Reentering the elevator, she pushed the button for the first floor again, deactivated her PNU, then ran out of the elevator before the doors could close. "That ought to confuse them for a little while."

"Confuse who?"

"The Regulators," she said, quickly taking in their surroundings. Another corridor. "Now come on." She took off at a run. "We need to find a stairwell."

Unfortunately, she'd just disabled her PNU to prevent the Regulators from being able to track her. That meant she couldn't rely on it to show her the location of a stairwell. It also meant, certain doors might not open for her. *Every* door might be locked to her, including the door to any possible stairwell.

"Right," Preston said. "I don't suppose you have a gun for me."

"No." Rylee didn't offer any excuses as to why. There wasn't time to talk about it. She needed to concentrate. As much as she hated to admit it to herself, without her PNU she felt handicapped. Why hadn't she thought to check for emergency exits *before* disabling her PNU?

They came to an intersection of corridors. Rylee halted, quickly considering each direction.

"Any suggestions?" she asked.

"Use your earpiece? Serg's on the line, right? He might be able to help."

Of course. She tapped the device in her ear. "Serg," she said. "We need to find a stairwell or emergency exit in this building. Any ideas?"

The line hissed before giving way to Serghei's voice. "You're the one with the PNU, and you're asking me?"

"I know," Rylee growled impatiently. "It's...not working right now."

"Interesting...Well, I don't have a schematic of the building in my head. I'd try the corners of the buildings."

"That's so helpful, Serg," she said wryly.

"Let's try this way," she said to Preston, motioning toward a corridor that looked the most promising, and took off running.

"By the way," Serghei added, "you do realize that the Regulators will be blocking all the exits, don't you?"

"I know," she said, and tapped her earpiece to shut it off. Serghei wouldn't be much use to them so long as they were inside this building.

Their corridor ran into a wall, and they were forced to turn right or left. Rylee chose right. Vaguely, she realized she was leading. Even though Preston had always been the leader of the Elect Hunters. What had changed? She didn't know that she wanted to lead. If they failed, it would be her fault.

Ahead, she saw a large white door with a metal crossbar. She pointed toward it. Preston nodded. It was the first door that looked different from all the others. There was no exit sign above it, or sign of any kind. This building was seriously lacking maps and signs. Perhaps the CA had them removed so that people were forced to rely on their PNUs.

They reached the door, and Rylee found herself actually praying that it would open for them. Miraculously, it did. Which was baffling. Then she realized that the stairwell door would probably lock behind them. Access to the floors was restricted, not the stairwell. If that proved true, they were trapped in this stairwell until they reached the bottom. If they even made it that far. Who knew how many Regulators were waiting down there for them.

Together they dashed down the metal stairs, Preston leaping down five at a time. The sound of their bounding reverberated through the stairwell like there was an army storming through. Not the ideal way to keep from being detected. But at this point, she counted on speed more than stealth to be their ally.

So far all her gambles had paid off. She just needed her luck to hang on a little longer.

Fourteen read a painted red number above the last door they passed. They'd only descended three floors and already Rylee felt sweat collecting on her brow. Fourteen more floors to go. They would never make it.

By the ninth floor, Rylee's legs were dead and her lungs on fire. Still, there was no sign of the Regulators. Shoving aside the pain and fatigue, she kept sprinting down the endless stairs with Preston.

Seventh floor. No Regulators.

Fifth floor. No Regulators.

Third floor. Still, no Regulators.

Were they actually going to make it? Rylee's hope swelled.

By the second floor, she believed they might actually escape. Then shouts erupted from below, as Regulators, armed with assault rifles burst into the stairwell from the bottom floor. Immediately, both Rylee and Preston turned to retreat for cover. At that moment, more shouts erupted from above them. More Regulators. Preston yanked on the door to the second floor, but he might as well have tried to move an iron mountain. The door didn't open.

They were trapped with nowhere to run, and only one gun between them.

FORTY-ONE

THE RAT MOVED with impressive speed and dexterity. Especially considering its cybernetic hind quarter. Grayson watched it dart toward his father with admiration. This whole thing was quite entertaining, watching his father's stone-carved guards scramble around like buffoons trying to capture it.

Of course, Grayson wasn't making their job any easier. And he had to concentrate hard to ensure that remained the case. So far, the first major test of his unverified code was going smoothly. Infected with his modified RARA virus, each of the bodyguards' PNUs was secretly lending processing power to slightly alter their perception, so that the rat appeared approximately ten centimeters offset from its actual location. The result—for them—was a rat that seemed to move faster than should be possible.

His father's men certainly believed the rat possessed a poison or PNU virus intended for their boss. That's precisely what Grayson wanted them to believe. The rat, however, served only as a distraction. A distraction for this next part of the show. His grand performance.

Was he really about to go through with this? At the graveside of his own mother, no less.

Now came the true test of his maverick coding. For more than more one reason, he hoped it would be over quickly. Even with his modifications to the code, he still ran the risk of depleting his energy level. Already he'd spent more than he had originally calculated. PNU energy consumption predictions were notoriously tricky to get right. Too many variables were involved. Simulation modelers often took days to produce a semi-accurate power-consumption profile for any sizable chunk of PNU code.

Preston steeled himself. It was now or never. Reaching into his pocket, he gripped the tiny pistol in his hands. Even though the temperature outside hovered below freezing, his hands were slick with perspiration. He'd never shot anyone before. Never even fired a gun, for that matter. If everything went according to his plans, he wouldn't have to.

Drawing out the weapon, he took a single step toward his father. Before he could raise the gun to his father's chest, the bodyguards reacted, abandoning their chase of Serghei's rat, and snapping their guns up before Grayson could blink.

"Drop the gun, William," Miles demanded at Grayson's left. "Now!"

Grayson didn't lower his gun. The five guns were not pointed at his head, but his father's. Neither his father nor his father's bodyguards realized it. That was the deception that his PNU — in concert with those he'd hijacked — was working furiously to create. A false reality. One where Grayson and his father had swapped places. His father still saw the real Grayson. But Grayson's virus was actively altering his father's vision to see his bodyguards' guns trained on Grayson instead of himself.

It was a tremendously complex altered reality to create. With millions of calculations and decisions per microsecond. Predictive movement algorithms ran for nearly every major object in the scene. All to make five men believe a lie and shoot their own boss. His father's PNU-enhanced reflexes might save him from Grayson's bullets. But there was no way he could dodge five bullets fired simultaneously.

"You can't kill me, son," his father said, neither his voice nor his face betraying a hint of fear. "You're an engineer, not an assassin. Put the gun down." It was his commanding tone. His, I'm-the-boss tone. The tone that got things done. The tone that had — more often than not — intimidated Grayson. Not today.

Grayson began to squeeze the trigger. His PNU reflected that subtle movement in the counterfeit version of himself.

"Drop the gun, Will!" warned Miles again. "I'll put a bullet through your head before you get that bullet off."

That was probably true. Only it wouldn't be his head the bullet would pierce. His finger stalled on the trigger. Was he really about to kill his own father?

Yes. I have to. There's no other way.

"Drop it now, Will!"

Forcing hot breath through his nose, Grayson tightened his finger, squeezing the trigger. He knew the bodyguards were doing the same. The trigger pull seemed to take a lifetime, moving a fraction of a millimeter at a time. Suddenly another strong breeze blew in from off the Puget Sound. And Grayson saw it, but too late. Too late to correct for it, to account for it. Too small for his algorithms to pick it up on their own. A piece of debris—a torn paper—caught on the wind. It sailed just over his father's head.

To the keen eyes of his father's bodyguards, though, that debris had just gone through Grayson's forehead. He was a good two inches taller than his father.

"Hold fire! Hold fire! Hold fire!" Miles and the others started shouting in unison, as they detected the discrepancy.

Grayson cursed, and pulled the trigger all the way. His father dodged. Grayson re-leveled the gun to fire again. Before his wrist could even recover from the recoil of the gun, a body that felt like a brick wall slammed into his side. Another of the bodyguards did the same for Grayson's father. They didn't know who was who, so they were pinning both of them. Grayson hit the ground with such force, the air was knocked from his lungs.

Stunned and struggling to breathe, Grayson tried to keep his virus active. Maybe he could still...something was wrong. His PNU had lost contact with his virus targets. And his own PNU energy was barely sufficient to process the simplest of commands. Any second, his PNU would force itself to shut down.

"Serghei," he grunted, "I'm down." *I've failed.*

* * *

Rylee's mind raced. They had nowhere to run. Only up the stairs or down. With Regulators waiting at each end. Within moments, those Regulators would converge upon them. And then there would be no hope. Rylee couldn't hold off an entire squadron of Regulators with a single pistol. Not without any cover. Not with gunfire coming from above and below. Not when the men were armed with assault rifles, tactical vests, and PNU-enhanced reflexes.

Their only chance was to storm one group of Regulators before the two groups converged. She cursed herself for not trying harder to bring a gun for Preston. The human body could survive a gunshot wound...or two. Sometimes more. So long as something vital isn't hit. There was no doubt in her mind one or both of them would get shot if they tried to fight. The only question was, could they overcome the physical and mental shock, and keep going?

Preston looked at her, his green eyes surprisingly calm. In that brief moment, they shared the decision. They would fight, or die trying. Rylee nodded. This was as close to a suicide pact as anyone could get.

Then Preston began tearing off his shoes, followed by his shirt.

"What are you..." Rylee began, her voice trailing off as comprehension dawned. He planned to throw them at the Regulators. A distraction. A weak, desperate distraction, but it was something. She didn't believe for a second it would truly help.

"Rylee Day and Preston Hyde," a voice boomed and echoed through the stairwell. "You are surrounded. Give yourselves up."

Right. Like that was going to happen. They were going to fight, not surrender themselves willingly to be Deprecated.

If she tried, she couldn't have found a worse place for a gunfight. With the steel staircase, and metal pipes everywhere, bullets were sure to ricochet like rubber balls in all kinds of wild directions. Maybe that would work to their advantage. Even with their PNUs, the Regulators wouldn't be able to dodge a ricocheted bullet.

If only she had her...

Idiot! Her PNU! There was no reason to keep it deactivated now. Using the one command that worked when the PNU was disabled, she brought her brain-enhancing abomination back to life. Instantly, she received a flood of PNU data. There were four Regulators below them, and three above. She also now knew their names. Lovely.

She whirled around and reached for the door latch, and pulled. Immediately, her PNU granted her access and the door clicked open. Not waiting for Preston to register what she'd just done, she pulled it open and dashed into the second-floor corridor.

"Come on," she shouted over her shoulder.

Preston recovered quickly from his bewilderment and chased after her.

"How did you—"

"Later!" she shouted, cutting him off. She would explain later. If there was a later.

She had her PNU now, no longer blind.

Desolation! How did I become so dependent on this blasted thing?

It would only take the Regulators a few seconds to understand what she had done. And these long empty corridors provided even less protection than the stairwell.

Where to go?

While getting away from the Regulators was critical, they still had to get out of the building. The stairwell was blocked. And the diagram of the building showed no other stairwells in a different sector of the building. The only other way up or down was the elevators. Those though...surely, they'd already been shut off.

"Here!" she said, grabbing a door handle at a dead sprint. Preston nearly slammed into her.

From their back, shouts burst out in a garble of sound as the stairwell door flew open.

"Halt! We'll shoot!" came a loud command.

Rylee didn't turn to look back, but pushed open the door, and ducked inside. A second later, Preston slammed the door shut behind them. Not that it would do much good. The Regulators would have access, wouldn't they? They could always break down the door.

Preston's gaze cast around the room, evidently attempting to find some means of escape. They were in a small office, with a few chairs, desks, and equipment, which Rylee had no name for. It looked like something Serghei might salivate over.

"Okay," Preston said. "I guess we'll make our stand here. Help me move these desks to bar the door."

"We're not making a stand here," Rylee replied, planting herself a few paces in front of one of the windows, and leveling her pistol.

"What are you—"

Bang! Bang! Bang!

Three bullet holes perforated the glass, a million white fissures spreading out like a tangle of spider webs. The holes formed an irregular triangle, about a foot apart.

Rylee's deafened ears rang from the gunfire.

Ignoring her ears and the muffled, urgent voice of Preston, she picked up a chair and heaved it against the glass, right where the bullets had struck. The chair burst through the window, shards of glass flying out in all directions. The resulting jagged hole in the window gaped just big enough for someone to leap through.

"We have to jump," she yelled, her own voice sounding distant to her ringing ears.

Then she leaned out through the hole. Thirty feet below, an empty street lay. Nothing but merciless black asphalt and concrete. Without giving herself time to realize how stupid her plan was, she jumped.

She'd never appreciated the feeling of falling. That torquing of the stomach as the body plummeted downward. More than once, she'd experienced it rappelling off the roofs of housing units in the slums. This time, she had no rope to slow her freefall.

The sudden rush of adrenaline to her system instantly activated her PNU's accelerated visual processing system. And though her stomach told her otherwise, she seemed to fall as an autumn leaf from a tree.

The ground seemed to approached slowly. She felt herself brace for impact. Her body's natural instincts took over. Additionally, she sensed something else kick in. Like an automatic engagement of a trained and highly calibrated muscle memory. Her legs pressed together, knees straight, but loose, feet flat. An instant later, she felt the impact of the ground touch the soles of her boots. Immediately, her knees bent, and her body listed to the side, falling into a side-roll as her shoulder made contact with the pavement.

A half-second later, her body stopped moving. For a moment, she lay there. All she could feel was her pounding heart against her chest. Did that mean the rest of her was broken, her body in so much shock it refused to process the pain? No. Somehow she knew she wasn't injured—not badly. Her PNU had protected her.

Preston.

The thought jolted her from the spot. She looked up just in time to see his muscular form leaping from the building. What had she done? Preston didn't have the benefit of the PNU to help him. Would he shatter every bone in his legs?

Helplessness and terror consumed her as she watched him plummet toward the street. She couldn't do anything to help. There was nothing around that she could use to dampen his fall.

A second later, Preston slammed into the pavement. The crunch and pop of bones made her recoil in horror. A piercing scream of agony shot out from Preston's gaping mouth.

She was at his side in an instant, checking his body for injuries, placing trembling hands on his arm.

"Argh!" he grimaced. "You couldn't..." His sucked in through clenched teeth, his entire face taut with pain. "...have chosen a...window..." He gasped. "...closer to the ground?"

"Is it both legs or just one?" she said, inspecting as much as she dared. Serghei was the medic. She didn't know anything about first-aid. "Can you walk? We need to get out of here."

"One. Ahhh!" He let out another cry. "No...prrroooblem," he said, gritting his teeth.

As much as she hated causing him any more pain, if they didn't get out of there, she might as well put a bullet in his head. Placing an arm behind his shoulder, Rylee helped him to stand, as he screamed in her ear. His weight startled her. Like a solid piece of lead.

"Let's get closer to the wall," she said. "Just put your weight on me."

The closer they could get to the side of the building, the more difficult it would be for the Regulators to get an easy shot at them from the window.

Limping and cursing with each step, Preston moved against the side of the building, where she propped him up.

"Halt!" a voice boomed from above. Rylee didn't even bother

to look up. Would the Regulators try and jump too? She counted on them playing it safe. Even though it would only take the Regulators a minute to descend the stairs and exit the building, it just might give her enough time...

She looked down the street and froze. Her Harley? Was this the side of the building she'd parked on? There it was though, in all its beauty. A mere fifty yards away.

"Come on," she said, positioning herself under his armpit again.

They were moving slowly. Too slowly. They needed to move faster. Already, she felt like she was half dragging him.

No other shouts came from above. Both good news and bad. It meant no one was likely to shoot at them as they mounted her bike. Probably.

Almost there.

Finally, they reached her Harley. Preston eased himself onto the back seat, as Rylee squeezed in front of him and brought the engine to life with a roar that was met with shouts of command from behind.

The Regulators. The Regulators carrying assault rifles, with accuracy up to four hundred meters.

"Hold on!" she shouted, as she laid on the throttle, racing away from the Regulators with a burst of speed.

Then the shots began to fire.

FORTY-TWO

Rylee's Harley was going ninety miles-per-hour before they reached the corner of Steele Tower. The thick November air felt as frigid as swimming through snow—without clothes on. She ignored the cold. The Regulators gunfire demanded her undivided attention. Bullets struck all along the street on either side of them. So far as she knew, none had hit them. Preston was the most exposed, his back facing the Regulators. If he got hit, would she even know?

Please, oh please, oh please…

Were they intentionally trying to miss? There were at least half-a-dozen Regulators back there. All armed with assault rifles with mounted scopes. *One* ought to be able to make a hit. Maybe the Regulators had orders not to kill. Maybe the shots were intended to scare them, or disable her Harley.

Whatever the reason—terrible marksmanship or bizarre orders—Rylee didn't slow down. Racing out of the side street, they crossed the main avenue running along the front of the CA's building. The gunshots slowed, and then stopped. For a moment, she thought they were giving up. A quick glance in her side view mirror killed that hope.

A pair of Regulators, astride electrocyles, zoomed into view behind them. And they were moving *fast*. Letting out a curse, Rylee twisted the throttle and leaned flatter over the gas tank.

"Give me your gun," Preston hollered over her shoulder.

What? Did Preston intend to try and shoot at them in his condition? Reaching around to her left side, she pulled out her pistol and held it over her shoulder. Preston pulled it from her grasp. A second later, two shots sounded in her ear. In her mirror, she saw the cycles swerve. Then another two shots.

Nine rounds left in that mag.

Three more shots fired. No contact. Not a surprise. Preston was shooting one handed, while hanging onto the back of a Harley barreling down the street at a near full throttle, with his leg broken into fifty pieces. Shooting at Elects, no less. The Regulators *had* slowed down some. That was good. They needed to get away, though. Lose these two, before more joined the chase.

Ahead, the street ended. They had to turn. Throwing on the back brake, she decelerated rapidly, then pulled the handlebars forcefully into the turn. The front wheel protested under the sudden change in direction as the bike leaned to the right.

Preston's strong arms wrapped around her torso like steel cables, as they raced into the turn. Even though she'd hit the brakes, her Harley was still moving recklessly fast for any kind of turn.

Rylee forced herself to stay calm. *The surest way to crash on a motorcycle is to panic during a turn.* A lesson her grandfather had drilled into her when she was learning to ride.

Biting her upper lip, she pressed her bike lower to the street. The corner of a brick building flashed by in a blur.

Preston screamed. Either from pain or fear, she didn't know.

At the apex of the turn, Rylee laid on the throttle again. The bike rocketed out of the turn, righting itself with the force of their acceleration.

They were alive. She had control of her bike. Those Regulators would never take a turn that fast.

"That was insane," Preston shouted in her ear, his voice almost entirely whipped away by the cold air streaming past them.

Through her side-view mirror, Rylee saw the two eletrocycles emerge around the turn. She'd been right. They did take the turn cautiously. Her risky maneuver had put more distance between them.

"We're going to do it again," she shouted over her shoulder.

"What!"

Before Preston had time to protest, she pushed the bike into another turn. His arms constricted around her middle again. This time they put even more distance between them and the Regulators. Despite the gravity of their situation, Rylee couldn't help but feel a thrill inside. Never had she driven like this before. She didn't know she could.

Another turn.

More distance.

It still wasn't enough, though. The slums were getting nearer. They needed to lose those Regulators.

Then she remembered Serghei. She'd forgotten to turn her earpiece back on. Tapping it, she said Serghei's name.

"It's about time you got back on the line," Serghei said. "You're in trouble."

"Oh, that's so helpful. Suggestions on losing these two Regulators?"

"Try using the Force."

"This is serious, Serg. Preston and I are dead if we don't get away." They rocketed through another turn, dodging a group of workers surrounding a manhole. A few of them dived out of the way onto the sidewalk.

"Feng is too far away to assist you," Serghei said. "Plus he's trying to help Grayson. You could—"

"Wait!" she interrupted. "What happened to Grayson?"

"Failed miserably. Apprehended by the CA's men. Everything's gone south. Anyway, have you considered a game of chicken?"

"Chicken? What are you talking about?"

Rylee took another turn.

"You know, where you drive at *them*."

"That's....that gives me an idea. I'm heading for the tunnel at Union Street."

"Ah...very good. Let me know how it turns out."

The line went dead. Rylee took the next left. Then another left, back toward the Elect sector of the city. Unfortunately, they would have to backtrack a fair bit.

"What are you planning?" Preston shouted from behind.

"Trust me," she replied. There was no time for explanation. Preston would figure it out once they got there.

The sun had broken through the thick blanket of clouds. A rare occurrence for that time of year. She intended to use it to their advantage. But they needed to keep enough distance from the

Regulators chasing them. She torqued the throttle and prayed no cars would cross in front of them at any of the intersections they were racing through. Even among the Elect, though, cars were rare.

The tunnel was just two blocks away.

With a hard right turn, they careened onto Union street. Ahead, the mouth of the tunnel loomed, the sun's rays casting a heavy shadow, hiding its depths. They plunged into the darkness, blind to the tunnel's innards until enveloped in the shadows. She intended to use that blindness to their advantage. The Regulators would not be able to see beyond the wall of shadows until they were in the tunnel.

Laying on the back brake, and downshifting, Rylee planted her left foot and whipped the tail end of her motorcycle around. Preston gripped tighter to keep from flying off.

"Get ready to shoot," she said, then took off, heading back toward the tunnel's entrance, toward the pursuing Regulators. Hopefully Preston got the idea of her plan.

They rounded the slight bend in the tunnel. The pair of Regulators raced toward them. Rylee backed off the throttle a hair. She didn't want to emerge from the tunnel's shadows prematurely, giving the Regulators advanced warning. Not when the Regulator's reflexes were PNU-enhanced. As it was, she didn't know if her idea would work.

"Take the one on your left," she shouted over her shoulder, as another idea came to her. Two birds with one stone. She shifted her bike to the right slightly, moving closer to the right-most Regulator. She only hoped she didn't break her foot—or crash—in the process.

They were almost dead-even with the Regulators now. Another second.

"Now!"

Even with the accelerated visual process of her PNU, the electrocyle on her right zoomed past with blinding speed. But her foot was ready. As the rider passed, the heel of her boot struck his knee. In her left ear, gunfire erupted.

Then they were out into the sunlight again.

Rylee didn't slow down. Didn't look back. The squeal of tires and crunch of metal told her all she needed to know.

"I think we got them," Preston grunted from behind.

She nodded, and turned them toward the slums.

Once certain the Regulators were indeed off their tail, Rylee spoke into her earpiece. "Serg, are you there? Preston and I are clear. What's the status on Grayson?"

The line hissed. "Well, he's a goner. Not much else to say. The CA's got him in one of his cars. The motorcade is headed back toward Steele Tower. I told Feng to pull out, but he's not listening."

"That's because you're not the boss, man," Feng said over the line. "I'm going to crash into the motorcade. Put a few bullets in some heads. Preferably the CA's."

"The Japanese call that kamikaze."

"I'm Chinese, tripe face."

"I know. I was only—"

"Guys," Rylee cut in. "Let's focus on the problem. Feng. Can you wait until I get there before you do anything crazy?"

"Just until the motorcade gets close to me. Why?"

"Just wait," she said, not wanting to say too much with Preston near.

"Fine," Feng replied. "But you'd better hurry."

Right. Hurry.

Her PNU energy was running low by the time she and Preston reached the slums. All the stress from their narrow escape had drained her resources. She would just have to manage with what remained.

Pulling to a stop in the alley behind Serghei's place, Rylee helped Preston off the back of her Harley. "Serg," she said in the earpiece, "I need you outside to help Preston. He's got a broken leg."

Preston handed her gun back. "Where's Feng?"

"Coming," she lied.

Preston's face squeezed up in pain. "Good," he groaned.

Serghei ran out of the warehouse a moment later. "What's with this team and lower appendage fractures?" he asked. "You could do something more original? A bullet wound, perhaps?"

"Just get him inside and take care of him, Serg," Rylee said, indicating for Serghei to take her place supporting Preston.

"Where are you going?" Preston rasped.

"There's something I have to take care of," she said. Then she turned quickly and strode to her motorcycle, hopped on, and sped away before Preston's shouts could make her change her mind.

FORTY-THREE

RYLEE FELT MORE than a twinge of guilt at abandoning Preston like that. Not a word of explanation. Truth was, she didn't think she could bear to face Preston with the truth. That she cared about Grayson. More than that, if anything happened to Grayson, she…well, she didn't want to think about it. Her heart was already overworked. She squeezed the throttle on her Harley. Why couldn't she hate Grayson like she was supposed to?

"Feng," she said. "What's your location?"

Her earpiece cracked a moment later. "4th and Stewart," he replied.

"I'm on my way." She tapped her earpiece off.

Feng was located back in the Elect sector of the city, a few blocks away from Steele Tower.

I need a plan.

She avoided the most direct route to Feng's location. It slowed her down a little, but she hoped to avoid Regulators.

Three minutes and seventeen seconds later, she turned onto Stewart Street, where Feng was hiding. An old beat-up van sat parked on the side of the street. Through the windshield, she saw Feng sitting in the driver's seat. He gave her a look that said he was tired of waiting.

Parking her Harley behind the van, she hurried over to the passenger door, and clambered inside.

"Took you long enough," Feng said. "Did you walk here?"

"I drove all the way from the slums."

Feng didn't look impressed.

"Well, I'm here," she said, tapping her earpiece back on. "Serg?"

"Uh…" Serghei's voice died out over the line, followed by some muffled voices mingled with the static. "Ry, what in Desolation's Thunder are you doing?" It was Preston.

She tapped off the earpiece. So much for that idea.

Feng's eyes grew wide, and he nodded in appreciation. "Man, he's angry. You just going to ignore him like that?"

"I have to. If they're not going to be useful, shutoff your earpiece."

Feng tapped his earpiece. "Mutiny," he said. "So, what's the plan, boss?"

She wished she knew the answer to that question. "How many cars are in the motorcade?"

"Three. The CA's car is the middle one. Should pass by on 4th Avenue there any minute."

Think, Rylee. Think! What to do? If they could stop the motorcade, maybe she could think of something. *That's it.*

"Feng, pull out into the street and kill the engine. Block as much of the street as possible. Pop the hood. Pretend the car is broken down. Shouldn't be hard with this piece of junk." Without waiting for a response, she jumped out of the passenger seat of the car, and dashed to her Harley.

A sickly rumble, followed by a puff of exhaust smoke came from the old van as Feng turned the ignition. One of its taillights glowed red, and the van rattled forward. With a sound of metal screeching across metal, the van came to a halt perpendicular to the flow of traffic. Then Feng climbed out of the cab, cursing, and limped over to the front of the vehicle.

It amazed her that Feng was able to walk so well with the brace. It was a shame Serghei's talents couldn't benefit more people. If he weren't forced to work on the scavenging crew, maybe he could. Then again, if Serghei weren't forced to work, he'd probably watch movies all day.

Straddling her bike, she pulled out her pistol and released its magazine. Only two rounds remained in it. She pulled out one of the jacketed hollow-point rounds and loaded it into the chamber of her Glock. Then she pocketed the magazine and pulled out her other one, still loaded with fifteen rounds, and jammed it into her gun. Another sixteen rounds. Likely, she wouldn't get that many shots off.

She started up her Harley, and pushed back the kickstand. Then she waited, scratching at the back of her hand.

A few seconds later, she heard the blare of a horn, followed by angry shouts. Her heart lurched. That was her cue.

She raced out and turned onto 4th Avenue. Three black cars of the CA's motorcade sat in the street, blocked by Feng's van. Right hand supported by her left forearm, Rylee began firing shots at the vehicles.

With a loud bang, she hit the front-left tire of the foremost vehicles. As a deterrent, she fired at one of the front windows. Gunning the throttle, she raced on past the first vehicle. Car doors flew open as the CA's gray suits prepared to return fire.

Rylee cursed. She had counted on them taking cover, rather than fighting back so quickly. She fired at the driver of the second car, who was using the door to shield his body. Glass shattered from the door, as Rylee's shots tried to find her target. This was stupid. Grayson was likely in that car. What if a stray bullet hit him?

The driver fired back at her. Three rapid shots. Rylee leaned hard to the right, attempting to dodge. Her headlight exploded. Another bullet struck somewhere lower down on her bike.

Desolation!

She torqued the throttle even harder, forgetting about returning fire. The driver of the last vehicle was shooting at her now too. There wasn't any way for her to dodge. The bullets were flying at her broadside.

More bullets struck her bike, sparks spraying in her vision. Suddenly, her front tire exploded. Fighting to keep her bike under control, she threw on the back brake. The bike veered to the right, ramming into the curb of the sidewalk with the flat wheel. The back of the bike flew up, launching her forward, over the handlebars.

Even with her accelerated visual processing still active, it all happened so quickly. Flying headlong toward the sidewalk, she attempted to calculate a landing. But her angle was too shallow. Arms out in front, they met with the abrasive concrete first. They buckled under the force of her momentum, but shielded most of her head from a hard blow, as the rest of her body flipped over.

She skidded for several feet before finally coming to a stop.

I have to get up. She was amazed to find she was still alive. Her gun. Where was her gun? She tried to sit up, but her body protested. Had she broken something? Everything?

Shouts reached her ears, as if uttered from miles away. A hazy face, shadowed by a bright sky, appeared above her. Then rough hands grabbed her by the front of her jacket and jerked her off the ground. A sharp cry pierced her lips, the pain in her body forcing the sound out of her.

"She's alive, boss," said a deep voice, clearer this time.

Then she was being dragged toward one of the black cars. A back door opened, and she was stuffed inside.

Warm blood ran down her arm.

More gunshots rent the air. *Feng.* What had happened to Feng? *Just drive away, Feng. Get away!* Where was her earpiece? Did she still have it?

She reached for the spot, ignoring the shock of pain that ripped through her arm. Gone. It must have dislodged from her ear when she struck the pavement.

There was a sound of a car crashing, headlights shattering. Craning her neck, she saw the lead car ram past Feng's van. Their own car squealed forward, pushing Rylee back into her seat. She turned as they passed the van, but she saw no sign of Feng. Had he managed to escape?

"You're more tenacious than I gave you credit for," said a voice next to her. "People like you are difficult to come by. I know, I always tried to hire people with your kind of grit and persistence."

With difficulty, Rylee turned her head to the right. Grayson's father, Nathaniel Steele, the CA, sat in the back seat of the car next to her. Disarmingly cold eyes took her in, scrutinizing her.

"It's unfortunate," he went on, "that I couldn't have found you sooner. I might have been able to use you in a less...disagreeable manner."

Disagreeable? He wanted to frame her for the murder of several high-ranking Elects, and he called it disagreeable?

Subconsciously, she tried to scratch at her tattoo, but her arm hurt too much.

The CA drew out a gray handkerchief, and attempted to bind her bleeding arm with it. She pulled away, preferring to bleed to death than have a rat touch her. No, rats were nice compared to him.

"I know you think I'm the enemy," he said, tucking the handkerchief back into his suit pocket. "But I'm not. If you and William had succeeded in your little plot to kill me, you don't want to know the destruction it would have caused. The Alliance needs me to survive. Sometimes, I must do hard, harsh things to ensure that survival. It's better than the alternative, I assure you."

"What do you want with me?" she snapped. The last thing she wanted to hear was the twisted lies the CA used to soothe his conscience.

"I want you to cede," he said, coolly. "Give up fighting against me. It's over. You've lost, Miss Day. Already, you've broken the terms of our agreement. But I shall show you leniency, *if* you do exactly as I tell you. And permit me to remind you that the life of your grandfather is at stake. I still might even manage to exonerate your friend, Mr. Hyde."

He paused, waiting for her to reply. She kept quiet, and turned away from his gaze. It was enough she was forced to talk with him, she didn't want to look at him, as well.

"We'll meet with the Regulators soon," he said, evidently reading her silence as a willingness to listen. "I will be handing you over to Chief O'Connor. She shall take you into custody, and eventually, interrogate you. At the very least, you'll be found guilty of conspiring in the assassination of an Alliance official, aiding in the escape of a criminal suspect, and obstruction of justice. Right now, you and William are the Alliance's highest-profile criminals. Threats to the stability and future of all its members."

Rylee's eyes flicked to the front of the car. For the first time, she noticed the rear-view mirror was pointed directly at her, the untrusting eyes of the driver fixed on her. Vaguely, she wondered why the car needed a driver. Weren't all the CA's cars autonomous? Perhaps the driver was there in the event—like today—

when the motorcade is attacked, and more evasive driving is required. Whatever, the reason, Rylee found the eyes on her unnerving.

"I want you, in that interrogation," the CA was saying, "to confess involvement in the spree of murders which Chief O'Connor has been investigating. She'll want details. Don't give them. I'll make sure everything comes out, in time. I want you to tell her, though, that Lieutenant Advisor Richard Straufmann is behind all of it. You were just a pawn. Do you understand?"

In answer, she flashed him a cold stare, then turned back to look out the window. They were nearly to Steele Tower by now. The Regulators would take her once they arrived. All would be over then. No, the CA was right. All was over already. She'd tried and failed.

"Don't expect your defiance to worry me," he said. "You may choose to keep your mouth shut. So be it. You doom your loved ones. Or you may be plotting to betray me again. Tell Chief O'Connor how I blackmailed you into killing my own son, that I'm responsible for all the murders. Go ahead and try. Believe me, I can make Chief O'Connor disappear just as easily as I can your grandfather. Besides, you have no evidence against me — aside from your word. And I have ways of altering PNU memory. No one will ever find proof of a single word I've said."

A smirk formed on his lips.

What she wouldn't give to punch him right in the mouth. She could barely move her arm, though. The amount of hatred she felt for him at that moment startled her. It was searing, tangible. It made her want to fight. To claw at his eyeballs. Bite and scratch.

Then the face of her grandfather came into her mind's eye. If she fought now, he would surely die. Her efforts would be futile. In her current state, she couldn't do any major damage. Besides, the gray suit in the front seat would have a bullet through her brain before she could even leave a nice scar.

Oh, Grayson! Why didn't you come up with another way to stop your father? Bullets had always been her answer to stopping someone. But the PNUs with all their subtle dangers and weaknesses…

271

Weakness. That was it!

Without giving warning, she pressed herself into the CA—ignoring the stabs of pain in her arms and side, and kissed him.

FORTY-FOUR

A HAND LATCHED onto Rylee's neck and yanked her back with such force she thought her head snapped free of her body. She let out a cry of pain. Another hand latched onto her arm, restraining her further.

"Miles, get back here!" shouted the gray suit holding her. "The girl's trying to attack the boss." Then he added in her ear, "not another move, or I'll break your neck."

Rylee didn't doubt it. Though, she was more worried about being choked to death, so firm was the man's grip on her neck. She didn't fight to free herself. She'd never intended to. Aside from struggling to breathe, her attention was fixed on the CA. Did her kiss work?

The CA was looking at her with a confused expression, tinged with…disgust? He seemed to be struggling to know what to make of her actions. The CA's bodyguard had thought she was attacking his boss, but the CA knew that wasn't true. At least, not directly.

"You…" he began to say, then paused. His eyes grew wide, and he struggled to swallow down air. "Peanuts," he wheezed out. Face reddening, his hands fumbled for something in his jacket pocket.

"What the devil!" The man holding her tossed her to the side. "Miles, the boss is going into anaphylactic shock."

The back door of the car flew open, and a different gray suit hauled her out, dumping her onto the pavement.

"Get his epinephrine injector," shouted the gray suit. "I need a med here, *now*."

Rylee watched as best she could through the gray suit's bulk. She saw the flash of something clear and cylindrical in the man's hand, just before he jabbed it into the CA's thigh. Would the injector still contain only water? Was Grayson's prank still undiscovered after so many years?

She wasn't sure it would work. It had only been a few hours since she'd eaten peanut butter with her grandfather for breakfast. But it felt like an eternity ago.

With the gray suits distracted, could she escape? She turned to look up the street. Several Regulators were running in her direction. On the other side, two more gray suits joined the scene. Not a chance.

The franticness inside the car increased. "He's not improving," the gray suit in the back of the car cursed. "Where's that blasted med!"

"Get him out of the car!" someone ordered.

"Loosen the necktie," another shouted.

Rylee was shoved out of the way, as several gray suits pulled the CA out of the car and laid him out on the pavement. Face red with hives, and eyes bulging from his head, the CA clawed at the men trying to help him. Mouth gaping open, the only sound that escaped was a thin wheezing. Sheer terror filled the CA's eyes.

"What is going on here?" a woman demanded, breaking through the small crowd. It was the Chief O'Connor.

"He's in anaphylactic shock," one of the gray suits said. "We need a med here five minutes ago."

"One is on the way," she said.

"It'll never make it in time," a familiar voice whispered in her ear.

Rylee jerked her head, and found Grayson crouched down behind her.

"How did you expose him?" he asked, talking quietly. "I assume you didn't have a handful of peanuts to shove down his throat."

"I'd rather not talk about it." If she lived through this day, she'd have nightmares enough, *without* remembering kissing Grayson's father.

"Are you alright?" he asked. "I thought you were dead for sure when you crashed. You shouldn't have come back."

"If PNUs can numb pain, I could really use that right now."

"Actually—"

"Forget it," she said between clenched teeth as she shifted her position, "my power's drained, anyway."

"Listen," he whispered, his tone more urgent, "maybe we can get away from here while everyone's distracted."

Placing a supporting hand beneath her bicep, he helped her to her feet. But they hadn't taken a single step before a hand seized Rylee's arm.

"You two aren't going anywhere," a voice said from behind. Rylee turned. One of the gray suits had apparently been watching them.

The urgency of the voices around the CA increased, bringing Rylee's attention back to the unfolding drama on the street.

"His pulse is weakening!"

"Blasted med, we're losing him."

Regulators and gray suits scrambled around the CA, frantically trying to save him, but having no means to do so. In the distance, the siren of a med van wailed through the chill air. In her mind, Rylee willed the med to miss a turn or hit a pothole and get a flat tire.

"He's stopped breathing!" one of the gray suits shouted.

A Regulator commenced CPR, but it was a futile attempt. It was too late.

"After all these years," Grayson muttered softly, "he never knew I'd filled his injectors with water."

Rylee sensed a note of sadness in Grayson's voice. And when she looked at him, she saw pain in his face. Guilt swept over her. As irrational as it was, this was Grayson's father. However terrible of a father, it was still his father. It still hurt to see him die. She leaned into him, hoping her nearness might bring him some comfort. In reply, he wrapped an arm and shaky hand around her back and side.

Before them, people continued to scramble around the CA's lifeless body. A single calm figure stood in that scene, arms folded, lips tight. Rylee caught the Regulation Chief's eyes for a moment. The woman looked at her with an expression that Rylee didn't quite know how to read. Was that...admiration?

"He's actually dead," Grayson whispered, as though he couldn't believe it to be true.

Yes, dead. The most powerful man in the Alliance. And she'd killed him.

The CA would never harm anyone again.

EPILOGUE

THE SOUND OF the metal lock clicking open made Rylee's head jerk up. It was a sound she'd heard too infrequently in the last five days since being deposited in a jail cell underneath Regulation headquarters. The sound reverberated through the metal and concrete chamber like a gunshot. Instinctively, she reached for the spot where she kept her pistol holstered before stopping herself. No gun. The click of the lock was followed by a screech of metal, as the outer door to the jail unit swung open.

Chief O'Connor strode through the open door, her heeled boots thudding on the floor. She wore a knee-length black skirt that hugged her thighs, a silver blouse, and her customary stern expression. The woman's appearance tended to baffle Rylee, who associated skirts with women like Adrianna. And in her mind, Adrianna was little more than a seductress of men.

This was the third visit from the Chief of Regulation since Rylee had been arrested for *suspected homicide*. The homicide of the CA, to be precise. A murder for which everyone—including Chief O'Connor—knew Rylee was guilty. Yet Rylee had not yet been executed or Deprecated. It was unimaginable for a criminal to sit in a jail cell for more than twenty-four hours before meeting with one of those two fates. The fact that Rylee had been jailed for several days spoke volumes about the state of the world outside her prison walls.

As Chief O'Connor had explained it before, the current political state of the Alliance was tenuous. With the CA dead, a power struggle for control of the Alliance had ensued, with several members of the Advisory Board attempting to maneuver themselves into power. One or two influential Elects outside the Advisory Board also sought to take control. Among the vying parties, there were those who denounced Rylee's actions and cried

276

for her execution, and those who denounced Nathaniel Steele and hailed Rylee a hero.

Rylee didn't know what camp Chief O'Connor sympathized with—if any. But she got the distinct impression that the woman was trying to help as much as she dared.

"My officers are investigating the claims you have made against the CA," Chief O'Connor said without emotion. "With the current political turmoil, it is difficult to make much headway. Your story does corroborate with that of William Steele's. However, it will be little help to you, as he's a suspected conspirator."

"Can you tell me anything about my grandfather or Preston?" Rylee asked. The same question she'd asked the last time. She knew Grayson was being held in a separate cell somewhere. And that Feng had suffered a gunshot wound in his shoulder, but was expected to make a full recovery. He was being held in a hospital ward.

Chief O'Connor pursed her lips, as if she was considering whether or not to say anything. At last, she leaned in closer and spoke in a soft voice. "Both are fine. Your grandfather has been assured of your current safety."

Then straightening, she took an abrupt step backward. "Have you thought of any other details that might aid our investigation?" she said, her voice back to its normal level and businesslike tone.

Rylee shook her head. She'd told the woman everything she knew, everything she could remember.

"Very well," Chief O'Connor replied. Then she turned around and strode toward the door. Just as she reached it, she paused and cocked her head to one side. "It might be hard, but you should consider yourself fortunate to be locked up. You are much safer in here than free on the streets." Then she unlocked the door—apparently with her PNU—and left Rylee alone with her thoughts.

Her grandfather and Preston were safe—for now. That was what she wanted. She could only hope that whoever replaced the CA would do away with Deprecation. If the new leader didn't—and if she ever got free—she would fight to make it so. She would never stop fighting.

ABOUT THE AUTHOR

MICHAEL KARR IS is a software engineer and science fiction author. By day he writes code to control drones or holograms, by night he writes books to control peoples' minds into reading more of his books. Like most authors—who try to pretend that they don't—Michael writes his own biographies. And in third-person, no less. He enjoys eating barbeque brisket and fish tacos from a tiny stand on the pier in Victoria, B.C. Until recently, he lived in Seattle, WA, where it really does rain nine months out of the year. Now he lives in Texas, where it rains only nine days out of the year. He's married and has five children.

AUTHOR'S NOTE

OKAY, NOW I'M going to switch to first-person, because that's more personal, right? In all seriousness, thank you for reading. If you've stuck with it to this point, then I must have done something right. It means a great deal to me. Even though this is not my first book, it's still a surreal feeling for me to have people I've never met reading my books. And by finishing this book you have become one of my favorite people on the planet. It goes without saying that an author cannot be successful without his readers. So, thank you again for reading. But an author also cannot be successful without those amazing readers—*you*—writing reviews of their books. If you enjoyed this book, I'd love to see your brief, honest feedback on Amazon.com.

Next, I'd really love to have you join my mailing list. Three reasons for that. One, it's the best way for me to stay connected my amazing readers. And two, because it's possible—with all you have going in if your life—that you'll forget about me and my future books, unless you have an occasional reminder.. You can sign-up for my mailing list by visiting www.michaelkarrbooks.com.

Michael Karr

Printed in Great Britain
by Amazon

20135054R00161